BRAM GAY

MICHAEL O'MARA BOOKS LIMITED

To my friends on and off the rostrum.

First published in Great Britain in 1996 by
Michael O'Mara Books Limited
9 Lion Yard
Tremadoc Road
London SW4 7NQ

A CIP catalogue record for this book is available from the British
Library

ISBN 1–85479–739–5

1,3,5,7,9,10,8,6,4,2,

Designed and Phototypeset by Intype, London
Printed and bound by Cox & Wyman, Reading

Maestro

is a work of fiction. Certain real places, buildings, institutions and orchestras being as central to fictional musical life as are Baker Street, New Scotland Yard and the Sureté to crime fiction of a certain genre, they appear in these pages; but my characters and events are entirely imaginary and bear no relationship to any real people, living or dead, nor to actual events.

Bram Gay 1996

PRELUDE
WINTER 1961

As the 707 lurched upwards and the black ant hill of Tokyo fell away, David Adams wondered whether he'd ever be at ease in the air. He flew as a matter of necessity; to the itinerant musician flying is as routine as the stockbroker's morning train and statistically, as he told himself for the fiftieth time, it's safer. Still, his fingers were always mentally crossed at takeoff; for him there was something unlikely about fifty tons of metal supported only by the vacuum above its wings.

If confidence was what the passenger lacked then Japan Airlines made up for it. For foolproof efficiency Japan took the biscuit – in the arts as in aviation. Three weeks in Tokyo, Kyoto and Nagasaki, four orchestras, six programmes, and hardly a nit worth the picking in any of them. No risk. Little excitement either, he reminded himself wryly.

Still, in an airline boring reliability was what he most wished. As the no-smoking light was extinguished, David relaxed into his recliner, grateful for the airline's hot towel and silently thanking Jane for her insistence on first-class travel. 'Never be seen to count pennies' she said. 'That's my job, part of what I do for my ten per cent. It's all tax-allowable. You're travelling as cheaply as a Japanese tourist.' So he sat, enjoying lots of legroom and an attentive stewardess while three hundred ordinary mortals bruised their knees in tourist.

Now a drink? Experience warned that alcohol increased jet lag, but on a twenty-four-hour flight the counterargument for anaesthetic was strong. Timely, the kimono-clad stewardess approached bearing a tray.

3

Champagne? Yes indeed. He sipped. It was the real McCoy, the widow's bottle.

First class was nearly empty today; four only, distant among twenty seats; one very English lady of a certain age, already deep in a book; a Japanese businessman devouring the *Wall Street Journal*, a Scandinavian beavering away silently at some figures, and one symphony conductor – himself – wondering whether to use the time learning a score or squander it on the film. This was not an option as a rule; a slow but thorough learner, David rarely had travelling time to waste. But thankfully there were two weeks before Boston, two weeks which the capable Jane, nursing her investment, had blocked all attempts to fill. There would be, for the first time in two years, if not a holiday at least a rest. He'd go home to Wales, to the hills and valleys where music was still a matter of brass bands and male-voice choirs, where the only Japanese were those of Gilbert and Sullivan.

Another world, the Rhondda of his childhood; an unlikely place in which to raise an orchestra conductor. Coal was what his home had been about. Coal had been his father's life and his grandfather's death. He'd expected nothing better. At home the notion that one could live by music was an exotic fairy tale.

The tray passed again, offering. He accepted. The great engines, menacing at takeoff, hummed reassuringly now. Through the window he watched silver wings gently flexing as the aircraft climbed and found its course. The sun was low on the horizon, never to sink below it on this polar flight, clouds a feather bed far below. Jet lag was for tomorrow, or the day after. For the moment relax and escape, forget . . . no, perhaps not forget. Memories awoke, champagne-stirred. Relax and remember . . .

The boy was feather-bedded, warm in the seaside cottage where Aunt Molly lived alone while her soldier husband was at war. The summer holiday nearly over, the two had celebrated his fifteenth birthday together with supper by the log fire under oak beams, remembering old times. The menu was simple, limited by wartime rationing, the talk wonderful. As a girl Molly had been sent in to domestic service in the London house of a great lady. There her unfailing good humour, lively dark eyes and coal-black hair had made her a great favourite with what she called 'the family'. In London she'd learned 'manners', bringing home style enough to set her apart in a mining community; not a snob, though, and with a natural grace which disarmed the envy of her less polished friends.

The great excitement of the boy's year was the day Molly arrived home for her annual holiday, laden with toys from Selfridges and telling stories of tube trains whose doors wouldn't wait, the Changing of the Guard, and the doings of the great.

Her cottage sitting room was all chintz and mahogany, beeswax and family pictures; the hostess relaxed in jumper and tweed, her hair piled high, her smile in the lamplight warm as her interest in his doings, her aroma mixing subtly with the woodsmoke as it drifted across the inglenook between their deep soft armchairs. The grandfather clock ticked musically, listening to their talk, its memory so much longer. There'd been sherry before supper, and after it a glass of mulled port, luxuries usually reserved for the family Christmas. It was all very festive, and before long David was more than ever in love with his aunt.

At length – they'd long since lost track of time – she'd said, yawning, 'Look, I didn't know what to get you for your birthday. There's a catalogue by your bed. Choose for yourself while you're here.' She raised a kind admonishing finger. 'Not too much money, now. Take it to bed and read yourself to sleep.'

Even in wartime that catalogue was page on glossy page of sheer magic. Down deep in his feathers David travelled a wonderland of toys, tools, clothes, and footballs, torn between greed and good manners.

Then suddenly he came upon unexpected delights of a different sort: page after page of ladies, underclothed to sell the pretty things which revealingly concealed their ultimate secrets. In moments he was alive with a veritable birthday prick. Untrousered in linened luxury he turned slowly from page to page, from knickered brunette to stockinged blonde, imagination rampant. He threw back the bedclothes in the nick of time. Gout after gout spouted, a mindlessly throbbing, endlessly leaping muscular heaving, his body tensing in uncontrollable delight. His eyes fast closed, every muscle from ears to toes in spasm, for minutes he lay, gratefully awash in repeated breakers of sensation.

Slowly he relaxed with a great sigh of relief and joy. Then he opened his eyes to see, framed in the doorway, Aunt Molly. There was a hundred-year silence. There lay David, his crime in his hand. There stood Molly, eyes like chapel hat pegs, hands to her mouth. And there on the floor by the bed was the catalogue open at ladies' underwear. Shock giving way to embarrassment, cheeks aflame, he reached blindly for the bedclothes, shaken and ashamed, searching her face for signs of mercy.

Her eyes betrayed her, sparkling under arched brows as her smile escaped her hands. Groping for the bedclothes still, he heard her command, 'Don't! You'll soak my sheets!' She waved a finger, hardly able to control her giggles. 'Just stay still!'

In a moment she was back with a warm wet flannel

and a towel. He made to take them, but no; 'Lie still or you'll have a wet bed!'

And so he was blanket-bathed and dried. He waited to be given the towel, as he so often had as a child to 'do the rest yourself'. Again no; his hands, his thighs, and his shamed sex were all delicately cleaned and dried. All done, she herself reached for the bedclothes to cover him. But under the influence of warm water and soft hands, irresistible pleasure had won its easy battle with his shame. His cock, recently shrunk to an acorn, was uncurling lazily but purposefully. Molly shook her head wonderingly, sitting down with a sigh on the edge of the bed.

'What a nuisance, to be a young man! Still, lucky for some!' There was a smile in her voice. Suddenly David realized that he was not in disgrace, that there was nothing to forgive. She looked at his levitating flesh. Not intimidated, it grew rather than hid from her accusing eyes. 'I suppose if I tuck you in you'll do it again?'

He gazed at her wordlessly, a new George Washington unable to lie, knowing there would be no sleep while his cherry-tree stood. 'Perhaps we'd better get on with it at once, then? Wait a minute.' She rose. In a moment they were in darkness, and the feathers adjusted again to her slight weight. 'Lie still now. Close your eyes. Think about something nice.'

His mind had room for nothing but the warm knowing fingers encircling him. In a few wonderful moments his back heaved again into the air, fresh warm rain falling thick. Reaching, he circled her neck, pulled her towards him, held her tight and kissed her; his first kiss, all others practice pecks for this one, full on lush warm lips, open and breathing hard. Her hair had somehow come down to cover them both, a fragrant curtain. Bliss.

They were fast together for an eternity. Gently Molly freed herself. In the dark the towel again.

'Now that will be enough for you, young man, and for me too if I've got any sense. Sleep now.' She was tucking blankets around him and fluffing his pillow. 'We'll talk about it tomorrow. No more of this tonight. Promise?'

He nodded in the dark. She tiptoed out. He was asleep before she reached the door.

* * *

A soft voice at his shoulder asked his choice of apéritif before dinner. Opening the menu, David wondered at the ingenuity which could provide such choice, miles above the polar snow. Melon perhaps? Then the beef, from Kobe, with a little claret. Cheese from France with . . . well, he'd finish the half-bottle. Recklessly he decided to go the whole hog, asked for a half of champagne with the melon.

The meal arrived, by airline standards a culinary miracle: wine at the right temperature, beef perfectly cooked. The cows of Kobe were massaged every day, it was said, for tenderness. With the coffee came a small interruption. Hovering, the girl offered another menu, asked for an autograph, 'for the lady in seat fifteen. She hopes you will not mind, sir?'

He'd been right, then, about the politely suppressed glance of recognition in the first-class lounge at Narita. He signed, 'With good wishes,' resisting the temptation to add: 'from a fellow-member of the mile-high club', because the poor dear might not understand the joke and might, just might, show it to someone who did. One couldn't light the blue touchpaper and run; not when one had signed the firework.

The messenger departed, no sign of recognition in her face, her composure impregnable.

After coffee, the drawing of blinds to keep out the ever-present sun, the offer of headphones for the film, the reminder of blindfold and slippers for those who wished to sleep. Cognac? He asked and it arrived in seconds. He'd have a little time with the flight magazine, six weeks old, with its optimistic preview of his Tokyo concerts, before sleeping, hopefully to Anchorage.

* * *

Soft autumn sunlight peeped through the curtained window, the sound of distant waves, sea birds, a child's voice on the beach below, and . . . a morning glory of more than usual impertinence, its head tasting the sheet and waiting confidently for encouragement. His remembered promise paled beside the greater one rising between his legs. Considering, his hand eased back volunteering skin. A rattle of teacups on the stair heralded Molly with a tea-tray, smiling.

'Tea and a biscuit. Sleep well?'

'Lovely, thank you.'

'Yes. I thought you'd died and gone to heaven.'

The two, he considered, were not always connected.

'Drink up then, Rip Van Winkle, and up with you. Breakfast in ten minutes. Try a shower.' There was a chuckle in her voice. 'Cold ones are best in the morning. There's a dressing gown behind the bathroom door. Quick now, or the eggs will spoil.'

Smiling at some secret thought, she went, leaving the door open. Already he guessed that women sometimes said 'don't' when they meant 'only if you must' and that he'd be forgiven . . . but he drank the tea and that ended the question. Into the shower, and downstairs in slippers and robe to the sunny loggia where breakfast was laid, fine china arranged with Kensington care among welcoming basket-weave and flowers.

9

Cornflakes, bacon and eggs, and conversation. School, his music, his hopes and, over the toast, his uncertainties. These were smiled confidently away. 'Don't worry your head, David. It will all come right. Take each day on its own, put one foot in front of the other. Not to waste time, that's the important thing. Time is what nobody's got.'

' "Fill the unforgiving minute"?'

She was pleased, amused. 'Ah! Read your Kipling, have you? Do you know about Judy O'Grady and the Colonel's Lady? No, they won't show you that one at school, I suppose. Still, you won't need Kipling to tell you that they're the same under the skin, I think.' She laughed at his puzzled face, shoulders back. It did wonders for her jumper, pulling his eyes over her wool, a different colour this morning. To hide his confusion he told her it was pretty.

'Prettier than last night's?'

'As pretty.' He lacked the confidence to tell her that the contents of her jumper would have beautified an army greatcoat.

'Last night's is in the wash, young man.' She sighed. 'Save a sheet and ruin a twinset.'

He remembered his passion, her breasts crushed to his body. 'Oh, I'm sorry . . .'

'Can't be helped. Truth to tell and shame the devil, I enjoyed it.' Suddenly she was serious. 'Fifteen yesterday. There's a law against baby-snatching, do you know that?'

'I know girls mustn't—'

'Nor boys neither, till sixteen. For that little accident last night I could go to jail.'

'Accident?'

'Oh, all right then, no accident; it was lovely.'

'Lovely?'

'Yes, lovely. Good God, boy, if men enjoy women surely a woman can enjoy a man?'

10

He remembered stolen moments in the lab after school, Julie's quick breathing, his hand exploring, her uncontrollable hips. Enjoyment, yes. But surely ladies, they'd be quite different?

She watched his face, reading his thoughts. 'But you are not a man yet, you see. Not for a year, in law.' She looked away over the sea, thoughtful. 'Perhaps you ought to go home . . .'

'Oh no! It's lovely here.'

A wry smile. 'So I gather.'

'It won't happen again. I'll never tell.'

A very straight look now. 'The first promise goes with a big pinch of salt. It takes two to keep it anyway, so who are you to say? The question is, can I believe the second promise?'

Desperately: 'I won't; I won't really. And I'm nearly a man. I *feel* like a man . . .'

'Sure you know how a man feels, are you?'

His face fell. She made amends with a quick peck on his cheek, teapot in hand. 'Don't look so down, David. I can tell you that you feel like a man to me. Nearer twenty-five than fifteen.' She was inwardly convulsed at some secret joke. Simmering down, serious again, her clear eyes captured his and held them fast. 'Men talk less than women, thank God. Look, we've got a week. It's time you knew some things.' His heart leaped. 'Not everything . . . but to have so much and know so little – well, it can be dangerous.'

'Dangerous?'

'God, boy, what's between your legs is the most dangerous thing on earth. It ought to have a notice: "Not to be used except at the right time, in the right place, with the right woman." '

'I thought it would all come naturally,' he said, wondering.

'Oh yes, naturally,' again that smile, 'or unnaturally.

And that is not to be recommended. But a little care and attention does no harm.'

A long silence now. He finished his tea, the sea washed the shingle, the birds cried. She got up, straightened her skirt, tucked in her jumper. She saw the appreciation in his eyes.

'Enough! We'll have a walk on the beach. You're here to get fresh air and exercise, not fumble around in bed. Go and get yourself dressed and decent, young man.'

Full of questions and hope, he went.

* * *

An hour to Anchorage. The arrow on the computerized map crept almost imperceptibly across the world, the journey of Marco Polo reduced to a metre and a half. A rattle of trays heralded breakfast.

Coffee, black and sweet, rolls, butter, cold meat with cheese. Jam. More coffee. Coming round now, and time to freshen up for landing. No queue for the small room. Time for JAL's plastic razor. A worshipping glance, half averted from seat fifteen as he passed. On the other side the financial virtuoso was still composing.

A change of note from the engines, white clouds hiding the sun at last. Down, down, fastening seat belts, the cabin crew sitting in matched pairs, hands folded, white-gloved for landing. Then again into the sunshine. Rocky mountains far, far to the ends of the earth, rocks and snow. Roads now, the hills smaller, flattening. Now rows of huts, the long runway with its tower. The great bird homed in, wings noisy with emerging flaps, wheels thumping down. One bounce, two, a third settling the matter. In the air deceptively slow, on the ground a racing monster.

Roaring reverse from the engines, brakes on. Slowly to a stop.

First class first out, down to cold concrete and all the fresh air a man could ask. A brisk walk to the building, up the stairs to the lounge replete with sofas, a smiling welcome at the frozen tip of the US of A. A very American voice asked, 'Mr Adams?'

David owned up.

'A cable for you, sir.'

He opened the envelope. Curious how a voice can survive the typewriter, and several thousand miles.

Sir George Box died this a.m. Please telephone Times newspaper, speak obituaries, waiting your time Anchorage. Then please telephone me. Grant.

His coffee growing cold, he sat for some minutes collecting thoughts for print. Nice of them to ask. The old man had taught so many good people. All busy, hard to track down before printing deadline. He was the lucky one with the on-the-ball agent. The woman never stopped.

The Times was grateful, hoped he'd had a successful tour. What could he say about Box? His influence, much more than purely musical; the stature of the man, his command of the British rostrum over a sixty-year span, his absolute values, the warm affection of players everywhere, his generosity to colleagues . . .

Far away the voice thanked him for his help and wished him a safe trip home. David was left with his memories of George Box.

A dinosaur, a lovable dinosaur, who'd never left the century in which he'd been born. That was his achievement: to have carried the best Victorian values into an age of compromise. To have talked with old men who knew Brahms and Wagner, yet to have played Berg with enjoyment and Stockhausen with conviction. A small man, military of bearing though the waistline of the light-infantryman of 1915 had thickened with age, walrus moustache completing the Blimp image, yet never a figure of fun, his natural dignity had shrugged off the attempts of generations of musicians to nickname him.

Times readers would be told of the iron discipline of his middle years, his selfless service to great orchestras struggling for survival, the glowing opinions of the great continental musicians. They would never know of the informal lectures given over good lunches to hungry students, the expensive scores loaned and generously never reclaimed. They would certainly never know of the advice he gave to David Adams on the day he ceased to be his pupil.

Sir George sat in his armchair, hand stroking his whiskers in the gesture famous on so many rostrums. 'Well, David,' he said, 'you have the prize you wanted. You've earned it.' His eyes twinkled. 'You've had the luck too, of course. Conductors rarely collapse on concert days for the benefit of bright young men who happen to know the work. Just as well, perhaps. But you have certain qualities the job needs; some I had to pick up the hard way.' David sat waiting, remembering the old man's famous advice given in his first lecture, that a conductor must never wear a watch nor a buttonhole, and *never bend his knees*.

'Your background gave you certain advantages. You've always known you'd have to work for what you want. You can't imagine the difficulty money imposes there.' He was right, David couldn't; but he'd always known that Box's family had money, a handicap he'd have accepted readily. 'You have the determination and the energy of what used to be called the work ethic. Then too you have a respect for the people who play. They see it and they like you for it. You learn from them and they give you a great deal. Now – three years in Vienna! Though I never cared for it much. Vienna thinks it invented music. I much preferred Heidelberg. More ideas and in my day better teaching too. But Vienna is the place today. Swarovsky will give you what you need. A fine teacher; all those fine pupils. First-rate chap. Mind you, it won't be easy, being the first British student there since the war. The opera is in ruins and the city is full of Russians. Still, the languages will be useful.'

He fell silent. Whatever was left to say he was not finding easy. 'One more thing, David,' he smiled, a smile of rare charm. 'I hope you won't mind . . .'

'Anything,' David said.

'Well, you're a handsome young chap, and you've cut a rare swathe here among the ladies. You'll go on doing so, no doubt. Terribly easy in our job, isn't it?' His eyes were watchful under beetling brows. 'That's the problem. You'll do well to remember it. Above all, never sleep with the orchestra.'

The boy was stunned. The old man saw it and laughed. 'Don't be too put down, David. You'll have your successes, conductor or not; but you'll never know, unless you choose well, whether the success is yours or that of the figure on the box. That would matter to you I think?'

It would. Of course it would.

'Yes. I think you like women, really *like* them. Very different from enjoying them. They like you too, and that matters.' Box walked to the college window, watched the members of the Philharmonic pouring from the door of the Albert Hall just a few yards across the road and turned. 'Respect, David. Respect is what it's all about, and respect is all of a piece. Look, when the second violin succeeds with a pretty cellist the success is personal. When the conductor is involved it's put down – fairly or unfairly – to power, money, seats at Bayreuth and Salzburg. D'you understand what I'm saying?' He smiled at David's embarrassment. 'The orchestra knows we are human, David, but they would prefer the man in charge to be a bigger person than they are. They know, in the end, that he's not; but the pretence is useful. It saves faces.'

'I'm sure you're right sir.'

'I know I am. I learned that the hard way too. One more word if I may?'

'Please.'

'Only one glass with dinner. There's nothing so valuable to a conductor as a good night's sleep!'

Laughing, they shook hands, friends. David walked from the room, out and down the college steps for the last time as a student.

* * *

Deep in recollection, he'd missed three attempts to page him. Now there was a minion at his elbow. He took the telephone, sensing trouble. He was right. Jane Grant was not pleased.

'Good morning. I've been calling for an age. Where'e've you been? Inspecting the bear?' The duty-free shop at Anchorage rejoiced in a vast stuffed polar bear in a huge case.

She was in her usual form, clearly. He smiled. 'Good *evening*, Jane—'

'Now listen, because this call is costing a mortgage a minute. John will be at Heathrow. He'll take you to The Smuggler.'

'What?'

'We have business at Glynde the day after tomorrow. I hope that's convenient?'

'No, actually. I was going home for a rest. To the sea at Southerndown.'

'Southerndown?'

'Yes. I haven't been home for a hundred years.'

'David, it's the same sea. We have a great deal to talk over, and not only at Glyndebourne.'

'Pop down to Wales. The change will do you good.' There was no chance, of course, but it was worth a try.

'Oh, come. This is important. Please, David. You can go on to Wales afterwards.'

He gave in. He always did. Twelve years with a first-rate agent and the habit had taken hold. He sighed. She heard it and the anxiety left her voice. 'Good. That's settled then. I'll be down on Monday evening for dinner.'

She'd allowed nicely for the jet lag. He'd be hopelessly fuddled tomorrow, useless for business. 'All right. Three days in Sussex. The rest down home. I hope *that's* convenient?'

His sarcasm was effortlessly dismissed. 'Yes, of course. Just don't miss the plane to Boston, that's all. Goodbye now.' She was gone.

The passengers were called for boarding. David joined the queue of four and walked out into the cold. The cabin was bright as the smiles of the new crew, lined up to welcome them. In minutes they were flying. It was time for lunch.

Southerndown, he thought, relaxing over his cognac. An age ago. He'd never been back since ... well, since.

★ ★ ★

Dressing, David heard women outside; a duet in contrasting voices, one Welsh, tuneful as chapel Handel, the other cut-glass. From the window he could see Molly at the gate, girlish in her warm woolly hat with the bobble on top, wellington-booted for the beach, her companion a tall blonde in a duffel coat. A golden labrador looked sagely from one to the other as they chatted, collecting words. Ready now, David approached diffidently.

Molly turned to introduce him. 'David, come and meet my friend Kate.'

'So! The famous pianist. I've heard so much about you. And how are you?' Her eyes were blue as the morning, her cheeks rosy, her hair beach-blown. Her face was welcoming, her hand firm, cool from the sea air.

He said that he was well, thank you, and Molly offered the opinion that he'd bucked up since yesterday. 'Poor chap's been down with the flu most of his holiday. Much more colour this morning. Wonderful what the sea air and a good night's sleep can do.'

He smiled, remembering.

Thinking it was for her, Kate returned one of her own. 'I'm sure he'll soon feel like a new man.' She winked at Molly. 'Like Mae West, perhaps?'

'Mae West?' Molly was puzzled, David too.

'Yes,' said Kate, 'she said she got up every morning feeling like a new . . .'

The two dissolved together into peals of laughter, quickly quelled by his visible bafflement. Sober again now. 'If you would like to practise, David, I have a piano.'

The last thing he needed: a cottage piano, ten years untuned perhaps, and a goggling audience of two. Eyes evasive, he patted the dog, which wagged a sympathetic tail. 'Thank you very much,' he said politely, 'but a few days' rest won't hurt.'

'Well, if you change your mind, just pop in. The kettle is always on, and music with elevenses would be lovely, wouldn't it, Molly?'

Worse and worse. The alarm must have shown in his face. Kate tugged gently at the leather. 'Come along, Soldier,' and the dog was up, head bobbing, tail fanning. They set off in opposite directions, the dog for the fireside, mistress in tow, Molly and he for the beach.

They walked in silence to where the cobbles tailed off into the sand, morning sun on their backs, sea breeze gentle on their faces. 'Like my friend, do you?' Molly asked.

'Posh!' he said. Posh was uncomfortable.

'Oh, not really. Not posh like Lady C. I mean.' Molly's lady was always Lady C.

'A bit too posh, anyway.'

'No. Her family kept a shop. She's only good-school-and-university posh, *trade*, not posh like class. She's the sort of posh you can easily get, young David, if you shape yourself.'

This was new to him. School teachers, bank managers and preachers were class up the valleys. 'What about *class* posh, then?' he asked, curious. 'How do you get that?'

She shook her head. 'You don't. Born with it, you must be. Talent will never get it; work won't nor money neither.'

He told her that this was not fair, that these people didn't sound very nice.

'There are all sorts of upper class. Some are nice and some are nasty. Anyway, they are better to work for than middle class, and much easier to get on with. Safe, you see.'

'Safe?'

'Yes. They know they've got you in your place, so they can afford to be nice, friendly even. But they never take you home to tea.'

It was beyond him, all this. He was curious about her friend Kate.

'Her husband drives Bob's tank. Uncle Bob's his gunner. We've loaned them both to General Montgomery for the duration. Jack's a Captain, very

19

important round here. That's why Kate's house is so nice. Houses go with ranks.'

'Class again?'

'Well, service class. It's not the same thing. Anyway, this house goes with a very nice man. So it's all right.'

'What did he do, before the war, I mean?'

'He was something at a university. So was she. You can ask her when we go.'

He murmured, noncommittal.

'Don't you want to?'

'Not much.'

'We must. Very bad manners not to. She asks about you a lot – your music, what you will do after school and all that.'

He had very little idea himself about all that. To play was enough, and to listen. So much music there was to hear, store up, think about. Where most boys of his age woke each morning hand-between-legs he woke tune-in-head too.

They walked along the waterline, skimming flat pebbles into the sea. Children were throwing a stick for a mongrel dog, wringing the wet best from the last of the holiday.

'Tell me,' asked Molly, 'do you think she's pretty?'

'Who?'

'Kate, idiot.'

'I suppose.'

'As pretty as the pictures in the catalogue?'

'How do I know? Her face is pretty, but . . .'

'I see. You will know better without her coat. Beautiful is all below the neck for you, isn't it? Did Mam and Dad never tell you anything?'

'About what?'

She sighed, mock-exasperated. 'About women. About men and women together.'

'Never.'

Another sigh, a real one this time. 'Well, when you

20

are interested in what's between a girl's ears as well as what's between her legs you are well on the way. If it is the same with her, grab her and hang on tight. There must be pretty young ladies at school?'

He told her about Julie. Things can be said while walking, eyes on the sand, which are impossible at any other time. Molly asked about Julie's family, her place in school, was she good at sports, did she like music?

She seemed to like what she heard. 'So, you're a lucky boy then! She's pretty, she's clever, she enjoys the things you enjoy, and she likes you. How lucky can a boy get?'

'I suppose.'

'I suppose too. Have you kissed her?'

'Yes.'

'Nice, was it?'

David hesitated. 'Yes . . .'

'Not too sure?'

'I liked it. But it was different from . . .'

'From what?' She stopped walking, faced him, obliging him to look at her. 'Come on, boy, tell me!'

To tell her that last night he'd discovered what a kiss can be was impossible. He hung his head, shuffled in the sand. She put a hand under his chin, tipped his face up, silent, her face serious. Then the space between them was gone and he was kissed again, on the beach. Only their mouths met, and for only the briefest time, but the kiss was full of promise.

They walked on, silent for a while. Then: 'You'd better tell me the worst.'

'The worst?'

'Or the best if you like.' Amusement in her voice now. 'You've had your hand under her clothes, I suppose?'

Reluctantly, in a small voice: 'Yes.'

'Ah. Did she like it?'

'I think so.'

21

'Don't you know?'

'Not really. She didn't want—'

'If she did she'd have been mad to let you see it. Inside her pants?'

'Oh no!' It was beyond imagining, or beyond expectation anyway; he'd imagined it often enough.

'I see. The lady kept her pants on. Very wise. More should do it. Do you think she knows what might happen if she were daft enough to take them off?'

'I wouldn't hurt her, she knows that.'

'No, she doesn't. She doesn't know a bee from a bull's foot, and neither do you. But a man can't be trusted, that she does know. The knowledge comes straight from Eve, believe me.' Again a long silence, then: 'Well, what about her? Has she put her hand—'

'Oh no! She wouldn't!'

'You asked her?'

'No. I knew she wouldn't, so I didn't ask her.'

'*There's* wise, I must say. But girls are just as curious as boys.'

He was surprised; still, she should know.

Seeing the look on his face she stopped walking and they turned to one another again. 'Oh dear, what an innocent!' Her hand ruffled his hair in a gesture he remembered from long ago. She pecked his chin, aunt-like, as they began to walk again. He waited. 'Not now,' she said.

'When?'

'Take time, greedy.'

They were back on the cobbles, the gate in sight. 'Time for lunch, nearly. You have some reading to do and I must go out this afternoon.'

Standing before the fire, warming, she put her arm round him in simple affection. 'You kept your promise this morning,' she said.

'Yes.'

'Easy?'

22

'No. Why?'

'Because I want to know if you keep promises.'

'Well, now you do know.'

She shook her head. 'I know I was just in time with the tea, that's all. Anyway, perhaps I'll ask you for a promise again. Now, get on with your book.'

* * *

It was a fine big house; the sort only preachers and bank managers lived in up in the valley. Kate Jones opened the door in a flowered dress, pleasure shining in her smile. The dog was equally pleased, exuberantly jumping up to welcome Molly. She produced a toffee from her pocket and the dog ran happily away to hide it.

'You ruin her,' said Kate. 'All those sweets. Very bad for her, and worse for her manners.'

Coffee was waiting. The room was unlike Molly's: masculine leather instead of chintz, the whole dominated by the personality of the man whose photograph hung over the big fireplace; a handsome young face confidently grinning at the world from the hatch atop his tank.

'That's a Sherman tank!' said David.

'That it is,' Kate replied, 'and all those little swastikas are for dead Panzers. Rather clever with a gun, your uncle Bob.'

'I'd rather be in the RAF,' he said. 'Flying a fighter.'

Molly now: 'Just thank God you are here on the ground, young man, where it's safe. Some of those Germans are quite clever with a gun too. Anyway, it will all be over before you are old enough for it.'

'Romantics, all of them,' smiled Kate, 'young or old. Big kids, that's all. If they could understand what it's really like before they start it they'd give it up once and for all.'

23

'Well,' reflected Molly hopefully, 'this lot will have had enough. There'll be no more for a while. Boyo here won't have to go killing Germans.'

'No job for a pianist anyway. David, the piano is at the back of the house. Down the passage, turn right, the last door. Help yourself.'

Nothing for it then; he must do the polite thing.

The door opened on a very large room, redolent of leather book bindings. On the wall to his left were bookshelves. The facing wall, with the fire, was shelved for volumes too. And sitting in state on a vast expanse of rug was a grand piano; a full-sized concert grand, black, shining, and awesome.

Sitting, David opened the lid reverently: a Steinway. His hand hovered over the keys, hardly daring to touch. Then a note, and what a note; a note which sang. He touched again, harder. It sang again, louder and longer. His feet found the pedals, experimented. The response was a new world, a door opening. A piano which liked his fingers it was, a piano with a welcome.

A chord now. It spoke of tuning, of people who cared. Beethoven, he thought, the *Pathétique*. Not hard, the slow movement, and this piano mustn't be insulted with mistakes. The notes sustained themselves, the great harmonies filling the room. Mozart now? The C major Sonata, scales trickling from his fingers like spring water off Cwmbach mountain. A piano to play for ever, never tiring . . .

He became aware of an audience. They were standing by the door, smiling.

'Surprised?' asked Kate.

He could only nod, beaten for words.

'You didn't expect so much music?'

'No.'

'It's all music here. Even the dog.'

'The dog?'

'Isolde.'

Light dawned. 'I thought Soldier.'

The women laughed. 'David, Isolde is a female!' Then taking pity, Kate added, 'Well, who would call a dog Isolde, I suppose? Only my Jack. There was a Tristan too, but he met a car and that was the end of him. Too much energy, like most young men.'

She was sitting with him now, the stool easily big enough for both. 'How about some four hands then? Brahms? Hungarian Dances?'

The music found, they were soon away. From Brahms into reductions of symphonies, a new experience. Who on earth could Mahler be? Such huge pieces, and like nothing else he'd ever heard. The morning passed in a flash. In the end Kate stopped, seeing the exhaustion he'd have died rather than admit.

'You play very well, David.'

'Thank you. And thank you for playing with me.'

'You read very well too.'

He told her of his teacher's advice, to practise the piano, not the pieces, because with enough technique he could play anything he liked; to read something new every day, learn a language he could speak with his fingers. All true, she agreed, and the best advice for players of any instrument. Did he play any other?

He was surprised at the question. Wasn't the piano enough?

'It's quite a lot.' She was thoughtful. 'But there's something to be said for learning how the others play, I think. I play the violin a little. Tell you what – let's have a go at a violin sonata. Game?' She produced a fiddle from a case under the Steinway, tuning it with care. 'César Franck. Do you know him?'

'No, I'm sorry.'

'Not too important, but his little piece in canon comes in handy. Look.' She produced the Franck

25

sonata with its last movement of no great difficulty and they began to play. Busy as he was he quickly realized that the violin was her instrument, began to work with her, supporting, arguing, giving, taking, loving it.

The famous movement ended. David looked round at Molly, standing silent, excluded. She collected herself, smiled, clapped. 'Lovely. Jealous, I am. Lovely it must be to play together like that.'

Kate was cleaning the violin carefully. 'Yes, it is. It brings two people very close. Jack and I used to do it a lot when we were students. We used to fall out about the music all the time. When we stopped falling out we knew it was time to get married. Anyway, it was the only way to get any real practice done, getting married. Arguments always ended up the same way.' Laughter again, excluding him in his turn. 'Molly, your David is a musician.'

'Talented, is he?' asked Molly.

'Oh, talent he has. Talent is not enough. He'll need luck too. Luck comes by putting a lot of work into a talent. David won't mind. Those fingers haven't come without a lot of hard work, I'm sure of that But he'll need advice. Your grandparents will have to think hard about it all, David, quite soon.'

He was thoughtful, walking back to Molly's. 'Mam and Dad, you know . . .'

'What about them?'

'They don't know about music. Music in chapel, in the male voice, of course. But not proper music, you know what I mean?'

She knew. 'We'll have to talk to them, David.'

* * *

A soft voice asking about his seat belt, indicating that he must adjust his seat for landing. A string of fairy lights below on the world's dark floor, then another, and soon a crazy checkerboard, the houses between anonymous in the black. Soon the whole earth sparkled with lights, some fixed and some moving. Down there clerks rushed for the 5.15, freshly powdered secretaries made for tea and the cinema. Out on the fringe where the lights faded into the countryside wives waited, schoolchildren opened their homework unconcerned at the huge aluminium bird dropping, dropping closer overhead. He thought, as he always did at this point, what a mess if one of these should come down on this vulnerable town, and what a miracle that it had never happened yet. Then they were at Heathrow and Japan Airlines were thanking them for travelling, wishing them a happy stay in London.

* * *

John was waiting. Tall, greying, immaculate in his blue driver's uniform, happy as always to see his friend, he seized David's bags for the short walk to the car.

'Good to see you, boyo.' They were long past formality, David and he.

'It's good to be back, John, I can tell you.' He settled into the familiar leather of Grant and Grant's ten-year-old Mercedes.

'I bet it is. I can't bear to think of Japan, myself.' John had served in Malaysia and associated everywhere east of Suez with jungles and bullets. 'Not going down home then?' As always when Welsh expatriates meet the accent surfaced very quickly.

'No such luck. The boss has other plans. The Smuggler it is.' He was very tired now, and The Smugger, a regular haunt during the Glyndebourne season, seemed suddenly very inviting.

The car nosed its way into the Heathrow tunnel.

John would expect an enquiry after the health of his pride and joy. 'Car still going well, is she?'

'Never better.'

'No need for a new one yet then?'

'No, see me out she will. Lovely old car.' So she was; luxurious enough to pamper any spoiled tenor, yet old enough to avoid giving the impression that Grant and Grant were doing *too* well. John eased the big motor into the outside lane. 'Not far to go, that's one thing. Back in Wimbledon by eleven.' The dashboard clock showed 6.30. 'Mind you, I'd have been happy to go down home. I like to see it now and then. Changed it has, David.'

How long had it been? Ten years? 'Not the same John, when the family's gone. Nobody there for me.' It was near enough the truth.

'Never was family with me. A lot of pals though.' John had been an orphan, and after the regiment Grant's had become his family. 'But never mind. Home is where you are born, see. I used to think of it in that old jungle. A coal tip would have been welcome, I can tell you.'

David asked about the rugby, the only game for Welshmen.

'Wonderful! Stradey Park nearly went up in flames that night we won. Mind you, the poor buggers didn't have a chance after "Cwm Rhondda". Shrinking in their shirts they were, just with the singing.' He laughed.

'How's the boss, John? Keeping well?'

'Same as ever. Never stops, boy. I wish she would, often. No life for a woman, see. Not natural. God knows she's got all the help she needs. Why go on all the time I don't know.'

'Like the Old Man?' David suggested.

'Different for a man. Work is for a man. Tell you

this too: easy for him it was. For her it is hard work. Hard work.'

'It's what she loves.'

'Oh aye. Some people love the drink, some work. Both can kill.'

It had killed GG at sixty, David reminded himself. Not so easy then, even for a man. John was ahead of him, far. 'What I say is, it is time, David.'

'Time?'

'To settle down, get married, have a family, with a nice home. Her artists won't keep her warm in her old age. Mind you, it's GG I blame, sending the boys away to college. The business was the place for them.'

Isaac, at thirty, was a rising barrister; Abe, his younger brother, would probably make Parliament at the next election.

'No use telling her. The firm is her baby, John. She looks well on it, I must say.'

'Oh yes. Mind you, she was always pretty. I used to bring her home from school in the country, in the early days. Lovely then. More now.'

'Tough though.'

John laughed. 'As old boots, boy! Pity it is she's not a bit more soft, for some nice young chap to get his hands on her, if you see what I mean.'

David knew. Discipline, control, were what Jane was all about, starting with her own.

'I spoke to her yesterday,' he said.

'Yes. Today it was here, of course. At Gatwick we were, waiting for the plane to Paris. Not too pleased, I thought.'

David sighed. 'Situation normal.'

'She'll get over it. Soft spot for you she's got.'

'Think so?'

'Obvious. Everybody else is business. Any problem for you, up she goes like a firework. Fireworks all round yesterday, though, over Paris. Nothing will do but she must be there. Back tomorrow, first flight. Pick her up from the plane. Then the office, then down to The Smuggler.'

David was dozing. He woke with a start when the car stopped.

'Mind yourself. Watch the old ice,' said John, already away with the bags. Reception needed only David's signature. John was halfway up the familiar stairs, ignoring the anxious porter. David followed, collapsed onto the bed. His friend smiled down from his six feet four.

'Well, boy! You won't be down for supper tonight, that's for sure!' From his pocket he drew a hip flask, poured a large one. 'Get that down, David *bach*, and get your head down after. Her ladyship will be here tomorrow, about six.'

David was asleep before the car reached the London road.

BOOK ONE
ENGLAND AND WALES
WINTER 1961

David slept through breakfast, waking bright as a button and marvellously pleased at having nothing whatever to do today. The Smuggler's efficient room service sent up tea and a pyramid of hot buttered toast with the newspapers. He showered, shaved and ventured into the January cold.

It was market day, the streets abustle with colourful stalls and townsfolk hunting for bargains. English voices and English noises, welcome sounds; the perfect antidote for the Ginza. The market pub served mulled wine, irresistible to freezing fingers. He quaffed happily with tradesmen and housewives, all bubbling and lively.

Mine host was sociable. 'Down from Town, sir?' he asked.

'Yes. Just a few days.'

'Business, no doubt?'

'No. Just a rest.'

'Nowhere better, sir! Plenty of good food, good sea air, and good ale too. I hope you'll enjoy it. Cheers!'

'Cheers!' he lifted his glass in response. Then out again, briskly round the town to the harbour, ears freezing, and back up the slippery hill to The Smuggler. Hearing the Hoover humming from his room, he picked up the newspapers and made for the bar. It was empty but for Harry, the barman, busily polishing glasses. Famous faces, ten-a-penny during the opera season, were rare as swallows at this time of the year. He was surprised and pleased.

'Cold enough for you, Mr Adams?'

'Indeed. Can you suggest a warmer, Harry?'

'Are you a connoisseur of malts, sir? We have the finest collection of malt whiskies in the county. Will you try my own fancy?'

'The best, is it?'

'The best is the one you drank last, sir. But you'll find this one goes down well.'

The liquid was almost gin-clear, slipping down with surprising ease, rich, peaty, and no bite. The aftertaste was a wonder. Harry shared his enjoyment.

'Come,' said David, 'have one with me.'

'With pleasure, sir.'

The drinks slipped down. Retribution was swift, reminding David of an empty stomach. 'What's for lunch, Harry?'

'Very nice steak and kidney pie, sir, here in the bar. Half the price without the tablecloth.'

Always first class . . . but it was good here, by the heaped fire, under black Armada-oak. Yes, a steak and kidney by all means. He settled by the hearth. The arts pages, as usual, were a source of amusement. Reviews relate to performance as pornography does to sex; the writer's fantasy, no more.

The pie was superb, going down well with a glass of claret. 'Now, sir, some Stilton?' Harry was making all the right suggestions. Perhaps he could tell David how to spend his afternoon?

'Have you seen Cocklesea?' he asked. 'The church is fine, and the town is lovely. Only two miles.' He glanced at the grandfather clock in the corner. 'You've just missed the bus, though. You can wait an hour or we can ring for a car?'

The days were short, the light soon fading. A car then.

Cocklesea was extraordinary; on a clifftop, in green squares regular as a draughtsman's dream, the church in the centre. David walked round the churchyard

34

wondering at the trim hedges, the tidy houses with loved lawns. Within the lych gate he stopped, leaning.

A cultured voice from behind: 'Quite remarkable, isn't it?'

He was an old man; very tall; with a stoop, smartly dressed in cords, and a hacking jacket over a pullover, his domed head bald as though tonsured. His eyes were clear, his cheeks glowed in the frosty air.

'Yes. Remarkable. As regular as Paris or Washington.'

A nod of agreement. 'This is much older than either, but not the original village.' The voice was soft, distinct, educated. 'Old Cocklesea is with the cockles. They built this one in good time and left the old one to drown.'

'No bells—'

'Under the sea? Nothing so romantic, I'm afraid. The church was always here, on the cliff. Come, let me show it to you.'

Willingly, David was led round the immemorial pile, shown the tombs of admirals, the gravestones of bishops and worthies long asleep. His guide stopped at an iron ladder set into the wall. 'I'm going up to wind the clock,' he said. 'Have you a head for heights?'

Carefully David followed him up and through a trap. There in its loft lay the daddy of all clocks; a machine in a great iron frame, a heart of drums wound round with ropes which disappeared through the floor to where the weights hung against the church wall.

Applying a handle, the old man turned easily, counting. Satisfied, he returned the tool to its place. David was silent, mesmerized by the great movement, its rocking escapement, its inexorable tick. Counting between beats he realized the machine was perfectly balanced. The old eyes saw his counting. A conductor

35

counts with his hands. 'Ah, I see you know about clocks?'

'No, but I know they must beat evenly.'

'And you know how to measure the beats I see.' He consulted a massive pocket watch. 'Shall we wait a moment and see the striking?'

A half-minute passed in measured silence. Then a whirring and a beating, a sudden movement of one drum, and four majestic strokes of a distant bell. Silence again, but for the tick, sweet and even. David tapped the rhythm on the stone, humming a phrase of Mozart in time with the beat.

' "To what am I now reduced . . ." ' said the old man.

David started, surprised, and finished the quotation. ' " . . . but to composing for a clock!" ' It was a line from a letter written by Mozart to his father; the complaint of a young man dying between the last opera and the incomplete Requiem, struggling to complete a commission from the owner of a mechanical organ. The old man smiled. 'A wonderful work, clockwork or not. Our organist gives a good account of it. You're a musician, sir?'

David offered his hand with his standard attempt at anonymity. 'John Davis,' he said. 'Yes, an amateur.'

The eyebrows raised quizzically, the handshake firm. 'And well read in Mozart.' He hesitated, then: 'My name is Jackson. I'm retired here.' He rose. 'May I offer you a cup of tea with some music?'

Some instinct, against all experience, advised acceptance. 'Thank you. That would give me great pleasure.'

They walked to a small house. Jackson produced biscuits, tea in mugs, and led the way to a warm sitting room overlooking the green and the church, all leather and walnut.

'That Fantasia,' said Jackson.

36

'Fantasia?'

'In F minor. For mechanical organ.' He was looking up something in a well-thumbed notebook. 'Have you heard it on the orchestra?'

David shook his head.

'Stokowski orchestrated it, among others. You may like it. I do. Here it is, anyway.'

They listened. Introduction, fugue, variations, double fugue, finale. Genius. Gratefully David stored the reference in his mind for future use.

Time was getting on. Rising, he offered thanks for a most interesting afternoon, looking anxiously at his watch and realizing that this kind man had taken him, as his mam would have said, out of himself for two hours.

'Glad to have met you, sir,' said the old man, leading him to the door. The car was waiting at the church.

Turning to go, David saw on the wall a familiar framed photograph; a very old one but a big print, all the faces clear. A concert platform, with a symphony orchestra. 'The Queen's Hall?'

'Yes. Wonderful old place. The perfect acoustic. Not the least of the good things Hitler spoiled.'

David stood a little closer, close enough to see the faces. There in the centre, on the rostrum, holding the stick, was the key, the face familiar from long ago. Younger far, but the same. He turned to his host, astonished.

The domed head nodded briefly, the old eyes bright. 'There's no escaping one's face, is there?' he said.

Thoughtful, David walked to the car.

$$\star \quad \star \quad \star$$

The red Porsche was outside, and as he came in from the car park David could hear Jane's voice at reception.

Two nights, possibly three. The bill to Grant's, with Mr Adams'. Yes, they'd both be in for dinner this evening. He stood at the passage end, admiring. She was not tall, but the proportions were perfect, surviving with ease the camouflage of her winter gear: white leather slacks, short boots, loose red wool from neck to hips, a white silk headscarf topping it off. Her face was hidden but he knew well the very dark eyes set in a creamy complexion, the mouth with its slightly pendulous lower lip, made for the flute, and the whole thing spoiled or made by the giveaway nose. He crept up behind.

'Carry your bags, ma'am?'

She turned, surprised. 'Oh, good. You're up and about.' He told her he'd been up and about all afternoon, picking up her two small bags. 'I'm on the third floor,' she said.

He put the cases down near the wardrobe, turning for a welcoming hug. 'Welcome back,' she said. 'It's been a long time.'

Yes, it had. Two weeks in Hong Kong, four in Australia, two in Korea, three in Japan. Long enough, certainly. He made a quick, easily evaded pass for her lips; a cheek was proffered. 'After the first three weeks one begins to wonder whether these islands are still afloat,' he told her.

She made a face, releasing herself to haul off the outer sweater, hair shaking down, 'Oh, come on. Japan must be fun. And all that Bondi sunshine, all those athletic ladies . . .' She sat own at the dressing table, hunting in her handbag for a comb. He told her that Japan had been fun the first time, that when one had seen one pagoda one had seen them all, and that Japanese ladies were not in the least attractive. Her face in the mirror, patting her hair, was disbelieving.

He gave her his pet theory about the Japanese – that they and the west had separated genetically at about the same time as had cats and dogs, and that the races now had as little in common as dogs had with cats. 'We walk on the same number of legs, eat roughly the same kind of food, keep themselves warm and dry by the same means, and that's about all. They're a different species. They know it. We don't. That's why they'll win.'

She shrugged. 'Well, happily for you and me they play the same sort of music, and as they seem to own about half the money in the world I propose to be nice to them.' Satisfied with her hair now, she turned on her stool with a grin. 'I'll have the fibs about boring old Australia and so on later. I have some telephoning to do. Meanwhile,' she produced from her bag a small sheaf of letters, 'these are for you. Not many, but one quite important, I fancy. Now, off with you while I get my act together. Can we perhaps meet at,' she looked at her wrist, 'six thirty?'

An hour with his letters, then. In his sitting room, by the fire, David opened them one by one, leaving the biggest envelope to the last. First a Cardiff postmark. Kate. Not a long letter, just her pleasure at seeing him in the news, her congratulations on his CBE, and hoping that if he was ever in Wales he'd telephone and perhaps have tea. There was some fanmail, with several requests for advice from aspiring conductors.

Then there was no escaping the brown envelope from Jane's brother's firm, the end of David's ten-year marriage. Poor Julie; what was it Moll had said? Pretty, clever, enjoys the same things, likes you . . . how lucky can a boy get? All true. More than pretty, ravishing she'd been and beautiful she still was. Such a wedding, in spite of her parents' doubts. They'd waited through his time in Vienna, until both their careers seemed assured, but her family had never believed it would work. A musician, a *conductor*? Why not something sensible, reliable? Nice people. How they must have hated him in the end. Now it would all come right for her; a new man in her life, the sort they'd always wanted. In her bed too. He probed the wound to see if it still hurt. No, it didn't. She deserved well and he'd failed her. Molly would hate that, felt she'd had a share in it. Wrong of course; she'd done wonders. How lucky could a boy get?

* * *

Showered and glowing among the feathers, released and relaxed, he was half asleep. A small noise on the landing and the door opened, closed. She was a presence in the room now; soft breathing and softer scents, a whisper of silk. He held his breath.

'Awake?'

'Mmmm . . .'

'Not reading tonight, then?'

The day had provided all the stimulus he'd needed. Lucky, lucky he. The bedclothes lifted and Molly sat, her warmth next to his, her legs tucked under her.

'A good day, was it?'

'Lovely, thank you.'

'Kate not too posh then?'

'A bit. But nice.'

'Yes, that's about it. Pretty too.'

'Yes.'

'Tell me what is pretty about her.'

'Don't know. All pretty, one way and another.'

'Never took your eyes off her. Quite jealous I am.'
He blushed safely in the dark and she chuckled softly. 'Well, she liked it, I could see. Soldiers' ladies don't meet so many handsome young men, you know.'

He was quick on the uptake. 'Oh, a man I am now? Yesterday I wasn't.'

'No, nor tonight, David. That's why you must

promise.' She was serious now. 'Not one promise, two promises. And not promises to break, but *real* promises.'

'I promise!'

She laughed aloud. 'There's easy! You don't know what the promises are, yet.'

'Whatever.'

'Think before you say it. Promise never to tell anyone in the world about what happened last night.'

'I've promised already.'

'But are you really sure?'

'*Yes!*'

'If you ever think about breaking the promise, remember it's mine as well as yours. It's between you and me for ever and ever.'

'Yes.'

'Now, promise that until you know how to be safe you will never . . .'

He waited, breathless. She was stuck now. 'This promise is for Julie really,' she said.

'Why Julie?'

'Her or any other girl.'

'What must I promise?'

'David, you know what . . .' she took a deep breath and plunged, 'What men and women do together?'

'Yes. Chance would be a fine thing.'

'Chance will come. And chance can ruin your life and some poor girl's life too. So when the chance comes remember that?'

'Yes, but I don't know—'

'Wise to know that you don't know, anyway. The answer is to use hands, boy, until it is safe. Hands are not so bad, are they?' Hers were under the sheet now, seeking him out, finding the sap still seeping. She smiled in the dark. 'I see. Missed the bus, have I?'

He said nothing. She bent, kissed him, and sap leaped again, regardless of sheets. 'So,' she said, busy

41

with a handkerchief, 'there was another bus.' He nodded, happy and grateful. 'Hands are not so bad, you see,' she said again.

'Lovely.'

'My hands better than yours?'

'Mmmmm . . .' was all he could muster.

She shivered. 'It's a bit cold out here. Move over a bit?'

He moved readily. She slid between the sheets, drew them up about them both. 'Cuddle up?' she suggested. Willingly he put his arms around her. She hugged, relaxed, released herself, lay back a little, away from him. Talk now. 'So, never inside Julie's pants, David?'

'Never. I told you—'

'Yes, I know you told me. So, a big mystery there, is it?'

'No.'

'No? So you've had a look round? Further investigation would be welcome, no doubt?'

He was silent. Her hands were busy below, pulling, adjusting. Then about her bust, buttons and strings. She relaxed again, reached for his hands in the dark, kissed them both. 'Come.' His hands were on her breasts now; warm, firm, pliant.

'Nice?'

'Mmmm . . .'

'Bigger than Julie's?'

'Yes.'

'So, her breasts at least?'

'Once.'

'Kiss them.'

He took her instruction for a question. 'No.'

'Not hers, fool. Mine. Kiss them.' She took his hand in her hands, led him. He kissed her, his excitement rising against her leg. God, she thought again, what a thing to be a boy and fifteen, so beautiful and so ready. Her nipples were hot and hard under his lips, swelling globes smooth under his hands. Her hands reached behind him, holding, her leg moving softly.

'Oh . . . I'm . . . I . . .'

'Yes,' she said, encouraging.

Again the miracle, his breath coming short and sharp, little cries escaping, warmth on her leg. He lay on her breast like a suckling child, his breathing slowing, coming down in a long dark silence.

Now he'd sleep. She would get up and go. In a moment, yes, go she must, otherwise where would it stop? The space between her legs, the ache in her breasts, spoke for themselves. So much restraint, so many months, the eyes of so many men. He was a man; a man with everything to learn, everything to do, but so much promise. She knew that if she stayed it would be as much for herself as for him. He must never know how much she had to give, how hard it had been to keep it from him. Kiss good night and go, then, leave him happy.

She leaned over, found his lips, kissed. Suddenly his arm was around her neck, the other lower, clinging, kissing on and on. Then her helpless response, holding tight, hips heaving to him, grinding. Would he never let go? Thank God he didn't know how close he was. She released him carefully, slowly, lay back again; a Rubicon crossed but the boats unburned. Long silent minutes listening to his breathing. Was he asleep now? She found his hand. It closed on hers. No, not asleep, waiting. She raised herself on her elbow, looking at him in the dark. 'Happy?' she asked.

'Lovely.' The whole world was lovely tonight.

She was a woman, and curious. 'How many times can you do it, David?'

'Do it?'

'Yes, you know . . .'

'Don't know. Depends.'

'Every day?'

'Oh yes.' The tone of his voice spoke volumes for the frequency.

She smiled in the dark. 'Do you know that girls do it too?'

'Yes.'

So he'd seen it happen, perhaps caused it somehow. 'David, feel.' She led his fingers to her waist. They stroked, smoothed, round to her hips and back, then again further, hesitating, taking nothing for granted, expecting her restraint, hoping and fearing. She lay back on the pillow, hands behind her head, trusting, his hands on her soft smooth middle. Softly, 'Lower, if you like?' Smoothing lower, meeting her hair, fingering, combing, curious. Such hands the boy had, pianist's hands, long fingers seeking, searching, shyly lower. Her legs opened of themselves, stretching, meeting his harder limbs. Careful now. She must be careful. His fingers met the lips, suspensefully dry but swelling in her hair. A fine line. Down, up, down again, hardly touching. In the dark the peach-skin parted, oozing juice, offering its stone. He stopped, wondering; moved, stroked softly. She held her breath. Lie still now, let him learn. His hand rested, covering her.

He spoke, unsure. 'Can I . . .?'

She kissed his ear. 'Careful.' Her hips raised themselves, offering. She was entered, deep. Time now to show him?

'Gently, David, very soft now. Higher, at the top, very, very gentle, gentle.' She was nearly there, mounting, breathless. 'Easy, round, round,' whispering, hardly speaking now. His fingers moving, moving, her hips suddenly wide, heaving, closing hard, her lips reaching as the massive climax struck, his hand trapped. Long moments as she thrashed, the boy helpless and wondering. Two people breathing, recovering, questioning, wishing, seeking.

She was first to speak. 'Now you know how it is with women, David.'

'The same as with men.'

'No. Not the same. With men a small thing, a squirting and a pushing. With us a world of difference, I'm sure. And not so often as with a man neither. It depends, love.'

'On what?'

'Oh, different things. Care. When, where, who. Love . . .'

'Anyway,' he said, 'it's lovely for both.' It was his favourite word tonight, and not far wide of the mark, she thought. Coming from love.

'Go to sleep now. I must go to bed.'

'No. Stay.'

She stroked his forehead, soothing. 'I can't. You know I mustn't. You'll play games all night. I must go.'

'Don't laugh. I don't want to play games.'

'I'm not laughing at you, love. But . . .'

'I'll come with you.'

'No, David. Only one man sleeps in my bed. You know what I'm saying, David.'

'Well, stay here. Stay in our bed.'

No, he didn't know. How could he know what a temptation he was? Our bed? Good God, *our* bed? What to do, what to say? 'Will you go to sleep if I stay?' She would creep out, once he was safely away.

'Yes, of course.'

He lay facing her. She turned away. His arms were around her. She reached to pull her silk down between them. Such a lovely boy, so big, so full of life, and so damned dangerous. She smiled to herself.

He was asleep already, breathing deep and even. How good to give such rest. In a moment she would go. She relaxed, moving his arms from her body slowly, slowly. His breathing safe, soft, slow, like a child . . .

Was it the sunlight which woke her, or the movement? He was still asleep, dreaming deep, his hips moving quietly against her, enormous in the silk between her legs. Oh God, what to do? She bent, affording safe space. Would it never stop? His arms holding tight, his breath hard in her ear, coming awake.

'Oh . . . what? Did I . . . did I?'

'No, love. Nearly, but no. It's all right.'

'Oh . . . I'm sorry.'

'Nothing to be sorry about. I was daft enough to be here, and you did what any man would do. Or nearly. My nightie saved it.' The material was cold now between her legs. 'David, look the other way while I get out, there's a good boy.'

'No, I want to look. Please, I want to see.'

Oh well, what point in denying his eyes when she had given to his hands? She sighed, surrendering. 'Oh well, look if you must, then.' She sat up, the sheet coming down with the movement. Her nightdress was a tangled mess.

'Let me,' he said.

'No. Leave it.' She lifted from the hem, raising over her head, her breasts lifting. Lying back, searching his eyes, finding what? Lust? No, wonder. Love? What was it, love? In his eyes adoration, feasting. Would he move, touch? His hands moved, touched her face, smoothed. Dear God, what a nice boy this was, what a nice man he would be. A soft kiss on her cheek now. She turned, rewarding, to kiss his mouth. His hand on her breast now, gentle, kind, but her nipple a diamond. She looked into his eyes still. Yes, love was there, kind honest love with the urgency.

She pressed him back into the feathers, his eyes still

46

on hers, waiting, wondering. She kissed him again as her legs came astride, holding him, placing. Down now, and he up into her warm space. His eyes, held by hers, opened wide as his hips heaved helplessly. She thrust down once, twice, then she was holding him while his flesh leaped within her, one, twice and again. So quick she thought, so quick. His breath came in throaty gasps, lungs gasping as though under water, then out with a rush as his arms grasped her falling body, turned her head, kissed her hard, violent, his teeth against hers. The coming, the never-to-be-forgotten first coming. It was done.

Her spinning head cleared slowly, slowly. What had she done, silly woman? Such a delight was silly, to give and receive? A crime and a delight, an offence and a privilege.

His arms were relaxing. She moved, relaxing with him, unsatisfied but happy. What a wonder, to give such pleasure again. So long since, and so hard to live without this giving. In a long silence she looked again at him, at his young face and lean body, he up at her.

'Well, young David, now you know.'

'Yes.'

She lay down with a sigh, spoke to the air. 'That's what makes the world go round.'

He was silent, waiting. There were small noises from the world outside. 'We must get up,' she said.

'It's early.' The pleading was in his voice, but she needed time; time to think, time to gather wits. 'Mustn't waste the morning. I'll have the shower first, make the breakfast.' She was up and away, escaping his hands. He was left with his thoughts, his discoveries. The shower stopped. He was out of bed and into the bathroom, hoping to catch her before she could escape, but no, she was in her housecoat and on the stairs.

Down again to breakfast in the sitting room, finding

her before the mirror, tidying her hair. She turned. He took her in his arms, hugged. She kissed his cheeks, auntlike.

'I love you,' he said.

She looked at him, smiled. 'I love you too. Always did, from a tiny tot.'

'Yes, but special . . .'

'Yes, special, but only on loan, for one week only.' Trying to joke now, keep a balance, busy with cups, teapot, mundane things. There was a call from the gate. It was Kate with Isolde; sane, life-saving normality. She'd invite her in, give her coffee.

Kate's eyes twinkled, amused. 'Lazybones, the pair of you. The day's half over.' Molly was busy still, hiding small blushes. He was into the eggs and bacon, shy. Isolde sat close to him, waiting for bits. Kate asked if he'd walk the dog today and Molly was quick to encourage.

Isolde was happy, swimming, retrieving her ball from the sea, shaking and splashing, showing off, the male company delighting her. They ran together, working up a heat despite the bracing air, a mile each way on the sand, and back to the house. In through the kitchen door to give the dog water.

There were voices in the sitting room. Kate first: 'His people, though. Will they agree?'

'I think so. He has only his grandmother, and I'm sure she doesn't know what to do with him. Someone must suggest it, if the talent is so big.'

'Molly, I'm quite sure. It's not just the piano, it's the sense of style, of judgement, the ideas. He mustn't be wasted. It's so easy to waste people.'

'Well, you'll have most of the afternoon. Find out for yourself. It's his life, no one else's.'

'You have no idea what he wants to do?'

'No, and neither has he, so far as I can see. He's in

love with his music. Otherwise he's fifteen, and you know what fifteen-year-old boys think about.'

'Such a beautiful boy, I must say. Quite trying, sitting on the same piano stool. Difficult to keep my hands on the keyboard at times.' They laughed together. 'He's a temptation. Still, safer with his Aunt Molly than with some other starved female.'

Molly now. 'Oh, he's only young. Quite an innocent. Mind you, they learn quite easily.'

More laughter, then Kate's voice: 'Yes, they seem to pick it up. Not that I've ever had to teach one. Mine have always come second-hand, if you see what I mean.'

Laughing again, then Molly. 'Mine too, all but one. I did once have a brand-new one . . .'

'Oh, golly, when?'

Listening, David's heart was in his mouth.

'Oh, not important when. But once.'

Kate mused. 'I'm not sure I envy you, on second thoughts. It could be rough.'

'No, honestly. It was . . . lovely, really.' Her voice was soft, a smile in it.

'Well,' Kate's voice was low, 'there are times when any nice safe anonymous man would do for me. It's been a long time.'

Molly was thoughtful. 'David now. So young and so far to go, no time to waste. All that can be such a distraction for a boy. Get in the way, I mean. It should be . . . oh, I don't know.'

'Disposed of,' chuckled Kate, 'so that they can get down to serious work? I'm sure it won't be long before some lucky girl has her way with him. I know a camp full of ATS who would be happy to educate him.'

'Well, tomorrow, it's back to school and the girl-friend.'

'Ah, there's a girlfriend?'

'I'm surprised there's only one.'

The dog was behind him in the passageway, butting him through the door. They tumbled in together. The two women were before the fire, empty sherry glasses on a tray.

Kate rose. 'The wanderer's return. If you'd like a few minutes more at the piano, David, I'll be in this afternoon.'

He looked at Molly. She nodded. 'It's my turn for the shopping. I'll be two hours at least. Go and practise, David. I'll drop you off on my way.'

★　★　★

In the friendly room the instrument was open already, some Schubert on the desk. Well, why not? He sat and began, the instrument singing to him in the familiar voice a century-and-a-half old, always new. Then to Mozart, from memory. The sixteenth sonata, with the variations in A major. At the end he felt her presence in the doorway, turned.

'You like him best, David?'

'Yes. But very hard he is.'

'Why, d'you think?'

'Not the notes. Just to get it right. Always different, every day.'

'Makes him interesting, though, doesn't it?' She was looking among the scores in the shelves. 'Do you know the symphonies?'

'Some of them. On the wireless.'

'The BBC has an orchestra in Cardiff, do you know?'

Yes, he knew, but it might as well have been on the moon. What he wished for was a symphony once a week, in the Workmen's Hall, Cwmbach. That would be the day.

Now she'd found what she'd been looking for, a

50

score of the twenty-ninth symphony. 'Do you know this one?'

He didn't.

'A little one, but lovely. My favourite, I think. Look, not many parts to play. You play the strings, I'll play the wind. Four lines for me, five for you.'

A new challenge, then. After a little it came easily enough, but the finale had too many notes for either of them, and the symphony dissolved in their laughter.

Her hand was on his shoulder. 'Let's have a rest, shall we?'

She led the way to the kitchen where Isolde was watching the kettle. She made tea, opened a tin and produced a fruitcake. David could hardly believe his eyes. Slicing, she said, 'We called this railway cake at school. We used to buy it at the station on the first day of holidays, waiting for the train home. It always reminds me of trains, holidays, school. My favourite cake, even made with dried egg.' She poured. 'David, what will you do after school, do you know?'

'Play, I suppose.'

'Is it a living?'

'If I'm good enough.' He broke off a crumb, generously dropped it to the waiting dog. 'I can teach. I can play at concerts.'

Kate mused. How to make the point without discouraging, that was the problem. 'Is the piano enough?' she asked.

'I like it. It's what I can do.'

'Yes, but there's far more music than piano music, and there are so many good pianists. Perhaps you shouldn't decide too soon. Look, if you aim for the top of the trees that's as far as you can go. Better to aim for the moon, perhaps? Why not take advice from people who know?'

'Like who?'

'I know the Professor at Cardiff, and the BBC

people too. Shall I ask them? Would your grandmother be offended?'

He shook his head. 'Pleased she'd be.'

'Sure?'

'Oh yes. She wants what is best for me. And not to go down the pit, you see.'

Reassuring, this simple confidence. 'Righto! I'll talk to my friends. If they have ideas I'll tell Molly, shall I?'

'Lovely!' Everything and everyone was lovely this week, one way and another. 'I wonder what I can do, though, except play.'

'We'll see. It will be the piano first anyway, so practise hard and do it as well as you can. But there will be lots of things to do after the war.'

After the war? He couldn't imagine a world without the war now, though he remembered the one before it, a world where the shops had oranges and bananas. 'Will it be better then?'

'Much better. People are making all sorts of plans. Much more music for everyone. And about time too.' She got up. 'Molly will be back. She'll think I've stolen you.'

Wanting to thank her, he couldn't find words. She smiled, knowing that words would come with the years, asking nothing now but his silent worship, the light in his eyes a reminder of her appeal to his senses.

On the way to the door a sudden thought: 'If you find you need scores, David, the symphonies, you know . . . they're all here. Well, not all, but the big ones – Mozart, Haydn, Beethoven, Brahms. All lying here waiting for Hitler to pack up, like Molly and me! So if you need one, ask!'

At the door he turned to offer thanks. Finally unable to resist, she took him in her arms and hugged him hard. For seconds she enjoyed him. Then they separated, a love affair complete in a golden minute.

He'd been dozing. It was 6.30. He threw on a suit and went to find Jane.

She was in the bar, drinking with Harry. Unusually for a woman, she enjoyed whisky.

'I see you've found it,' he said.

'Harry's whisky? Yonks ago. After my father, Harry's the best judge of a malt I've ever met. Come, join us. Cheers!'

They made small talk for a time by the fire, until an influx of talkative regulars provided the privacy they needed. Then: 'It really is good to have you back,' she told him.

'It's mutual, believe me,' he said feelingly. 'It truly was too long this time.'

She was concerned. 'You really don't enjoy travelling, David, do you?'

'I don't know, truth to tell. Before Vienna I'd never travelled at all. Since then it's been work always. Airports, hotels, concert halls . . . it never stops.'

'It's a problem. The money is abroad. What can I find you to do here, d'you think?'

'Something uncomplicated, like Music Director at Covent Garden and Chief Conductor of the LSO at the same time. Then perhaps I could travel for fun, to see whether I like it.'

She laughed. 'Hang on a mo, until I find my magic lamp, and all will be well. Until then I'm afraid you'll have to up and go when asked. Anyway, for what it's worth, our man in Tokyo has been making appreciative noises.'

'Mmmm. I'm still fooling them, it seems. But it's good to be home, or nearly. Home properly in a day or two if my slave-driving agent will kindly let me off the leash.'

'Well,' she said carefully, 'there are things to do first, please. I'd meant to tell you over dinner, but . . .'

'Now, please?'

'*Figaro* at Glyndebourne, summer after next. We have to talk casting tomorrow. You have a choice of producer, what's more.'

'What it is to be well-managed. Congratulations.'

Pleased with the compliment, she was too honest to accept all the credit. 'David, it's not down to me, really.'

'Bunkum! The whole thing's been down to you, from the very beginning.'

'Well, in a way. But there is a point where the thing takes off. We're not promoting you any more. The work just comes in and we choose the best. No one can *sell* a conductor to Glyndebourne, nor to Philip.'

The name halted the glass, halfway to his lips. 'Philip? How did Covent Garden get into this conversation?'

'We're invited to see your old friend from Dresden conduct there on Wednesday. *Figaro*, coincidentally. Supper afterwards. It can only mean he wants you.'

'But for what?'

'I'm not psychic. You'll have to wait and see.'

'Nothing on the grapevine?'

'Lots, but we never trust the Garden grapevine. Wait and see. There'll be a game to play. There always is with that man.'

They were called for dinner. 'But we haven't ordered,' he said. Jane coloured, a little embarrassed. 'I hope you don't mind. I know you love the lobster and it takes so long . . .'

David took her arm. 'As I said, what it is to be well-managed.'

They went in. It was still early, and pleasantly quiet. They sat near the fire, the blaze from the logs highlighting Jane's hair. Beautiful, he thought; a really lovely woman.

The wine waiter poured. David offered her the glass and she sipped thoughtfully, nodded.

'This thing about whisky,' he asked, 'did GG really know about it?'

'Absolutely. None better. He took it up because it was the British thing to do, like cricket and rugby. Frankly I'm not sure he ever understood either game but he understood Scotch all right. The only drink, he used to say. The best collection of malts in London is in my cellar, or was until the boys started borrowing it. I learned quite a lot. That one—' she gestured in the direction of the bar – 'was a Glen Grant, the same age as me. I know because it was the bottle that came out most often at home.'

She knew her wine too, and he sipped, mentally congratulating her on her choice, watching her unwind.

Something he'd always wanted to ask her. He hoped this was a good time. 'Your father. Tell me . . .'

'Well?'

'Didn't much like me, I think?'

Her smile was frank. 'Nothing personal. You were his big mistake, that was the chief reason. Not your fault.'

'Really? I thought I'd done him proud.'

'Oh, you did. That was his problem. He never believed the British could produce a conductor, a real one. Not enough opera, he used to say. Opera makes conductors and there's not enough of it here. Then there was the name. He said the only British conductors to make it internationally had been Stokowski and Barbirolli. How would he sell a David Adams? That's why he gave you to me to run. He was sure I'd lose out.'

'Well, he went too soon to see you win.'

'He'd begun to suspect I might, actually.'

There was a thoughtful silence. Then: 'I owe you both a great deal, Jane.'

She gave a good imitation of her father's cartoon-Jewish shrug of resignation, palms raised. ' "Just business," he'd say, if he were here.'

They were into the lobster now, and the wine was doing its work. She was leaving the office behind. There was a long silence, excusable in the presence of so good a meal and such fine wine, then she was looking at him pensively over her glass. Apprehensive? Yes, a little. Well, give her time. Time and a small nudge.

'There was another reason, then?' he suggested.

'Another . . .?'

'The chief reason, you said. So there was another.'

'Oh. Yes. There was, I think, though he never spoke of it. He thought you were dangerous, you see.'

'Dangerous?'

'To women. To me.' She was demolishing her lobster skilfully. 'Are you surprised? Surely not. Your performance is no secret. Even as a student it wasn't. He'd done his homework, you know. And I am a woman.'

'I'd noticed,' he said.

'And therefore vulnerable.'

'The least vulnerable woman I know,' he said.

'I see.' There was a sudden edge to her voice, betraying a strain he hadn't suspected. He quickly turned the conversation to safer subjects.

With the arrival of the cheese she asked, 'Are you glad it's over?'

'I am indeed,' he said. 'Please don't send me to Japan again for twenty years.'

'Don't fence, David.'

'What? Oh, Julie, you mean?'

'Yes.'

'It *is* over, that's the thing. I have these impressive papers from your learned brother to prove it.'

She turned up her nose, unconvinced. 'I know what the papers say; what about the gut?'

'The gut has known it was over for some time.'

'Free, then?'

'Yes, free. I hope she'll be happy. It's all I ask, that she'll be happy now.'

'Don't be too hard on yourself. It was six of one . . .'

'And half a dozen of the other? Not quite. Only one on her side, rather more on mine. But hers counted. Mine didn't.'

'Did you seriously expect her to accept that yours didn't count?'

'Why not? I know that they didn't. You and I know women who can and do accept such things.'

'Unusual women. It isn't the way women tend to see these things. It's not something I could accept.'

'Perhaps not. But you know the business. You know how it is.'

'Yes. And I know some people who've come through it with sixty years of fidelity.'

'I tried. You know how close Julie and I were. We'd survived a lot. Ten years waiting to marry, from school through college and Vienna, while she qualified. Her family made it as hard as they could.'

'Did you really wait?'

'God, no! No two people were ever so mutually explosive, or so sure of each other.'

'Why, then? Where did it go wrong?'

'There wasn't a single point where it went wrong. Not like the *Titanic* and the iceberg. A marriage can spring a tiny leak and one day you wake up with your feet wet.'

'But where was the leak?'

'I don't know. I haven't thought it through.'

'That I don't believe,' she said. 'You've thought it

through from the inside, as your friends have tried to from the outside. We thought you two would survive. We thought you had it sorted out.'

He was irritated. 'So, my friends know the answer?'

'No, of course not. We've seen the obvious things. They don't provide the answer.'

'Tell me what my friends can see.'

She was wary now. 'David, it takes a very strange man to be a successful conductor, you know?'

'It's an odd sort of job, certainly.'

'To control like that. With no authority beyond what you can deliver from your head, with your body and hands. Words don't work, even. The job consumes people totally. Is there any energy left for the rest of your life?'

He smiled, trying to keep the conversation light. 'My wife – my *former* wife – might say I had too much energy.'

'That's the other thing. You people are so often dynamite with women.'

'Dynamite?'

'Yes. The biggest stag in the herd, you see.'

He shrugged. 'Groupies.'

'No. You know very well that's not true. Quite clever women.'

'Don't exaggerate, Jane. Conductors are not magicians.'

'The good ones are, in a way. David, I'm talking about instant attraction, unreasoning attraction, the sort that gets you into bed with the wives of cultural attachés.' She laughed at the surprise in his face. 'Our man in Tokyo was very informative, you see.'

'All right. A fine concert produces adrenalin, a hundred times as much in the conductor as in the audience. Women feel it. They know it's waiting, bottled up.'

'Indeed. My father taught me never to knock on

the greenroom door too soon after the concert. Winding down can be a very immediate matter, it seems.'

'Jane,' he said, throwing caution and good manners to the wind together, 'there's another factor. Good conductors have lots of money.'

She stopped eating, folding her arms defensively. 'My God, do you really dislike women so much? Have all your women been whores?'

He must press on; he had no alternative. 'No I don't, and no they weren't. But if you're right, and the biggest stag gets the pick, by your own reckoning it's the power, the money, the influence . . .'

'So, you take the pick and give nothing? Nothing beyond exciting company and good night? And afterwards home to the little woman who knows, of course, that you've just been out to stud but it's nothing that *counts*? I'll remember that next time you make your routine pass.' Her face was flushed. All this was much nearer the bone than he'd realized.

Very well then, the truth, if she must have it. 'Jane,' he said seriously, 'I've long since given up hope of getting you into bed.'

'So, why the routine?'

'Never routine, since you ask. I put my arms round you from time to time, usually after concerts, from good old-fashioned gratitude. I *am* grateful, you see. You don't seem to mind, and it's no hardship, I can tell you. Then the other thing takes over, that's all.'

'After old-fashioned gratitude, old-fashioned sex. I see.'

'It takes over because you are beautiful, because I've wanted you from the first day I saw you. It stops because you wish it, because you are not to be trifled with. Anyway, you seem to enjoy it, in a limited way.'

She applied her napkin in a thoughtful silence. A decision to be made, he thought, watching her; a fork in the road.

The waiter was at his elbow. 'Your coffee is ready, sir, in the lounge.'

They were sitting in the deep cushions, cups filled, before Jane spoke again. 'Yes,' she said quietly. 'I'll accept that. I do enjoy it, and the limitation was essential.'

He nodded, carefully skirting round her past tense. 'I know that.'

'You never seem to wish to press on, David.'

'Because I'm sure you don't wish it. We stop because it's what you want. Persuasion would be impertinent and probably impossible. What can one do but stop?'

'But you could have, you see.'

'Persuaded? I didn't know.'

'Easily. And if you'd known?'

He put his arm around her shoulder and kissed her cheek. 'Jane, you are no one's one-night stand.'

'But I am, of course, sometimes. Surely you realize that?'

He felt a sudden chill, deep in his gut. 'No, I don't realize it.'

'There are very few virgins past eighteen, outside nunneries. Women need men. Better still, a man.'

His voice was tired. 'Yes, all right, I believe you.'

'But you wish me to be a virgin, at twenty-eight?'

'Jane, this is an impossible conversation. You are entitled to live as you wish. So am I.'

'Yes. I always have been, and from today you are too. That's the problem.'

His mental fog was thickening by the minute. Jet lag catching up? he wondered. 'Why?' he asked. 'For the love of God tell me why liberty is a problem?'

She settled back into the cushions, hands folded carefully before her, eyes frank. 'Because I've wanted you since the day we met; because now, at last, I'm allowed to say so; and because I'm afraid that I'll never be free of you if we once sleep together.'

'I didn't know,' he said, very tired now, 'that you wished to be free of me.'

'Idiot!' The exasperation in her voice turned heads at the other end of the room. 'I don't. Of course I don't. But I can contain what I feel, so far. It's under control. When I hear stories of diplomatic wives in Japan, of record producers in Los Angeles, of sopranos in Prague, I can say – oh, that silly man, he can't refuse a pair of legs; one day he'll grow up. I can laugh, or at least pretend to laugh. But can I be sure that I'd feel the same way tomorrow, after a night together? You think I'm no one's one-night stand. Well, where I'm concerned, neither are you.'

'You're asking for commitment, I think,' he said.

She laughed. 'Commitment? You don't know what commitment means, David. No, I'm not asking *you* for anything. I'm asking myself whether I could be happy in a relationship with a man who can't be trusted out of sight.'

'And you know you can't.'

She sighed. 'I wish I could. Sex as a recreation doesn't interest me. Sex with you will be another matter.'

'Will be?'

'Yes. Unless you decide against it.'

'I'm to decide?'

'Yes.'

'Not a bit fair, are you?'

'I think it's entirely fair – to you. You have to decide whether you're prepared to put our present relationship at risk.'

'Jane, after this evening our relationship can never be the same again, anyway.'

She shrugged. 'Oh, I don't know. It rather depends on one's discipline, doesn't it?'

Yes, thought David, it rather does; and discipline she had in spades. Professionally she'd survive easily without him. Emotionally, well, she'd cope. But he, without her? She was right. Truly he was more at risk than she. She was smiling quietly, following his thoughts. 'Fair, then?' she asked.

'Fair? I don't know. Look, reason is one thing. You could be hurt.'

'Yes. I think that's very likely, one way or another. I'm prepared for that . . . So what happens now?'

He looked at her; the marvellous shape in the twin-set and tweed, the perfect legs properly together, the dark eyes watchful under the luxurious black hair. 'Jane, I'm only human. There are limits . . .'

'Yes, I know, and the cultural attaché's wife is five days ago.' She stood up. 'Take your time, David. Think about it. I need perhaps a half-hour anyway.' She consulted her watch. 'If you don't appear by eleven I'll read myself to sleep.'

A bleep on the bedside telephone. Blindly he picked it up. Jane's voice, office-sharp. 'D'you know what time it is?'

'Sleepily. 'What . . .?'

'Nine thirty. The middle of the day. I've had a walk and read the arts pages.'

'Good God!'

'We have very little time before the bacon stops sizzling. I'll see you there in ten minutes. Jump to it.'

He showered, shaved, donned slacks and a pullover. She hovered outside the restaurant, newspaper in hand, wifelike in tweeds and warm ribbed stockings, her hair up in a bun, and they went in together. The dining room of last evening had been screened to half, but their lateness provided privacy from all but a last handful of residents. The waitress approached, menus in hand, and Jane ordered confidently for them both, juices, cereals, grills, with toast and tea.

'I'm terribly hungry, it seems,' he said, surprised.

She was embarrassed, a little. 'You can eat or you can nibble as you wish. If you're stuck I'll eat your toast. I was merely trying to avoid your asking me whether I drank coffee or tea in the morning and whether I took sugar in either.'

He laughed. 'Darling, you're trying to look domestic!'

'I'm trying not to look like a seduced secretary, is what I'm trying to do.'

'Does it matter so much?'

'Of course. One mustn't embarrass people.'

'The waitress will have seen it rather often, you know.'

'Then she'll appreciate my attempt at tact all the more.'

He gave up the unwinnable argument. 'Where did you pick up these seduced-secretarial skills, may I ask? Does *Woman's Realm* give tips?'

'I don't know. John Updike does, rather. You'd know, if you read anything but Kraut philosophers.'

His German, begun in Vienna, was constantly polished in that way. He nodded in the direction of the approaching tea. 'That young lady needs neither Updike nor Schopenhauer to tell her how it is with us.'

The corners of her mouth turned down, disbelieving. 'Psychic is she? Or does my worshipping gaze give me away?'

'Neither.' There was a space while dishes were arranged, tea poured, busy steps retreated, all ears. 'Darling, if you wish me to remain anonymous you'll have to keep my face off the front page of the *Sunday Times*. You are no doubt registered as Miss Grant? Look, hotels like this provide beds largely for people to make love in. They are not in the least embarrassed, I promise you.'

'You don't give a damn what they think, do you?' she asked seriously.

'What do you think they think?'

'That's very obvious indeed, if you're right.'

'They think we slept together, and they think you are a very lucky lady.'

'Bloody conceit!' She was really cross now. Time to retreat and retrieve.

'I didn't say that you *were* lucky, only that they would think so. They don't know that behind the famous face is a pitifully inadequate human being, a pain in the neck, utterly dependent on his talent for acceptance, exploiting an impressionable and beautiful lady.'

'And a disaster in bed?'

'Right!'

She smiled over the rim of her cup. 'I'm not really good at all this.'

'I'm very glad to hear it.'

'But of course you get lots of practice.'

He put down his fork, suddenly depressed. 'Jane, it was lovely. Don't spoil it, please.'

There was a silence while she sipped tea, thinking, adjusting.

'Yes, all right,' she agreed, 'it was lovely. You were lovely, we were lovely. More lovely than one could ever have hoped.'

And that was her problem, it seemed. He remembered that look, eyes wide with surprise as her arms had closed around him and her lips searched for his. He'd left her, with a soft undemanding kiss, in the early dawn; fluffed her pillow, tucked her in, exhausted, relaxed. Poor Jane. Poor wonderful, clever, astonished Jane. He reached for her hand. She looked round, alarmed, but the room had emptied. He kissed her fingers in a long silence disturbed only by the murmur of distant kitchen voices.

She retrieved her limb. 'Come along,' rising, her voice unsure. 'You must get some air. We'll walk down to the sea.'

'Oh, will we?'

'Yes. If you anticipate further adventures at half-past ten in the morning, abandon hope. Whatever the inn thinks of us I have no intention of advertising.'

They donned scarves and coats against the winter air and stepped out on salted pavements under icicled gutterings. Down the hill and through the old town to the harbour, boats bobbing on the rising tide, then up the hill to the castle with its view over the sea.

'I read a book about all this, about this coast, once,' she said.

'One of my brothers', yonks ago. About smugglers. It was a very masculine house, ours. I read a lot of boys' books.'

'I gather they read a more colourful list today. Lawrence, even. Joyce.'

'Very hard going, that. The juicy bits are famous, but too far between. A bit like Wagner, really.'

'I didn't know you liked juicy bits. Tell me more.'

'All will be revealed, I expect, if you stick around.'

He promised to stick around as long as he could. She sighed. 'Ah, but your agent, clever girl, will soon wing you away to Boston.'

'I'll be back.'

'In two months. Leaving me with a problem, perhaps.'

He was aghast. 'Darling, I didn't ask —'

'Oh, not that problem. That's well in hand. I knew it would be this time or never.'

'So sure?'

'Yes, of course. For how long do you think you could go on fumbling under my skirt in greenrooms and limousines? Anyway, I'm safe as can be. So have no fear.'

He turned her, took her in his arms, kissed her and hugged her tight. He spoke into her hair. 'This conversation is creating a certain demand, love.'

She leaned against him. The demand was evident. She smiled. 'Not gone off me now that you've had your wicked way, then?'

'We've hardly begun, believe me.'

'Oh, I think we've begun all right. But we can't continue just here, I fancy?'

'You're right — too cold. And silly when we have a bed waiting.'

She made a face. 'Even sillier when you and I have to be at Glyndebourne in an hour.'

'Bugger Glyndebourne.'

'No, it's Bognor.'

'Bognor?'

'Yes. Bugger Bognor. George the Fifth and all that. He didn't much care for Bognor.'

'You've lost me.'

'Obviously,' she sighed. 'Too much Nietzsche, too little English history. Never mind. Come, we must pop over and decide casting for your Mozart. That's why we're here, darling, remember? Business?'

So they got out her Porsche and motored over for lunch at Glynde; producers with the apéritif, sopranos with the pâté, baritones with the beef, and her eyes glowing the whole time with excitement for the project. A blind man would have seen them for what they were, and their host had no illusions.

'Marvellous, isn't she?' he asked as Jane absented herself briefly before leaving.

David agreed carefully. 'Yes, marvellous. She could cast *Figaro* without me. I sometimes wonder if she could conduct it. And in business, well . . . I'm so lucky to have her.'

His friend laughed. 'Business apart, and you are right, she is a wonder, you're lucky. So is she, perhaps.' David enquired with his eyebrows. The two turned to the window, out of earshot as she reappeared. 'The wrong man could do a lot of damage. You won't, I hope and believe. If I'm wrong, expect assassination from any one of a hundred friends.'

'Pistols at dawn on the croquet lawn?'

'Assassination comes in appropriate forms. Rest assured, my talented friend, you will certainly not conduct anything of mine again if you let that lady down.'

She bubbling, David thoughtful, they drove back

to The Smuggler. Parked, they sat snug among slow snow.

She turned to him. 'What were you talking about?'

'Which . . .?'

'Oh, come on!'

'Oh, you mean . . .'

'Indeed.'

'Some things are not for your ears, darling.'

'I'm entitled. He's business. Read the small print.'

'You get only ten per cent of everything.'

'Try me with my ten. I'll work the rest out for myself.'

David gave up. 'Just a warning that if I hurt you he'll hang my guts from his proscenium.'

'Oh, I'm to be hurt, am I?'

'Curiously, he thought possibly not.'

She shrugged. 'I let myself in for this. No room for Dresden ladies in my business, David, I promise you.' She was suddenly thoughtful. 'It was good of him, though. He's a lovely man.'

'Hey, I'm the lovely man this year.'

'You are *the* lovely, lovely, *lovely* man. Different thing entirely.' She leaned towards him, offering her lips. He accepted readily. When they came up for air her hand held a parcel, brought from behind his seat.

'Late Christmas present?' he asked.

'Hardly. Shostakovich, for Boston. You've done no work at all on him, I think?'

'Shostakovich now? Slave-driver!' His disappointment was comic.

'Just looking after my meal ticket. Shostakovich until six thirty. Then cocktails.'

'In my room, then.'

'Not Pygmalion likely. You get lucky, if at all, after dinner, not before.'

'So proper.'

'And so prudent. To eat nicely one must sit comfortably.'

'Flattery will get you anywhere, darling.'

'In that case be flattered out of my car and into your score, please. Lollipops later.'

'Promise?'

'Quite unnecessary, don't you think? With a fast lady, down at the seaside?' And with a quick peck and a wave she disappeared stairward.

* * *

Head down then on the conductors' treadmill, the essential miracle by which the composer's pen is translated into memorized sound; never easy, there are many approaches to it. Some – and because of his command of the keyboard this solution was the one David often and pleasurably adopted – play the score on the piano, the struggle to adapt and confine so many parts within two hands providing first-rate food for the memory. Others, pressed for time, play recordings, a second-rate trick rarely admitted for shame's sake. Today David simply read and imagined sounds; the slow solution but the best. That which goes in slowest sticks longest. Some composer, Dmitri Shostakovich, he told himself over his afternoon cup of tea. Anyone who could distract a man at such a time was not half bad. He was well away, the music and its attendant problems filing themselves in his head, hands instinctively moving, commanding the invisible orchestra, when the phone brought him back from 'A Soviet artist's reply to just criticism' with a jolt.

'Time,' Jane suggested.

He'd play her game. 'Look, I'm very much into this, and there's half an hour left.'

'Where are you in the work?'

'Nearly at the end of the first movement. You know, where the horn goes up . . .'

A giggle from the other end, then: 'He can try again tomorrow. Look, you've just got time for a shave and a shower . . .'

'A shave?'

'Please. I was sandpapered last night. No doubt you are expecting to get quite close to me this evening?'

'I rather hoped, I must say.'

'Well, then. And this is to be a very uncasual dinner. A black tie would be nice.'

What it is, he thought, to be involved with the woman who organizes one's entire life. Leaving Dmitri among a chaos of notes and coloured pencils he made for the bathroom and at 6.29 presented himself, bowtied.

At first David thought the bar was empty. Then he saw high heels below a great leather wing-chair in the corner before the fire, its back to him. He crossed the room. Sensing, she rose, lovely in a green silk sheath which showed every line of her body and yet stayed miraculously within the bounds of good taste, her hair a simple miracle. Around her neck a single rope of pearls. He stopped and looked, admiring. She was pleased.

'Like it?'

'I hope that's evident.'

'I'm carefully not looking that closely. Not polite, you see. You'll have to tell me, I think.' She handed him the waiting dry Martini and sat again, silken legs conspiring softly.

'I think,' he said, 'that you are the most beautiful – '

'Ah, I see. Like Brahms? The symphony you like best is the one you played last night, they say.'

'In that case you are all four symphonies.'

'Thank you. Can I have the Variations too, please?'

'If you like. And the *Academic Festival Overture*, as in all the best recorded cycles.'

'Cycles are for riding. Is it true there's a bike in every orchestra?'

'I expect so.' She was much too good at this musical badinage. Across a low table, her legs whispering reminders with every movement and her breasts promising through the silk, how could a man cope? He decided to make a move for the table. 'We ought to order, perhaps?'

'All done. For seven o'clock.'

'Such precision.'

The clock struck. They got up as though summoned. He took her arm. At the door she turned to the staircase, away from the restaurant. 'Look, darling, there's just something I must do. Can I use your room for a moment? It's much closer.'

He followed her upstairs, key at the ready. But the door was open, logs glowing, the room softly lit, a waiter inside, smiling. The table was set for dinner, candles beckoning, the first course ready, the remainder in a trolley.

'Pleased?' Jane asked.

Poleaxed, he grunted a throat-clearing reply. The waiter gone, she was leaning against the closed door, smiling, utterly successful, radiant, a cream-filled cat. He advanced. She put up defensive hands. 'Uh-uh! Not now. There's a tournedos, among other nice things which would spoil. And you are not to ruin the best hairdressing in Sussex just yet. Make yourself useful with the champagne.'

'Two bottles?'

'And a very good claret. And cognac, very old indeed.'

'Not afraid of the traitor, then?'

'Good God! The man's read Shakespeare. No. Our defence is sure, as the old hymn says.'

71

'Such confidence.' They sat and started on the bisque.

'Truth is,' Jane said, 'I half hoped the question would not come up this evening. I'd have you know, my inconveniently adequate love, that I'm a little out of practice for exercise on the scale of last night.'

'Oh, love, I'm sorry . . .'

She made a face, dismissing his attempt at sympathy. 'Do try to look a little less pleased with yourself.' She was smiling broadly now. 'But perhaps I should have kept up with my ballet.'

'It's among the better reasons for sending young ladies to ballet class. Often counterproductive for boys.'

She laughed. 'Not always, believe me. And the scope for the survivors . . . Anyway, in the end the mechanics of the thing are the same for the wives of Methodist ministers as for prima ballerinas. A little pain and a lifetime of—'

'Love?'

'Love?' She was suddenly serious. 'It means so many different things. To me it means commitment. You're not ready to commit to me, David. Perhaps you never will be.'

He got up, walked round the small table, bent to kiss her. It was an expression of affection mixed with an acknowledgement that last night had been very special to her.

'Damn you,' she said at length, mopping with her napkin. 'Ruined my lipstick.'

They finished the steak in a thoughtful silence, each seeking the way forward, each giving the other time to find it. The Stilton now.

In the end he said, 'Jane, I don't know what can come of this. But if you wish to think all I want of you is business and sex I'll try to pretend it's true.'

'Pretend?' She waited, a small commitment hanging on his reply.

'Yes, that would be a pretence, certainly.'

'No. Don't pretend, now or ever. Promise me?'

'Willingly.'

'Good.' Her mood lightened. 'My dress, tell me!'

'What?'

'How much you like it, idiot.'

'Like it? I adore it. I can't think how you got into it.'

'Simple.'

'Good. I rather hope you'll show me. In reverse, of course.'

'I mean the dress is simple.'

It was very expensively simple, he realized. It would take a very successful conductor to maintain this woman in the manner to which she was accustomed, financed as she was by fifty talents.

'Your figure is amazingly demonstrated, yet . . .'

'Art, of course. But I daren't put on weight. So not too many meals like this. And not too much . . . Is it true that fucking fattens?'

The shock showed in his face. She laughed. 'Oh, love, even nice convent girls have to use the word. There is simply no other. Try for yourself. Try shagging, screwing, try being *had* . . .'

He was appalled. 'Darling, none of those things must ever happen to you,' he said. 'I give in. If anyone can beautify the word you can.'

'Agreed then.'

Over coffee, back to the subject. 'But do tell, *does* it fatten?'

'Perhaps. Happier is often fatter. A little fat is a small price to pay, d'you think?'

'I don't know yet. All I have to show for last night is a bruise or two.'

He got up. 'Something better can be arranged, perhaps?'

She was not to be rushed. 'Sit,' with a wave to the sofa, 'and I'll bring cognac.'

He sank into the vast settee. She brought liquid amber in surprising goblets.

'Waterford?' he asked. 'This hotel has style, love.'

'Not Waterford; a long way east of there, and the style is mine.' She sank beside him, holding the glass to the candlelight, diamonds sparkling through the brandy. 'My mother's glasses. They come out quite rarely.' She hurried on, sidestepping the question in his eyes. 'Now a little music, I think.'

In her other hand the switch for the hi-fi. A quick finger and Mozart, the slow movement from the twenty-first piano concerto.

'My love,' he remonstrated, 'you're right about nearly everything, but Mozart is not music to make love to.'

'Indeed not. And I'm not about to be tumbled on a sofa, between brandies.' She snuggled close, kissed him briefly, and they sat in the glow of the fire while the magician weaved his infallible spell. Her hand, he discovered, was on his thigh. His, round her body, nursed a breast. The music died softly.

'Perfection,' he said, waiting.

She turned again to his ear. 'Only one movement. Five minutes of total provocation is quite enough for me,' she moved her hand, exploring, 'and there are indications that my breast was too much even for Wolfgang.'

David got up, drawing her with him. 'Come to bed?'

'If you like. But I wonder . . .'

'What, love? If we don't get there soon . . .'

She laughed. 'I don't believe you. Look, it's warm by the fire.'

'But you were not to be tumbled . . .'

'No, but . . .' She looked, smiling, at the deep sheepskins before the fire, irresistible. Freeing herself she put out the lamp, joining him again before the fire, the only light now. A long kiss, arms round his neck, legs wide, stretching the silk, a mixture of aromas in his nostrils, one made in France, one unique. He breathed deeply, inhaling her wanting. She moved even closer, hips rising, finding, fitting, settling. From her waist his hands moved lower.

'God, what a woman you are.'

'Mmm . . .' She released him, tugging at his tie. 'You must hang that suit. Can't have you dining out with blue-rinsed Bostonians looking like Moss Brothers on New Year's Day.'

He sighed. 'Do you never close the office?'

She pushed him towards the bedroom. 'Go, while I do that.'

In the next room the coverlet was turned down, the light low. On the bed a small cataract of white lace. Her weekend bag was by the wardrobe. He put on a dressing gown and rejoined her. She was standing before the fire, as he'd left her.

'Now, have I seen the last surprise?' he asked.

'Not quite. Look, I hope you don't mind my moving in? Anyway, the boats are burned. I have nowhere else to go tonight so I hope you're not about to throw me out into the snow?'

'Not for some considerable time.'

'Promises, promises,' she laughed. 'Now, just take the comb out, love?'

A small movement and the dark crown fell about her shoulders.

'And the zip, please.'

It was quite a long zip. There was a buzz in the movement. His hand travelled slowly down her back. Stopping in the small of it he kissed her there. She shivered.

'Cold?' he joked.

'Oh, get on with it, do.'

75

His journey ended in the happy place where cheeks divide. Before he could realize the absence of any other clothing she shrugged once, and the gown was a green pool around her feet. High heels, sheer stockings, and pearls.

'Well?' There was a breathless silence. She was looking at his face in a distant mirror. She smoothed back her hair, breasts rising with the movement, then turned. 'Come on, kiss me.'

They were as close as two people can be without becoming one, kissing, tasting, stroking, her hand inside the silk on his back. He kissed her breasts, she stroking the top of his head as he reached low. Her hips offered a little, volunteering. His hand moved still lower.

'Please,' she said, into his mouth.

Carefully he palmed her, kissing, the movement all hers, a hand on his head crushing her mouth to his. Knees giving way, they subsided onto the rug, breathing hard, her eyes bright, flushed, soft, happy.

A log moved in the grate, making a small November of sparks. He watched the flickering reflections on her skin. She found him, stroked softly. He luxuriated, happy to follow where this whitest of witches might lead.

She looked at the hard flesh. 'A moment, love,' she whispered. 'Something I must do.' She was up and into the bedroom.

Long seconds, alone by the fire. Then she was standing in the doorway, little more than a silhouette against the soft light behind. The lace covered her from neck to floor, her two hands raising the hem, bridelike, tiny frills at each wrist. The lace hid nothing. Her nipples, her mound with its luxury, every curve displayed for his astonished eyes.

'Like it?'

He could only nod, wordless, knowing that he had seen, would see, nothing more simply beautiful.

'There's a satin slip for church. Then, without the satin . . . sensible, don't you think?'

Rising he made to take her in his arms but she was with him again on the rug, raining kisses. Her eyes wet, she clung like a lost child for moments. He lay under her, wondering.

Her kisses moved lower, her hands finding him again. He ached as he had not done since he was a schoolboy. Her hand on him, nursing, then her breath. He looked down at the lovely head moving small. Deeper now and sweeter. Feeling the quick muscle she raised a little, tasting once, twice, three times as he subsided, exhausted, taking him softly into her mouth again for comfort. The world stopped turning. Now her mouth was close to his again.

'Darling,' he said, 'thank you.'

'No need, you see,' she said. 'I can't help any of it.'

'No?'

'No. It's meant, surely.' Then, practical again. 'Now, love, the second bottle!'

'Watch out for the traitor, I keep telling you.'

'We licked him once. We'll do it again. Against such a combination what can he do?'

Smiling, he got up, rescued the bottle from the ice, stood twisting wire, watching the firelight in her hair. He filled the glasses, gave her one. She sipped and he asked the question. 'A wedding gown, love?'

'No questions tonight. After the wedding perhaps.'

'After the wedding?'

'Oh, all right, after the consummation thereof.' The champagne was bubbling in her voice now.

'I thought last night . . .'

She drank deep. 'Let's not stand on technicalities, darling. Last night was for me. I needed to know. Tonight is for us.'

He emptied his glass. 'Yes, I see. In that case the gown . . .'

'It's quite clever. Buttons in all the right places.'

He made to investigate but she put down her glass, lay back, a lacy wonder amid the fur. 'Leave this to me, love. Look.'

The neck unbuttoned, the breasts were unveiled again, nipples hard. He took them in turn into his mouth. Her hand rested for a moment in his hair, stroking, then back to its task. Uncovered to the waist now. She reached, pulled up the remaining lace. 'Look,' she said again.

He looked, kneeling between her thighs. In its bed a beauty of shining mother-of-pearl between full lips, a natural pearl above. He kissed it, but her hands were raising his head. 'Enough, darling.'

He watched her face in the firelight, her lips moist, forming words. Hardly a whisper now. 'Enough, David. Now, now . . .'

He kissed her. Kissing, she found him, her hips moving, placed him. Her hands on his back, her eyes open, watching his face. He moved a little. She sighed, tensed, relaxed, gave a little. His iron sank deeper into the tight warmth of her. Higher, higher, slowly, her legs wide, their hair tangled.

A whisper: 'Still, darling, can we . . .' They hung, waiting while the world turned. 'Now, just a little . . .'

He moved, pressing gently, then slowly back. Her hands held him, afraid to lose him. He pressed again. She sighed, relaxing. Again the slow sweet slide, again and once again.

A small quick movement. Softly but urgently she said, 'Darling, don't wait. Now, now . . .'

He plunged once, twice, three times before the storm burst. At the last, raised on his hands, her body supporting him off the rug at her hips, tensing again and again while she sobbed and clung.

How long they lay absorbed in one another they were not aware. Then her voice in his ear, softly. 'Hey, Gulliver, we might move, I think?'

He was still hard, a welcome witchcraft. They rolled together. She lifted slowly, kneeling, looking at his pride, smiling a new smile. 'I thought it went down at this point? Practice not always like the theory then?'

'Most theories collapse if extended long enough.'

She touched, stroked, more in affection than wanting now. 'Impressive, I must say.'

'Happy?'

'Mmmmm . . . wonderful. Wonderful thing for a woman to have.'

He laughed.

'Darling, bed would be sensible, don't you think?' Jane asked.

Bed would be welcome. The rug was softer when she was on it, he on her. He got up, unseating her, led her willingly to the bedroom. She discarded her lace, its purpose served, and climbed in. He watched as she arranged herself as though for sleep as does every animal in its way; on her left side, an arm under her pillow, foetal. From behind he embraced her, one hand to her bush, one to her breast.

'Sleep now?' he asked.

'Soon, love,' she said. 'Not quite yet, but soon . . .'

He waited, but there was only her deep breathing, asleep like a child.

« 3 »

It was a bird that woke him, singing on the thatch outside the window. David lay listening and remembering in a room grey with filtered sunlight. Nature's alarm excepted, the silence was complete.

Jane was sleeping as he'd left her, the sweep of her back towards him, bones just visible under the satin skin. He kissed her there. She gave no sign, her breathing smooth and even.

Bright sunlight edged the curtains. Should he wake her? Since it was irresistible perhaps it was justified? Potent reasoning, straight from the groin.

He came close and low behind her, rising on an elbow to look at her face, relaxed, soft, trusting. His hand, passing one firm breast, stroked the other. Still nothing disturbed her even breathing. He settled deeper into the bed, curling his legs behind hers. To fumble would wake her, to press . . . He shifted slightly and was received into remembered sweet softness. Rest now, her body a soft delight against him. Quietly he pulled down a pillow for his head. He would stay until she woke, a moment or a lifetime.

Lying still he sensed a soft pulsing, hardly felt, growing, growing. He pressed, gently hard, to feel it, feed it. Somewhere inside her warm stillness a tight ring was forming. Moving now, pulling, rippling, relaxing, again and again. Suddenly she was awake, with little cries half alarmed. 'No, no . . .'

'Oh yes,' he begged, 'Yes, yes, yes . . .'

A sudden blossoming of the lotus, a small scream – 'Darling, darling . . .' and their ecstasy flooded as she sobbed into the pillow.

Slowly, slowly, their breathing subsided. Still linked in the ravaged bed, relaxed, wondering, they heard the chink of china, a rumbling of small wheels.

'God!' she said, sitting up, glorious breasts dancing. 'They're setting breakfast! Darling . . . oh, how awful! My God, they must have heard . . .'

David mustered what feeble reassurance he could, realizing that she'd given a new and delightful meaning to the word 'cockcrow' this morning. 'Not a chance, love. They've only just arrived, and the walls are very thick.'

She was out of bed now, opening curtains, a small flurry of activity to cover her embarrassment.

'Darling,' he said, 'whatever they've heard will hardly be new to them.'

'Well, Casanova, it's new to me. Whatever will they think?' She stood at the window, arms crossed over her breasts, hands grasping shoulders, tense, looking out over thatched and pantiled roofs, the snow almost thawed, a glory in pink and dark brown lit through sunny lace. Slowly the tension left her. He saw it go, went to her. She turned, put her arms round his neck, breasts tight to his body. He kissed her, wrapped together, held her for a while, content. Then he said, 'Look, this Casanova thing . . .'

'What?'

'Don't think – '

She laughed. 'That it happens all the time? With all sorts of ladies? Of course not. Nothing like *this* has ever happened to you before. Nothing like it has ever happened to anybody. We're unique.' She kissed him again, long, slow and deep. His body stirred again, ambitious.

'Down boy!' she commanded, starting back, mock alarmed. 'Time for breakfast. Race you to the shower.' They reached it together, showered and towelled companionably. Half dressed they sat and ate.

81

The serious newspapers had come up with the meal. She turned the pages busily, devouring concert reviews with the toast. He remembered the reason given by a famous colleague for never reading his press reviews; that when a man had spent the night with his wife he ought to talk to her in the morning. The role-reversal amused him. She looked up.

'You're looking awfully smug over there. Is there a joke, or are you simply pleased with yourself?'

Since explanation would have been too complicated, he chose the latter. 'Of course I'm pleased. With us. It takes two to tango.'

'We seem to be up for a *Come Dancing* prize, you mean?'

'Revelation on revelation. Convent girls have smutty minds, it seems.'

'Oh, we have our moments.' She put down the paper, asked seriously 'But I'd like to know . . .' She was colouring a little.

'What? Ask and it shall be revealed, if within my modest grasp.'

'Well, have you always been . . . or often, even . . .?'

'So successful? No.' He shook his head. 'No, of course not.'

'So I may really be lucky?'

'*We*, love, not just you. Anyway luck is usually a combination of talent and application. Of your application I shall say nothing in case you ask for an increase on your ten per cent.'

'Please feel free to comment on my talent.'

He thought for a long time. She waited, half smiling. Taking refuge in an old joke he said, 'Love, if the Almighty made anything better he's been keeping it to himself.'

This was no way out and they both knew it. She was waiting still.

'My dear,' he said eventually, 'how do I know? You are the first woman to whom I've ever made love.'

They sat silent and still for a minute. Suddenly she was up and making for the bathroom. He followed, concerned. 'Darling, I'm so sorry. I don't know what I mean, truly.'

She was mopping eyes furiously, sniffling and swallowing, pulling together the self-reliant Jane. 'No,' she said, 'you say all the right things. Too bloody clever by half, you are.'

'Darling, I thought you were happy.'

'Damn you, I am happy. That's the problem. I've never been half so happy. I came here expecting to be bedded, simply, and I find myself . . . I'm just not . . . Oh, I don't know.'

He led her back to the comfort of the sitting room, settled her on the sofa, regret at having got her into this warring with the delight of being with her. There was nothing to say. Wisely they held hands, silent.

Eventually Jane said, 'Perhaps I should go home. There's such a lot to do in the office. Three days away is a nice theory but I wonder, seriously, whether . . .'

It was nonsense, he knew. She'd learned, from the chaos which followed GG's sudden death, to appoint and delegate. But the choice must be hers.

'If you wish, of course. I'll stay here and make love to Dmitri.'

'Dmitri? Oh, him. You'll need the Britten concerto too. I'll have it sent.'

His heart was in his boots. She got up, walked to the fireplace, stood for long moments looking sightlessly at *The Destruction of the Orient* hanging above it. Eventually a long sigh. She turned, quietly resolute, her voice low. 'GG said never run away.'

'We all run, one way or another. He ran, once.'

'Oh yes, he ran. Even then he never forgave himself for running, avoiding the obligation to die with the rest. Problems must be faced, he used to say, and the earlier the better. And one other thing.'

'Yes?'

'He said he regretted the things he hadn't done much more than the things he had.' Suddenly her mind was made up. 'Come along, love, let's get out of here.'

They were closing the door, wrapped for the street, when the telephone rang. Pencil and notepad materializing out of the air, Jane sat listening intently, taking notes. Marvellous, David thought; the Pavlovian reflex applied to business management. Her responses were brief, monosyllabic, until the last. Then, 'Thank you. I know he'll be pleased. Yes, tomorrow evening at six. Goodbye now.' She put down the handset, walked to where he was leaning on the mantel, put her hands on his shoulders. Now she was all control and decision. 'A televised memorial for Box, love. In Cardiff with the Welsh Philharmonic and Chorus. I know you would want that?'

Not this week please, he told himself. 'Why the rush, and why in Wales?'

'Because it works. He was to conduct a Mozart Requiem there on Sunday. It's almost rehearsed. You get three hours with the choir tomorrow, six on Friday with the orchestra, six on Saturday, performance in the Cathedral. There'll be an audience.'

A relaxed schedule, designed for an octogenarian conductor. It would be easy, if Mozart ever was. Still she saw his reluctance.

'An honour, love,' she said.

'I'm free, that's all.'

'Don't be churlish. There are four others free, or could be if asked. One more of mine even. You've been chosen. Anyway, you'll have your days in Wales. It's what you wanted, surely?'

He'd developed an attachment to Sussex in the past

84

thirty-six hours. Still, she was right. He must pack and go. She was calling her office already.

'. . . to pick up Mr Adams at one tomorrow, coming on from Gatwick after dropping Mary. Cardiff by five, latest. What? Oh, he can be back in Town by supper time. Friday's schedule can stand. Just a moment – ' She turned. 'You won't need the car?'

He was tempted. He knew John would have loved three days in Wales, but it wasn't on. 'No. I can cope,' he said. The Philharmonic would supply if necessary.

'All settled then?'

'I suppose.'

'I'll come on Sunday, of course.'

'No. Saturday, please.'

She looked up, surprised at the decision in his voice. 'If you wish,' she said.

'I do wish. I wish you could come tomorrow, or on Friday.'

'No, really.'

'Come on, love; you have the time, you know you have.'

'No. Three days for the art of love you can have and welcome, but three days mooching about your rehearsals like some sort of groupie, no. I'd be famous. So would you. Bad for everyone. I'll go back to Town tomorrow and do some work.'

She was right, but the disappointment in his face moved her. Arms round for a hug, she said, 'Only two days, love. In any case I need time.'

'Time?'

'To think. I've been on this roller coaster and I need time between rides to decide whether I'm going round again.'

'To hell with it,' he said, holding her tight. 'This can't stop here.'

She kissed him quickly. 'Yes, yes it can if you and I decide. I don't think it will, do you? But we both need a little breathing space – or at least I do. Look, I'm trying to hang on to my head, that's all. We know where we are, just, but we don't know where we're going, or even if.' She put a finger to his lips. 'Don't argue. If you must debate, do it with yourself. That's what I'm going to do, for a day or two, or a month or two, or whatever it takes. Come on. Time for some air.'

Outside on the hill she asked, 'I wonder if the hotel ever hear from that waiter?'

'Which . . .?'

'Pinkie's waiter.'

'Oh yes.' David remembered a handsome eighteen-year-old who'd caught the eye of a famous lady producer during the Glyndebourne season. To everyone's astonishment they'd married and he'd been in attendance at the great opera houses of the world for some years. 'He's in America.'

'With Pinkie still?'

'Oh no. That's over. She fell for a Lohengrin in San Francisco, so all change. He's fine, though. She set him up in a Chinese restaurant.'

'For God's sake, a Chinese restaurant?'

'In San Francisco. He married a delightful Chinese lady and they're employing her family. It's a very good restaurant. It's becoming a chain. He's doing very well indeed.'

They laughed together at the extraordinary world which travelling artists create for themselves and at the generosity of one traveller to another.

'Extraordinary woman,' said Jane.

'Yes.'

She looked at him sharply. 'Do I detect a note of censure?'

'Well, it is an odd way for a woman to behave . . .'

'No. Nothing odd about it. If she'd been a tenor with a waitress who'd have been surprised? For how long do you people do without sex on your travels, anyway?'

'Don't. There isn't an answer. We're all different, love.'

'That's true, at least,' she conceded. 'Listen, until this week I'd no idea of the pressure. Now I know how inadequate the five-fingered widow is.'

'Flattered I am.'

'I'm not flattering, love, I'm disturbed. Life on tour must pose difficulties for a man *or* a woman with a high sex-drive. That I can see.'

'Looking for the answer?'

'It's your problem. I'm by no means committed to sharing it. Find the answer for yourself, David.'

'Love, perhaps?'

'Nonsense. You were in love with Julie since school. To you love doesn't entail sexual commitment.'

'So, I'm not capable of – '

'Not what I said at all. But on past evidence . . . Perhaps it depends on the relationship, on the way it works, on the honesty of it. Perhaps it takes two. But I'm beginning to understand the lack of conscience in a starved man.'

They were walking slowly, high above the sea. 'David,' she said, 'I can go on as I am if I must. It's what I'd expected to do. I offered no commitment and asked for none. But I wonder . . . I wonder if we know each other at all.'

'I thought we were fairly close.'

'Sarcasm I can do without. Look, are you sure you know me, even?'

'Pretty well.'

'Sure, are you? You've seen the business and the brain and you've had the body, at last. But until this week I've kept you well away from me, myself, in many ways. If we're going further with this . . . well, there's no time now. It must wait. Where will you stay in Wales?'

'There's a pub called The Dragon at Cowbridge.'

'Will it do?'

'We working-class boys have a certain tolerance. Anyway, I won't stay in Cardiff.'

She knew his dislike of hotels where he couldn't escape other artists. 'I'll book it from the office. You'll be in late tomorrow evening?'

'Tennish.'

Back at The Smuggler it was time for lunch. The steak and kidney was still available and still recommended. She set to with gusto.

'Gives one an appetite, apparently,' she said as the last mouthful disappeared.

'I couldn't eat another bite,' he said.

'Neither could I. I have in mind more of something quite different.' She glanced at her watch. 'I have an hour before the hairdresser.'

He was taken aback. She saw it in his face, laughed. 'Poor dear. Hard on an old man? More than you bargained for?'

'Oh, I don't know,' he said, rising.

'But you have work to do. Cardiff will lose you some learning time.'

He made a face. 'It's one o'clock. I'll work from two until five, perhaps?'

'I'll go up. Have a quick one with Harry. See you in ten minutes.'

She was in bed when he arrived. 'Darling,' he said with a grin, getting out of his clothes 'you look very married, tucked in like that.'

'Appearances deceive. Married means pyjamas, I think? The sheets are all I've got on.'

They made slow, thoughtful, utterly satisfying love, resting afterwards interwined, tongues teasing occasionally. Two o'clock chimed in the distance. Jane

showed no sign of rising. Her hand enquired suc-
cessfully.

'Such energy,' she said. 'Are you always like this?'

'The inducement is unusual.'

'Thank you.' She was reaching for the bedside telephone, exposing a paradise of back. He moved closer
with intent.

'Wait, do. I must call the hairdresser.' Reception
answered as he found her. 'Oh . . .' She gave her
instructions, breathless and disjointed. Putting down
the phone she turned, thumped his chest with furious
fists. 'Bastard, they must have heard.' Now she was
laughing, tears running, rolling her body under his.

'Whatever will they think?' he asked. But she was
already too busy to reply.

* * *

Jane was waiting in the car, its engine rumbling, huge
wipers dealing contemptuously with the newly
resumed snowfall. David threw his topcoat into the
space behind the seats and climbed in, wishing for
once he was shorter. Once in, there was comfort
enough, a cocoon of warm soft leather. She swung
out and down the hill. He felt he should be driving
and said so.

She shook her head. 'No, really. I like driving. I'm
a terrible passenger and it's no distance. We have two
hours. Easy.'

Not that easy, he thought, what with the snow and
the early start at the Garden, at the tail of the rush
hour. Still, it was good just to sit and let the countryside fly by in the gathering dark. Fly it did, once on
the motorway. He asked whether she ever had trouble
with the boys in blue.

'All the time, but I look suitably penitent and they
let me off, usually.'

She was in a knitted woollen sheath, scarlet, restrained but expensive leather at the waist, equally expensive silk at the throat. Black silk legs in sensible shoes for driving, red heels sitting pretty on the mink behind her seat. A lady from a Porsche advertisement. Yes, they'd let her off, usually; but not always.

'Don't miss them tonight. You won't be so lucky.'

'Whyever not? Rarely fails, I promise you.'

'When did it last not work?'

'Three months back. Driving his nibs from Heathrow to Town, late in from Paris for his press conference.' His nibs was her name for her best investment, Ardiles, an Argentine conductor of immense prestige.

'There's your reason. The solo lady is vulnerable. Driving a friend she becomes a show-off, fair game.'

She sighed. 'Perhaps you should be driving, after all?'

'Oh no. This way I get to look at the Grant legs. Such delights ought not to be reserved for policemen.'

Her hand waved dismissively on the way to the audio button. 'Enough. Let's do some homework, shall we?'

Beethoven, 'Emperor' Concerto. Within half a minute David recognized it as a performance of his own. Technically the pianist had been superb, musically a nightmare. He'd spent that day defending Beethoven, to little effect. Entertaining for the orchestra, but hardly music.

'Like it?' she asked as the first movement ended.

'Not a bit. Let's find something else.'

'Oh no. Millions suffered, why not you?'

The second movement was worse than the first. 'She was impossible,' he said.

'No. Unmusical, silly, wilful, and not to be worked with again, but not impossible.' The finale now.

'Oh come on, darling,' he remonstrated. 'What can one do with a pianist who is all hands and no brain?'

'One can go with it.'

'Then the whole bloody mess gets to be my fault?'

'Not at all. D'you really think people would believe it?'

He couldn't think why not, and he said so. She glanced, slightly worried, at the clock. It would be touch and go to make it in time in this weather and thickening traffic. Then back to the attack. 'That performance did no one any good. If you'd let her have her head you'd have got full marks for technique at least. The nonsense would have been down to Miss Fingers. Otherwise you become a bad accompanist, which you are not.'

He was not altogether pleased. 'Tell me, do you dispense wisdom of this kind to all your artists?'

For a moment her eyes left the road, met his in the glow of the dashboard lighting, just a little afraid of having gone too far. Then: 'Not all of them. Just the ones I sleep with. I'd rather hoped that gave me – '

He gave in, laughing, put his hand over hers on the gear lever, feeling the car's vibration through her fingers. 'It does, love.' Especially, he thought, when she was right. She smiled, relieved.

The traffic building up through Blackheath, he could feel her concern in her driving. The fast car was a handicap now, every driver competing, reluctant to give way. He realised once more how much he disliked London; its confusion, its mess, its dirt, no place for a boy from the green hills. Now the traffic was thinning; Waterloo at last and over the bridge past the Festival Hall, merrily lit for pre-concert diners, into the tunnel and up into Kingsway. Thankfully parking was not a problem this evening; the private space at the side of the Opera House was waiting. Jane side-slipped neatly into the slot with a small grin of achievement.

'Six-fifty,' she said, reaching for her shoes with one

hand and removing her pumps with the other. 'Time for a quick one?'

The barman in the crush bar, a virtuoso at late arrivals, produced a gin and tonic as though from his sleeve. 'And for you, sir?' he asked, professionally declining to recognize his customer. David asked for the same and downed it quickly.

Jane was slower. 'Come,' she said. 'I can smuggle mine into the box with luck.' They made their way along the Grand Tier, Jane waving away an anxious usherette with the confidence of long practice.

Settling, waiting for the house lights, David remembered why so many friends insisted that just to be there was worth the price of the ticket. Smaller than La Scala, less spectacular than the Paris Opera, despite its antique inconveniences it was a perfect setting for opera.

There was a stir at the pit door behind the timpani where the conductor awaited. He looked up from his programme to catch the effect as the lights went to half, the theatre a heartbreaker in soft red and gold. Magic.

The old man's progress to the box, with failing eyes and shaky legs, was very slow, but the applause sustained him the whole way. He grasped the pit rail, turned, bowed twice, picked up the stick, the orchestra attentive, tense. With hardly a movement, barely audible, the *Figaro* overture began.

Fascinating, David thought, the fingerprint of each fine conductor on the orchestra. Here was velvet Mozart, a big string body in the old tradition, lush wind, lovely stuff which would be patronized in tomorrow's press as the forgivable foible of an old man. The production was ageing and conventional, the cast old friends made in a dozen places and twenty different operas. He sat back to listen, eyes on the house and its audience, returning often to his companion sitting rapt and upright in her chair, watching, listening, absorbed. Measuring talent perhaps? Wondering whether this or that younger member of the cast was ready for greater things or should wait a year or two? Or was Mozart winning over business? He hoped so.

They'd been invited upstairs for the interval; a tortuous journey, but they were already there when the old man arrived on the arm of a friend, sinking gratefully into soft cushions, accepting a glass of mineral water. Pleased to see David, kissing Jane's hand with old Viennese courtesy, he was desperately tired already. David wondered at the sheer guts which pulled an octogenarian through such a marathon.

They told him of their enjoyment and talked of the production. The old man thought it was nice, better than most. There was too much production and too little music nowadays. Was he enjoying the orchestra? 'Very good, very good. Not Vienna, not perhaps Dresden, but good. And thank God it never changes. In Germany on the first night they give us a new Mercedes but on the second – '

'A very old Volkswagen!' David finished the conductor's in-joke with him and they laughed together.

'Yes,' said the old man, 'here it's good. I'm happy.'

Turning to Jane, sitting silent while they talked, he asked, 'Now, please tell me about this young lady?' He'd missed her name, David realized. He explained her again, his agent, Miss Grant.

'If she is as clever as she is beautiful you will both make your fortunes!' was the response. Jane blushed fetchingly. In the distance they heard the first bell. David made to say goodbye, but he'd lost the old man. He was silent, looking hard into Jane's face, his hand to his mouth. When he spoke again his voice was curiously low and small. 'Miss Grant? Miss *Goldberg* . . .?'

She nodded.

'So . . . after so long.' Rising from his chair he carefully crossed the room. She rose to meet him. They hugged. He kissed her on both cheeks. She held him, as slow to let go as he, her face a rare mixture of emotions. David felt himself curiously excluded, almost embarrassed.

The old man looked at her, at David, back again to Jane. 'Does David know?' he asked.

She nodded. 'David knows a great deal.'

'All?'

'Not quite.'

'Ah. You are waiting for the right time?'

'Yes. Yes, I expect I am.'

'Do not wait, my dear. Tell him, for both of us. I am very old. He is a good friend, with far to go, and I would like him to know.'

She nodded quickly, holding both his hands in hers. They looked at each other silently, she half smiling, he grave. 'So,' he said, nodding slowly, 'one did some good things, so long ago.'

There was a soft tap on the door. He released her hands reluctantly. 'Time,' he said. 'Please excuse me. So many stairs. This is not a House for old men. Goodbye now.' Leaning on his help, he made slowly for the door. Turning, he raised the finger which had launched a thousand evenings. 'Look after her, David.' The door closed behind him.

Jane looked at David, he at her, the air full of questions. 'Not now,' she said. 'Not here. Soon, perhaps, but not now. Please, David.'

'Promise?'

'Yes, soon, yes.' Another bell. She took his hand. 'We'll be late. This opera won't wait for you, maestro. Let's go.'

Down the stairs then to another act. Then to the crush bar with the punters. The barmen were the fastest in London, but it paid to skip the applause and get there first. No place for conversation, this. They made their way to the stairs under the chandelier and sat down, glasses in hand, close to the wall, safe from passing feet, looking down on the throng.

'I think you've never really approved of all this?' she asked.

He was only half with her, the questions in his mind abstracting him. 'All what, darling?'

'The people, the clothes, the money, you know?'

'Here to be seen, of course. So many others kept out by the cost. Not the House's fault, but wrong, absolutely, yes.'

'Are you sure they're here *just* to be seen? Isn't it an awful lot of opera to put up with, just to show off a new dress?'

'Oh, come on. Look around you. This is the *in* place to be. The opera lovers are upstairs.'

'The rich oughtn't to be allowed opera then?'

He saw the trap too late. 'Opera is for everyone.'

'Oh, good. That's all right then. For a mo I thought you wanted the rich kept out. Look, they can pay for it, so they get it. That's life. Would two thousand coal miners enjoy the opera *more*?'

'We'll never know,' he said, defending feebly.

'But we do know. They'd enjoy it just as much. Darling, it's your class thing coming out.'

A disability her background didn't allow, class. She could never understand why it caused him such problems. His retreat was disorganized. 'I can't think what you see in a working-class boy like me, really, unless it's a certain limited talent . . .'

'In bed,' she said. Two ladies climbing by to the balcony looked round as though stung, but Jane was undeterred. 'Indeed you have, and not bad on the rostrum either. Curious thing . . .'

'What?'

'Well,' as they got up in response to the bell, she

95

straightening her dress, 'the two have something in common. I mean,' she said over her shoulder as he followed her down the stairs, 'you'd look rather silly doing either by yourself.'

* * *

After the opera, to supper with the cast. Not a grand affair, but a long table in a small Italian restaurant. The talk was relaxed, of families, absent friends. No shop now, except to congratulate their host on the smooth running of his House, famous among artists for its planning. Philip was urbane, thoughtful, untired, though he'd been at his desk, they knew, since eight thirty that morning. Knowing David and Jane had far to go and that the others would unwind for hours, he suggested he might walk with them to the car. So they bade their friends goodnight and walked through the market, quiet now.

'I hear you'll be at Glyndebourne soon?' His grapevine was infallible. 'You must be busy now. We have so few conductors of our own. I hope you'll find time for us, too?'

What style, thought David, to offer so rich a prize with such diffidence.

'After Glyndebourne, of course,' Philip continued. Yes. Of course. He must be watched first, the option kept to some extent open. 'We can't think earlier than three years, and I suppose you can't either. I wonder, David, if you'd like to work with the big man?' It was the code for a very famous tenor.

'I would, of course.'

'He'd like to sing *L'Africaine* here.'

Meyerbeer? David confessed cheerfully that he'd never heard a note of the work.

'Perhaps you'll think about it?'

'Of course I will. And thank you.' They'd arrived

at the red demon, crouched and ready for flight. A handshake, a kiss for Jane, and they were away.

For a while she was silent, then: 'What an operator, isn't he? Quite the best.'

'As all the world knows. Well, I suppose I can learn the piece.'

'Yes, of course. But there are questions . . .'

He would leave the whole thing to her. 'It's your percentage,' he told her.

'And your future. He needs you for that piece. The very top people won't touch Meyerbeer, and Fatso won't work with a nobody. Leaves a few like you.'

'The need is mutual,' he reminded her.

'Yes. The only question is whether we accept before or after we get a better piece.'

Ah, he smiled in the dark, the regal *we*. A battle royal there'd be, with her opponent playing it his way for his own secret fun, the lollipop safely up his sleeve from the first.

The snow has stopped. 'There'll be ice,' he suggested, with a view to self-preservation.

'*Will* there? My dear, all one needs is a pair of skates. It's frozen hard.' She was losing no time, though. All the stories he'd heard about rear-engined cars surfaced in his mind. Jane adjusted her seat. 'I know about these things. I was rather well taught. Close your eyes if it worries you.'

They were at The Smuggler at 1.15, sixty icy miles in seventy-five minutes. Jane strode to the door, satisfaction in every step, and upstairs two at a time, pouring a nightcap almost before her coat was off.

Emerging from the shower he found her sitting on the bed, glass in hand, watching television, still dressed. 'Hard to unwind,' she said.

He told her it had been some performance.

'Yes. Lovely Mozart.'

'I meant the Monte Carlo Rally.'

'Oh, that. I'm sorry, I do show off rather. Then it winds me up.'

Television politics in the background, he lay on the bed in his towel, sipping his Scotch and wondering how to get her into bed.

She got up, stretched, and let down her hair. 'Wind me down?' she asked. 'Unless you're too tired . . .?' Legs braced, she was looking quizzically at his wrapped body. 'Still interested in the Grant legs?'

A distinct possibility, he told her.

'Let's see how far up they go.' Her hem was rising. Up and up, past stocking-tops. He realized with a rush of adrenalin that she'd been nude under the dress all evening.

An age later he suggested, 'Bed, love?'

She stirred, looked into his eyes, smiled a slow smile, her body relaxed, soft, savouring the decline inside her, hers and his. He made room to open the bed, covered them both.

'Thank you kindly, sir,' she whispered.

4

Having woken to the sound of Jane's voice, David showered and threw on a dressing gown. She was sitting at the telephone, arguing in animated French. Without the language it was impossible to know whether or not she was winning, but her colour was up and when she replaced the phone it was with a gesture of satisfaction. He gave her a short round of applause.

'So!' she said. 'Conscious at last. How men do sleep, it seems. I'd almost given up hope. Breakfast is here.'

He offered the first kiss of the day. She turned, collected it on her cheek. So, he thought, not this morning. He waved a finger. 'I do believe you got up early – '

'To avoid a repeat of yesterday's performance? Don't kid yourself; work to do.'

She told him about the Paris problem over tea and toast. It was an old story; a dissatisfied conductor who'd walked out. Her job, as a panic-stricken opera house saw it, was to get him back in. It was impossible; he'd drawn the line, vanishing in the direction of Cannes with the latest lady in his life, leaving the theatre to explain as best it could to a perplexed public. He'd be 'indisposed' no doubt.

David admired her French. She accepted the compliment with assurance. 'Got it at school, with lots of French holidays. German I had from a child. At home there was only Hungarian. Funny thing, that; GG was so determinedly English everywhere else. Except the accent. That he never lost.'

David remembered the MCC tie, worn like a decoration. 'Why did he never go back?'

She shrugged. 'One day, he always said. But he'd had such a hell of a time getting out, I think he felt it would be tempting providence to go back again, however things changed. And he was sure nothing had changed. After Nazis, Commies, he used to say, and there's no difference. He'd have voted for anyone who promised to widen the Channel.' She pointed to a bulky parcel fresh from the post. 'There's your Mozart. I'm going early, to make sure you read it.'

She'd packed while he'd slept, he suddenly realized. She was still talking about his arrangements. 'John will come at one. You can talk rugby all the way home.' She was putting herself together for travel, slipping on the sensible shoes. There was a knock on the door, the porter for her bags. Then the bags were gone, the door closed.

'Can your lipstick be spoiled, d'you think?' David enquired hopefully.

'None on, actually,' she said, leaning on the door. It was a very long kiss, ending only a second before she came back for another, longer. He hadn't dressed. His urgency was obvious, and she was breathing hard. He reached for her. She grinned. 'Back to groping in the greenroom? Darling, be quick.' Her skirt was up, legs wide. A long deep sigh, 'Oh, my dear . . . now, now . . .' and she was shaking in his arms. Loose against the door, she'd have fallen had he not held her.

He held her for a very long time. She looked down at the sad remnant, smiling. 'I wonder whether that's really the end of him for today?'

'Depend on it,' he said.

'Darling,' her smile was a little cry, 'all I can depend on is that he'll be there when I need him.'

'Well, that's something.'

'In view of the demand, you mean?'

'That too.'

'D'you know,' she was hunting in her handbag, 'I'd quite decided it wasn't to happen this morning?' She was mopping with a tissue. 'It must stop somewhere, or nothing gets done.'

'So, why no pants?'

'Changed my mind. Woman's prerogative, I'm told.'

She produced knickers from her handbag and slipped gracefully into them. Her dress straightened, she put her hands on his shoulders, kissed him quickly, affection replacing passion, sighed. 'Oh dear, this is going to be such a complication, love.'

'Don't worry about it. It's quite a nice complication, don't you think?'

'We'll see. I must go. I'll be with you on Saturday, in time for lunch.'

* * *

'Done her good it has,' said John as they sped west. 'Just came in as I was leaving. Looking much better for it. Two days' rest down here, lovely for her.'

David wondered whether the office would reach a more informed conclusion. 'Perhaps she did well in Paris?' he ventured.

'No, no. Paris is still steaming. Glad to have her back they were, to do her own fighting, I can tell you.'

'Enjoys a good scrap, doesn't she?'

'Oh yes. Like her father, see? Terrible losers, mind you. No rugby in Hungary, of course.' They laughed together. True, GG'd had very little practice at losing. He'd been the Hungarian who went into a revolving door second and came out first.

'That car, John. How did the old man feel about it?'

'Oh, hated it he did. Sure she would kill herself.

Only agreed on condition she would pass all the schools first.'

'Schools?'

'Advanced driving. Then the Police. Two days they had her sliding round in her old Volkswagen. Then she had a whole holiday in Bavaria in the winter, with people from the car firm. He used to say the lessons cost more than the damn car. Daft, boy! He'd have bought her a Mercedes without a murmur, but no, no. Nothing would do but this silly thing with the engine at the back and no room for a suitcase.'

'Drives it well, though.'

'Oh, marvellous, of course. Well, you'd expect, wouldn't you? That's her problem, isn't it?'

'What?'

'Does nothing badly. Must be best at everything. P'raps that's why she stopped, with the flute. Always somebody better, see. GG knew that. That's why he didn't push her to play. Knew she'd get hurt.'

'Well, there's nobody better in her business.'

'No, I s'pose. Or if there is, she don't know or she won't see it. So that's all right. She's happy. Happy enough this week, anyway.'

David suddenly remembered Kate's note. 'Cup of tea, John? I have to make a telephone call. Something I forgot.'

'Stop in five minutes. Plenty of time.'

Kate was surprised and pleased, and even more pleased to hear what was afoot. 'So, we had to kill poor George to get you back to Wales! You can't imagine how often it's been tried, David.'

He could. He wondered how many others Jane had sent in his place while shipping him off to more exotic places. He'd be tied up this evening until nine.

'Perhaps we could have a bite together tomorrow evening?' he suggested.

'Lovely. Where shall I find you?'

He told her he would stay at Cowbridge. She was delighted. 'Just like old times. Too cold for the beach, though. And there's only me here now.'

'Oh, you'll do,' he said.

'Well, let me give you a meal here at home.' She felt his hesitation. 'I've got help, it's no trouble.'

'Sure?'

'Of course. We've such a lot to talk about.'

'Well, come in time to hear the end of rehearsal, then we can talk about that too.'

'Tonight? I'll come and collect you. It's no distance, and no bother. Unless you prefer to stay up, gassing to the establishment . . .'

'Only too happy to escape.'

* * *

They were waiting; General Manager, the Leader of the Orchestra, and Chorus-Master, their genuine pleasure making David feel almost guilty at his long absence. He was shown to comfortable quarters for coffee and biscuits, ten minutes head-down, and a wash and brush-up. Then on the pip of six to rehearsal.

A hush as he entered. The ice would need breaking; people must relax to sing. He adopted his best valley accent. 'Good evening, ladies and gentlemen. I feel a bit like the Prodigal Son . . .' There was a general laugh. They knew the form.

They knew their Mozart too, he found. A few minutes to make contact and the whole work clicked tidily into place. Marvellous. He relaxed, the work becoming a pleasure. At the break the Chorus-Master was waiting, anxious.

'My dear chap,' said David, 'they are lovely. You should be proud.'

The man was relieved. 'I'm glad you're happy.

They've worked hard. I know you'll have a fine Requiem.' By 8.15 David knew he was right. There was little left to do now but what would come right when the orchestra played. He thanked them. They applauded and went home happy.

Then the remembered voice was behind him. 'Is Mozart still so hard, David?'

She was very little changed; fifteen years and a lost husband had dealt mercifully with her. A little more weight, a few lines, but still beautiful. He gave her a hug and a kiss. 'Different every day,' he told her, smiling.

'That's what makes him so interesting, you know.'

'Oh yes, the most interesting.' They laughed together. The manager arrived and David began to introduce her.

'No need, David. Kate is more at home here than I am – I've only been here ten years! Now, both of you, a quick one? I know you'll be anxious to get away. It's been a long day and we want you in good shape tomorrow.'

They sat over a drink, catching up. David told them of his debt to Wales for those Saturdays when he'd been allowed to watch the BBC orchestra rehearse, talk to conductors and players. What a bore the student can be, he now knew only too well; so many questions asked of people who were themselves groping for solutions. He'd been so lucky, and so lacking in practical gratitude. Yes, he must talk to Jane.

Kate drove a vintage MG. What was it about women and sports cars? he wondered. They were quickly at the old pub, fifteen miles up the coast. Sitting in the quiet bar over whiskies, the years rolled back.

'It's all very different,' Kate reflected. 'Funny thing, we came for the war, but it became home. Molly would never have left it but for the need to be near the hospital, and there was no point in my leaving once Jack was gone.'

She had no problem now in talking about her tragedy; the tank alone in the desert, Bob found two days later, nearly dead, his spine wrecked. He'd never walk nor even stand again, nor live far from his doctors. Jack, unscathed, had tried to walk to find help and was never found. 'I was lucky in a way. I wonder whether I could have borne it to have Jack crippled – whether he could have borne it either. Moll has been wonderful. She's well supported by the service, of course, but it must have been hard.'

Kate had made a new life. Music had made her many friends. 'Life goes on,' she said, 'and the days pass very quickly if one never stops working.'

He was intrigued. 'No new man, then?'

She smiled. 'You'd have expected that?'

'Why not?'

It had been so good, she said. It could hardly be as good again. Of course there'd been men; she was human. 'But, you know, it's not easy. People get set in their ways. In a marriage both must bend. I'm not sure . . . Anyway, who wants a bendable man?' The double entendre amused them both. 'I'm not sure I can bend either. I get by. But, you never know! Now, tell me, how is it with you?'

He realized how out of touch they'd been since his college days. He told her about the divorce. She was sad.

'Oh dear. I saw the wedding pictures. She was lovely. And clever too. And you waited and waited . . .'

'All a mistake, perhaps?'

'Who knows? How could either of you know how life would turn out, what a conductor's life would mean for a wife? Exciting for you, forever on the go. Bloody for her, believe me. I've had my share of waiting.'

'No choice, you see, until something worthwhile turns up at home.'

'May be a long time. We're not famous for encouraging our own, are we?'

'No. Perhaps I should live abroad. Jane could easily find me something in America.'

Kate's ears pricked up, almost visibly. 'Jane?'

'My agent.'

'Oh. Jane Grant. Tough cookie, isn't she?'

Tough? He remembered his soft Jane and smiled. She saw it. 'Ah. Important, is she?'

'Vital,' he said. 'I depend on Grant's, utterly.'

Wisely not pressing, she turned to practicalities. 'They'll send a car for you tomorrow, I expect? I'm stuck until lunchtime. Then I have some teaching in Cardiff, so I can bring you out again. We'll have supper and a long talk, Now, off to bed.'

With a wave she was gone.

5

Good players adjust to new conductors very quickly. In fifteen minutes David and they were old friends. It was a band well supplied with experience, primed with a dozen or so bright young people. David enjoyed his morning.

Over lunch the manager was enthusiastic. 'Not enough of you people about,' was his only complaint. 'There's no performance without conducting. Unfortunately, outside London we get only the up-and-coming. Once they've made it they're too busy.'

Well, thank God there were opportunities for the young, thought David; it was not so long since he'd have given both legs for a concert in Cardiff, but that was not the message his friend wanted to hear. He took the bull by the horns. 'I know. That's life, and life's never fair. You must try to find the carrot which might make Cardiff more attractive than Tokyo. Not just to me but to Grant's. Talk to Jane tomorrow and see what you can sort out. But she has my book full for two years, with options coming in all the time. You need a project. Something good for me, good for you, something which only you can offer.'

The man was thoughtful. 'Not easy,' he said.

Neither was Mozart's Requiem, and the solo singers were waiting. The voices were first-rate. An afternoon full of excellent sounds and happy people. Kate watched the last hour, waiting afterwards while various players came to raise points of technique. The last, a fetching lady viola, gave up only when Kate's fidget became noticeable.

In the car, waiting for traffic, she said, 'It's always a lady last, I expect.'

'What?'

'Enquiries about bowings, dynamics, all that.'

Smiling, he told her he hadn't noticed.

'Oh, come on! That one tried all the angles. Busy with her legs every time you stopped to discuss. Not half so interested in your ideas as in what you might do with a free evening. I almost left you to it.'

Yes, he'd enjoyed the legs. 'Wasted effort,' he said. 'Golden rule, never sleep with the orchestra.'

They were away, the little car making too much noise for conversation. Soon they were in the village street, passing Molly's old house, then into the drive of the bigger one. David prised himself out of the tiny door and she garaged the car. Key in the lock, she said, 'Welcome back, David.'

In the sitting room little had changed; only the picture was missing. She saw his look. 'I found another place for him. He used to be company. Afterwards . . . well, one doesn't need a constant reminder. Now, would you like a shower?'

'Wonderful.'

'It's at the end of the passage. Upstairs belongs to someone else now. Too big for me by myself. Off you go, while I get supper.'

When he returned she was sitting, drinks waiting.

'Seems like yesterday,' Kate smiled. 'You've grown a bit. We knew you were going to be a big chap.'

'It helps in the job, I think.'

'Does it? Some of the small men did very well, surely? Toscanini, Beecham, Barbirolli . . .'

'Exceptions. Anyway, they were the aggressive sort – Napoleons. Times have changed. The days of *do it my way or else* are over.'

'I must say, you seem to have the orchestra on your side.'

'The only way to work. Nice people. I'm enjoying them.'

'They enjoy you. Try to find a little time, now and again – '

'Oh, the pressure's on. They'll have to talk to Jane. I'll do what I can, but I mustn't commit myself without her. She'd hate it.'

They were halfway through supper before Kate returned to the subject. 'Sounds a hard lady, Miss Grant.'

'No. It's a tough business, though. She does a great job for me.'

'You were lucky to find her, then.'

'It was the other way round really, but you're right. It was luck. Grant's came to the famous concert. The pianist was one of theirs.'

'The evening when Box conked out?'

'That one. Bartok Concerto, Brahms' Third.'

'Terrifying.'

He considered, remembering. 'Concentration is the thing. I had nothing left to be nervous *with*. And the orchestra was wonderful. It would have been quite hard to get them to play Brahms badly. Anyway I conducted Box's performance, not my own.'

'Very different?'

'I hope not. The old man was usually right.'

'So you were snapped up?'

'Hardly.' He remembered the edgy afternoon at Grant's, the old man's long inquisition, Jane sitting silent across the room, taking notes. A disaster, he'd imagined. Then the letter offering another discussion, the meeting with Jane alone, her unpromising and distant attitude. Then the work. First a trickle, then a steady stream, now a torrent which might drown a man. 'He didn't want me. Jane had the job of selling me.'

'But there's an absolute famine of good conductors.

You know the bandroom joke? The question, what it is the great conductors have in common?'

He knew it only too well. 'They're all dead, you mean?'

'It's nearly true.'

'I'm hardly among the great.'

'Obviously not, since you're still alive.' They laughed together.

She got up. 'Now, some unfinished business. Come on!'

She led the way to the big warm room with the piano. 'Franck Sonata. All of it, I hope. How are the fingers? Can you cope?'

He could, easily and gladly; he had so few opportunities to play nowadays. She was a delight, so musical a player, and in fine form. Rising at the end he kissed her gratefully on both cheeks. She took him by the hand and they went back to the fireside.

'Tell me about the golden rule, David.'

She'd lost him, or he was still lost in the music. 'What . . .?'

'Not sleeping with the orchestra.'

'Oh, yes. Box's advice to departing students. He thought it a very bad thing.'

'To *all* departing students?'

He'd never wondered. 'I imagine so.' He sat up straight. 'Surely it wasn't special advice for me?'

She thought it might well have been specially for him, but no need to decide this evening. 'Is it? A bad thing, I mean.'

'I expect so. I don't know. I took the advice.'

'Lots of opportunities, though?'

'I suppose. But there's a curious defensive mechanism which switches off dangerous possibilities. I reckon fewer executives sleep with their secretaries than the popular magazines would have us believe.'

'So you really were not sorry I was waiting?'

'Good God, no. It wouldn't have been on.'

'Because you thought I might be available?'

David put the glass down with care, giving himself lots of time.

'*Might*? You *were* available. There you were. Here we are.'

'So, sleeping with me was at least a remote possibility?'

'*Is* it?' he asked.

'Oh yes. The last time you were here I wanted it very much. I still do.'

'But – '

'No. Not then, and not now. Not then for Molly's sake and yours too. Not now for . . . well, I'm not sure why not, but no. No.'

'You knew about Molly and me?'

'Oh yes. That morning, d'you remember, when I popped in and chased you out to walk the dog?'

'She told you?'

'Lord, no. No need. I could see it. Look, we'd been together, Molly and me, for eighteen months, without the men. It wasn't easy. I'm not cut out for a nun. Moll certainly wasn't, you know that.'

'Molly? But it was all for me, surely?'

'Mmm . . . half-and-half.

'She needed a man, I can tell you. And that morning the release was so obvious in her face.' Kate smiled, remembering. 'All the edges gone. So soft she was. She looked five years younger. And you! So pleased with yourself! I was embarrassed at first, then green with envy. You were almost dragged into bed that day.'

'I wouldn't have been hard to persuade.'

'But I couldn't have faced Molly, you see. Also, it would have been awful to have you think that all women had round heels.'

'I see. Well, you haven't.'

111

'No. Not all. But not so square as you might think, if we know we can get away with it.'

'I wonder if we ever do,' he said.

'But we think we do, at the time. I gather you didn't, in the end.'

'It wasn't just the women.'

'They'd have been too much for most wives, surely?'

'Perhaps. But Julie knew me very well. Even when I was in Vienna, I . . . we were a long time apart, you know?'

'D'you think it's easier for women?'

'No. But people are easier on men. Women don't get away with it, and you know that. So you have this necessary discipline.'

'It's not just what people think, David. We blame ourselves. We feel ashamed. Molly did, of course.'

'I hope not. I didn't think – '

'No. How could you, at that age? But she was ashamed, certainly. It was a long time before she understood that I didn't blame her.'

'She was lucky to have you.'

'We were all lucky to have each other, weren't we? It must have made a difference to you, the experience?'

'Yes, it did. It has.'

'Good. Her justification – to herself I mean – was that she wanted to put the problem behind you, leave the field clear for work or whatever.' She poured cognac, in cut glass. He must ask Jane about those glasses, he thought, and the lace.

'I know,' he said, dragging himself back to the present, tired now. 'Did either of you really believe in that?'

'Well, didn't it work?'

'Not in the way she wished. It gave me a lot of confidence, though. Enough to make me a menace to every girl in sight. Tell you something else. They *knew*. They can feel it, the difference, as though we hang out a signal: come on, girls, I can solve your problem, show you what it's all about.'

'So, we were wrong?'

'I don't know. I might have worked just as hard if I'd stayed with the five-fingered widow until I married, but the result wouldn't have been the same. Confidence breeds. Nothing succeeds – '

'Like success?'

'Yes. Three nights with Moll may have produced a conductor in an emergency. Who can say?'

'Poor Moll, it wouldn't be easy for her to live with what she did. Easier for me, far. No Welsh Methodist bunkum about my family, you see. I'd have done it and enjoyed it. So would you.'

'Oh, I fancy Molly enjoyed it all right.'

'Mmmm. But she was worried silly afterwards, I could tell.'

'About the law, yes.'

'A bit. But mainly old-fashioned conscience.' Kate refilled their glasses. 'Anyway, it was all for the best.'

'I hope so,' he said, 'but I wonder if Julie would think so.'

'Did she know? About Molly?'

'No. No, of course not.'

'But you think it was all part of a disaster for her?'

'Julie's all right now. She has what she needs, some-one to come home to, someone who comes home to her, not a voice on the line from Sydney or San Francisco.'

'No kids?'

'No. We decided against, until I could settle down. She had her research. Kids would have been someone else's job if we'd had them, with an absentee father and an absorbed mother. Not fair.'

'So you were not what she needed, ever?'

'No, not really. There's only room for one career in a marriage I think. It wasn't until we were married

113

and busy that we found that out. If her folks hadn't been so obstructive . . . we were a determined pair, you know. The parents were an obstacle to be overcome, like her studies and mine. Things to be beaten so that we could do what we'd decided to do, years earlier, regardless.'

'But you were in love, surely?'

'Yes, we were. Puppy love at first, then real interest as we realized we had talent, both. A mutual admiration society with sex thrown in. I was away so much, and every time I came home was a honeymoon. But life's not a honeymoon, is it? It's routine shared, small problems sorted out. I can only throw money at difficulties. If we needed a carpet, she chose it. The house was decorated – while I was away. I didn't think about it, share the mess. It wasn't fair, any of it, but what could I do? She had her work *and* the marriage every day. I worked in a cocoon, with a marriage to come home to.'

'Lonely for her?'

'Not only that. She felt excluded. My life's a solo experience. There's no way into it for anyone.'

'Forgive me,' asked Kate quietly, 'but would you share it if you could?'

'It's not possible. The nearest one can get is to manage it.'

'Miss Grant, then.'

'Jane is the perfect manager.'

'And that's all?'

Evasion was impossible. 'No. Not now. Jane *is* in the picture, but only now.'

'Is she what you want?'

'You're about to tell me that the rebound is dangerous.'

'Very. But she knows you well? No illusions?'

David smiled. 'Yes. She knows the worst.'

'And how well do you know her, David?'

114

'Not at all, she says.'

'Bright girl. Do I get to meet this wonder?'

'After the concert, I expect. She'll be here tomorrow.'

'Good.' She looked at the clock. 'Come on, I'll walk you back.'

Getting up, they were very close. She put her arms round his neck, his went round her. She'd been owed the kiss a long time, and it lasted. 'Mmmmm . . . irresistible, nearly,' she said, carefully light. 'Such a beautiful man,' releasing him. 'Easy for me. But you have problems enough. Make me a promise though?'

'Anything.'

She chuckled. 'Be careful with that *anything*. But if it doesn't work out, come and play another sonata? Unless I'm too old?'

'You'll never be too old,' he said, shaking his head.

'Balls. Come on. Back to The Dragon with you.'

* * *

David could sleep, as his Mam used to say, hanging up on a clothesline; catnap, given half a chance, in an hour's break between rehearsals and leap up all bright-eyed and bushy-tailed for the next three hours, no problem. But tonight he was in trouble. Was it that he'd subconsciously expected to sleep with Kate?

How had she guessed that women had been part of the trouble between Julie and him? Women seemed to get into his head with amazing ease. As Box had said, he liked them. He'd had very few men friends, and none he could call close. Masculine friendships are built on common ground, and conductors had so little in common with the rest of the human race. Only freaks conduct, he told himself. Or was it that con-ducting produced freaks? A famous player had once told him that while he knew many conductors, there

115

were none with whom he could contemplate a two-week holiday. All very odd people, conductors, he'd said, 'even the nicest ones. Including you, David.'

With women he could relax, perhaps because to him, difference was what the relationship was all about. Women expected nothing in common, except an unspoken and usually unfulfilled mutual interest in sex. Was it Wilde who'd said that it was impossible for a man to follow a woman innocently up a staircase? Women were not disturbed by difference, and because of his work he was more interesting than other men to them.

Then there was the power thing. Men, even friends, resent power; but for women it was the great aphrodisiac. The thing went back to the neanderthal with the biggest club. But surely a man should be loved for himself, not for his work? Otherwise the job became the man. Without it he was less than the least of those who existed as themselves, as real people.

Ten years of reassuring applause, and still this need. What was it that he needed? To prove that he was human, that music moved him, too? Did women make love to him because they thought he was extraordinary, while he made love to prove that he was not? Or was it much simpler; did it happen because he was handsome and couldn't resist a good pair of legs?

No. Not that, anyway. All his women had been bright; all charming and clever people. There'd always been good conversation in the morning. For the bimbos there were autographs, nothing more. Still, they'd made it easy. Sometimes, taking a bow, he felt as though he had the choice of half the audience; the half in skirts.

It was not a physical dependence anyway. That could have been solved with ease, a matter of money. He remembered his first visit to Japan, when a light-hearted remark to orchestra management had produced two delightful ladies waiting in his suite after the concert. What a night it had been, Japanese efficiency in these matters knowing no bounds. Those had been the only paid ladies in his life. He'd been embarrassed to find them there. To pay them, even to telephone them for himself, would never have entered his head.

The Diplomatic Corps, whose hospitality to visiting artists is legendary, was sexually out of bounds except by specific invitation, endorsed in triplicate on Embassy notepaper and signed by their partners. Dangerous people, diplomats; influential at long range. On this trip his fall from diplomatic grace had come on the very last evening. She'd been the Italian wife of a Northern European cultural attaché. A lovely girl, she'd been pursued by every unattached diplomat and many of the others, but her virtue had been famously impregnable, her husband the most envied of men. Diplomatic ladies are the toughest and sometimes the most exploitative alive under their suave exteriors but this one was, as our Ambassador had memorably said, 'What we used to call a good girl, I think?' At three dinner parties David had achieved no more than a handshake, her eyes modestly downcast. Then fate supplied the fuse and the subsequent explosion had been appropriately Vesuvian.

There'd been some confusion over David's car, and as Tina was to attend the concert she'd been sent to collect him. All went beautifully if uncommunicatively until the intermission, when he'd looked for the score of the final work. It was every conductor's challenge, Stravinsky's *The Rite of Spring*, and a last-minute look at the score was a superstitious ritual of his. Alas, the music had been left in the car. Tina, dispatched posthaste to the parking lot, returned distraught. The score was safe enough on the car seat, but she'd lost her key.

Every conductor intends one day to conduct *The Rite* without a score, but never today. A prudent man might have kept the audience waiting while the car was burgled. He couldn't do it to Tina, now in a state of panic-stricken collapse. He'd had the desk taken away.

He'd survived without putting a wrong beat down, the last three awful minutes with his eyes closed. Sheer terror, but it had looked well. The orchestra stood to applaud, and audience reaction was the sort Karajan might have expected after a good Mahler Nine.

David had walked back, after seven bows, pleased with himself but very weak at the knees. Tina had been there, waiting. Hardly was the door closed than her arms were round his neck, her lips seeking. He leaned; it was all he could do. Her face was tear-stained and wide-eyed with admiration, whether for his kindness to her or for what she considered an enormous feat of intellect he didn't know, but the reward she offered was unique. Are diplomatic wives more expert at removing formal evening wear than most? She undid his collar and his flies with one movement, or so it seemed. Jane was right; unwinding can be very urgent. He was ready, Tina even more so, hauling at her gown, kicking off her pants. She was beside herself, her immaculate English lost. '*Caro, caro mia . . . bravo . . . bravo . . . bravo . . . grazie –* ' and in moments she was subsiding, only standing because her hold on his neck was so firm. There was a knock on the door. He disappeared into the toilet to repair the visible damage while she made what futile gestures she could to propriety.

The next half-hour was taken up with the usual congratulations and autographs. Someone asked about his car. 'It's not necessary,' she said. 'I will see Maestro to his hotel.' He surrendered to the diplomatic inevitable and they'd made torrential love until the light came up. He'd no memory of her leaving, only that he'd overslept, just making the plane.

He was just about to board when she arrived in the VIP lounge, looking rested, charming and demure as ever in a business suit, carrying the famous score. Her apologies for the misadventure of the previous evening were modest. 'I hope Maestro will forgive me?' She was back in character, eyes lowered. Bowing, he kissed her hand. The Second Secretary, there to see him off, shook hands gravely, his face admirably disciplined.

Why, tucked up in his Welsh bed, was he now questioning an episode which most men would have remembered with pleasure and gratitude? What was so wrong in enjoying women? Who, for God's sake, would have refused poor Tina? What rational wife would have blamed him for what had happened?

David was almost asleep when the telephone rang. It was Jane. 'Were you asleep?'

'Nearly,' he said, yawning.

'I rang earlier. In the interval.'

'The interval?'

'There are other concerts, you know. And other artists. I've had an evening at the Albert. Did they keep you nattering?'

'It was a good evening.'

'Not too good, I hope.' She sounded worried. 'You haven't made any silly promises?'

'No. The pressure is on, though.'

'Of course.'

'Don't worry. It wasn't that sort of evening anyway.'

'Oh? Are there diplomatic wives in Cardiff too?'

'They follow me about. Won't let me sleep.'

'Time I came down, is it?'

'Darling, it was time yesterday. Get the car out and come now.'

'Tomorrow. In time for lunch,' she said.

'Good. And tell the office you won't be in on Monday.'

'I won't?'

'No. We have things to talk about. Welsh things. Hungarian things too, if you're ready.'

There was a pause, then: 'I'm ready.'

'Good night now.'

'Night.'

Then at last he could sleep.

6

They'd progressed to the day of judgement, the trombonist sounding the last trump, when Jane arrived. Facing away from the door, David was aware of her presence through the eyes of the orchestra. For the space of eight bars they played and sang by radar, without eyes for the music or the conductor. Glancing round he saw her, in jeans and a tank top, immersed in a score. There are times, he thought, when plainness is useful in a woman.

Kate arrived soon after. In the break they were waiting together, chatting easily, getting along well. They all had tea, listening to a tape of the rehearsal, checking the radio sound. It was fun for David hearing the two women debate it together. Both had ears. So had the BBC's engineer, and he'd take precious little notice of either, judging by the surreptitious grins he exchanged with David.

By lunchtime all was in splendid order, so no need to work this afternoon; tomorrow's polish would be enough. Nothing pleases an orchestra more than a cancelled rehearsal, leisure gained the best way, by working for it. The church emptied with such speed that he wondered whether Wales were playing the All Blacks today. Kate and Jane reappeared. He told them he'd given everyone the afternoon off.

'Lazybones,' said Kate. 'Don't you like Mozart any more?'

'Mozart is not to be liked or disliked,' he told her. 'You know that.'

'Ah,' smiled Jane 'a fact of life, like Mount Everest.'

'And income tax,' Kate added.

He was more interested in Welsh mountains today. 'Can that funny car climb Cwmbach mountain? A proper hill, that. Not one of your alpine molehills.'

'You're not serious?' asked Jane.

Kate had seen the look in his eye. 'Oh, he's serious all right. Go and look at his valley. It's not far. You'll just have time before the light packs up. I must go home, wash my hair, do a little practice. See you tomorrow.'

There was a motorway up the valley now. In the old days the road and the river all crisscrossed the railway madly the whole twenty miles, like a crazy game of snakes and ladders. Now it was fast but much less fun. They drove all the way to the top and up the hill road beyond. Among the too-tidy trees of the forestry they found a track which took them to the edge of the mountain. There below was an abandoned mineworking, marked by two great steel winding-wheels set in concrete.

'The Tynybedw pit,' he told her. 'It means the house in the birches, or the larches, I can't remember which. My grandfather was working down there when I was born, and my father with him. They were together, two miles down, the day the old man was buried by a fall of the roof. He fell on his back, only his head and shoulders free. Four hours it took, digging him out. Can you imagine four hours, looking up at that roof and wondering?'

'No,' she said quietly. 'That I can't imagine.'

'Only Dad and Dada got out alive. But for that chance . . .'

'Chance, yes.' She looked at him in the half-light, the streetlamps winking now, down in the valley. 'Life is all chances. If they'd died, who would have paid for your music, I wonder?'

'Don't wonder,' he told her. 'Two and sixpence a week on a widow's pension? Not likely.'

'No. Then the chance that your aunt had a friend, who thought you had talent and who knew the right people. It was a violin sonata, wasn't it? Franck? You dictated style to her, she said. A musician with a mind of your own, even at that age, even in new music, even before you could find the right notes. An astonishing mind for one so young and inexperienced. So she thought, anyway.'

He shrugged, deprecating. 'Sounds like Schumann's description of the English: musicians who made many mistakes but with great feeling.'

Jane laughed, but insisted. 'The ideas, she said. The ideas were the thing. She knew the piece long since, but you gave her new ideas about it.'

'Wasn't it much simpler?' he suggested. 'Two frustrated women longing for a youngster to help, one way or another? Still, lovely, isn't she? Kind, thoughtful, sad still.'

'Sad? Tell me. And *two* frustrated women?'

It was quite dark now. He could see, far down the valley, the lights of the street where he was born. A little train was climbing the single track up the valley, its carriage lights bright; the train which had taken him to the seaside long ago. It was time to tell her.

She was silent when he finished. He reached for her hand. She turned to him. 'Astonishing. A week to turn a life.'

'Every life turns somewhere, surely?'

'No.' She was thoughtful. 'Many lives run on railway lines, sidings here and there but the destination never in doubt. But to discover a talent, make a decision for someone else, shape him . . .'

'Did they really, d'you think?'

'Yes, of course. Kate made the decision for you. Your aunt . . . now her decision . . . You told Kate about me?'

'Yes. You don't mind?'

'No. No, she's close.'

Only the lights now, the valley black as coal.

'What did she think of us, your Kate?'

'She asked if I really knew you,' said David.

'Clever. What did you tell her?'

'That you were sure I did not.'

'You do in a way. In another way not. It doesn't matter.'

'It mattered three days ago. Why not now?'

'Because I know myself well enough for us both. Trust me.'

'Do you know me?' he asked.

'Yes, I do . . . now.' She was suddenly practical. 'I'm hungry. Love and Mozart are all very well but the odd steak wouldn't come amiss. Let's go down, shall we? Tell you what, though, I haven't been kissed today. Gone off me?'

'Fool,' he said. 'Come here.'

They made good time down the hill and up the other side, over to the coast.

She changed for dinner. No way, she said, that she could drink a decent claret in jeans. He told her that her hopes of a decent claret in this little town were slim indeed. She smiled pityingly.

'Essential, a good bottle. If in doubt it makes sense to bring one's own. It's breathing already.'

The story which unfolded over the steak and mushrooms was of another time, another world.

'My father was a Jew, of course. His father was a rabbi, quite an important figure in Jewish society in Budapest. GG was the first of three sons. They intended him for the synagogue, but from an early age he would think about nothing but music. As a child he would sit and tinkle endlessly at any keyboard he could find. There was lots of music among family friends. They encouraged him, taught him music, gave him books to read. He sat down one day in a small café and

124

played. He was so tiny, David. People were fascinated. They gave him money to come back next day after school. He was a working musician at seven.

'Grandfather was not too pleased. The family was not so rich that they could afford a long training. But there was no stopping him, and a family with money admired his talent and paid for his place at the Conservatoire.

'He made a reputation, and they began to think this was not so bad an idea after all. They were proud, the way Jewish families are with bright kids. Then he met mother. She was a singer. He used to say she made his life one long song. But she was a Catholic. You know what that meant, David?'

'Trouble?' he suggested.

'You can't imagine how much. You don't know what it meant, what it still means, to be a Jew in Eastern Europe. Here a Jew is an Englishman with a funny nose, someone who goes to church on the wrong day and does business with his chums rather than with you. Someone who doesn't mind when you make jokes about him. But in Hungary then a Jew was another sort of *being*. Even if his family has lived there for a hundred years he's just a Jew, to be suffered as long as he isn't too much in evidence, too successful, too noisy. GG was never a Hungarian like my mother. Until you understand that you can't get near understanding the pogroms of the old East, still less Hitler's philosophy. Their Jews were not *human*, you know, just very intelligent animals who walked on two legs. And that was not the worst of it. My mother's father was an Austrian diplomat, with one brother a colonel in the army, another a cardinal, a prince of the Church. They were rich, influential people. Such people didn't encourage their women to marry Jews in Budapest in the years after the first war, let me tell you.

125

'For a while the families played the situation very coolly, waiting for good sense to intervene. But both sides were terribly ashamed and embarrassed. Neither could even mention the other at home. Both homes knew. My parents were honest kids. They wanted only to graduate, marry, make a living and have children, all the things ordinary folks do, and these two families were determined to stop them. GG's money, Jewish money, stopped. He went back to playing in cafés to pay his fees. The worst thing was that he was a good Jew, and she a good Catholic. It was hell, he used to say, facing his father and friends in the synagogue, she going to confession, neither willing to give up the other or their beliefs.

'When the pressure got too much they ran away. They found jobs in Vienna, at the opera, he on the music staff, she in the chorus for a while, until the babies arrived. They told both families where they were, what they were doing. They didn't mean to get lost, just to take the problem away. The families could tell whatever polite evasions they wished to their friends. They were both success stories anyway, working in that famous opera house so young. Only the relationship was shaming, and that was never talked about. It was convenient, it worked, but neither family ever saw either of them again.

'At least they could marry,' he said.

'Oh no. How could they? In the end, neither could accept the other's faith and neither could believe in a civil marriage either. They just did without. Love had to be enough.'

'Strong people.'

'Yes, strong. Their love was like a wall around us. Home was full of love and music.'

'But you can't eat either . . .'

'Oh, they were not short of money, in a modest way. Things were harder when the kids came and

126

Mother couldn't sing. For a little while Father played in a café again. We used to eat there once a week, in the café where he played. I can see it now, lots of big mirrors, gilt lamps and white linen, waiters in aprons and a cimbalom player in the corner. A Hungarian restaurant. It was important to them that the children knew how to behave in a restaurant. A musician has status in Vienna, the only city where you could dial A on the phone and get a tuning note, you know? The most musical city in the world.'

'And the most anti-Semitic in civilized Europe.'

She nodded. 'If it's possible to be anti-Semitic and civilized. They got the best of Mahler, then chucked him out. They built the finest orchestra in the world on Jewish string playing and then stood by when the Jews were taken off to camps. Even when I was a small child I felt it. We were not to be played with, not to be taken home. Still, Father made progress. Soon he was conducting in small theatres, assisting great men in the State Opera. He had real talent.

'Then one day there were swastika flags everywhere, people going about in brown clothes and raising the right hand. Suddenly even the nicest people were, well, politely distant.'

'Couldn't you all have gone away? I mean, before the thing got really nasty?'

'Mother wouldn't believe it. Lots of people didn't, to the very end. It's not easy, I suppose, to admit to yourself that the nice young man you went to school with a few years back is busy killing people. They knew Jews were being sent away, but only to the east, where they'd come from. Not altogether a bad thing, perhaps, lots of people thought. GG had lots of Jewish friends. He knew much more than we did about what was going on. He was left alone because he had powerful friends at the opera, for a while. Then people stopped employing him. People were dismissive at first, then ugly. It was worse and worse. In the end he ran, as you know.

'Both my parents were in the plot to save us. At first mother didn't believe the need, but in the end she agreed that he must go. She was right. If he'd stayed we'd all have been finished, like his family in Budapest. It was your friend from Dresden who got him out. The opera was in Zürich for two weeks, the old man conducting. There was sickness. He insisted on GG as a replacement. Of course there was no sickness, no emergency. The point was simply to get him out. It was a terribly dangerous thing to do, the sort only the very important *could* do. They were needed, you see. The Party had lost so many famous artists, and the ones who stayed were vital. They've always been blamed for not clearing out – and it's true that some stayed for the good jobs left vacant, rich pickings – but some stayed because there was work to be done, things to preserve and protect. Who can judge them? Anyway, GG went to Switzerland and never came back. Even then he'd have come back, he said, but for the letter.'

'What letter?'

'From Mother's people. They were watching, God knows how. Perhaps they were even part of the plot. The colonel was in the SS. He must have known what was happening to the Jews. He was a good man, hanged for his part in the Generals' plot to kill Hitler.'

'My God,' David said, 'it's like something out of a novel.'

'But it was *real*. Real people were dying, love, millions of dads and mums and little kids. We had a half-chance of survival without Father. That was what my grandparents wanted, to get him away, forgotten, married to someone else, anything. Mother could still have married. There was a letter waiting in Zürich telling him that we were finished, the whole family, if he came home, promising that we'd be cared for if he went, telling him to go. There was money waiting in a Swiss bank. What else could he do but run?'

'To England, though?'

'Yes, but the idea of losing us completely never entered his head, nor Mother's either. She stayed in Vienna, wouldn't go home to Budapest. She was right. God knows how we'd ever have made it out of Hungary. Anyway, the promise was kept. Whether it was the Party through the Colonel, or the Church through the other brother we never knew, but the knock on the door never came. We were in Vienna when the Russians arrived. We left it in '47.'

'Nine years,' he said.

'Yes. Mother had one year to live. GG used to say it was the only year in which he really lived too. He'd done well. There were an awful lot of Hungarians in London and many of them in the arts. They helped. After all those years of being a Jew he became one of your men with funny noses who go to church on Saturday.'

'Oh, darling,' he said, 'GG was as Jewish as all-get-out.'

She grinned. 'Well, we insist on advertising. A little antagonism feeds us. What else would we have apart from a talent for music and money?

'The war made a mess, of course. He was sent to the Isle of Man with all the other potential spies. D'you know, some of them expected to find gas chambers there? What they actually did, in the war, was to sit down together, teach and learn. There's a top man in Oxford today who says his best university was on the Isle of Man. GG taught music and learned business. What he wanted more than anything was to join the army and kill as many Nazis as possible. But the best they would allow was ENSA, playing to the troops, you know, then helping to manage it, and finally into the Arts Council. They needed people like him, with background and languages. There was a shortage of musicians too. England had a lot of catching up to do.'

'It sounds a little like the Kryshkov story,' he said.

'Isn't he a trombonist —'

'In the Phil. Polish. Played in an army band in '39. Captured by Jerry. They offered the alternative of a prison camp or one of their bands. He chose to play. Then he was captured again, by the British this time. He finished the war in ENSA too. I wonder if they ever met? Great player, Kris.'

'It toughens people up, David, all that. The ones who came through did it in a big way. The fact that most went under is never noticed by the envious.'

'Are we envious, really?'

'Oh yes, of course. Especially of successful Jews. But there is an acceptance of talent here, and the British admire resilience. They'll play merry hell about successful people and then say, "Mind you, you've got to hand it to him . . ."'

'The boys did well too.'

'It was nearly too late for them. They were very Jewish-Hungarian young men.'

'But they made it.'

'Survival is the name of the game. We've had a lot of practice. But people were wonderful. We got a lot of help from GG's friends. In a year the boys were just romantically foreign. Attractive, that. They did terribly well with the ladies. I got to be plain British. Plain Jane.'

'Oh, come on!' He had to laugh.

'You think I try too hard not to be Plain Jane?'

'We are what we are, love. The thing is to enjoy being yourself. You can't be anyone else.'

'I know it. I haven't learned to enjoy it, that's all.'

'Who has? Not I for sure. I haven't learned to enjoy

anything but music, and the better I do it the less I enjoy it.'

'That's what the artist gives up in return for the talent,' she said. 'Fun. Ordinary enjoyment. You lose out, there. But music isn't all you enjoy, surely?'

'Tell me.'

'Women?'

'Every man enjoys women. Biology, simply.'

'Every man enjoys sex, or nearly every man. Nearly every woman too. Not the same thing at all. No, you enjoy *us*, women as people. You don't understand us, of course, but no man does, ever. The nice thing is that you don't really try. You just allow yourself to be charmed.'

'I see. I've been had, have I?'

She smiled. 'Ah . . . you've wondered about that?'

'Last night, oddly enough.'

'After talking to that clever lady? Well, you were long enough getting there. Yes, I think lots of your women have had you. All that power on the box, all that authority. Yet all we have to do is cross our legs and you're sunk. Men *are* had by women, all the time.'

'If you're right I don't like women.'

'But you do. What you are learning to dislike is yourself. Or at least, your own weakness. Look, you know I adore having you make love to me. Only a week and I don't feel complete without it. Neither of *us* is had by the other. But that's so easy to forget when ordinary sex comes as easily as it does to you. I love you, David and I'm just as sure that you love me, in your own way, but I'm not sure what that means to you.' She reached for his hand across the table, held it tight, suddenly vulnerable, looking for reassurance.

'Neither am I,' he said with a sigh. 'I know the not-complete bit. I've been there before, a long time ago. I lost it under a great deal of pressure and too much absence. That's my excuse anyway. What you are asking is whether this time instead of getting lost it will grow until no other woman can attract. That's what you want.'

'It's what every woman wants.'

'Well, at eighteen I'd have made the promise and forgotten it next time I went up the college stairs behind a skirt. I'm old enough to know better now.'

'Old enough to avoid the promise? Or—'

'Mature enough to keep it? How do I know? What certainty can I offer?'

She shook her head, slowly. 'Don't offer the uncertainty as a challenge, David. I've had a gutful of uncertainties. If you can't provide certainty then please go away, leave me alone. I know how to deal with that.'

'You know? You're certain you can deal with it?'

'Yes. Inside myself there's certainty.'

Her grip on his hand was almost too tight now. He kissed her fingers, put them on the tablecloth and covered them with his own.

'No,' he said. 'Inside yourself there's control, and even your control has limits. I can offer you nothing but what your intelligence already knows. That and what your body is saying, and your intelligence is already reminding your body that there are other men; nice, trustworthy, reliable, safe other men. But you can't organize the risks out of your life.'

'You're telling me that I must gamble or leave the table,' she said.

'It's not even that simple. You can't leave the table. We're all chained to it. All we can do is play the hand as wisely as we know how. I won't play the game for you. You'd never forgive yourself for letting me do that. You have one great advantage. You deal most of my cards.'

There was a bell. Somewhere a barman was calling,

'Time, gentlemen . . .' Yes, time. They were both very tired. She smothered a yawn.

'Bed?' he suggested.

'Yes, if you still want me after all that.'

* * *

Much later, luxuriating with her arms around him, he asked about the lace.

'My mother's lace, you see. And the glasses. The lace was my grandmother's wedding gown, and her mother's too. Before that . . . anyway, it was meant to be passed down. When Mother ran away it was given to her sister, but she sent it to Mother, with the glasses. There was a message, that she would know when to use them. She kept the note. I found it when she died.'

'Did she? Use them, I mean?'

'Yes, of course, once. She was meant to break them in the traditional way.'

'But she didn't?'

'Perhaps there was a greater need, to hang on to anything of the old past she could keep.'

'Oh, good,' David murmured. 'I'm not one for breaking beautiful things.' Her body was moving again, and he held her more tightly.

When she spoke again, she was half asleep. 'I hope . . . I'm too beautiful.'

Sleepy, he was slow to understand. 'You are very beautiful,' he said.

'Mmmmm. But too beautiful to break?'

She was asleep before he could find a reply.

7

A kiss and the rattle of a teacup. Blindly David put up an arm to pull her down for an encore.

'Tea's made,' Jane said. He opened his eyes to find her jeaned and jumpered.

She kissed him again, lightly and briefly. 'It's eight o'clock.'

'Rehearsal is at . . .'

'Three.'

'Come back to bed.'

'Things to do. Drink your tea. I'm going for the papers. Breakfast at eight thirty? See you there, love.'

He drank the tea and ate the biscuit, got up and opened the curtains to look down the village street. There was Molly's grocer's. He remembered Molly's tea and biscuits. Poor Molly. Such generosity in the beginning, and such helpless need in the end. He'd felt like God that last morning. Love, simply. Then the silent drive to the station. How she'd clung, in the cold waiting room. The only people waiting, they'd hid in the corner where the booking clerk couldn't see, kissing like a courting couple, desperate to retain an imprint, something permanent to take away. They'd kissed again through the carriage window. Tearful she said, 'David, David *bach*, be careful, be good, don't spoil . . .' but the train was moving, taking him back to his boy's life, her home to wait for the brown envelope with the letter telling her that her husband would soon be home, but . . .

Shower, shave, throw on slacks and pullover. Down for breakfast. By the fire Jane had done with the juice and cereals already.

'Have you ordered for me?' David asked.

The paper lowered to disclose smiling eyes. 'No, she teased. 'I've given up the domestic act for the wicked lady. If you like, I'll even ask whether you take sugar when the tea comes. The disapproval at reception is really something.'

'Surely not. They must be used to it, even here?'

'I wonder. The woman at the desk makes her feelings very clear.'

'Perhaps we should've bought a ring? Welsh Methodism goes very deep.'

'Hmm. Is that what it is? I think she needs a man, that's all.'

'Jane, your cynicism beggars belief!'

The grills were here, enormous. Two eggs even. Tasting, he realized they were fresh this morning, unheard-of luxury.

'It's a hard world for ladies, David. There's a toughish centre under the peaches and cream where our own sex is concerned.'

'But last night was all about exploiting the male. Now you produce this poor soul who *needs* a man. What changed?'

'Nothing,' she said, pouring tea, a practical hand steadying the lid of the pot. 'There's no contradiction. We're not team animals like you people. Managing men doesn't preclude competing with women. Anyway, if she'd been as thoroughly satisfied last night as I was she'd smile at me this morning. And at everyone else, too.'

'Thank you for that, anyway. But you're simplifying madly.'

'Yes, I know.' She buttered toast, spread marmalade reflectively, bit and swallowed before returning to the fray. 'And a lot of complicated things are becoming simpler.' She was munching happily. 'How far is it to the sea?'

'Two, three miles. Not far.'
'Too cold for a walk, d'you think?'

* * *

They parked the car where the sand began. A short
walk round the headland and the beach was revealed.

Jane stopped, delighted, clapping gloved hands.
'Love, it's marvellous. I never imagined.'

It was a wonderful stretch of sand, and never more
beautiful than in the cold light of the January morning.

'The best beach,' David told her, pleased with her
pleasure. 'Better than Copacabana. Shorter of course,
but in Rio you have this wall of high-rise hotels, end
to end. And Southerndown is always quiet, even in
summer. No funfair, not even a pub. Nothing.'

They walked for a little, holding hands. A flock of
sheep on the sparse grass above the dunes complained
half-heartedly at their approach and began to move
slowly away, their shop steward leading.

'So,' she said, 'Molly's beach.'
'Yes. It seems an age ago, and yet only yesterday.'
'I was in Vienna.'
'At school.'
'Well, sometimes. Have you any idea what Vienna
was like then?'
'Tell me.'
'No. Not today. There are things to tell, though. It
was worse for a while under the Russians. Especially
at the beginning, when we were just fair game for the
army. I was a little girl. Thank goodness I was just a
bit *too* little.'
'Oh God,' he said.
'It wasn't for long. They soon had it under control.
If it's discipline you want, try the Red Army. There
were British and Americans too. Not always nicer than
the Reds, unless you find rape more acceptable when

136

it comes with a smile and a bar of Cadbury's. Ugh! No, I'd rather forget Vienna.'

'But can you? There must be scars.'

'If there are you've seen them. One didn't warm to men for a long time after. But my father was a man to hang on to. That was the happiest day, tumbling off the boat at Dover. There he was, waiting. Older, greyer, amazingly prosperous, but still my father.'

'A new life,' he said. 'What a problem. The language—'

'That was the least of it. You can't imagine how different the British are from the rest of humanity and how hard *they* are to learn. Nicely different in some ways but quite impossible in others.'

'Not easy, digging new roots.'

'We didn't. We don't, and we won't. We've given up trying. I'm only half a Jew, but quite rootless in a Jewish way. The idea of reliance on an environment, on places and attitudes, on a language even, is foreign. Unfair, the way we've been blamed for being separate, when we've never been allowed to join.'

'The chicken and the egg? But you really are different, you see. There is something fascinating about the Jew. It's part of your attraction for me, the difference, one I'll never understand.'

'Yes. We've been raped a million times for that reason, love; for the taste of the dark secret, the forbidden. Hitler forbade his master race to marry Jews, but a rare old time was had at the point of the bayonet, I can tell you. I'm not surprised you can feel it. But I am glad you own up to it.'

Own up? He was owning up to many things in his mind, though not ready to tell her. She was becoming too big to work *round*, rationalize, set aside until the next convenient time. The whole business of travelling, learning, meeting people, the concerts, all this giving of himself, was assuming the aspect of a nuisance. He wanted to stop, look round, breathe and think. He wanted to *talk* to this woman, the woman he'd thought he knew. There was so little time, his unforgiving minutes. Suddenly he remembered Molly's Judy O'Grady and the Colonel's Lady. Yes, he'd discovered.

'Come back,' she said.

'What? Oh, I'm here.'

'Barely. Look, the past is done, David. It's a bit like playing, you know. If you think about the mistake you just made you make another and another. It's the *next* note that counts, all the time. Come on, relax. Get some oxygen into your day.'

'It's a day I could do without,' he said.

'Nonsense. It'll be lovely. An occasion. You should be so lucky. Enjoy it. I will.'

They turned, and she became practical. 'Now, the day goes like this. Coffee, drive down, a few words about Box to the camera. Then a light lunch. Rehearse, how long?'

'Cameras will want an hour,' he guessed. 'That will do for me.'

'Right. They've arranged a room for a nap. Safe until six. John will deliver your clothes. I'll collect you. Performance at seven, over soon after eight. Then a reception, the City, the BBC, the University, you know the form. Then drive back to Town.'

'Tonight? I must travel tonight?'

'I think we should get away. God only knows what you'd promise them after a drink or two.'

'I see. I'm not to be tempted.'

'No. Business is for me. I'll look after it while you're working or sleeping. If there are loose ends they are not to be tied over a drink.' She held up her hand, knowing what was coming. 'I know. I know you want to give them something. For some silly reason so do I. It's just that I'm more likely to come up with a sensible gift than you are. You're too Welsh for your own good, love.'

'I'll sleep all the way home,' he warned.

She grinned. 'Not the way I drive.'

* * *

As usual, David enjoyed talking to the camera. It helped when the interviewer knew his job, and this chap had come well-briefed. As the piece was going out live the producer needed a clean five minutes, without edits. He was in luck today, and the end of the take produced a sigh of relief.

Politely evading an invitation to lunch, David was quickly away with Jane for an omelette in the greenroom.

'Bags of time,' she said, clearing away. 'Well done.'

'We try to please,' he said, kicking off his shoes and putting up his feet on the sofa-bed.

She smiled, reaching for a blanket to cover him. 'You're doing pretty well this week. Now, twenty minutes. Every little helps.' She turned down the light and left him to nap.

John woke him, bringing his clothes. His pleasure in being 'down home' shone in his face, and his Welsh accent had taken over completely. 'Sorry, David *bach*, but time it is! Suit is pressed, and shirt, lovely! Don't get it all creased now, or the missus will never forgive me. Watching she'll be on the television tonight.' John's Mary had been doing for the Grant family almost as long as he'd been driving for them, and a Grant artist's needs were those of the family. He hung the blacks in the wardrobe, gave the shoes a quick rub, sitting to chat while David put himself together.

'Good week, boy?'

'Great, John. I like it here.'

The old man was smiling, a little shy for the first

time in their considerable friendship. 'Lovely that she could come down too. Done her the world of good it has.'

'Wonderful what sea air and a good night's sleep can do,' David told him, remembering Isolde, her sympathetic tail, and the walk on the beach.

John agreed. 'Do it more often, David. Nobody else can stop her old gallop, see.'

'I'll do what I can.'

'Very grateful they'd be, in the office. A bit of peace and quiet now and then. And her so happy, boy . . .'

'Yes.'

John was hesitant, not knowing how to go on. 'David, pleased GG would be to see her now. And Mrs Grant.'

Knotting his tie David saw in the mirror that his friend's eyes were wet. Sentimental lot, the Welsh. Silently they shook hands.

*   *   *

Television had done well with the church, avoiding most of their customary mess with cables. Three cameras, two of them out of sight and none of them mobile. He gave silent thanks. Talking to the camera was one thing, playing music with a camera looking up one's nose was quite another.

There was an air of quiet satisfaction in the orchestra and chorus, reminding him again that orchestras love to play, that singers love to sing, that it was what people came into the business to do. They worked quietly and easily while the cameras found angles and technicians moved seats for the best shots, soloists at half-voice and leaving out the most strenuous passages. They were satisfied quite soon. He thanked them all for a fine week's work and for making him so much at home.

The leader rose, a small package in his hand. 'Mr Adams . . . we'd like you to accept a little present from us all here, something to remember us by and to bring you back as soon as you can. I know you like a game of rugby . . .' He was unpacking and offering a Welsh tie. David took off the RCM he was wearing and tied the new one to tumultuous applause.

Back to the greenroom with Jane. 'Such nice people,' she said, pouring tea. 'They like you. I wonder if you know how lucky you are to have roots.'

'I know it,' he said, 'and now we both know. Let's do what we can, shall we? There must be time for work here.'

'And a walk on the beach?'

'Yes. That too. That is what I'd like. Please arrange it.'

'Instructions now?'

'Please, Jane. It's important.'

'I know, I know.'

* * *

Jane had this knack of waking him with a kiss. Eyes closed, David reached for her. She evaded him easily. 'Mozart first, love afterwards.'

'Promise?' He opened his eyes. She was in a black suit, silk blouse and stockings to match, her hair pinned up. Mind-blowing. 'Kiss me again, anyway?' he asked.

'Oh no. Black is sexy, huh? We're going to church, remember? You have forty minutes to the red light.'

When he emerged from the shower she was tying a black lace headscarf, adjusting it with care in the mirror.

'You're serious about all this, aren't you?' he asked.

'Serious? How?'

'Church. The Requiem, all that.'

She was checking seams now, a splendid thing to watch. 'Oh yes. I forgot. For you it's just music, isn't it? Lovely sounds, good tunes for the voices, great writing for the orchestra. Nothing more.'

He thought it was a little more than that, and he said so.

'Yes, it is,' with a tuck at a rebellious hair. 'Much more, for me. It's where I get closer to Mozart than you ever will, my darling. Wolfgang and I are about to pray for the souls of the departed, not least that of George Box.'

'He wasn't a Catholic, anyway.'

'All the more in need of our prayers, poor chap.'

'I'll never understand you people,' he told her. For him religion was just so much more luggage to carry.

Jane shook her head sadly. 'Never's a long time. You'll come close to it in the end. I hope we can get a priest to you in time.'

'He was fixing his cravat, never an easy matter. 'Let me,' she said. 'Come here.'

He turned from the mirror and she managed it effortlessly, fastening the waistcoat over the silk. She stood back to admire her work. 'Splendid. Razor, please.' She tended to the back of his neck, the bit the audience sees. 'Now, one more thing.' She took from her handbag a small blue box. 'Something of GG's,' she said, her voice very small.

David opened the box. A diamond pin. 'Oh, love,' he said.

She was watching him carefully. The stone was spectacular. GG's taste in jewellery had been famously over the top. 'Look, if you don't like it . . .'

He thought again of Box's advice against wrist-watches, buttonholes, and such things, and hoped he'd have been forgiving. 'My love,' he said, 'I'll never wear a cravat without it.'

She put the pin carefully into the tie, tactfully half-burying the stone in its folds with a smile. He put on the jacket and she turned him to the mirror. 'Yes. Rather well turned out, I must say. You're in good shape.'

'Exercise,' he explained.

'Mmmm . . . we know what kind. It does seem to work. Look, I want to kiss you, but please behave. We mustn't be late.' She put her arms round his neck and they kissed. Her tongue encouraged, almost, then she broke away. 'God,' she said, breathless, 'it's too much, isn't it?'

'Hardly *too* much, but I'd like as much as possible, please.'

She looked at him in silence for a moment or two, her hands on his shoulders, about to say something important. There was a knock on the door. It was John, with the car. Sensing the atmosphere he was a little embarrassed. Jane was immediately all practicality.

'We're going with John. Lots of photography, some of it outside, probably. Hard to look the great conductor, climbing out of the Porsche. Is there a change of suit?'

'In the vestry, hanging,' said John. David looked at her, questioning.

'You'll need something more formal than those,' Jane explained with a nod to the discarded casuals John was carefully packing, 'but less formal than these.'

She'd been right about the photography. There were several flashes as they alighted, one only too obviously for Janet's legs in their black silk. For the photographer's personal collection, David thought, none too pleased. Then they were within the church, meeting the Dean and his friends. Jolly people, clerics, David reflected. Well fed, relaxed as only performers can be who are guaranteed repeat performances however badly they do it and however small the audience. A good life. This one seemed genuinely happy to have them in his church. Jane disappeared to her seat, David smiling inwardly as clerical eyes followed, giving ecclesiastic approval to her suit and the figure within.

The organ murmured distantly. All was ready. David followed the verger down the aisle, the people rising in a welcoming shuffle. To the rostrum then, turning to bow to the verger, then to the orchestra and singers. The players sat, the choir remained standing. A red light winked. David raised his arms and the music began.

Is it an act of God, when a performance so far surpasses expectation? Or the result of concentration so complete that the performers are almost able to stand back to listen to themselves? The Requiem found its home in church. Somewhere during it David found himself promising never again to play it in a concert hall.

At the end he stood silent for long moments, putting down the stick very quietly, almost afraid to break the hush even with so tiny a noise, an almost literal dropping of a pin. He turned. The Dean was in his pulpit, giving the Blessing, his voice at once present and remote over the electronic relay. The people were standing, the verger waiting. David followed him down the aisle. For a moment there was no sound but for their feet.

Then from the organ came a thunderous F minor. It was the Fantasia for Mechanical Organ. A tidy solution to a nearly insoluble problem, one of the few works which could follow the Requiem, and in a week of personal coincidences a nicely tied loose end.

Into the vestry, subsiding into a chair, David would have killed for a drink, but the congratulations were waiting – the solo voices coming in behind him, Dean and clergy, leader of the orchestra, and outside the door an interminable queue for autographs, each with a word of thanks.

At last they were changed and away. He settled into

the deep seat with a sigh of relief. But Jane had an urgent worry.

'Listen, love, things to tell you and no time. Just take it as it comes tonight, please? I wanted time for an announcement, but there's no holding them. They want to do it tonight.'

He was in a private fog, as so often after working. He let her ramble on. 'If I haven't got it exactly right we can fiddle with the bits and pieces later. The thing is just to look happy. Please?'

Even in the darkened car her anxiety was palpable. He took her hand, hardly aware of her words. 'Jane, when did I ever argue with you about work?'

'You don't. But I don't often move so far and so fast. I just hope I've got it right, that's all.'

Pulling himself together he pecked her cheek reassuringly. 'Don't worry. You're never wrong about these things. Now, tell me what you can. It wouldn't do for me to look *too* surprised, would it?'

But there was no time, the journey too short. They entered the reception to a round of applause. The Lord Mayor was charming, his Mayoress gushing, both proud that a Rhondda boy had done so well. Speeches now. After the Mayor, the Welsh Arts Council in person. David, aware of Jane's nervous edge, wished he could hold her hand.

'. . . An evening to remember . . . an inspiration to the chorus and orchestra . . . a worthy tribute. Now I can say that this is the first of many occasions like it. David is to be with us next year, and every year for a long time, for one month every summer. He will be chief guest conductor of our orchestra for the next five years and I hope for much longer.'

There are various kinds of applause. There was real warmth, real enthusiasm here. David's turn now. He thanked them all for their welcome and for their work, the orchestra, the chorus and the solo voices. He told them that he'd felt at home, not only because he *was* at home but because there had been a real musical understanding here. He looked forward to being with them again and to many more evenings like this one. It had been a lovely performance, one he'd never forget, but nothing to do with him; the composer had been speaking for himself . . .

Lots more applause. Circulating with the Mayor, David saw Jane across the room. The black headscarf had gone, the suitable suit becoming high fashion with the change of a wisp at the throat.

'Well done, David.' Kate was at his elbow. He kissed her on both cheeks. She blushed becomingly, waving to Jane. 'She is really extraordinarily lovely, David. And terribly clever. You are a lucky man, d'you know?'

'Yes. I do know. I just hope she's got all this right, that's all. One day she's warning me about my enthusiasm for Wales, the next she's signing half my life away to Cardiff. How was it, Kate?'

She smiled. 'Oh, not bad.'

'It felt too good to be true.'

'True enough. Listen to the tape and decide for yourself. But would I lie?'

No, she wouldn't. 'Well, it had very little to do with me. They were all so good. It all came right at once. It happens.'

She made a deprecating face. 'Not very often. Your special trick is to get out of the composer's way and let him get on with it.'

'Thank you,' he said, knowing her compliment was sincere. 'I really don't know any other way.'

'Don't look for one. This will do. It's a curious approach to Mozart, though.'

'Why?'

'Unusual, anyway. Most people play Mozart on their knees, in a kind of terror, as though he's too fragile to touch.'

He laughed. 'That won't do. Nothing to be afraid of. He's not at all a bad sort. Just go up to him, shake him firmly by the hand—'

'And say, "Shwmai"?' she laughed with him.

Then there was a thoughtful silence. Quietly she said, 'Moll will be glad.'

'Ah. You were never sure, were you?'

'Sure?'

'Whether all that was good for me or bad?'

'No. Neither of us. If she's been watching she'll be sure now. I am. I've been sure for some time, but mine was the easy bit. Moll's concern was different. But if she could see you two together—' she waved at the approaching Jane – 'she would know it's all been for the best.'

Jane was back, taking his arm. 'Come to rescue him, have you?' asked Kate.

'Yes,' she said. 'Can't be trusted, you know.'

'Only the boring ones can,' said Kate. 'Oh well, no sonatas tonight, David. You'll be off soon if you're wise. This will go on and on. You know where you're going, Jane? Won't get lost?'

David looked puzzled. The two women laughed.

'He doesn't know,' said Jane. 'A night of surprises for the poor man. But you're right, we should be away. And thanks,' she took Kate's hands and kissed her, 'for everything.'

In the car, with that gutsy subdued roar following them up the London road, 'I hadn't realized how fagged I would be,' Jane said. 'There's no way I could drive to Town tonight. It's a hotel in the Forest of Dean. Kate's idea. One hour to bed, that's all.'

David was being shaken awake. In ten minutes they were between the sheets, for once too tired even for each other.

8

The view of the Wye from Symonds Yat is very special. David and Jane sat, hatted and wrapped against the frost of the morning, their breath rising in clouds.

'Quite a week,' she said.

'Yes, one way and another.'

'Not at all what you expected.'

'No.'

'Happy?' she asked.

'Don't know when I've been so happy.'

She made a brave attempt at a wry face, handicapped by an immense scarf. 'Well, there was that week at Southerndown.'

He laughed. 'That was quite different.'

'Mmm. I can imagine. It must have been bliss.'

'For a day or two.'

'Then it was Julie's turn. You had it made, young David.'

'Yes, I suppose I've had all the luck. We've both been lucky, one way and another.'

'Lucky? GG used to say the Goldbergs had used up all their luck, staying alive, so we mustn't hope for more. Now we must work, he said, work to deserve our luck. So we did, all four.'

Not without success, David thought. A successful barrister, a prospective politician, and the most influential arts management in England, all in a little over ten years from scratch. Yes, work, and for the old man killing work. 'It can't have been easy,' he agreed.

'No, it wasn't. But it was wonderful to put all that water between us and such pain. We had this tiny flat. It seemed like heaven. GG gave us all tube money and sent us out to find out how to live here. We went to Tussaud's, the Tower, the British Museum . . .'

'Curious thing. I've never seen them.'

'The British never do. It was a great way to learn English, though. Then off to school.'

She'd never spoken of school except in general terms. 'Tell me about it,' he asked. 'Fun, was it?'

'Yes, most of the time.' She seemed a little reluctant to go on, then: 'It *was* a convent, you know . . .'

'Funny place for a Jewish girl.'

'One doesn't have to be a Catholic to go to a convent school. But Mother wished it. She said the boys were her contribution to the chosen race, and I was to go to heaven her way. It was my choice too. I fell in love with the place on sight. GG didn't mind, so long as the music was good. Nuns are lovely, not at all what you'd expect. Wonderful broad minds, and the most forgiving people, so forgiving that hurting them is unthinkable. It makes them wonderful teachers.' She was silent for a while, then: 'I learned the flute at school.'

He remembered what John had said. 'Do you never play now?'

'Never. I wish I could. My fingers itch for the thing sometimes, but it's agony playing badly when one's played quite well, and I couldn't keep it up without practice. I tried, but it's no use. I can't bear to hear myself. So I don't.'

He remembered his school in the valley, where the only music was class singing. 'Did the nuns teach?'

'Only the piano, theory, and the voice. The singing in chapel was really something. There were visiting teachers for everything else.'

'Everything?'

'Well, all the ladylike ones. The broad minds didn't run to lady trombonists.'

'So who—'

149

She named a very famous flautist. 'He wasn't famous then. But he was such a beautiful young man.'

David remembered him from college. Handsome, talented, charming, all the gifts.

'I worked so hard for him and it went terribly well. We were sure I was to be the flautist of the century for a while.'

'So, why not?'

'My fault, of course. We were such good chums. It developed, you see.'

Ah, thought David. Here it comes.

Her voice was very small in the still air. 'I remember the day he kissed me, the first time. It all sounds desperately corny. I expect it happens all the time – kids and teachers, I mean. He was correcting posture, standing behind me, holding my arms. I turned round and it happened.'

There were birds, the sound of running water and a train whistle miles away across the river. A man with a dog on the far bank stopped and threw a stick into the icy water. The dog plunged. Jane shivered, in sympathy perhaps.

'I was sixteen. Sweet sixteen, never been kissed, literally.'

Bastard, David thought. 'Not a very nice young man,' he said.

'Nice? What's nice got to do with it? A healthy chap of twenty-five spending a day each week in a nunnery with six nubile flautists? The nice thing was his moderation, surely? He might have had us all.'

He said nothing. She read his silence. 'No, I don't think he did. I hope not. But I was crazy about him. He was my first man, you see – hard to forget.'

'I'm surprised it wasn't seen and stopped. How did it finish?'

'He married. Look, let's be fair. There were no

150

promises, no words even. We never talked, just *did*. He couldn't help himself, and I certainly couldn't.'

David wondered how hard the man had tried. She was on his side, though. Amazing people, women.

'I was very young for my age. He was the first man I ever related to, other than my father. I thought these feelings were for ever. Love, I thought. How could there be anything more? Then I discovered he was to be married. Because lessons were to be cancelled for the honeymoon, that's all. He never told us.'

David waited.

'I felt so inadequate, such a child, so *toyed with*. On the day of the wedding . . . we had this lovely park, lots of trees, a lake and a weir. I still don't know . . .'

'What, love?'

'Whether I fell in or . . .'

'Well?'

The words came with a rush. 'Whether I meant to do it. I was fished out by two nuns. They must have run half a mile to get to me. Lovely people.'

All sorts of women under those habits, then; some of them remarkable.

'I remember coming round in the san. Reverend Mother was there, with Matron and the doctor. Then, hours later, GG, furious, of course. A lack of super-vision, he said. I was half asleep, and trying not to wake up while they talked. I'm sure he never realized what had happened, not sure even they did. After that John came every Friday to take me home for the weekend. My friend never came back to teach. We weren't told why, or even if there was a reason. I went to the Academy on Saturdays for the flute.'

'No professor trouble?'

'Oh no. It takes two, and I'd been inoculated. They must have felt the chill.' She smiled, remembering. 'I think most people did.'

David remembered their first meeting. He'd felt it

too. 'Yes,' he said, 'you were a cool lady. But with time, surely . . .'

'Mmm. Time gave me a perspective, true.'

'I'm glad,' he said.

'That's not at all what I mean. I mean I came to accept that a man can be such a child, close to a woman. I learned to make allowance for that. I've been making allowances for you for years. Even last week, when I heard—'

'Will I never hear the last of that lady?' David asked, rather short now.

'Eventually, no doubt. But when I heard I thought: oh, that man, he's incurable. A good pair of legs is all it takes. What hell to be married to him.'

'Sure?'

'Less sure than I was. But there's life outside the bedroom and the concert hall. It could be hell, yes.'

The cold was getting to him, and he wasn't ready for this discussion. 'Walk back?' he suggested, standing.

She rose to face him. 'In a moment. There's something else.'

He waited, holding her hands. She took a deep breath. 'Since then, there's been no one.'

He stood amazed, hardly believing his ears. 'No one? How? Jane, it's been—'

'Twelve years.' She smiled. 'Makes me almost a double virgin, doesn't it?'

'But you told me . . .'

'If you'd known, would you have come to me?'

He shook his head; not a negative but a vain attempt to clear it. 'I don't know. Yes, I suppose. I don't know. Jane, how—?'

'Not now. Time for coffee in the lounge, I think?'

They walked in silence.

Sitting in enormous chairs either side of a roaring fire, they had the lounge to themselves, and cognac with the coffee. He was pensive, she reflective.

'I couldn't bear men, you see. Not for years. I missed out socially, at the Academy, avoiding men.'

'Boys, surely?'

'Is there a difference? When do you people grow up? Is there ever a time when a man won't put his hands into a girl's pants? They thought I was stuck up, of course. All that money, you see. It was easy to play it safe.'

'But for so long?'

'Why not? It gets to be a habit. A girl *can* keep her legs closed when she has a good reason, and there are always very good reasons. Mine was an extra reason: to avoid being let down again. Emotional giving upsets lives, gets in the way. I did without it. Work does wonders. I was determined not to fall for it again anyway. My head would dictate, that was the plan. Marry sensibly, at the right time. Someone would be allowed into my life but not into my head.'

He was appalled. 'But one can't plan these things.'

'Oh yes. One can build a wall and keep people out, even quite close people. It works very well. People hurt themselves on the brickwork, and the inside can bruise one too. But it simplifies life, lets one get on with things. Then you turned up. You were a problem.'

'Solved, now, anyway.'

'Oh no. A far bigger problem, now. The sex I wanted – still do. It was time. I'd begun to wonder . . . For years men kept me at a distance. After a while that began to worry me, that they didn't try.'

He smiled. 'I'm not surprised, Jane. It would have taken a lot of confidence, even early on. You terrified me. Look: a man is afraid more than anything else of being put down. We make passes only when we are nearly sure we'll score. You're just too strong, too able, too, too *much*, dammit.'

'So what must a girl like me do? Tell me.'

'What you did with me. Make the move herself. Proof of the pudding, Jane; I'd never have done it.'

'Never?'

'No.'

'And that's all?'

'Yes. Thank God you didn't find the answer earlier.'

She was silent for a long time. Then: 'Look, I have to control this thing if I'm to stay sane. You'll go off to Boston. In three days you might be tucked up with someone else. You could come back married, even.'

'Is that likely?'

'I know it's possible.'

'You think I can forget this, then?'

'Perhaps you can. I don't know what you can do. How many times have you made love to a woman while thinking of another, a picture behind closed eyes?'

'It happens, I suppose,' he said, wishing her knife were a little less sharp and a little further from the bone.

'Yes, I'm sure it does.' She paused. 'I see him sometimes.'

'See him? Why?' He was alarmed.

'Oh, not in *that* way. But it can't be avoided. He's very important now. Quite hard to hear a week's concerts without seeing him. He never speaks. I can see the wish in his eyes, though.'

'What about your wish?' he asked.

'I stopped wishing. I took up working instead. But it wasn't fair, was it, any of it?'

'No, it wasn't. Life isn't fair. Things happen to the wrong people all the time.'

She nodded, finding the idea attractive. 'You mean that what happened to me might have been good if . . .'

'If it had happened to someone else? Possibly. It happened to me, didn't it?'

'Yes. Your wonderful aunt.'

'No one seems quite sure it was good for me, on the other hand.'

'It was, I'm sure. But there's the sex difference. And that you knew from the first that you couldn't have her. And the fact that she loved you.'

'Think so?'

'I have to think so. The whole thing would be intolerably ugly otherwise.'

'And he didn't love you?'

'No. He loved sex, that's all.'

A waitress, coming to clear away, caught the word, stopped short in the doorway. They fell silent, enjoying the glowing coals and the cognac warming them from within as the crockery was taken away. The door closed.

'Tell me,' asked Jane, 'is it something you might have done?'

He thought carefully. 'I don't think so. Anyway I had my schoolgirl. She was enough. Then there was college.'

'And no shortage there. Not a jealous girl, Julie.'

'No. She knew, and she was sure of herself. Sure of me, too.'

'Lucky Julie. Until the luck ran out.'

He was surprised. 'Ran out? Julie's luck didn't run out. Julie had ten years with me, doing what she believed she wanted. Now she has what she really wants.'

'So, it was your luck that ran out.'

He got up, crossed the room. She put up her face for his kiss.

'My luck hasn't run out, my love,' he said. 'Someone up there has always looked after me, and he's still doing it.'

She kissed the hand she'd been holding. 'Such a nice man, and such a gift for the right word, on and off the television. David, there are so many questions, aren't there?'

'It takes time,' he said. 'Could be fun finding the answers, don't you think?'

'Time's what we haven't got. Never will have.'

'We've made some. We can make more.'

'Is that what you want?'

'What I want is not to spoil what we've got.' His arm was round her on the sofa, her cheek close for kissing. As he leaned she turned. He kissed her again. The kiss blossomed.

'I see,' she said with a grin. 'All this talk of sexy schoolgirls, that's what it is?'

'I'm just a man, you know. We're like that.'

'We've checked out of the pub already.'

'We can check in again.'

'That would be advertising.' Her cheeks shone. 'To hell with it,' she said, taking his hand. 'Come on!'

★ ★ ★

'Wonderful' she said, drowsing.

'Mmm . . .' He lipped a nipple, his hands smoothing fine fur.

'I can't think how a girl did without it.' Her hand was in his hair, encouraging. Her thighs stretched a little, giving him room.

'So you're not thinking of giving it up?' he suggested.

'Oh no. You told me the secret. Ask for it and it comes. I can do it any time now.'

For a moment he thought she was serious. He stopped grazing abruptly and sat up. She laughed. 'It was your solution, David. Ask, and if they've got enough confidence . . .'

He pretended to rationalize. 'You'd be pursued, endlessly. It takes time, sleeping around. As much of a distraction as a real commitment. An immense professional nuisance. Professional suicide, even.'

'Perhaps. But organization is my thing, you know that. Now I know what fun it can be. All work and no play . . .'

'Bunkum, Jane. You knew about the fun, if that's what it is, from the first time that damned flautist put his hand between your legs. You can do without it.'

'But why? Why do without it? I like it. I feel better for it. It's good for me. We can *all* do without it. Even you could, if you made half an effort, but you don't.'

She was well over the top again, he thought. 'Do you imagine I never sleep by myself?'

'Of course you do, often. When you must, and when you wish it. But do you ever sleep alone *on principle*, David?'

'It's not like that. It happens. It seems good and right at the time. It hurts no one. This has hurt no one.'

She considered while he prayed she would not apply the logic too closely, but as always she read his thoughts. 'Another notch on the bedpost, then?'

'You know very well . . .'

'I know nothing for sure. Nothing. And how can you be sure this won't hurt me?'

'All right, we can't be sure. You said yourself that you *expected* I'd hurt you. God knows, I don't want to hurt you. Or anyone.'

Her smile was wry, remembering her own miscalculation. 'Ah. But I was fairly sure you couldn't. I meant to enjoy you and I wanted you to enjoy me, but I had no intention of letting you over my wall, you see.'

Yes, that was Jane, he told himself; she thought she could manage anything, anybody, including herself. Well, she'd learned. 'You thought you could light the blue touch paper and enjoy the pretty firework from a safe distance?'

'Yes.' She nodded. 'Yes, that's about right.'

He got up on one elbow to look at her as she lay with an arm over her eyes, providing the dark she seemed to need. 'And the bang was bigger than you expected?'

Her arm moved. Their eyes met. 'Much bigger, that's the truth. I got my fingers burned. I neither expected it nor wished it. If I'd known I wouldn't have done it, perhaps. David, now I want what you've given me. I want it very much. But I can't share it. I want it all, or you can give it all away to someone else, or spread it around in your generous way and forget about me.'

Her eyes were fixed on his face. Crunch, David boy, he thought. Well, she was never one for leaving loose ends, and if you thought you could fly away without tying this one you must have been crazy. He took a deep breath. 'That's as close to a proposal of marriage as I ever expect to hear,' he said.

Her voice was quiet, controlled, decided. 'I'm a Catholic. You can't marry me. It's not marriage I want, it's commitment.' She stood up. 'Now, we have arrangements to make. I hope my office hasn't given me up for dead.'

*　*　*

While she worked he walked. When he got back, she was nearly through, sitting by the fire, telephone in hand and pad on her knee. He sat opposite, reading her outline for his annual time in Wales with its carefully guarded commitments to schedules, programmes, tours, broadcasting, television, and the escape clause which would get him away should Bayreuth offer, as they both knew it soon would. Not the richest of contracts but a clever one; the choice of repertoire was his within reasonable limits, and he needed room for experiment now. A commitment, but he owed it.

Lunch was quiet, the oncoming separation looming large. They talked of work, of people and places, their minds busy with the problem with which neither could help the other.

Two o'clock. She put down her coffee-cup, smiling a little tensely. 'Look, I must go. So much to do. So have you. You've neglected poor Dmitri and his symphony.'

'I can learn in the air.'

'Yes, of course. John will collect you at five. Heathrow in plenty of time. Mary has everything packed.'

'What it is,' he said again with a small smile, 'to be well-managed.'

He carried her bags to the red car. She sat, engine grumbling at the delay, window down, making a polite and businesslike goodbye. He wanted to open the door and wrap himself round her but everything about Jane begged restraint now. He pecked her cheek through the small space. One more wan smile and she was away.

*   *   *

There was fog on the motorway, but they had the time, so no worry. John was concentrated but relaxed, the professional.

'Terrible timing, boy,' he grumbled. 'Come home too late for one match, off to America before the next.'

'Got to work for my living, John, like everyone else. Tell you what – make a list of the dates next season and we'll tell Jane to keep them clear . . .'

'Oh, I nearly forgot. Letters in the bag with the music.'

David took them out, curious. All his business affairs taken care of by Jane's office, letters – fanmail

and professional scrounging apart – were always welcome. One hand he recognized instantly and put aside
for a quieter moment. They were turning into the
airport now, stopping at the entrance. John summoned
a porter and the luggage disappeared to check-in.
They said goodbye with a grin each way, shook hands,
and David made his way to the VIP lounge, certain
of a long wait in the fog.

Settling into his recliner with a gin and tonic, he
took the letter from his pocket. A loose end? No,
those were for the legal people. Something more then,
unexpected, disturbing. Oh well, face it. He took out
the closely written pages.

Dear David,

Your Mozart was lovely. You have such a gift. We
always knew that, didn't we? No wonder you give
yourself to it so completely. It must be irresistible.

Please give my thanks to Isaac Grant for making
divorce so painless. And thank you too. It's just in
time. Arthur's folks are so old-fashioned. A prema-
ture baby they'll believe, but there are limits.

It's such a *responsible* thing, to be having a child.
It's what life's all about, at the time at least. Even
from the first moment, the unprotected moment.
Commitment, I suppose. It's what I've always
wanted, I know that now. Home, kids, all that. I'm
a homebody, would you believe? Lucky I found out
in time. I'll play house with the kids and wait for
him to come home and look after us. He always
will. He's like that.

I worry about you, though. I would like you to
be as happy as I intend to be, but you give yourself
no thought at all. Life is very short, David. You
need someone. But she'll have to be very special.
You need a lot of looking after, more than I gave,
but it is a woman's job. They've always done it,

haven't they? Your aunt, and her friend with the advice and the contacts. Then Jane. No men in your life except GG, and he kept you at such a distance, didn't like you very much. Afraid for his wonderful daughter, of course. Always terribly nice to me. Funny man, but so clever. You know how much you owe him, I suppose? Don't think that Jane did it all, will you?

I hope you will find someone, someone important, I mean. The unimportant ones will always find you. Bees round a honeypot. I never really minded them, although I expect people think they were the trouble. Not at all. But I need someone to look after me too. I'm not a support machine. I needed one, that's the truth, and I've got one now.

Jane, I wonder? Odd girl. I can't get close to her. No one seems to. Even you. If she could think for a moment about anything but business she might be right for you. You are two for a pair. Neither of you has time to live and neither of you seems to know what you are missing. Think about it, David, before it's too late.

Well, it's over. We had a special place and a special time, and we don't resent one another. People expect it, but we don't, really. I know the others were not important. Trouble is, I don't know exactly how important *I've* been. And the other thing I'll never know is – would you have played the field if you'd thought it would hurt me? I hope not.

We will always be part of one another and of one another's lives. I'll come to your concerts. Funny thing – my folks looked forward to my being Lady Adams one day. They think your K's inevitable. I suppose it is, after a CBE so early. I do hope so anyway. The one thing about our marriage they liked. Now I'm to be Lady Graham instead of Lady Adams, and in only three days' time. What a short cut! What all this has done for gossip in Cwmbach I can't imagine. They'll get used to it I expect.

That's all. Just a thank you, for one thing and another. But do look after yourself. Just stop for a breather now and again, look round, take time to live if you can.

Much love of course,

J.

'Mr Adams,' said the voice. He looked up, from miles away. 'I'm afraid BOAC won't get you out for an hour more. Possibly two. But we can get you a place on Lufthansa, leaving almost immediately, if you'd like that?'

The three other travellers were astir already, making for the door. David hesitated. He had this superstition about planes, and changes of plan disturbed him. In any case, he had his scores to read and it was comfortable here. A sandwich and a drink, and he'd have to sleep in the air anyway, whatever time he flew. And again when he arrived. The time lost meant nothing. 'Thank you,' he said. 'I'll wait.'

She seemed disappointed, surprised. Perhaps the change had been a lot of trouble. 'As you wish, sir. I'll call you when we have news of your flight.'

He settled to his score. He was in learning mode now, lost to the world. It was what he did well. Ever since he'd first seen that little Mozart A major in Southerndown all those years ago he'd been able to escape into a score for however long it took. Black spots on paper, marks made by other chaps, all over the world, for three hundred years or more, especially for him to read, turn into sounds.

* * *

He was the only passenger in first, or was until the

late arrival turned up. They were closed for takeoff and his stomach had begun its customary wind-up when the doors were opened again. Footsteps on the stair. Having helped himself to the nose seat where the legroom is best he didn't look round. Then the voice. 'David?'

'Jane?' He had the mad thought that he'd left something behind and she'd come to deliver it. Then he knew they were moving and the stewardess was urging her to sit, fasten her seat belt. She sat. Neither spoke until they were up and away.

Then she asked, 'You don't mind?'

'Mind?'

'I'm not in the way?' She took two glasses of champagne from the proffered tray and passed one to him.

'No. No, of course not.'

'I can't live with loose ends. Not if they can be tied.'

'I know.' But two weeks in America wouldn't tie them, he knew that too.

'So I thought a few days more. There's always work to be done in Boston, New York, Philadelphia. It's not wasted time, once in a while.'

'Of course not.'

'Will they feed us soon? I haven't eaten since lunch. Sat twiddling thumbs and thinking, you know . . .'

'Yes.'

'They think I'm ill. In the office, I mean.'

He shook his head, trying not to smile. 'No. They think you've got a problem and they know you'll solve it in your own way, in your own time, that's all.'

'Then I heard you were delayed. Tried to catch you in the lounge and couldn't. Bought a ticket. Seemed to be the only thing to do.'

'No bags?'

'No. Nothing.'

'Ring Mary. She can put something on the morning flight.'

'Yes. What a thing, to be well-managed.' They laughed together.

Supper arrived. He discovered an appetite too, and they disposed of it quickly. She pushed buttons and her seat moved back. He did likewise. The cabin staff, invisibly aware, cleared away and reduced the lighting. A polite voice asked if there was anything more? They shook their heads and the presence evaporated.

'Has she really gone?' asked Jane quietly.

'Not entirely. Wouldn't get far without a parachute anyway. But she won't come back for some time unless one of us pushes the button.'

'Aware of a certain need for quiet, is she?'

'Something like that.'

She sighed. 'Oh good. Look, I have to powder my nose. D'you think you can stay awake until I get back?'

'I'll try,' he said.

BOOK TWO
GERMANY AND AUSTRIA
SUMMER 1963

9

When the summer breeze from the Bavarian hills drops it can be very hot. Nothing to be done, then, but sit in the shade with a cool drink, sybaritically towelled after a post-rehearsal shower. Not, after all, a bad life, conducting; better anyway than digging coal, like his father before the war took him. David wondered again – the thought was irresistible in this country – whether that charming violinist from Dresden, or perhaps that ageing trumpeter from Berlin, had pulled the trigger that killed Dada. Then he wondered whether the bright young timpanist with whom he'd had this morning's sharp exchange had the same thought in reverse. Ah well; a nation which could brew like this was not all bad.

He sipped appreciatively. Curious how despite his rugby-playing youth he'd never been fond of English beer. Here the stuff went down like nectar, with a certain soporific effect. A reason perhaps for the orchestra's lack of response after the rehearsal intermission? Which of his colleagues had said after a German tour that the orchestras there had too much time, too much money, and too much beer? Well, with nothing to do until Jane's arrival this evening he could afford to drowse.

The view from his balcony had probably not changed since the house was built two hundred years ago. From his eyrie under the wooden eaves David could see over the red-tiled roofs, past the church with its onion dome, to distant rolling, heat-hazy hills. Somewhere over to the east, tucked into a fold of the land, the Munich-Berlin autobahn occasionally hummed softly. It carried little traffic here, so close to the border.

A green country, green as his own. Softer though; no rocks here to challenge the schoolboy, but more trees, and not the Rhondda's forestry-commission sort in their ordered ranks but God's own firs in happy disorder. Ferns, too. Tall, springy ferns. Ferns to cushion a fall, five foot ferns, ferns in which a boy could hide, a boy and a girl together . . .

* * *

'Hot,' said Julie.

David lay propped on an elbow, watching her, a handkerchief over her face to keep out the sun, sensible print dress properly drawn over her knees, hands meeting behind her head, drawing up her breasts, small but perfect under the cotton.

'Rhondda weather,' he said. 'Rain to drown us most of the time. Drops like birds' eggs. Then it roasts us for a change.'

'Sun for school. Rain for Sundays usually,' she said, drowsing.

Half raised, he could see over the ferns and down the hill to the houses. They'd come further than usual, almost to the crest. The view stirred a memory. 'When I was little my grandfather carried me from our house to the top without stopping, on his back. I can just remember. I was four, I think.'

She considered. It was the sort of thing a miner would do. Her doctor father would hardly have climbed so far, with or without the boy. One culture for muscles, another for brains. But the boy had both. Where had this miner's son found his extraordinary talent for music? Her people thought little of it. No money in it, that was the trouble. She wondered yet again whether he could be persuaded out of music and into something sensible. But no, not now; it was too late, since the weekly trips to Cardiff, the lectures, the days watching the orchestra. 'He must have been strong,' she said.

'Strong?' His mind had wandered.

'Your grandfather.'

'Oh yes, strong. Soft with it, mind you. Mam gave him a hard time, trying to be hard for them both. Then the dust got him and he wasn't strong at all. Couldn't walk up the hill to our house, at the end, without a spell.'

Silent in the sunshine, he remembered the last talk with the old man. Certain he seemed that David would never have to go down the pit; and when his father came home from the war he must tell him it wasn't worth it, not for all the money in the world. He must never go down again and David mustn't think of it. Stick to his music. Mind you, what they'd wanted, a big boy like him and with a talent for the game, was to play for Wales. But never mind. 'Do what you want to do, boy. Lucky to have the chance. Very few have it, David. Make the most of it, now, remember.'

Next day when David got up for school the old man was dead.

'He liked me to play to him,' he said. 'Little pieces. Simple music. Nothing complicated. Gave him a lot of pleasure.'

'That old music, David – is it a living, d'you think?' she asked.

He toyed with her hair. 'Have to be, won't it?'

'My father doesn't think so.'

So her family talked about him? 'Why do they care?' he asked, curious.

'Because we are together a lot. Too much, they think.'

'Do you? Think we are together too much, I mean?'

She sighed. 'Daft you are, sometimes. If I thought that, would I be here?

A long companionable silence now. He would kiss her soon, she knew. One of the nice things, that he was not quick, nor rough. She could set the pace. Yet since last summer he'd been somehow more positive, more sure, not just with her, but in everything. Her friends at school felt it. Curious how they flocked and he didn't care. Always polite, with a smile for everyone; but only two ideas in his head, his music and her, and the music always first. Music he had in plenty. How long before . . . well, she was always in charge, six months older than he.

The ferns rustled. She sensed his body closer. He saw her small smile, recognized her anticipation. Behind closed eyelids she felt his hands lift the corner of her improvised sunshade, exposing her lips, folding the cotton over her eyes, doubling her dark, kind. Happily blind she felt his lips, soft knowing butterflies on hers, bringing her nerves alive, soft messages spreading. Not demanding, only making aware, offering. Presents they were, and welcome, his kisses. She put a hand to his neck, rewarding him with a firmer pressure, her lips opening to taste. He smoothed her hair, kissed her eyes through the cotton. Soon there would be his hand. Yes, now, lightly on her knee where the dress had lifted with her movement.

If she protested he'd stop, she knew. Why, though? It was quiet here, secure. Why refuse what she'd allowed in sudden forbidden corners? In any case it was time. Time for her. Time for the assurance her body asked. And for him? God knew he'd been patient.

She kissed him again, and with the kiss his hand moved higher, to the warm firm thigh. Her breath came in a quick intake. His other hand was still in her hair, stroking. There was a line connecting his lips with his fingers, passing through her centre, feeding her. Her breasts were suddenly hard under the cotton. He must see, her dress was so thin. But he was so close now, he'd see nothing. Feel he might. Suddenly she knew she wanted that, that she should feel his feeling her there, on her breasts. Her legs opened a little of themselves, and his hand moved higher still, almost to the cotton. Show, him, then? Her hand went to a button, then another. Another still? No; now he would do it for himself, for them both. Yes, open now to the waist, her small white underthings shining in the sun. Still she lay blind in the green ferns, her half-smile an invitation.

Bending he kissed the skin above one breast, then the other. Her practised hand moved briefly and the cloth fell away. Again his lips on hers. Such patience he had, that he could wait to thank her with a kiss before bending to his feast. Such luxury. A long moment before the butterfly settled on her nipple, teasing. The tension rose between her legs. Now the other breast. God should have given him two tongues, she thought, to pleasure. Each was jealous of the other.

His hands, permission given, were busy with her buttons, braver, lower. Now she could feel the hot sun on her body, now on her legs. Still his lips on her breasts, on her mouth now open wide, sharing breaths. Her legs opened, knees rising a little. She put his palm soft on her middle, her hands away, trusting.

Their mouths joined as his hand found the soft hair, discovering the moistness. His fingertip dipped, collected, then again then to her bud as his tongue tasted hers. Her legs spasmed and suddenly her hands were pushing the cotton.

The kissing stopped. She steadied her ragged breathing, half glad of the respite yet wanting more, completion. Now his lips were at her breast again, his

171

hand palming her mound between explicitly stretched legs. Oh God, she must come or die, perhaps both. The tide flooded, her hips heaved, her hands holding his head, protesting but pressing, his hands beneath her holding, lifting, his mouth sucking while the whirlpool of her world spun, the mountain beneath them swaying.

Subsiding now, her eyes fast shut, half ashamed and half exultant. He was kissing her again, proud, leaving his hand to console her. Softer, softer, eyes coming awake, smiling into his.

'Oh, David, what a boy you are, and where did you learn such a thing?'

More kisses, kind and sweet. 'Comes naturally, doesn't it?' he said.

She wondered, without doubting; it was not a day for doubting nature, with the ferns rustling in the mountain air, the birds singing, distant sheep querulous. They looked at one another for a long minute, silent.

'Thank you,' she said.

He lay back in the green, relaxing but not relaxed, his pressing problem unsolved, eyes closed against the sun. She sat up, bent to kiss him briefly, folded her handkerchief, put it over his eyes. He smiled. He'd lie quietly now while his body subsided and she put herself together . . . The ferns rustled again. A hand at his belt. He started up, but she restrained him. 'Shh now. Be still. Let me.'

He lay back. His body felt the sun. Only his shirt now, and that unbuttoned. Close, she wondered at the veined stem. She was so small, yet it was possible, she knew. He could almost feel her breath. His hips rose, begging, his knees tensing, vibrating. Would she kiss him there?

Suddenly his hands were everywhere, pushing her away, his body turning, almost too late. A gout of liquid, warmer than the sunshine, then another, another and another, feeding the ferns. By some miracle she held him still, feeling the pulsing of the self-minded muscle as it hurled seed into infinity. Wonderful, wonderful! God, to be the receiver of such a thing!

He sank back, breathing hard, blowing. Their eyes met. 'That came naturally too,' she said, answering his unspoken question.

They kissed, each thanking the other for such an understanding, such care. A lovely boy he was, she thought for the thousandth time.

'Time to go down?' he asked, speaking to her ear.

'In a minute. Take time. Rest for a little while?'

He was enervated, his eyelids heavy. She lay half over him, a leg between his, spreading her dress. He drowsed, half awake, her breathing soft in his ear.

Almost dreaming he felt her hand again, nursing, soothing, encouraging. His flesh woke willingly. He lay still, grateful, tasting her touch. Then he sensed her shade keeping out the sun, felt her lips on his, opened his eyes to find her poised over him on one arm, her other hand holding, placing, searching, finding.

'Julie!' he said.

'Shh . . .' Sinking down, her face tense, a soft obstruction now, her weight on him, pressing, pressing, and giving. 'Ohhhhhh . . .' she breathed, 'ooooh . . .' Then it was upon him, his body helplessly heaving into hers, she clinging, clinging, two people adrift in a universe of their own making, throbbing, clutching, one body for the first time.

They slept. The sun deserted them little by little. The coolness woke her first but she would not move to disturb him. Then he stirred. Her cheek was touching his, wet.

'Crying?' he asked, concerned.

'No. Not now. A little bit, at first.'

'Did I hurt you?'

'Hurt myself, didn't I?' She sat up, mopping between her legs.

They dressed, she quickly and efficiently, David much slower.

She watched him. 'Not very practical, boys' things, are they?'

He smiled. 'Wouldn't like me in a kilt, would you?'

She giggled. 'Oh . . . I don't know. Handy, sometimes, I should think.'

He was dressed now. 'What will we do?' he asked.

'Do?'

'If we have a baby.'

She smiled, liking his *we*. With the female wisdom of a thousand generations she saw the male helplessness. Muscles, brains, instinct, yes, but no common sense. A lot of use he'd be if it came to a baby. 'Not much chance, so don't worry.'

'Not much chance?'

'No. The right day for it, exactly. Not much use studying for a doctor, is it, if I can't work it out? Right day, right place, right weather. Right boy too.' She laughed, kissed him lightly and quickly. 'Everything right.' He reached for her, but she freed herself, giggling. 'No more for you today. Sore I am.'

'Sorry, love,' he said, penitent.

'No need. My idea it was, I told you. Glad I am.' She stood, brushing the green from her dress, a creased wreck now. A hand to ruffle his hair, his head close.

They started down. Sometimes they'd raced to the bottom, careless of falling, risking limbs and heads. Today they were slow, helping each other, aware of a new need to consider, be careful. No talk until they reached the gully behind her big house. It was dusk now, dark in the shade of the trees where they stopped,

174

as always, to say good night. They kissed, considerately.

'No good making promises, David,' she said.

'I suppose.'

'I don't want anybody else is all I can say.'

'Nor me.'

★ ★ ★

He'd been dozing. The telephone was ringing. He got up, not quite steady, telling himself he must beware of the beer, and picked up the noisy nuisance. Jane, hardly audible against the autobahn background. 'At last! I've been ringing for an age, David. They were sure you were in. Busy?'

'Asleep. It's the local brew. Puts one out.'

'Ah. I wondered . . .'

'I know what you wondered. No. No company except the flies. Where are you?'

'Bamberg. Trouble with the *Polizei* coming round Frankfurt. With you in half an hour.'

'Have you eaten? Shall I order something?'

'Well, I'm hungry, yes. No, don't order anything. Let's see how it is.'

'Okay.' So she'd be here soon. Still hot and a little fuzzy he made for the shower. Bracing himself, he turned to cold and pushed the button. Yes, cold. Good though. Back to the towels, once more in touch with himself. Dress? Well, shirt and slacks perhaps. Keep cool and like the boy scout be prepared. They hadn't been together for six weeks, before Prague and the Provence Festival. With Jane one could never be sure how it would be.

The exhaust was personal as her voice. The red Porsche beetled in, her small figure with hair tied back and wraparound sunspecs visible through the open roof. Parked, she climbed out, took off the specs, looked up and waved, made for the door and reception. Anticipating her problem, he made for the stairs, two at a time.

Her bell had already summoned Frau Blink, proprietor, receptionist and sole attendant at this time of day. Yes, Fräulein Grant was expected, and yes, there was a room at the top of the house as she had asked. No, unfortunately there was no one to help with her bags. Under Blink's carefully dispassionate gaze David held out his hand for her keys and went to open the jaws of the red monster. Three pieces of Gucci's best to haul up those stairs. One at a time, and the rest when convenient, he decided.

She was inspecting Bavaria from her balcony when he arrived with the bag. 'Well,' he asked, 'will it do?'

'Not a bit sure,' she said. 'People seem to stay up the Bamberg road, at – '

'I know. With every opera director from Glasgow to Athens.'

'Good for business?' she suggested, turning, taking off the headscarf and shaking down the dark hair.

He shrugged. 'Who needs it? Let's develop a certain scarcity value.'

She shook her head. 'You really are too big for your Welsh boots, young David.'

'I have this very clever agent lady. Look at the diary. How much time do I have in the next three years?' he asked.

'Oh, all right, Toscanini. Have it your own way. I suppose you'll soon be able to do without us. What a life! We take a chance on a talent, and if we're right it gets independent. Our failures we're stuck with.' She came in from the sunlight, held out her arms for a kiss. It lasted and lasted. 'A long time,' she said eventually.

'Much too long.'

'Oh, time flies . . .' She laughed at his reaction.

'Come on, man, show me the shower and take me to bed. Then perhaps we'll be able to think of something besides how long it's been.'

He sat and watched her shower. A wondrous sight, hair down, not troubling with soap, relishing the hot water as it eased away the long miles from Ostend. She emerged from the stream, pushing back her hair, looking for a towel. He wrapped her and carried her out through the door to the sunny balcony, depositing her on her lounger.

'Hey!' she protested. 'A little too public, surely?'

'You're well wrapped,' he said. 'Just lie and dry. It's what the sun's for, love.'

'You're getting old,' she said, half-accusing and half-joking, 'or you've been busy elsewhere. A year ago you'd've had me before I put a leg out of the car.'

'It crossed my mind,' he grinned back, 'but Bavaria is a very proper place. Sex in the car park is not encouraged. Here, let me dry the odd bit.'

'Oh. I have odd bits, have I? Well, dry the odd foot if you must. Then get me to bed, idiot.'

He dried the odd foot, then the odd leg, and somehow between the odd thigh and the odd hip he found himself immersed in her. The whole thing from blissful entry to total exhaustion took less than two minutes.

'So,' she decided, relaxed on the very large bed, 'not busy elsewhere!'

'Not since lunch, anyway.' It was a question she never asked seriously, since she wished neither a serious answer nor a lie.

'You, on the other hand, may have been having it away with all your conductors, not to mention the *Polizei* on the autobahn, and a poor innocent man would knows no better.'

She pulled a face. 'That policeman. No hope for him. Smiled sweetly, fluttered the eyelashes, flashed

177

the knee, nothing doing. Wanted his money. The number-plate was a giveaway.'

'A xenophobe?'

'Among other things. Did I speak German? No, I told him, just to make life difficult. He spoke only autobahn English, he said, but that was okay because every day he had the same conversation. I was driving too fast in a temporarily restricted area. Told me my speed, did a lot of sums, asked for a hundred and ten marks. I had only a hundred in cash, so he took ninety. Said the German police would like me to have enough money for a coffee at the next *Rastplatz*, so that I would please stay awake and not make a nasty mess on their nice clean autobahn.'

'A practical race. Perhaps you should have answered him in German. Might have been cheaper.'

'I don't like them, that's the truth. Especially in uniform, with black leather boots.'

It had shown, probably, hence the fine. He gave her hand a comforting squeeze. 'Try to be nice to them, Jane, just for a week?'

'Oh, have no fear,' she assured him. 'I can be nice for as long as it takes, given a sound business reason. Now – my tummy says it's time to eat. Here, or out?'

'Here I think, tonight. Good plain cooking, and you wouldn't believe the local wine.'

'Right. Be good and bring up the other bags while I put myself together?'

When he got back she was sitting before the mirror, fixing her face. He sat to watch the finishing touches. She eyed him in the glass. 'Well? Ravages of time not too obvious yet?'

He'd seen no change in the past two years, since they'd become lovers. Still the pocket Venus with the dark hair, brilliant eyes, the giveaway nose and full lips, a beautiful face. There'd been a certain softening; but that had been his doing, he knew, and he sometimes doubted that anyone else ever saw it. 'You'll do, love,' he said.

'For a day or two, no doubt. I have this advantage, that I tend to disappear before you begin to wish I was a blonde.'

'Ten a penny here, blondes,' he told her. 'Valkyries everywhere. Too boring.'

Downstairs, Frau Blink was pleased to see them. 'Good evening, Herr Adams, Fräulein Grant. You are just in time.'

One table remained, in the corner. These were largely local folk out for the evening, any festival visitors being halfway through *Tannhäuser* now. Talking in English they were isolated from the room, or so they thought. Then a polite voice from the next table asked, 'Please excuse me, but may I ask for which opera you are in Bayreuth?'

He turned. A middle-aged pair, neatly dressed, he greying, tall, she plump and rosy with a happy smile beneath horn-rimmed specs. Oh dear, conversation. Well, at least they hadn't recognized him.

'Of course. We are here for *Meistersinger* only,' he said.

'Ah. We are most fortunate. Tomorrow, *Lohengrin*. Then we must wait for three days for *Meistersinger*. So lucky to get seats. Have you come from London?'

Curious, how foreigners always asked. The positive answer was the easy one. Had they been to Bayreuth before? Yes, once, last year. They too, only once, for their honeymoon, for *Meistersinger*. And each year since they had again asked for tickets. Now, on their silver wedding, they were lucky at last. So they'd cancelled the planned second honeymoon in the Caribbean to relive their *Meistersinger*.

'You must go to Nürnberg on the day before the opera. Until you have seen the city you cannot understand what the opera means, really. But this you know, if you know Wagner.'

Yes, he knew. Jane was silent, listening, reserved.

The meal over, he asked for a carafe to take up.

'Your place or mine?' he asked, as they climbed the stair hand in hand.

'Yours, I think. I'll be a minute or two,' she said at her door.

He sat on the still-warm balcony in the dusk, waiting. Ten, fifteen minutes? Was she asleep? Telephoning, more likely, said experience. Then the communicating door opened, the surprise complete.

She wore a kimono from his previous Tokyo trip, a vision in mother-of-pearl silk, embroidered with delicate flowers below the obi. Her hair was pinned up, her hands folded, hidden in the deep sleeves.

'Well?' she asked, standing framed in the doorway.

'I've seen nothing more lovely in my life,' he said.

'Ah . . . Japanese silk more beautiful than Hungarian lace, then?'

His guts stirred at the certainty that under the silk there was nothing at all. 'Honestly, love,' he said, 'I don't know. Perhaps it doesn't matter what it is, so long as you're inside it.'

She sighed, coming closer. 'Men. We take all this trouble. No sooner do we get it on than you want to take it off again.' She turned, mannequin-like, arms extended to show the wonderful sleeves. 'I hope you approve?'

He offered her glass. She raised it. 'Cheers.' She quaffed. 'Small world,' she said, 'Hungarian Jew, British passport, sitting in Bavaria in a robe made for a Japanese lady a hundred years ago.'

Not the time to remind her that she wasn't really a Jew, since her mother hadn't been one. She had this trick of being a Jew or a Catholic as the fancy took her. 'It looks right,' he said, 'so it must *be* right.'

They sat drinking the wine. It was dark now, a glow in the far distance reminding them of the little town in which nothing happened except Wagner. David got up, stooped to kiss her. Her arm was round his neck, not letting go until she'd had her fill. Into his ear she said, 'Have you ever had a Japanese lady?'

'You know very well,' he said, 'that I've never had any lady but you.'

She shook her head sadly. 'Such a wonderful shameless liar. And so successful with it. Come, bedtime.'

As he turned from fastening the double door the silk was slipping from her shoulders, the hair coming down before the long dressing mirror. He crossed the room, stood behind her, kissed her ear.

'Happy?' he asked.

'Like coming home,' she replied.

She slipped easily under him, hand seeking and finding. A small movement and they were joined. Into her like silk, tight enough to milk, warm enough to melt.

'Love you,' he said into her ear. She was already nearly away. Then, drowsing, she murmured the words which stayed in his sleepy mind, to come into focus with such clarity as he woke.

'Love you too . . . and I'm sorry, love.'

« 10 »

'Erika? I'm sorry to ring so early but . . .'

Bayreuth's favourite voice smothered her waking yawn.

'It's okay, Jane. David still sleeping, huh?'

'Yes. Erika, how's he doing?'

'What d'ya expect? The man's got talent, he's got charm, he knows the opera, he knows how it is with German orchestras and it took him about thirty seconds to realize this one's as smart as he is.'

A sigh of relief. 'Success then?'

'With the orchestra and the chorus, sure. Never wastes a minute, always half an hour extra for tennis. Some of these guys will always do it again if there's time. Not this one. When he's finished he stops.'

'So, no trouble with the orchestra?'

'One snarl-up yesterday, that's all. Nothing really.'

'Tell me?'

'Just a timpanist late back from a smoke. Misjudged the time, y'know how they do? Stopped the rehearsal. Then the boy said the wrong thing.'

'The boy?'

'The player. He's young.'

'I see.'

'So David blasted him in his best German. Over the top I'd say. Worse because he's always polite, and they like that.'

'He'd better apologize?'

'No. The form is that the fixer speaks to the boy and the boy makes the move. If David can handle that the show is back on the rails.'

'I hope so. Now, what about the cast? Happy?'

'Oh, sure. The calls with piano were great. Makes a difference, y'know, when the conductor plays the thing himself, and without the score too. Singers have to memorize so we like it when the conductor does. Frankly, I wish I was in his *Meistersinger* instead of the other piece.'

'So there's nothing I have to say to him?'

A pause now. Then: 'Well, he's giving the producer hell.'

'Stolz?'

'Yeah. It's his first time here too. His *Meistersinger* doesn't fit with David's. Oil and water. It's an old story.'

'But it's not like David to fight people.'

'Fight? More than one way to fight, y'know. He doesn't argue, just does his thing. His thing is natural, and the cast likes it. About half of what Stolz did in production has stuck, and that's the half that suits David. When the man gets uptight your boy's all innocence. Water off a duck, Jane. I've watched it in rehearsal.'

'Bad for David. All the German houses love producers.'

'Not much fun for the other guy either. But they're a complete mismatch. David is just not interested in his ideas, Jane. In fact he's not interested in anything Wagner didn't write.'

That was the truth of course, and Jane knew it. 'What can I do, Erika?'

'Do? Nothing. If there ever was anything it's too late. One of them had to win. It'll be David's opera. Stolz has nothing left except his pictures, which are great. Don't worry, sweetie, the whole damn thing will be wonderful. Hard on Stolz, but the musicians around the place are smiling. We've had so much producer-opera all over the world. Time for the composers to get something back.'

'You're sure there's nothing I can do?'

'Nothing. Relax, Jane.'

'I'll try.'

She put down the phone. The last thing they needed, a scrap between David and the producer; an operatic commonplace, but avoidable here, surely? What could she do? If Erika was right, nothing. Cross your fingers and pray, Jane.

She woke David with a cup of tea, sitting dressed on the edge of the bed. He pulled her down with a hug, a hand between her thighs, and she wriggled happily against it before freeing herself. 'Come on lazybones. Rehearsal at ten, and I have to be at the Festival office at ten-thirty.'

Extraordinary, he thought, the effect of her being here with him. He'd managed himself perfectly through weeks of work, never a stitch dropped and never a minute lost. Now his watch had ceased to count. The day was for her to arrange.

He showed her the quick way to the Festspielhaus, cutting across country and coming in through the car-park. She drove as always with marvellous precision, frightening stray ducks and the village postman en route, and inserted her machine into the space allotted without apparently glancing into the rear-view mirror.

'Off you go, maestro,' she suggested, 'and try not to upset them this morning. Wagner is their business, after all . . .'

The orchestra was waiting down in the cave, the leader smiling politely as ever, tuning ending as David reached the rostrum. They shook hands again, David wished them a good morning, and they were away into the final scene of *Meistersinger*. In came the guilds one by one with faultless precision, the chorus singing and placing themselves perfectly. The sound was simply stunning, all the more impressive because

David knew they were pacing themselves for *Lohengrin* later.

On to the end of the work, and coffee-time. As always David queued with the players and as always someone foiled the gesture by bringing a cup to him. Oh well, perhaps the democratic conductor really was bullshit anyway? He sat down at the nearest empty place.

'Mr Adams,' said a voice at his elbow, 'I'm sorry, really.'

It was the timpanist, yesterday's sparring partner, offering his hand. David shook it warmly, smiling. 'I didn't mean to bite,' he replied, 'but the language is not quite perfect, you know, and we misunderstand sometimes.'

It was a good enough out, and willingly accepted. 'My name is Hans,' said the player.

'A good name for this opera.'

He laughed. Yes, they called him Sachs sometimes in fun, but his name was Hans Keller. David realized that he was being invited to call the player by his given name, a formal privilege in Germany, and requiring a formal response. 'You must call me David. Whenever I hear *Mr* Adams I look for my father.'

'Oh yes. But here we are always so formal, you know? It's one of the things which makes us Germans, as you say, a bit stuffy?'

'Congratulations on your English. It makes me ashamed of my German.'

'Your German is fine – for an Englishman.' They both laughed.

'For one year I was in London, after the *Hochschule* studying.'

'At the Royal College?'

'Yes. But there is a wonderful player of my instrument at Covent Garden, you know? From him I learned much more.'

Yes, David knew. He'd tell the man, one day, if he could do it without embarrassing him.

'May I say that your Wagner is good?'

'As often as you like,' David responded, laughing.

'I'm a new boy here. Four years only. I cannot talk about so many old men, like my colleagues. But we have played *Meistersinger* much less well, this I can say. It will be a fine evening.'

'Of course it will, with so fine an orchestra and chorus and a wonderful cast.' They shook hands again as the bell rang for work to resume.

David had nothing to say to the orchestra, confident that he could make the remaining corrections with his hands at the general rehearsal tomorrow, when they would play the complete opera. The producer, as usual, had a great many criticisms. It was not his rehearsal, but David's. Still, that was life in the German opera house, where the play's the thing and the music often comes second, so he suffered in silence. Such awful psychology, he reflected. If conductors behaved like some of these chaps what monumental balls-ups there would be.

Back again to the scene, and once again a clean run. It was 12.30. He sent the musicians away to their rest and went up the long ramp into the sunshine.

Jane was waiting, leaning by the car, one knee raised to hook a heel on the sill, her knee-length linen coat a vivid white against the red, the walk across the yard giving him time to enjoy the picture. No way, he thought, to hide this woman. Just as well she was beautiful.

'Bone idle, you people,' she said as he climbed aboard. 'Always out early. Just look at them, pell-mell for the bar.'

'They've done the work,' he said, fastening his seat belt as the car accelerated down the famous hill into the town. 'They know the piece. If I go on they'll decide I'm still learning it. Wouldn't do. At the moment I seem to be winning.'

'I see. Pleased, are you?' The eyes hidden behind the sunspecs gave no sign, but there was a smile in her voice.

'It seems they are pleased with me.'

'That troublesome timpanist tell you, did he?'

He was stunned. 'How . . .?'

She laughed. 'Love, surely you know Germany better than that? The form is everything here. Your fight yesterday was famous. The apology was inevitable. Now you can call him Hans, and he can call you David – off the box, anyway.'

He was not sure he liked this. 'We'll never understand these people,' he complained. 'Must formal mean insincere, then?'

'No. He had to apologize or he just might not come back next year. He was not obliged to be complimentary, if he was.'

'Yes, he was.'

'That's all right then. Darling, you're doing beautifully and they're all terribly pleased. You can buy your timpanist a beer next year, have no fear.'

'Dammit. I'm contracted for next year. You know that.'

She looked at him in wondering disbelief, changing the while into second gear, to leave a surprised Mercedes standing at traffic lights.

'Tell me, love, how long have you been in this business?' she asked.

'Fifteen years, I suppose . . .'

'And you don't know yet that no one appears here for the second year unless the face fits in the first? Oh, come on, darling! They go down with the flu and so on, in May or June, or they beg to be released for other things. This place is not everyone's glass of schnapps, you know.'

187

Too many questions here, apart from the one which had started the day. They were on the Ringstrasse now, intimidating the lunchtime traffic, no easy feat in this nation of autobahn aces. 'Are we in a hurry?' he queried. 'Where are we flying?'

'Thought we might have lunch at the Hermitage, and a walk in the gardens? I haven't seen it since . . .'

'Well?' he prompted.

'Trying to remember. I was very tiny. My father was on the music staff here. We all came for the summer. Before the trouble.'

'You must have been very tiny indeed,' he said.

'Oh yes. Three, perhaps. But some things I remember. There are pools, a cascade, and an indoor fountain in a great stone room.'

The Hermitage was almost asleep in the sunshine, the courtyard empty and the restaurant quiet. Over lunch they talked business. Jane had had a good morning. Her arrangements for the recording, his first recorded opera, were first-rate. There was a television possibility too. But the great man had been vague about the future, waiting for the proof of the pudding, the first night, before committing himself.

If all went well, what would he offer?

'Whatever it is, short of a *Ring* Cycle or *Parsifal* at least, we don't want it, David,' she said firmly.

He was taken aback. 'Hey, clever lady, Bayreuth before Japan any time.'

'You can always *come* here if you like. You don't have to *work* here unless it suits you, surely? You're not about to become part of the Bayreuth set, conducting some opera or other every year forever, the sort of conductor who'll do what they ask in return for a nice summer in Bavaria. No. A big one or nothing.'

She was right, of course. The thing could become a trap – beautiful, but still a trap. She went on. 'Don't forget there are other festivals waiting. Bayreuth in means Tanglewood out . . .'

'Have I been asked for Tanglewood?'

'Not yet. But it will come. Then there's Salzburg, and Munich. Locking yourself up here can be a mistake, unless the work is a plum.'

'Love, Salzburg is for Grand Old Men. And they won't give me a Bayreuth *Ring* for a very long time.'

'No, they won't. Probably not until you are a music director with your own house. But if you have to wait then so must they. I think another opera after four or five years, and a *Ring* when you're sixty.'

'Sixty?' David had never imagined being sixty.

'Long-lived lot, conductors,' she said. 'You'll make ninety on present form. Lots of exercise and so on . . .'

'I've heard that certain oil millionaires have a system for staying young,' he said.

'Ah yes. The one where the boys are supplied with a different eighteen-year-old each year of their lives, and the youth rubs off on them?'

'Seems to work.'

'Hmm. I'm told it ages the girls.'

'So that's where your wrinkles are coming from! You'd better look out, young Jane.'

'Oh, I'm looking out, constantly. For a safe, reliable man. One I can trust out of sight. Not this Welsh conducting genius with equal talent for the ladies . . .'

The girl was hovering with the bill. Time to walk, he suggested. Out then into the sun, around the great rococo circle to the pool.

'You'll never trust me, Jane,' he said.

'You've never asked me. When you ask me . . . until you ask me, the question doesn't arise, does it? Where there's no commitment . . .'

'There's no breach. True.'

'And, since you don't ask, you don't want the commitment.'

'Don't I?'

'No. No, you don't, of that I'm sure.'

'Why not, d'you think?'

'I'm not sure. I don't want to explain it. I might be wrong.'

'Try,' he said. 'You may be right.'

'Well, wishful thinking, probably. But I'd like to believe it's because you'd hate to let me down.'

'And so long as we're not committed that can't happen?'

'Right. Nothing to apologize for. Nothing to regret.' Hand in hand they'd reached the long natural pergola of beech, dappled sunshine on the path between the trees, leading to the gazebo at the end. 'Never to say sorry,' she finished.

Now, he thought. Now's the time. 'Last night, dropping off to sleep, you said you were sorry.'

Her eyes were wide now, startled. 'Did I? Why?'

'Yes. Why?'

She turned and began to walk. There was a ten-pace silence. Then in a small voice, looking carefully down at the gravel path. 'I can't think.'

'Yes, you can. Thinking's your thing.'

'I mean I don't know. How can one know, half asleep?'

How indeed? His own sleep-talking had been the first crack in the security of his marriage. All the more need to know, then? Or better left? When she was ready, if she was ready, she'd tell him. They reached the gazebo, secure amid dense foliage, and stopped. Her arms reached for him, a plea in the gesture. He tugged her around the curve of the leafy wall, safe from sudden eyes at the end of the long walk, and they kissed. She sighed, relieved. His hand went to a button of her light coat and slipped inside. She welcome his touch as they kissed again. Then she was suddenly resisting. 'No . . . no . . . not here love,' and she pulled away, buttoning quickly. 'It won't do. People.'

'To hell with people.'

'Yes, and to hell with a *Times* headline about a famous conductor done for indecent exposure at a German festival, too. Some things we can fix, but that might be tricky.' She buttoned her coat and they walked again, out into the suddenly dazzling sunshine, among the flowerbeds to the head of the cascade behind the fountain. She made to walk down the steps. He told her that once down, there was nowhere to go but up again, a long climb in this heat. They turned to walk back to the car.

'One thing I don't understand,' he said.

'Only one? Lucky you,' she replied lightly, finding her key. He turned her and she leaned back on the red beast, smiling up at him.

'How it is that you reduce me to the helpless quivering lust of a sixteen-year-old?'

'Fifteen, I thought you were, the first time?'

'Yes, all right. That kind of lust.' He took her hand and put it on his trouser-front.

Laughing, she squeezed briefly. 'Poor boy. I'd be happier if I thought I was the only woman who could do it, but I'm not one for kidding myself.' She kissed him, lightly and quickly, and slid into the car.

They drove back in silence. Climbing out of the town, traffic thinning, he put his hand on her thigh, where the coat rode up. She smiled briefly, patted the hand and lifted it back to where it belonged.

The house was quiet, as always in the afternoons. The door closed behind them. She leaned on it and he kissed her, long and hard, she busy with buttons the while, first hers and then his. Her arms dropped and the coat with them. Still kissing they fell on to the bed. 'Now, love,' she said.

They were still and silent for a long time. Then: 'Good . . .?' she breathed.

He nodded. Better than good. Utterly relaxed now, they rolled apart, holding hands, breathing deep. Quietly she said, 'I really don't believe this happens to other people, do you?'

When he woke, evening was drawing in, cool. She'd covered him with a duvet. He could hear her, on the balcony, talking softly into the phone. The business voice. Three Janes, he thought. A Jane for me, a family Jane for a few close people, and business Jane for the rest. Discipline. More of it than he could ever summon, except at work. Then it was easy; music's discipline, not his own.

Quietly he crept to the shower, made himself presentable. She was waiting when he emerged, changed into wool for the evening, with two glasses of champagne. Such timing.

'Such good ideas,' he said.

'That's what I do . . .'

'For your ten per cent!' They laughed together, sipping appreciatively.

'I think I could get used to this,' she said, walking to the open balcony door.

'But it's usually said to be a boring place,' he reminded her, following her outside. 'People come for their opera and vanish again, down to Munich, Nuremberg, Rothenburg . . . all the pretty places.'

'Rothenburg?'

'Rothenburg on the Tauber. Lovely little town, unchanged since God only knows when, town walls intact, a picture-book really.'

'Can we go?'

He thought quickly. 'Certainly. Tomorrow, after the general rehearsal, we could drive there and put up, see the town in the evening, drive to Nuremberg next day, come back early for supper.'

'Are we really going to Nuremberg for the day before *Meistersinger*?'

'Yes. You'll love it, I promise.'

'I wonder . . . Very odd things happened in Nuremberg when I was a little girl in Vienna.'

'Darling,' he said, 'Hitler's dead.'

'Is he, now?' She leaned on the wooden rail, completing the picture he'd admired yesterday, against the low sun. 'What a simple man you are, David love. Hitler will never die. There's a bit of Hitler in each of us. Quite a lot in some of your friends here.'

'But, darling,' he remonstrated lightly, 'this is the most civilized country.'

'Civilized? Civilization is a millimetre thick. All that beastliness appealed to some amazingly civilized folks.' There was a sadness in the dark eyes, a sadness beyond his means to relieve.

He took both her hands in his. There was a long silence, then: 'If Bayreuth makes you unhappy I won't come here again,' he said.

'Nonsense. It's important to you. Anyway, I don't have to come when you do.'

'But you do,' he said, unable to resist the double-think.

She laughed, then finished her champagne and glanced at her watch. 'Time,' she said. 'You haven't forgotten we're entertaining this evening?'

He'd been trying to forget. Never a social animal, he'd kept a low profile for the past three weeks. Now, with most of his work done, good manners demanded that they dine some of his colleagues who were conducting in the present season. Jane had chosen the famous country hotel below Bamberg. Best bib and tucker, then, and get rid of his five o'clock shadow. She was already prepared, with only her hair to finish, so she sat at his mirror while he dressed, her conversation a catalogue of those invited and their affairs, professional and personal. By the time he was ready and dressed there was little he hadn't heard about his guests, their backgrounds, their status and their prospects, if any.

It was what the German tourist trade calls a Romance hotel; an eighteenth-century interior, lavish with carved limed-oak, ornate mirrors, farmhouse-heavy furnishings and inch-deep carpet. David and Jane arrived early. Sitting over cocktails he watched her silent assessment and smiled. 'If your nose were flexible enough I think it would actually turn up, Jane. Right, was I?'

She conceded. 'Right you were. It's an opera set.'

'*Rosenkavalier* with Park Lane plumbing?'

'Mmmm.'

'And crammed with faces, a duet at every table.'

'And an act in every suite, I imagine.'

He shook his head despairingly. 'What convent girls imagine—'

A voice at his elbow. 'Good evening, Mr Adams. How very kind of you to invite us.' He rose. First to arrive, the Bergers were the guests on whom the evening would turn. Rudi Berger, the House's chief resident conductor for some summers past, was safely established at fifty in his own State Opera directorship, with a busy touring diary. His wife, a tall blonde fifteen years his junior, wore a silk creation whose simplicity spoke of serious money. Relaxed, assured, she greeted Jane warmly. 'My husband tells me that you are the most successful lady in the arts in London. And so young, and so beautiful! My God, how is it done?'

Another voice now, older and less successful with its English; that of Hans Schmidt, who had joined as music staff thirty years ago and remained, year after year, growing into the House conductor, picking up the big works as the visiting geniuses gave them up. 'It is done I think by very much hard work, and also by the hard work of the lady's father. Of hard work he was not afraid, this I remember.'

Jane turned, astonished, to be introduced to the small grey man who'd arrived with his even smaller and greyer wife. 'Surely you don't remember—'

'Gregor Goldberg? But of course, and his lovely wife too. We were here together. You were very small. Your brothers used to swim'—the word came out as *schvimm*—'with my two sons. I hope they are well?'

'A very pretty little girl, I remember so well,' put in Mrs Schmidt.

'Then he went away, of course, to England.'

'And we,' put in Mrs Schmidt, 'have been here all the times. Good times and bad times.'

'You must tell us how it has been,' said the old man, 'but I am happy to see that the times have not all been so bad for you and your family.'

'Hi there!' Unmistakable voices from the door heralded the two music staff who had provided David's backup during rehearsals. Jonny Johansson, from the Royal Danish Opera, and Nancy Gee, from New York, arrived arm in arm. Their collaboration had blossomed famously, Bronx extroversion and Danish athleticism providing the House with amusement bordering on panic when matters reached the stage of having to knock very loudly on studio doors and waiting to a count of twenty before entering. The Great Man, it was rumoured, had said a few words – at second hand, naturally. Now their antics divided the House, proper Germans disapproving, the international set loving the whole picture. Tonight they were at their most formal as they greeted Jane, Jonny frankly admiring and Nancy's obvious reserve causing their host an inward chuckle.

Their table was ready. The menu was vast. 'Oh dear,' said Jane, 'such temptation. Two weeks here and I'd need a new wardrobe.'

Two pairs of eyes, Nancy's and Mrs Schmidt's, looked again at Jane's dress, their expressions suggesting alternative homes for the present outfit.

Berger was encouraging. 'I think you are one of those ladies who can eat absolutely anything and get away with it. In any case, fast tomorrow! Tonight, eat and celebrate the great success of your friend David.' He raised his apéritif. 'Let's drink to the success of our new *Meistersinger* and a new friend for the *Festspiel*.'

Dinner was a nice mixture of German politeness, Austrian charm, Danish humour and Bronx scattiness. Berger knew London well. Nowadays he was an occasional visitor to Covent Garden and the Festival Hall, and like all continental conductors he admired London's ability to provide so much music. 'A fifty-two-week music festival, really. It says much for the British.'

'Not the land without music then?' asked David.

'Of course not. Schumann was quite wrong.'

'But so little money for the arts,' put in Jane.

Schmidt was thoughtful. 'With so many orchestras, all making a living, all playing well, why complain? If you can do this without asking for money from the State, that's good I think.'

'Perhaps,' she agreed, 'but very hard work.'

Leaving the men to Jane, David applied himself to the ladies, who were predictably less enchanted by her. They were pleased to be at Bayreuth again; a recurring family holiday, it was so much nicer than following their husbands to the Far East or America, the necessary alternatives in a conductor's summer. Mrs Berger still regretted the loss of her promising singing career, and, much older, Mrs Schmidt was quietly content to observe them all, perhaps wishing that fate had provided her husband with the extra ounce of special talent which might have raised him to the jet set, and her with him. All were frankly envious of David's developing reputation in the USA and – Nancy especially – incredulous of his dislike of all things transatlantic.

The conversation would never have reached Bayreuth had not Jane taken it there. Then they enthused about its musical qualities while politely admitting its drawbacks.

Berger was philosophical about the orchestra. 'It's not so easy for them, after so many seasons here, to think again. And new ideas can disturb good technique . . .'

Schmidt was more direct. 'If you leave them alone they'll look after you. They are concerned with your performance. It's theirs too, and they have to live with it when you've gone.' It seemed every part of David's work had been reported back and scrutinized. So, Bayreuth had found him interesting at least.

Over coffee and cognac Berger was complimentary. 'It will go well for our friend. He conducts with his hands, not with his mouth. Not a man who rehearses without reason, yet not one who accepts what he should not. Bayreuth will like him because our orchestra really knows Wagner. Here it is only important to perform well, rather than to teach new tricks to an old dog. You have made a mark on *Meistersinger*, David. Now you have only to give maximum in performance. They will be surprised, I think, because you have not yet shown the steam which you can raise. It is there, waiting, I know. That is a very English way. It is perhaps not always the best way in Germany, but it will succeed here.'

The evening, David sensed, was over. A toast, perhaps, and in German, a small thank you to six nice people, five of whom had conversed in a foreign language for two hours past. 'My friends, let us drink to the Master, to Richard Wagner, and to the wonderful House which gives pleasure to so many . . .'

197

Before the glasses could be raised came a transatlantic coda: '. . . and work to us guys!'

The laughter saw them to the car. Jane drove back in a reflective silence, not commenting until they were relaxing over a nightcap.

'You're glad that's over?'

'Yes. Always hard work for me, these things. Nice people, though.'

'Worried, I think?'

'No. Not at all, I promise you,' he said, surprised.

'Not you. Them. Quite funny really. The orchestra knows there are not enough good conductors, but conductors think there are too many. Some people would be quite happy if your *Meistersinger* were nothing special.'

'Who cares?' he asked. 'I have to conduct the piece. Good or bad, but it will be mine.'

'Oh, it won't be so bad, I fancy.' She sipped thoughtfully at her cognac.

'The Bergers are nice,' he suggested.

'Secure, you see. Schmidt a little less successful, so a little less comfortable with new talent. He's the sort of man every opera house must have for backup. Very sound performances; not inspired but clean, tidy, reliable.'

'Very German.'

'That's what Bayreuth is all about. Salzburg is about Mozart, composer to the universe. Bayreuth is for Germans. We overhear Wagner. It's all for them, really.'

'Love, don't you think you take all that a little too much to heart?' he suggested gently.

She smiled her wry smile. 'But that's where the problem is. In my heart, in my guts, in my lungs, where my grandparents got the gas.' She saw his appalled face, crossed the room to sit on his chair-arm and kissed his cheek in apology. 'I'm sorry, love, really. Perhaps if I'd spent more time in Europe I'd have come to terms with all that. But not yet. Belsen is just down the autobahn, after all. Just give me time?'

'Jane, you can have the time and anything else you need, but I begin to feel like pig-in-the-middle.'

She put down her glass and slipped into his lap, arms round his neck, head on his shoulder. 'Explain, please?'

'Well, on the one hand I have an audience which hears wonderful music, a heart-warming plot, beautiful pictures, and a happy ending; on the other, people like you, who suspect every word and every note of fuelling race-hatred, who cringe at every idea in the piece. What am I to think? One or the other is right about Wagner . . .'

'Perhaps. Or perhaps we're all wrong. We'll never know. Anyway, your position is simple. Delivering the music will take everything you've got. It's not for you to explain. That you can leave to the producer. Heaven only knows he's got enough ideas and to spare.'

'I'm entitled to a point of view surely?'

'Yes, a personal one, not something you can sell to either side. Anyway, your point of view will change.'

'Will it, now?'

'Many times, I hope. You have time. Perhaps it will become clear in the end. Who knows?'

A Bayreuth *Meistersinger* can go by itself, the reason they'd given it to him, David knew. It was the safe piece for a new boy. Well, he was not too green to recognize the big problem, its length. If the climactic third act is to achieve its effect the first and second must be restrained. His first act was a calculated understatement, even less vigorous that morning. He'd never been one for giving his best performance three days early.

He was reassured by the atmosphere at the coffee break; not that he was looking for reassurance; he was already thinking himself into the second act. This was his longest opera – everyone's longest – and pacing his concentration over a six-hour span was not easy. He remembered the wise words of a conducting elder statesman, that a comfortable pair of shoes was essential for Wagner. Even tired feet could be a dangerous distraction.

Jonny and Nancy were constructive; some small changes in balance here and there, a little more time for Beckmesser in the song-trial perhaps? Otherwise nice. They were soon into the second act.

By its last scene he was beginning to feel the whole thing was just a little too good. Perhaps the chorus would muff the final riot, to give them something to improve at the premiere? No; these people were bombproof. So he relaxed, let it run and the inevitable happened. Jane, watching and listening from above, heard his mistake, one which would have stopped most performances cold. It made no difference; the orchestra and chorus coped and all was well. He thanked them as he left the pit, applauding as he stepped down.

Over lunch before the two-hour marathon of the third act Jane was subdued, disinclined to comment even when led, sensing his isolation, the impossibility of useful comment now. It was all his own work and going according to plan; he believed he knew what to do in three days' time to turn up the gas and boil the kettle. He was abstracted, remote, coming to earth only when the bell rang for resumption.

'Bags packed?' he asked.

'Mmm. In the car. Can we get away quickly?'

'Not sure,' he said. 'There's certain to be something. If not from me, then from Stolz. He's on edge, you know. It's his debut here too. Trying much too hard. The piece isn't that complicated, but producers must try to do something new to justify their existence. Anyway it won't take long. Come if you like?' She nodded. Now it was time to finish the work.

There was rather more than polite applause as he went in, she realized thankfully. The third act prelude set the scene, the act flew by, and very soon the cast and he were thanking each other in the anteroom. The atmosphere was relaxed, easy, pleased. Then Stolz arrived. His displeasure was all for the conductor. Arriving late, Jane heard his voice from the doorway and beat a tactful retreat, though not out of earshot.

'So many things! Where can one start? All because of this pressure from the orchestra. Too much sound, always pressing, no time for my work to take effect, no sympathy for the play. *Meistersinger* is not a symphony concert with voices. It is an important statement of German art . . .'

The Sachs, Wagner's cobbler-philosopher, an old Bayreuth hand and a veteran of many producer-conductor spats, came to the rescue. 'Herr Stolz, may I have one word?' All eyes turned to the speaker, and

Jane's ears strained to catch the words. 'I must say that I have been completely happy. David makes not too much sound for me, and always he gives me time to sing. Almost he is a singer himself.'

There was a murmur of agreement. The Eva added her point. 'For me there are no problems.' Their polite insistence in speaking English was touching, thought Jane. The soprano voice went on: 'For me it has been a happy experience. The music goes well, naturally and simply. This will be a fine *Meistersinger*.'

'But the play. The play has no direction.' Stolz turned directly to David. 'You will not wait for me. My work is for nothing, entirely.' Jane, outside, could hear that the poor man was terribly worried. She crossed her fingers as David took the plunge.

'Ladies and gentlemen, we are all tired, and naturally in so long a work Mr Stolz has not seen everything he would have wished today. If I am at fault,' turning to his critic with an apologetic smile, 'then I am truly sorry. You must all feel free to play the piece as Mr Stolz wishes. I'm here to make the music work, that's all. You have two days still. I need nothing, musically. Do as you will with the play. I am sure all will be a great success on Thursday. Let's say no more about it now. It's been a delight to work with you. I wish you all a great evening, and many more.'

Jane waited at the door.

'Marvellous, really,' she said, starting the car. 'Hardly a snag until that nasty in the third act. It wasn't there yesterday. How did it happen?'

He laughed. 'It didn't happen. It was necessary, so I made it. Just a bar of three dropped into five minutes of fours. General rehearsals mustn't go as well as that one, darling. Not good for anyone.'

'Oh come; superstition surely?'

'No, the truth. If everyone feels safe someone will go to sleep, sure as eggs are eggs. Now they've decided

I'm a risk after all, they'll stay awake. Staying awake is a priority.'

'But it might have stopped the show, David.'

'Anywhere else it might, true enough. Not here. They are very good at what they do. Chorus too. Is there any sound like it on God's earth?'

She was worried at the implications of all this. 'David, it won't help your reputation here . . .'

He shrugged. 'Every orchestra likes to think it's cleverer than any conductor. Especially this one, in this piece, and me British. A good one on Thursday and all will be forgiven. In fact they'll think they did it for me. It all helps.' She was not convinced, he could see, so he tried again. 'Jane, routine is death, especially here. They are amazingly safe performers and they know it. Orchestras in Germany sit like Fafner in the cave, nursing their gold, you know, complacent. And when the conductor, especially the young conductor, comes like Siegfried to wake them up, they usually say *Who are you, child? Go away. Don't disturb us. If you do it will be the worse for you.* But if they are woken up . . .'

'They become the Friendly Dragon?'

'Usually.'

'And the risk is worth taking?'

'Wait and see.'

She was silent for a while, digesting all this. Then 'You really didn't know about Stolz? That he was miserable as hell?'

'One gets used to a certain level of dissatisfaction from producers. They have ideas and we need them, but they don't have the musical imperative to drive them. We do.'

'But here, you know, ideas are terribly important?'

'Always, in Germany. But the score is still the only thing the composer left us. Everything else is some-

203

body's else's invention. A musician must draw the line.'

'Trouble, then?'

'No. We'll play it terribly well, they'll all sing their hearts out and everyone will love it. The production too, you'll see.' She wondered at the musical certainty which had rendered him insensitive to Stolz's three-week struggle. True, these collisions were an inevitable part of opera everywhere, but generally it was the conductor who had to give. 'Ninety-nine per cent confidence, your business, I think,' she said.

'Ninety-nine point nine.' They were cutting across the hills, away from the traffic. She'd done her home-work, knew the route. Just as well, since he was utterly bushed.

Jane was still puzzled. 'Surely you knew he'd com-plained endlessly for two weeks, ever since the first stage rehearsal?'

'No. Look, this opera is important to us all. We've all got strong opinions about it, the cast too. I've given in endlessly, so long as the music hasn't suffered.'

She shook her head. 'No, David. You've had your own way from start to finish.'

'But surely,' he said after a space, 'I've got it right. That cast is the best in the world. They wouldn't have given so much if I'd got it wrong.' He was desperately tired now, and the car was a humming hypnotist. He began to nod. She saw it. 'Push the button, love, get your head down . . .' and he knew no more until they were passing under the Town gate at Rothenburg.

In the hotel yard under the timbered beams in the dusk, porters bustled with their bags. To her alarm he threw himself on the bed. 'Shower' she said, making for the bathroom 'and a good dinner. Then a walk, then a drink, and then bed.'

'Enjoy all that, will you?' he asked, yawning as he threw off his things.

'I will, I will.' She stood in the doorway, holding a woollen sheath, her choice for the evening. He went back to her, held her very tight. She felt the inevitable stirring below. 'Down, fido.' She pushed him into the shower. 'I'm famished.'

So was he, he suddenly realized. Unusually, too, he was taking an age to unwind. He preferred to come down with a crash, over a sizeable Scotch. This time, wound up over a six-hour period, he was still tight as a drum. She seemed equally tense, and the meal was unusually quiet. At last, over the second cognac, he began to come down. She felt it, took his hand across the table. 'Better, love?'

'Thank you,' he said, grateful for her understanding. 'I'm coming round.'

'Takes time. You've been winding up for three weeks in that hothouse.' And he was still winding, she knew, for the premiere. 'Exhausting.'

'Oh no. Not at all,' he remonstrated. 'They were lovely. The cast were sweet the whole time and the schedule makes life very easy. Only one small spat with a player, and even that was useful in the end. But I didn't even notice Stolz's problem.'

'That was part of his worry, of course, that you didn't. But it must have told on you both.'

'Well, perhaps. Look, it's almost dark. Shall we leave the walk for the morning?'

She would have none of it. 'Absolutely not. I need it, even if you don't. I'll just pop up and get my coat.'

Five minutes and she reappeared in the white button-up, a scarf around her hair. It was July and still very warm even so late. They walked down the street past the Christmas shop with its candles, cribs, and angel-carousels. She stopped to look, delighted and amazed that Christmas could support a shop all the year round.

At the edge of the town they met the gate and the

wall. Up the steps then, in the dusk, to the watchmen's walk of long ago, under the long roof, once thatched but now pantiled. Arm in arm, no words now. Every so often they came upon a tower, with steps to the street, and at the furthest turning point they looked out over a deep wooded valley. Distantly the church clock struck. It was the time of the *Meistersinger* Night Watchman. The magical notes came instantly to them both, and David sang quietly:

'Hear people!
Ten has struck from the steeple!
Guard your fire, guard your light
That no one comes to harm!
Praise God, the Lord!'

Jane drew him into the curve of the tower, leaning on the wall, a silhouette against faint distant streetlamps. He kissed her. Releasing him, she asked seriously, 'D'you never stop, David?'

'It's all music, you see,' he told her.

'Yes, I do see. For you there's nothing else.'

The sadness in her voice eluded him. 'It's what I understand, what I can do. We must all do what we're good at, mustn't we?'

'In that case I must look after your diary . . .'

'And your ten per cent.'

'Nothing more, then?' There was something in her voice he'd never heard before.

Concerned, he held her close again, speaking into her hair as her arms circled. 'Jane, you know I love you, surely?'

In your way, she thought. But if one took away business and bed, what would be left? 'Do you know what love is?'

'I'm not even sure I know anyone who does,' he told her.

'I know. I've seen it. My father and my mother, they knew what it was.'

'They went through the fire. Perhaps one needs the fire to prove it.'

'But love, there *is* no fire for us. We're secure, we have money, we both have the success we looked for.'

'Shouldn't we be grateful?' he asked.

'Oh, I don't know. Perhaps. I wish . . . I wish . . .'

He kissed her again, to stop her wishing. Her response was immediate, feeling for him with her body. They were quite alone. He held her tighter. She clung. He opened the top button, then another, to kiss above her breast. Her hands were suddenly busy below. The coat was open, she was drawing the tight dress up above her hips. Now she was close, hands searching.

'Darling, wait,' he suggested.

She was leaning on the parapet.

Her voice was soft, breathless. 'No. Now, please?'

He held her, or she would have fallen. Minutes passed. She looked up, mouth open. He kissed her again, a long soft kiss.

I love you, he thought, whatever love is.

'Oh, David, it's been such a day.'

'It has,' he agreed, bending to arrange her dress, kissing the velvet round of her body before covering it, buttoning her up, pecking her cheek. 'I had no idea . . .'

'That I was in such a state? Darling, don't you know how important all this is to me?'

'Of course it is,' he said. 'Look, I won't let you down. You know that.'

She turned away. 'My God, is that what you think this is about? Business? I care, damn you, I care! I was more nervous today than anyone in the theatre. About what? Money? Another date, another dollar? God, no. I just want you to succeed. I want you to be happy. Why? Because if you are happy then we can be happy together. But you don't care, *you just don't care*. You don't even know how I feel.'

She was crying into her hands now. He reached for her, held her head to him, soothing helplessly and uselessly as she cried, quite alone, beyond his reach. In a space the sobbing and heaving slowed, she took his proffered handkerchief and put herself together. One deep breath and then, 'I'm sorry. I'm such a fool. Such a day. I'm so tired. Take me back?'

12

His watch, propped up on the bedside table and viewed through one focusing eye, showed 9.25. He could always sleep after work, and yesterday had been work, certainly.

Returning from his shower, David found Jane still asleep. Beautiful, her head on the big pillow, black hair disordered, curled and relaxed, catlike. Time for the Sleeping Beauty trick, or they'd get no breakfast. He sat down softly, bent and kissed her cheek.

'Mmm . . .' Eyes closed still, she raised her arms from the tumbled linen, put them round his neck and pulled him down. One arm left his neck, pulled at the bedclothes, making room. He lay for a moment before whispering into her ear 'Love, it's nine thirty-five . . .'

She blinked awake, shook her head and sat up, her surprise almost comic. He grinned. 'I'll ask them to send breakfast up, shall I?'

'Oh no, we can catch the dining room if we're quick. Be a love and get the papers, would you?'

English papers here? Not likely. It was a ploy to get him out of the way, he knew. Once out of bed she hated to be seen first thing in the morning. He slipped into slacks and shirt and went down the vast staircase to reception. Yes, there were English papers. Only two, and a day old, of course. Browsing through *The Times* he was called back to the desk. There'd been a call for him. Would he or Fräulein Grant please telephone Bayreuth urgently? He could do that now, of course, from the foyer box. They would find the number, it would be no trouble.

The *Festspielhaus* was wide awake and waiting. A

call from a Mrs Jones, who would like to hear *Meistersinger*. She could come on the first evening or the second. There were no seats possible for the first, and they asked confirmation that he wished this lady to have a seat for the next. He told them that yes, he did wish it, and asked them to give Kate his Bayreuth number so that she could find him when she arrived.

Jane came down as he left the box. 'Trouble?' she asked.

'No. Not at all. I'll tell you over breakfast.'

The restaurant was thinning now. They addressed themselves to the muesli, the rolls and the cheese. 'Well?' she asked.

'Kate. She'd like to see the opera. I told them to arrange it.'

She sat up straight, alert. 'She's coming from Cardiff?'

'I suppose.'

'Didn't you ask?'

'No. Does it matter?'

She swallowed the last of her coffee and stood up. 'Come on, upstairs.'

'Where's the fire?'

'Must find her.'

Bayreuth had kept the number, a Salzburg hotel. Kate answered.

'How lovely to hear from you,' said Jane, 'and how utterly and typically thoughtless of David not to ring back himself.' He could just hear the laughter at the other end. 'You know you have a seat? I won't be here after the first night. He'll need someone to keep him away from all that Bavarian food.' There was a response which made Jane giggle. 'Not to worry. It's a terribly long piece. He'll be much too tired.'

There were so many questions. How long would she be here? Would she like to hear *Lohengrin* on Sunday? Yes, of course David could arrange that.

Where would she stay? Nothing arranged? Then of course she must come to Altdrossenfeldt. Of course there would be a room. There was always room for friends of *Festspiel* conductors. That was settled, then. Down with the receiver.

'How lovely! She's at Salzburg with friends. She can drive up on Friday. Can you keep her amused until Tuesday, d'you think?'

Well, the place would fascinate Kate and he had nothing else to do.

'You don't look terribly pleased,' Jane said.

'Pleased? Oh, Kate is lovely. I'm never good at surprises, that's all.'

She sighed. 'Don't we know it? Well, come along, let's go shopping for Christmas.'

They spent an hour in the Christmas shop. Candles, carousels, wooden toys including a night-watchman and a Sachs who smoked their tiny pipes from a tablet popped inside, a glorious pile of boxes which she gaily asked the shop to send home. Then to the church with the immense carved wood altarpiece, the *Rathaus*, and coffee in a small street café.

'Lovely, lovely,' Jane said, relaxing in the sun. 'What a pretty place. Thank you so much for thinking of it. I'd never have known.'

'There are quite a lot like it,' he said. 'Kind of us not to throw bombs at them, wasn't it?'

'Did you care, really?' she asked.

'Not at all. So few of us had been here. To us Germany was just a place full of Nazis. The more we killed each night the happier we were. I remember it very well. Kate's husband killed lots. My uncle was with him. They were very good at it, in their tank.'

'And it didn't keep them awake at nights?'

'No. I don't think so. They'd rather not have been there at all, surely, but they were in the service and

211

there was a war to fight. I reckon their one thought was to get there and back alive, that's all.'

'A remote control war, for them.'

'Until the shells hit them. Then it got rather personal, didn't it?'

She was pensive. 'Not as personal as pushing a hundred people into an iron box and switching on the gas, though. That's what one never understands; that these civilized, charming people could do that.'

'Yes.'

'They must have known, surely?'

'Oh yes. Whatever they say, however they argue, they knew.'

'You're getting there,' she said, putting down her cup.

'Where?'

'To the point. To the understanding that if civilized people can do it once they can do it again. And perhaps not only these people but yours. We know that. It's why there is no trust in us, why we defend each other. Because in the end we know . . .'

'That no one else will? But we do. We defend Israel.'

'Oh, all *that* takes is money, and we have all the money, you see. Bring the problem closer, David. Look at the people who don't wish to live next door. They defend Israel because they'd like us to go and live there and because they think Arabs are even less sanitary than we are . . .'

He put his hand on her arm, stopping her. 'Darling . . .'

She blushed. 'I'm sorry. I do go on, don't I?' A long uncomfortable silence, then: 'I promise you I don't inflict this on anyone else.' Again he waited. 'As a matter of fact there is no one else I can . . .'

'I know,' he said. 'I know. But don't let it spoil the good things around you, love.'

'For me nor for you. I'm sorry. Come on, let's walk the walls. The view must be stunning in daylight.'

Up then by the gate, and the long walk round the old town, surrounded this morning by energetic young people with cameras. Yes, the view was wonderful, looking in at the old buildings or out at the green country. Reaching the scene of last evening's exploit she produced a miniature camera from her handbag and David was comprehensively snapped.

'There ought to be some way of leaving a mark,' she said.

' "David and Jane were here." '

'We could ask the Town Fathers to permit a small plaque.'

Knowing his ineptitude with a camera she asked help in snapping them both from a passing tourist. He stopped her German in midflow. 'I'm so sorry. I don't speak German . . .' and they all dissolved into laughter.

The picture taken, they completed the circuit, tired now, and went back to the hotel. It was almost time for lunch. She disappeared, then returned dressed for the restaurant, with two glasses of bubbly.

He tried to pull her down. She dodged, prepared for his move.

'It's the twinset,' he laughed. 'Never could resist a twinset and pearls. Highly stimulating gear for the working lad. Very top drawer.'

She sighed. 'Oh dear. For one lovely moment I thought I'd produced the reaction myself. Well, now we know. For you heaven is a Jaeger shop.' She sat on the edge of the bed to finish her drink.

'I think,' he said thoughtfully, 'that what's under the twinset makes a difference.'

'Oh, half of humanity has what I've got,' she pointed out lightly.

'All right then. *Who's* under it.'

213

'You wouldn't try to fool a poor unsuspecting girl, sir, would you?'

He put down his glass and reached for her hand. 'I'm serious,' he said.

Jane had this nuisance-making tendency to face issues after a glass of wine. 'Yes. Yes, I suppose. At least you're *more* serious.'

'Explain?'

'Yes, if you really wish it.' She thought for a moment, then: 'How many women have you had, David?'

'Oh, come on, darling! I don't keep a book . . .'

'Like Leporello's book for Don Giovanni? All right, I know you're more serious about me than the others.' She was silent for a space, then: 'I said once that I couldn't bear to share you. I told you that if that was what you intended then you must leave me alone. But here we are, two years on. And when I've gone in a day or two . . .'

'Don't go. Stay with me.' He tried desperately to keep the thing light.

'Why? To keep you in order? Can't you do it alone?'

'Darling, this is utterly different.'

'How different? Tell me how different.' Her voice was low.

He took her hand. There was no responsive squeeze, just compliance. 'For everyone there's someone. Someone different, someone important, someone to come home to. Different.'

'So, I'm to come home to after the others?'

'No. You're never away, always with me. Part of me.'

'Even when you're making love to someone else?' There was sudden steel in her voice.

'I'm sorry,' he said, beaten.

'Sorry you make love to—'

'Sorry that you're hurt.'

She was silent, steadying herself. 'No commitment,' she said. 'No commitment so no need to say sorry.'

'Either way?' he suggested.

'Neither way. But I'm not a civilized agreement. I'm a woman. I have choices, I have decisions to make.' There was something in her hand, something small and brown and rubbery. 'Do you know what this is?' she asked.

He sat up, surprised.

'Our amorous activities of the past three months have been controlled entirely by this little gadget. Rubber has one great advantage. It can be abandoned, selectively if necessary. David, I'm going to have a child.'

For the first time in her life she saw colour physically drain from a face. For a full half-minute he could find no words. Then: 'How? We've been so careful . . .'

'No. *I've* been so careful, surely?' she smiled. 'I'm sorry, love. Wrong end of the stick. I don't mean I'm pregnant. I'm not, as far as I know. But I intend to be. I'm telling you so that you won't feel caught out when it happens. *If* it happens.'

He shook his head, relieved beyond words but baffled. 'Why, love? What for?'

'I'm thirty. If I'm to do it I must do it soon. And I must do it, you see?'

'No, actually. You needn't,' he said.

'Not for you to say, love. My life, my body, my decision. And I can't leave it much longer.'

'A child should have a father, Jane.'

She winced. 'Don't I know it? I did without mine for long enough. My mother was two parents in one. I can do it if I must.'

He was all at sea. This was a new Jane. The other Jane was his support, his stability, the solution to his problems, the pivot on which his life balanced. This one was careless of his needs, making a problem for him to solve.

'How will you manage?' he asked.

'I'll have all the help in the world, a birth at a clinic looked after by the best obstetrics in London, a nanny . . .'

'Yes, all right. All right. You can organize it. You can organize anything.'

'Organizing is my thing?' The steel was back in the quiet voice now, harder and sharper.

'We both know that, love.'

Now came the explosion. Controlled, in a low voice, precise, the blowing of a valve long screwed down. 'Don't you see that there are things which shouldn't be organized? I'm a woman. A woman like all those *disorganized* housewives who make themselves happily available night after night to husbands who cheerfully fill them up at bedtime, or over the kitchen table, believing that whatever happens things will somehow pan out *without* organization, that kids are what life is about, worries and all, and that two secure people can see themselves through anything the world can throw at them? They are the people who make the world go round, David, not us.'

It was too sudden, not something he could talk about without trapping himself, making her angry. 'Jane, we're not like—'

She was in control again, the tears leaving her eyes and her voice. 'No, of course we're not. We're too well off, too comfortable, we have too much to do to live like *people*. But I want the best of what they've got, and I'm determined to have it, don't you see?'

'Yes. I see.'

His trying to placate was transparent, the more irritating because she loved him, needed his support. 'No you don't. You think it's a piece of female nonsense, hysteria. It's nothing of the kind. Perhaps it's my Cath-

216

olic mother coming out, the piece that says sex must bear fruit, or perhaps it's my Jewish father, the bit that says getting out of Nazi Germany was not for nothing, not to die without continuing the race as so many did. Whatever it is it's very deep and very important. I'm not going to argue with it, and I'm not going to listen if you do.'

She got up, searching for her handbag, finding what she needed, her nail-scissors. One quick jab, so savage he winced, through the centre of the rubber. Several snips reduced the cap to scrap for the waste-basket. Crossing the room she disposed of it there, turning with a defiant grin.

'Gone, one safe lady.' Her grin softened to a smile as his face fell, and she sat again, holding his hand. 'Oh, not to worry too much. The dates are all right, until I go, anyway. But when I come back I'll be a risk. In fact rather more than that.' She put her hand on the back of his head, stroking, consoling. A quick soft kiss on his cheek. 'Think about it,' she said. 'You're not to be trapped. And you know I won't marry you. But I'll have my child, perhaps more than one, who knows? Yours only if you wish it. If not, then—'

It was more than he could take, suddenly. 'For God's sake, don't. I can't bear it. Don't even talk about it.'

'We must, love. Because I'll do it if that's what it takes. Look, it's more justifiable than spreading one's legs for fun, which is what ladies do all the time, surely?'

'You and I are not just fun. We make love. It matters.'

'Yes it does. That's why it's to be your child, please, if you will. Otherwise I shall have to collect from someone else. But I love you and there's no room to love anyone else.'

'It could grow. The father of your child would be special, always.'

'A risk. A risk I'd have to take.' She came close, put her arms round him, hugged him tight. 'Nothing changes, David. We're still ourselves and we have each other. Perhaps we always will. I'm a pushover for famous conductors, so long as they're Welsh Rugby enthusiasts, working at Bayreuth.'

'Not too many of those about.' He hands were on her skirt, inching the hem upwards as she stood.

'One's enough.' A kiss, then a longer one. 'I thought we were to have lunch,' she said.

'Lunch will wait.'

* * *

Eventually they slept. Lunch became early dinner. Then a relaxed drive to Nuremberg, to a small hotel under the castle walls and a drink high above the city, the lights sparkling in the warm dark.

'A timeless place,' he said.

She was amused. 'You're a hopeless romantic, d'you know?'

'I'm entitled. I'm a Celt.'

'Oh? That's what it is? I'm not sure what I am. Not a romantic, anyway. For me history's fact.' She gestured to the walls towering above. 'There's a convenient mist between you and the people who built that heap, isn't there?'

'Yes. Yes, I suppose.'

'Like King Arthur, all that nonsense?'

'A bit, yes.'

'Picture would have been clearer if they'd had the nerve to pop over for the odd scrap in Sussex or Kent?'

He laughed. 'We'd have chucked them out. We've always been good at that.'

'But not infallible. Anyway, they didn't. The Channel has kept history at a polite distance, hasn't it? Well, since they couldn't swim in their tin suits they trotted over to Hungary instead. My folks found them decidedly unromantic, I can tell you.'

'On the credit side, all that art, all that literature, all that music.'

'Oh yes. Every stream in Austria plays the Pastoral Symphony, doesn't it? Well, I won't complain. It's made us both a bob or two, I agree. Especially this year, the Wagner.' She looked at her watch. 'They're well into *Tannhauser* by now.'

'And tomorrow *Lohengrin*. It was my first Wagner. Must do it again one day.'

She smiled. 'When you are Music Director in . . . let's see . . .'

'Vienna? The Met?'

'Let's not get carried away. Berlin would be enough. Covent Garden would be nicer, of course.'

'There's a queue.'

'It's what his nibs wants, above all, Covent Garden.'

'Ah! and how is the Argentine genius?'

'In Salzburg. Well, I think.'

'With his lovely wife?'

'No, with someone else.'

'Anyone we know?'

'A new one, I gather. He didn't say who.'

'He has a talent.'

'For the ladies, even more than for the orchestra. Still, Martha seems to put up with it. Keeps him young, she says. And he always comes back.'

'Yes. He always will, so long as she takes it with a smile. Is it true, the story about the way he met her?'

'No secret. They joke about it at dinner-parties even.'

'On a plane? Truly?' David was incredulous.

'Truly. Between Buenos Aires and Lima.'

'Over the Andes? A long trip, that one.'

219

'Yes; very boring. She was just out of finishing-school, coming home from a visit to relatives. He was on his way to the Teatro Colon. She was only superficially finished going up, she says, but thoroughly so coming down.'

'It must have been a quiet flight.'

'Often is, in first class. I seem to remember . . .?'

'Yes. And then he married her.'

'Yes. With amazing speed.'

'And they're happy?'

'Happy? Nuts about each other. He dotes on her and the boys.'

'Despite . . .?'

'Yes. Well, I suppose when a girl picks up a husband that way she has few illusions about his probable fidelity.'

'So, it works for some people.'

'And you'd like it to work for me?'

'For us.'

'What more do you want? Do I complain?'

'I want you to be happy.'

'I'll be happy with my baby. Or babies. It may be habit-forming. I want a family of my own, that's what. And I'd like my very own man. I don't like sharing you with . . .'

'Darling, am I so bad?'

'Yes, you are. When I've been gone a week there'll be someone, won't there? Someone who *doesn't count*, poor dear. Well, so far as I'm concerned she'll count.'

'Jane, I love you, really.'

'It's the reassuring *really* I don't like. Come on, we don't have to talk about this. I'll put up with it. I said I wouldn't but I do, more fool me. When I won't, then you'll know.'

He reached for her hand. 'Listen, Jane, I can't imagine being without you.'

'I know that,' she said. 'That's the difference. I've given a lot of thought to being without you because it may be necessary and I've had some experience of being without people I love. It takes practice, but I can cope. And don't worry. You'd find another lady, or fifty of them, and there are other agents. They'd queue up to have you.'

'Don't for God's sake. None of this is necessary.'

'Isn't it?'

They were paging Fräulein Grant, Fräulein Grant . . .

She got up, waved at the man. A telephone call. He sat alone looking out over the city with its spaces where great buildings used to stand, wondering how long it would take, what these people would build, how it would be in the time of five Bayreuth seasons, ten, twenty. Then she was back, excited, a little breathless.

'How well do you remember your *Lohengrin*?' she asked.

'Pretty well, why?'

'They want you to do it tomorrow.'

He laughed aloud. 'They can't be serious.'

'Never more so, I promise you.'

'But why? It's Schmidt's piece.'

'He's ill.'

'He has his cover. They're well up to it, surely?'

'Yes, but they need a name, tomorrow. Some sort of state visit. The cast is asking for you. The orchestra too.'

'Are you sure? What cast?'

'Well, Erika's the Ortrud. Didn't she sing that with you in San Francisco?'

'Yes. Yes, she did. It's a hell of a time ago, Jane.'

'Then that's where the pressure is. A difficult lady, our Erika.'

Such a long time ago, he thought. Was the work

safe? If it was safe anywhere it was safe at Bayreuth. She sat, silently sharing his inward debate, weighing the risk with him, waiting. She saw the decision in his face before he spoke.

'All right. Tell them I'll do it. But I must have the cast for two hours with the piano.'

She was smiling broadly. 'No need. I told them to assume a positive unless I rang back at once. The cast will be on stage at ten thirty in the morning.'

'Damn,' he said, looking at his half-empty glass. 'I'd have loved another before bed. Now you'll have to finish that one.'

'My pleasure,' she said.

13

It was a happy, relaxed supper. Five of the world's great voices, one relieved conductor and his equally delighted agent. Their host was expansive. 'It's been an exciting evening, my friends. What a good thing you could be with us, David, and how wise it was of you, Erika,' with a smile to the lady on his right, 'to suggest that he should be asked.'

The given name was not lost on David, but he was careful not to presume its significance. He knew, too, that Erika had done rather more than *suggest*. 'Erika's confidence was very flattering, sir. *Lohengrin* is the only other work of Wagner I've conducted. And that was—'

'A hell of a time ago,' said Erika. 'Too long. In San Francisco. And it was a wow there too.' The voice, mellifluous in song, was almost Brooklyn-abrasive offstage.

'Yes. I remember. A production I didn't like, but musically fine. Except that the sound of the orchestra was not what I like in Wagner.'

David sprang to the defence of the American orchestra, anticipating and defusing a more spirited defence from Erika. 'Well,' he said, 'I like orchestras to sound ethnic. That way I know where I am. If they sounded alike all over the world there would be very little point in any of us travelling, surely?'

The baritone, Erika's compatriot, was amused. 'Oh yeah? You mean like the old tourist gag, the brasses have more vibrato than the tenor so this must be Paris?'

'And the oboe sounds like toothache so it must be

223

Vienna?' Jane suggested. There was a general laugh, and for some minutes there were jokes at the expense of the orchestras of the world. David brought them to a halt with a compliment for the Festspiel Orchestra, 'the orchestra which made this evening possible.'

General applause followed, to their host's obvious pleasure.

'Now,' he said, 'let me say something which I intended to say only tomorrow, after *Meistersinger*. David, you are a true Wagnerian. They are very rare. To succeed here it is not enough to conduct the piece well. At Bayreuth, where we search constantly for new ways to express the work of the Master on the stage, conducting can be – what is the English expression – a mixed blessing? When a conductor's work survives the *sturm* of the production, when the artists on the stage are completely with him, then he is a Wagnerian of the first class.'

More than polite applause now. Something of significance was coming and the table was all ears. 'David, you will always be welcome at Bayreuth. It would be a pleasure to have you back in three years, when your *Meistersinger* passes to someone else, for another opera,' he held up his hand, halting whatever response might be impending, 'but I know that Miss Grant' – with a smile for Jane – 'will already have decided that this would not be wise. So let me suggest something else. In four years, when you have had two years away, please come for *Tristan* . . .'

The rest was lost in general applause. Jane looked up, startled, then down again, depriving David of a response on which to build his own. One must be contrived though. He looked down at his glass for a while before answering.

'I am truly grateful for this wonderful gesture,' he said, 'and I hope that what you ask will be possible. But some promises have been made, particularly in my home in Wales. Above all, the Promenade Concerts are special occasions for me and for my friends. We'll talk about dates and occasions . . . Meanwhile may I say how grateful I am to you, sir, for your confidence and to you all for your wonderful support this evening? I have been made to feel very much at home in Bayreuth. Now,' he rose, 'it's late. I must sleep, or tomorrow will be so bad that you will never want me here again.'

He subsided into the Porsche with a sigh of relief. 'I don't know which is hardest, conducting the piece or saying the right thing. I suppose he didn't ask you about that *Tristan* before chucking it at me?'

'No. He didn't. Not fair at all.'

'These people never are. How they love playing God.'

'Never mind. You said the right things. We must clear the way for *Tristan*. Not too soon, though. Perhaps a year later than he asks.'

'Jane, please don't lose it. It's such a piece. And sometimes the only thing is to *let* these people play God.'

'Yes it is, and no I won't. But it must wait, probably.' Her mind was already busy, calculating the possibility of recording his *Tristan*. If the date was right and the cast available . . . this man was getting her into deeper water than anything in her previous experience. For the first time she wished GG was here to steady the boat, keep her feet dry.

The car was purring up the gentle hill to Drossenfeldt. He was exhausted, nearly asleep on the short drive. The house was quiet. They climbed the stairs in a hush and she opened the door. 'Shower? A nightcap?' she suggested.

'No. Just bed. I'm bushed, absolutely.' Sitting, head drooping, hands on his knees, he was making no effort to undress. She started on his buttons and he took

225

over, dropping clothes everywhere, finally rolling into the bed she opened for him. In moments he was asleep.

She smiled her wry smile, then hung his clothes carefully before going to her own room with its unused bed. She felt curiously lonely, the strain of the evening unrelieved by physical and mental draining as his had been. On impulse she picked up the telephone. Somewhere she'd scribbled the number. She looked at her watch: not quite 11.30. An uncivilized time to ring? No, why not? She found the number and dialled. The answer was immediate, suggesting a bedside telephone. Her conscience leaped, but Kate's voice was cool. Not so cool, though, when she was recognized.

'Jane! Is something the matter?'

'No, nothing. It's been a wonderful evening, Kate. You can't imagine what a clever boy he's been. How was your concert?'

'Fine. Von K. and the Vienna Philharmonic. Bruckner does go on a bit, though, doesn't he?'

'An acquired taste. I have to admit he hasn't got to me yet. Look, I just have to talk . . .'

'Of course. Talk away.'

'Stop me if you're embarrassed, or—'

'Jane, for the love of Mike please stop, or I'll be out of bed and driving to Bayreuth tonight!'

'Oh, Kate, you were asleep.'

'No. And, in case you're wondering, there's no one else here. So press on.'

'Kate, you know him better than anyone.'

'No. I've seen very little of him, darling. If anyone knows him it's you.'

'Kate, I wonder.'

'But you two are obviously in love, Jane. One only has to see you together . . .'

'God, is it so obvious?'

'Daylight, my dear. Gaga, both of you.'

'Oh dear.'

Kate chuckled. 'Anyone who's been there can see it. We're all envious as hell.'

'Such problems, though.'

'Of course. What one really wants in a man, even in a very exciting man, is a Rolls-Royce. You've got a Le Mans Jaguar. Difficult, I should think.'

'You can't imagine.'

'I think I can. But from where I'm sitting it sounds like fun.'

'Oh, it is. In a way. He's such a talent.'

'I *think* you mean—'

'I meant the musical talent. With the other thing I don't have so much experience . . .'

'Ah.' Kate was silent for a space. 'That can be a problem, can't it? You wonder whether he's so special, or whether it's just that he's the only one . . .?'

'Sometimes. Kate, does that sound awfully ungrateful?'

'No. Simply Jane-practical. You don't forgive mistakes, Jane, do you? Especially your own.'

'Dear God, am I so hard?'

'On yourself, very hard indeed. If you were as hard on everyone you'd have given David up long ago.'

'Perhaps I should?'

'Don't ask me the big one, Jane. Not fair.'

'But I want him, you see.'

'Well, I must say you seem to have him, darling.'

'All of him, I mean.'

Kate was silent, thinking.

'Still there, Kate?' Jane asked, thinking she'd lost her.

'Still here. Look, I'm not sure we ever get *all* of them. Do they get all of us, d'you think? Can one own a person?'

'But he's got all of me. It's not fair. Every time I

227

try to retrieve part of me he gets it back with such ease.'

'The right man can cure practically anything in bed. It's important, Jane, believe me.'

'To everyone?'

Kate laughed. 'You're not a biological freak, Jane, just lucky. No hangups, apparently.'

'Masses, once. He's killed them off.'

'Sounds lovely.'

'That's the thing. It's so important. To us both, I mean. How can a woman think straight?'

'With her knickers off? She can't, darling. But we mustn't let on. If they all knew that they'd work much harder at it. Mustn't give the chaps all the advantages.'

'But it must wear off, surely?'

'Is it? Wearing off, I mean?'

'How can it? We're not together enough. He said once that in his marriage every time he came home was a honeymoon, he was there so little. Isn't it the same now, with us?'

'Is it?' Kate smiled to herself, playing the psychiatrist's unfair trick, asking questions, never giving an answer. 'Is that how it feels?'

'Well, not exactly, because when we are together he's always working and I'm as caught up in that as he is. More, I sometimes think. But when the door's closed . . .'

'Good, huh?'

Jane sighed. 'Unbelievable. To answer your question, no, it seems not to wear off.'

'So what are you worrying about? He loves you, we can all see that. Any advance on the present bliss can only come with time. There are no cast-iron guarantees, you know.'

'That's his line. A gamble, he says. No certainty of winning.'

228

'He seems determined not to encourage you, I must say.'

'He is. Doesn't he want me?'

'Yes. He wants you, and he wants you to be happy. But he's not going to kid you, Jane. And whatever happens will be your decision.'

'Is that fair?'

'Does fair matter? It's inevitable, that's the point. Some women a man can tell what to do. Not you. And there's the other thing, that he can't be sure either, and he won't be completely responsible for a mistake. If mistake it is.'

'Damn him, he can do without *anybody*. I think he could go on for ever, just making love to the orchestra.'

'More than anybody he needs the right woman. He knows that.'

'Do you think he makes love to me as a relaxation, to get himself a better night's sleep, and a better concert tomorrow?'

'No. That may be the reason he makes love to other women. That and the physical pleasure of it, the endless variety of experience which seems to come to him, the sheer *fun*. But surely he makes love to you because he loves you. *As well* as all the other reasons.'

'Sure?'

'Am I sure he loves you? Yes, I am.'

'I don't understand any of this.'

'That there may be other reasons for going to bed together? No, of course you don't. But you must try, I think. There are lots of aspects to sex. For some people it's never exclusive.'

'But mine must be, Kate. It really *must*.'

'Sure?'

'Oh yes. I half-tried. I couldn't go through with it.'

'Does he know? Have you told him?'

'Nearly, but no, not yet. I must, mustn't I?'

'Why?'

'Only fair.'

'Fair? What's fair about worrying him? And what's clever about putting your relationship at risk?'

'You think I mustn't tell him?'

'I know you'd better think twice about it, Jane. It might be impossible for him to take. Especially if you're as important to him as you wish to be. And you are, I really believe that.'

'And if I'm not? Then at least I'd know, wouldn't I?'

'You'd give up what you have, just to know?'

'Oh, Kate, I don't know, really . . .'

'Just think again. Do what you will. It's your life, Jane. But don't do it in a hurry or because it's on your conscience. Your conscience is there to worry *you*. No one else.' Kate waited, but there was no response, no decision. Her voice lightened. 'Anyway, you can't give yourself lightly. That you've found out.'

'No, I can't, and I'm glad.'

'And you feel entitled to expect the same . . .'

'Yes, of course.'

'Very conventional.'

'Yes. That's what I am, conventional.'

'Pooh! Jane, your whole situation is as unconventional as can be. Conventional girls lose it at school and have three or four chaps before getting married and getting kids. Then if they're lucky they get the conventional, twice-a-week reminders of how they got into this thing. If they're unlucky or careless they lose their men, more or less, sooner or later, one way or another. None of that will do for you.'

'But, Kate, I want kids. Or at least a child.'

A long silence, then: 'Don't we all? No, I suppose some don't. I know I did. I wish I'd been given one. God knows . . .'

'Well then?'

'It's easy for you. No trouble, except the business inconvenience. People will say unpleasant things, but so what? You won't be listening. So long as you're sure you can cope, perhaps without a father for the child, get on with it.'

'Yes, I've warned him that's what I intend to do. With him if he's ready for it, otherwise . . .'

Kate was shaken. 'My God! How did he take that?'

'I don't really know. He has a wonderful way of burying reactions. Perhaps he could cope with it.'

'Careful, Jane. You may be facing more choices than you think. You might have his child and keep David, or you might have someone else's child and lose him, or then again you might have David's child and still lose him.'

'You think that's the way to lose him?'

'Might be. Remember, the child may become a substitute for him. They often are. Marriages have crashed that way. Irregular relationships must be even more vulnerable, surely?'

'Not sure.'

'Well, he does seem to have written off his marriage easily. But one can't be sure how he really feels about even that. Anyway, you think you're more important than Julie.'

'Yes, I am. I think.'

'Don't be sure. Jane, what do you really want of David?'

'I want him to settle for me. Give me a family, a home with him, a life like any other woman. And, of course, I want him to become the very best at his job. But that's not a problem. He'll do that anyway.'

'And by settle you mean no other women, ever?'

'Yes. That's what I want.'

'Well, darling, you want a hell of a lot. One day, in a more liberated or less private world people will get round to an honest study of marital behaviour, and there'll be shocks for both sexes. What you *can* achieve is an honest relationship, where you know the man and his failings and your own capacity to cope with them.'

'And that's the best I can hope for?'

'Some people would say it was rather a lot.'

'My parents had a lot more.'

'Don't idealize. Every marriage has problems.'

Jane was very tired now. 'Kate, you are altogether lovely and so kind. Such a help.'

'I'll be there the day after tomorrow. Will I see you?'

'Probably not. I must catch the evening boat. Look after the boy wonder, will you?'

'Yes, of course. Go to sleep now. Big day tomorrow. Wish him luck for me?'

'Can't. We haven't spoken, you and I.'

'I see. Well, I'll be thinking.'

'Night, Kate. And thank you . . .'

14

She woke to bright sunlight, voices in the yard below, goodbyes and hellos, a lorry driving by. What time? Nearly ten. She smiled to think he'd slept so long. What an evening that had been. She threw on a housecoat, tied up her hair and went to wake him.

He was dressed, sitting on his balcony, drinking coffee, a score open on his knee. He waved at the steaming percolator. 'Help yourself. Thought you'd deserted me.'

She poured, sipped appreciatively.

'I looked in,' he told her, 'but you were dead to the world.'

His smile was one of the nicest things about him, she thought. In her world so many smiles stopped short of the eyes. 'There was a time when that wouldn't have stopped you,' she reminded him.

'Yes. I remember.' He closed the big book, tapped it affectionately. 'But you had serious competition this morning.'

'Big day today.'

'Mmmm. Biggest for a long time.'

She toasted him in coffee. 'To even bigger ones, maestro. Now, breakfast is over. What happens this morning? It's a lovely day. D'you feel like walking?'

He looked at his watch. 'Yes. Not far, though. To the church, perhaps?'

Five minutes for Jane to dress and they were away up the hill. It was a slow walk and a quiet one, signs that the work of the day had already taken him over. A lucky man, she knew, to have this gift of concentrating the stress out of his way. So many artists would be unbearable now, on edge.

'That "maestro" of yours,' he mused at length. 'Very suspect. I think British orchestras only use it when they can't remember the conductor's name.'

'Different here?'

'Here they never forget names.'

'But how they adore titles! My father's chief was *Herr Generalmusikdirektor* to everyone.'

'And his wife *Frau Generalmusikdirektor*, no doubt. Incredible, isn't it? In London it's always first names, even if you are Music Director at the opera and a knight of the realm to boot.'

'One day, perhaps . . .' she said.

'Ah. Want me safely under lock and key, do you? Where you can keep an eye on me?'

'Oh,' she waved a dismissive hand, 'there'd be no keeping you in order, I fancy. One could try keeping you in a state of total exhaustion but that wouldn't be too easy either.'

He considered this option with what appeared to be complete seriousness. 'Sounds attractive,' he said at length, 'but would it be good for the job, d'you think? A man has to stand up to conduct. There are limits.'

'So. That's why—'

'Why I didn't disturb you? No. I hadn't the heart. You seemed to need the extra three hours.'

'Three hours? You've been up since *seven*?'

'I had to get one opera out and the other one in.'

'I hope you've made it?'

'I hope so too. We'll see, won't we?'

The church was small but beautiful, with woodcarving older than the building itself, a fine screen and brightly shining plate. She was at home in church, where he was a mere admirer of lovely things, taken a little aback when, in the little white porch, she covered her head, and genuflected on entering. It sobered him a little, reminded him of unresolved differences.

★ ★ ★

Out again in the warm sunshine a faded signpost suggested a way home across the fields. Her eyes enquired, his nod assented. Soon the path entered a wood, dapple-lit by the high sun. The church clock chimed. 'Eleven' she said. 'What time's lunch?'

'Twelve fifteen. An omelette, salad, some fresh fruit, and a small glass of wine for me. Whatever you wish for yourself.'

'I see,' she said. 'I'll settle for your sort of lunch. Then what?'

'Shower, sleep until three. We'll leave at three fifteen. Time for the usual politeness. Four o'clock we play.'

They'd come to a space, with a comfortable-looking tree. 'Would a five-minute sit ruin that precise schedule?' she asked.

The sun was overhead, the sky cloudless, the shade welcome. They sat propped against the tall fir, his arm around her, her head on his shoulder. There was silence but for the slight breeze at the very top of the trees, a buzzing insect, and a bird.

'The woodbird,' she said.

He shook his head. 'Wrong opera. I don't get a *Ring* until I'm sixty, remember?'

'Never mind the Ring. Listen to the bird.'

They listened. 'No use' he said. 'To understand the woodbird you have to kill the dragon.'

'Problem. First find your dragon, Siegfried.'

'It's done by blowing one's horn, I gather.'

'No horn handy?'

'No. And no horn player either.'

'Then you'll never know, will you?'

'What won't I know?'

'What the woodbird is trying to tell you. Where Brunhilde is, on the fiery rock.'

'I think on the whole she'd be a bit much for me.'

'Ordinary mortals easier to cope with?'

'Much.'

'That's a relief anyway. Bayreuth is full of Brunhildes, and I'm leaving tomorrow.'

'But I'm to be looked after, meantime.'

'Kate as Sieglinde' Jane suggested.

'No. Sieglinde died when Siegfried was born. Gutrune perhaps.'

Jane frowned. 'I don't much care for Gutrune. Decadent creature. Always suspect her of having it away with her awful brother.' She was warmed by the earth, the warm air, and his closeness. She snuggled a little closer. 'Darling, do you think you could leave Wagner for a mo?'

He turned to look at her as she laid her dark glasses carefully on the grass. 'Been a long time, has it?'

She made a face. 'Don't be smug. Alright, irresistible, it's been *too* long. Just kiss me, will you?'

It was a long kiss, longer than he'd intended. 'Mmmm. Again, if you like?' She was smiling, sensing he was hooked.

'Darling, we're out of doors, in broad daylight. . . .'

'Mmmm. . . . think you're too old for this sort of thing, do you? Come on; we won't frighten the birds.'

The nearest human being was driving a tractor, so far below them that the noise was hardly audible. Oh well, in for a penny . . . by the time the second kiss ended they were horizontal, one of her legs between his, her need becoming evident.

'Darling' he said 'we have this hotel, quite close . . .'

'No.' Her mouth was close to his ear. 'Here, now.' She took his hand and placed it on her zipper. It slid down almost of itself. He lay back on the green, she half over him, her arm under his head, her mouth on his, giving a great sigh as his palm covered her. Long silent minutes, the trees whispering, only the birds watching.

Slowly she came to, braced herself on her elbows above him.

'Lovely, lovely' she said. 'D'you know, I thought I'd get used to this? But no . . .'

'In that case you're lucky.' He drew down her head for a reassuring peck.

'I've heard that before. But it seems I get luckier.'

'It may even be true, then. Look, we have ten minutes before the omelette. Punctuality, politeness of princes, not to mention conductors.'

'And their agents?'

'And their agents.' He got up, offered her a hand. She straightened her skirt, brushed the dry grass from her clothes. 'Wait a mo, David.' She was picking bits from his shirt. 'Wouldn't do to shock Mrs Blink.'

* * *

'No coffee?' Jane asked after lunch.

'No. Keeps me awake. I must sleep now. What will you do for two hours?'

'Business.' It amused her always, his complete lack of awareness of her other preoccupations, the affairs of other artists.

'Oh. We'll go up then.'

While he showered she closed balcony doors to keep out the village sounds, drew the blinds, making a comfortable dark. Towelled dry, he settled into the feathers. She was halfway to the door when he spoke. 'Jane?'

She turned, stood by the bed.

'Jane, I love you very much, do you know?'

237

Accustomed to the flip and undemonstrative David, she was taken aback, the tears starting to her eyes.

'Yes, I do know.'

* * *

She was still working when he appeared, spruce and relaxed, ready for work. No need to dress in this theatre, the only one in the world which concealed the orchestra completely. She remembered Toscanini's famous description of Bayreuth: six weeks without a bowtie. There'd be a dinner suit to throw half-on for the third act, donning the jacket and tie for his curtain. Meanwhile sports clothes would do. Jane had changed already into a cocktail dress, smart but relaxed enough for this operatic marathon. She put down her telephone, glanced at her watch. 'Tea?'

He shook his head. 'There'll be a cup waiting. Let's go, shall we?' She put on her light coat. He picked up his own, a precaution against the cool of the night into which they'd emerge, and they made their way to the car.

She drove quietly, matching his mood. The whole day had been paced, everything saved for the hours to come. He was physically relaxed, mentally concentrated, gathering forces, a state of mind she could feel and marvel at. It was the secret, of course, the reason for the strength of his work, the mental approach which produced the very best at exactly the right time. No words now. No need.

The great redbrick building was buzzing with a kaleidoscope of people, the souvenir postcard-shop doing a roaring trade, the policemen shepherding the endless queue of cars to the park on the high field. On the pavement the hopeful ticketless waved their notices of 'Suche Karte' as each car stopped to put down smartly dressed ladies. Through the stage door then, into orderly and purposeful quiet, up the stair to the peace of the greenroom.

Tea arrived as they did; Earl Grey in bone china, two cups, milk and lump sugar. Bayreuth did everything well, down to the sponge cake. She poured while he sat to read the telegrams and cards wishing him well, the encouraging messages taped to the champagne bottles on the sideboard. He passed her two cards with a smile. One from John and Mary reminding him to convert all the tries. One from the orchestra in Wales, wishing he was there or, better still, that they were here. He put down his cup. Standing, he took her hands in his, serious now. 'Well, Jane, you made it. Congratulations.'

She was moved. 'We made it together, David.'

'No. I just conduct. Lots do. But GG would have been surprised, wouldn't he?'

She walked to the window, looked out over the small paved courtyard, bounded by its green hedge, to the milling people beyond. 'Yes, he would.' The idea of a Brit in this holy of German holies would have been beyond her father's belief.

'The next bit is my bit,' he said.

'Yes. I'll go down, shall I?'

'Might be as well. You know the way? Shall I ask them to put you through the pass-door?'

'No. I'll go round and in with the rest.'

'Sure?'

'Yes. One should. I'm just audience now.'

She turned at the door. He went to her, hugged her tight. 'Thanks for everything, Jane.'

Down and into the milling crowd then. Curious, she thought, that despite an orchestra of a hundred, a huge cast of singers and a vast chorus, one man would be quite alone.

* * *

'Oh, *what* a clever man!' They were alone at last, free of the theatre, the delighted cast, the thronging, clamouring audience, the superlatives of the supper table, just Jane and David to celebrate the triumph of the evening and their delight in each other. The champagne cork popped. She raised her glass. 'To you, David.' Her eyes were shining bright, her face flushed, proud.

'To us,' he suggested. They drank deep. He poured again. 'Now to Richard Wagner?'

'All right. I'll drink to the old rogue,' said she. 'And one more toast. Defeat to the traitor!' They laughed again at their private joke.

'Darling,' she said, flinging herself on the bed, pumps flying into a corner, 'come and kiss me. You may save a life.'

'Once,' he said. 'Only once. So much to talk about . . .'

It wouldn't do for her. 'Nonsense. Love first, talk afterwards. You're needed, love, urgently.'

He sighed. 'Oh dear, these schoolgirls with their appetites . . .' He joined her on the bed, kicking off his shoes, and for a space they were lost to the world.

Eventually the room stopped spinning. 'Well,' David said, amused, 'it's a very long time since I made love with my pants on.'

She giggled. 'Likewise.'

'Yours seemed to have been designed for the purpose,' he observed. 'Mine were definitely not.'

'Mine were not actually *designed* for it, I think,' she told him, 'but selected, I admit, just in case . . .'

'Of an attack in the greenroom?'

'One hoped, love. But here they don't give one time, do they? I must do something about it, contractually.'

He laughed. 'Can you, do you think?'

'It's a must. Absolutely. It was difficult enough keeping my hands off you this evening. After *Tristan* it would be quite impossible. I'll have a clause reserving the greenroom for thirty minutes after every performance. Now, I wonder whether you can perform one more miracle this evening?'

'We try to please,' he said.

'Mmm . . . we succeed, what's more. But can you undress without disturbing that wonderful thing?'

'Unlikely, I fancy.'

'It's just that it shows very little sign of decline, and it is so very welcome where it is.' Provoked, he kissed her again, began to move gently. Hers was a reluctant protest.

'Mmmm . . . darling, quick was lovely and necessary but slow needs . . .'

So he lifted himself, enjoying her unwilling release, kissed her again, and sat up. He looked at her, she at him, smiling. 'Lovely, lovely man.'

'You said that before, somewhere.' He was discarding clothes. She was slower, stretching catlike.

'Lots of times,' she said. 'And you're getting lovelier, I do believe.'

'No regrets about the great flautist then?'

She turned, dress in hand, standing in bra and pants, surprised. 'Good God, no. Do you really think—'

'No, I don't.' He lay propped on an elbow to watch her. 'Not the same Jane as that one.' Not the Jane of two years ago even, he added to himself.

'Improved, have I?'

'Impossible.'

'Flattery will get you everywhere, but what are you talking about?'

'Different. My Jane now.'

She'd rid herself of her underthings. Her bush, at his eye-level sparkled in the soft light. He reached for

241

her. She evaded him with a small movement. 'No. Not yet, please. I'm not a bit sleepy.'

'I thought you had something else in mind.'

'Indeed, indeed, but you were right – there are so many things to talk about, and in the morning . . .'

Yes, in the morning she'd be gone. He got up, collected a wrap. She was at the balcony door. He put out the lamp, realizing that she'd be silhouetted for anyone outside. 'Warm,' she said. 'Come outside?'

He gave her his robe, warmer than hers, and they went out into the warm summer dark, shielded by the deep wooden rail from eyes below. It was very quiet. Not a place for noisy night-birds, Bayreuth, and here they were miles out of the town, its lights a faint rosy glow in the distance.

She held his hand, between wicker armchairs. 'Wonderful music, David.'

'Yes, it is.'

'Always knew it was. But tonight, I can't tell you . . .'

'You cried, of course?'

'How did you know?'

'At the chorale? Everyone does. Everyone of sensibility. Even hard cases, people who've been everywhere and heard everything. Wonderful sound apart, it's the truth of the piece, I think. The truth of that moment. The Masters with their singing rules, the knight with his problem, the ladies with their needs, they're a microcosm of their society, the town locked inside its gates, inside its ideas. That chorus, with its big simple tune, reaches out to bigger problems, *everyone's* problems. We're all bound by rules, still kicking against them, still failing, still leaning for support on one another. We identify with it, you see. For two minutes the audience is in the opera. When we cry, it's for ourselves.'

She was silent for a time, gathering thoughts. Then: 'But that awful man never recognized any sort of common humanity. Never in his selfish life. He had no loyalty to anyone or anything but his own talent.'

David shook his head. 'Too hard, Jane, too hard. He was loyal to his country, to Germany. He suffered for it all his life, chased out of Dresden after helping to stir up that little revolution. He was a German when most Germans were Bavarians, or Prussians, or Württembergers, long before the idea was fashionable. When it was treasonable, even.'

'But he hated my father's people.' Her voice dropped. '*My* people.'

'Some of them gave him a bad time. You mustn't blame him for the doings of men who came fifty years later. Hitler enjoying *Meistersinger* doesn't make Wagner a criminal. And he gave his last work, the one he loved best, to a Jew to conduct, here in Bayreuth.'

'So I'm all wrong about him?'

'Who knows, really? Look, let Wagner stand or fall *by the work*. It's given us all a new dimension in which to live.'

'I hope you're right, David.'

'Because you can't resist him either?'

'No, I can't. Not tonight anyway. And some of that is your doing. You're altogether *too* good at this.' She got up, looked away over the dark country to the distant lights. 'I hope you're right,' she said.

He stood behind her. She leaned. He kissed the top of her head, then her ear, then her cheek as she turned a little. 'I just think the man's had a hard time from the thinkers, Jane. I'm a musician and I'm on his side. I'm sorry for his mistakes, but we all make them.'

'You've thought, though.'

'Yes. Of course. And I feel for you and your problem with him. You'll never lose it.'

'Sure?'

'Absolutely, yes. You envy my roots, my sense of belonging.'

'Of course I do.'

'But your roots are as strong, darling. It created you. It feeds you, sustains you, as my roots feed me. You mustn't lose it, even if you could. You can't anyway. When you heard Sachs's monologue, all that about holy German art and the German people, you felt threatened?'

'Didn't you? I hoped you'd feel it, like me. Surely everyone must who isn't German?'

'Yes. In a way. But it was a German speaking, a German trying to put Germany together, not a man trying to murder the rest of us.'

She turned in his arms, held him close, her mind coming to terms with his words, his ideas, his picture of her. 'You are such a nice man,' she said. 'I once hoped I'd be able to get over you. Now I know that I won't, that I can't, that I won't even try.'

Commitment, then. He was moved, moved but unsure of his right response. She saw it.

'Darling,' she said, 'once you told me it all took time. I was in such a hurry, then. Take all the time you need. I'll be here.'

15

'You must have started very early,' said Jane. 'It was so good of you.' They sat on the terrace of the Cathedral at Bamberg, looking down over the town, watching the busy boats on the river, the old bridge with its Town Hall placed halfway across.

Kate smiled over her coffee cup. 'Not a bit. It *is* a long way, of course, but when I've had a long way to go I prefer to drive early.'

'Lovely little thing, your MG,' smiled Jane. 'It has style. Very British. Makes one quite envious, really.'

'Only in England, believe me,' said her friend. 'Here one's in constant fear of getting run over by something bigger going at twice the speed. But it's a delight to drive, and there's a wonderful impression of speed even at seventy. Now come on; tell me how it's been.'

'Well, you know he took over *Lohengrin*?'

'We heard. News travels fast in certain circles, I needn't tell you. And the *Meistersinger* seems to have been the event of the year.'

'Kate, it was such an evening. I was at the pit door when the orchestra came out. Their faces! Smiles everywhere!'

'Yes. It's the acid test,' Kate agreed. 'The orchestra is never wrong about a conductor. Now they'll want him back, sure as eggs are eggs.'

'That we know already. There's to be a *Tristan* quite soon.'

Kate put down her cup, clapped her hands. *Tristan*! My God, what a thing!' Then, part of her enthusiasm evaporating, she added, 'But it means another lost summer for our people. Oh dear. Jane, he means so much to them. It's all gone so well.'

'Not to worry. First thing, when I get home, is to rearrange that year. Something will have to go, but not that.'

Kate sighed with relief.

'Don't worry. He gets very Welsh every year in the spring. Can't wait for his walks on the beach. I sometimes wonder if he'd disturb his Cardiff time even for the Berlin Philharmonic. I get jealous sometimes.'

'Jealous? Of Wales, or of the folks?'

'No. Of him, simply. He has this tremendous feeling for his home. Must be a wonderful thing.'

'Yes. I lost mine, with Jack. Life seemed to stop, you know? For a long time. When it began again I was a different person. Quite alone. It was a while before I could be with anyone or anything. I was afraid of losing it all again. I didn't allow anything to grow, just in case.'

'You had Molly.'

'No. Molly went to live close to the hospital. They still do, with the boys, in their little bungalow. He wasn't expected to live so long. She keeps him alive by sheer determination, I sometimes think. And the boys are lovely kids.'

'Not easy, nursing him and bringing up twins. She must be quite a character.'

'She is, believe me. Bright as a button, never the slightest sign of self-pity. And she's such a tiny thing. Still looks like a schoolgirl, in the right clothes.'

'She must love him very much.'

'It's mutual. They dote. But it's a hard life, Jane. I know she sometimes wonders which of us is the better off. But the boys make it worth while, she says. And of course he adores her. No woman was ever so much loved. Such a wonderful man; generous and forgiving, you know . . . But how is it with you two?'

Jane took in a huge breath and let it out through pursed lips in a comic gesture of despair. 'Kate, how does a woman cope with such a man?'

'Ah, bad as that, is it. Impossible to live with, unthinkable to be without? That one?'

'That's the one. The very man. I was too carefully brought up, Kate. Sometimes I wish I'd had ten before him so that I could put him into some sort of perspective. He's exactly my man, except he has the morals of a sheik. I don't know how to cope with that.'

'Most of us would say hooray, throw the bonnet and the knickers over the windmill, enjoy him for as long as it lasts. Look, he's exactly your kind of man: a virtuoso conductor, good in bed – I assume he really *is* good in bed? – and gaga about you. Marry the man and have done with it. What can you lose?'

'I don't know. Is it that simple?'

'Well, what *can* you lose? It's a serious question, Jane. You're worried about the possibility of losing something or other. I don't know what, but something. Think about it.'

Jane thought. This was not the time for an argument about the morality of the second marriage, and Kate would think it a silly one anyway. What was it she might lose? 'I don't know, really.'

'It's not for me to tell you, Jane. You have to think it through.'

Jane thought aloud. 'My freedom, anyway.'

'Freedom for what? To sleep around? But you never did anyway. Sounds like *luurve* to me.' Kate shook her head sadly and they both laughed. 'What have you lost so far, Jane?'

'Well,' said Jane 'I've lost my self-control, that's for sure.'

'Aha! Now we're getting there. Just how do you mean that?'

Jane considered. 'In lots of ways. I can't get enough of him, physically, for a start.'

'Well, he'll enjoy that, surely?'

'Yes.'

'So?'

'You're right, Kate. It *is* a matter of control lost. I don't control my life now. Before David, to leave the office for anything but business was unthinkable. Now I cut and run whenever he's about.'

'Bad, huh?' Kate was amused.

'Yes. GG would have hated it.'

'Sure?'

'Oh yes. He put the firm before everything.'

'Before your mother?'

'Mother was different. She was ill, she needed him. He worked all night to spend the day with her. They had so little time. There's no comparison, Kate.'

'Well, perhaps. But what harm is this doing? Business going to the dogs, is it?'

No, Jane admitted to herself; the job was doing splendidly. Her people were growing every day in skills and responsibilities, less and less dependent on her.

'Come on, Jane,' pressed her friend, 'surely it's a good thing to let the reins hang loose now and again if you have the right folks around you? And you have, of course. We all know that.'

'Well, in a way. The thing is so much bigger now. GG did it all with one good secretary. Now it's much more complicated. Some of our artists need a person to themselves, almost.'

'Like David.'

'Yes, like David.'

'Will you give him to someone?'

Jane was surprised. 'David? How could I?'

'Easily, if you wished it. You don't have to book his dates because you sleep with him, Jane.'

'But he's mine, Kate. Always was, from day one.

248

GG wouldn't touch him, didn't want him. If he comes, he said, he'll be your problem, Jane, not mine.'

'I know the story. But are you sure you know why?'

'Yes. GG thought he was trouble, one way or another. Talented, but trouble.'

'Woman trouble? Lots of men are trouble in that way. Especially in this business. There's a lot of stress about. One way or another they have to blow. Sex is among the less damaging explosions. If you managed a pop group you'd know.'

'I do know. And David's stress is my stress, when I'm with him.'

'Mmm. And the explosion too, of course.'

'Yes.'

'If GG was so sure David was bad news, why did he take him on?'

'Oh, bad news but good business. He couldn't resist real talent, that's a fact. Anyway, I bullied him.'

'All right. But why give him to you to manage? If he thought the man was trouble, I mean?'

'To teach me a lesson, I sometimes think. So that I would really see David, as he was. So that there would be no illusions. I'd learn the worst.'

'Perhaps. Well, have you learned?'

'Kate, you think GG intended all this? You think he *wanted* David for me?'

'Don't ask me. Ask yourself.'

'I can't believe it, Kate. My father really liked Julie. He'd never have done anything to hurt her.'

'No. And he knew you wouldn't, either. That knowledge would make the thing possible. Perhaps he knew you would wait. Some things are very easily predictable, you see. David would never have left Julie, but her leaving *him* was always on the cards. Your leaving him is on the cards too, isn't it?'

Jane was startled. 'Leave him? How? What for?'

'For the same reason Julie did. Because you want a

life outside the job. You want kids, and a man to come home to. Look, as you describe him he's got two talents, music and the other thing.' She shook her head. 'Pretty boring in the end.'

'Kate, I really believe he loves me.'

'I told you already. If that's enough for you, it's knickers-over-the-windmill time. But you've still got yours on, because you're not sure it *is* enough, are you?' She looked at Jane, a picture of confusion, and smiled. 'Come on. It's not so bad, love. You're having a wonderful time. Stay with it.'

'I could lose him.'

Kate was moved by the dejection in her voice. Such a clever girl, this, and such a problem she had. How to give the right advice? Dare she give any advice at all?

'You can't keep him locked up. You can't be with him all the time. And you can't get closer to him than the thing which finally counts to him, his music. You will always be number two, in that sense.'

'Always?'

'Yes, always. It's what made him, you see. Without it he'd be digging coal. Without it he wouldn't have a personality at all, not one that any of us would recognize, even himself. Without it even *you* wouldn't know him. You're lucky, being in it with him; you can share it at least, but you can't take its place. And the risks come with it. Jane, you know all this. I don't have to tell you.'

'I think what you are telling me is that I can have him on the terms Julie had him, no more.'

Kate raised a warning finger. 'Careful. I don't *know* that. It seems to be true, doesn't it? But it only holds good if he's learned nothing, or if he wants no more than that.'

'Kate . . . can I ask? He'll talk to you, won't he?'

'I don't know. If he does I'll listen, of course. Look,

one thing: you have to understand how it is with men, the sex problem. They don't have our hangup, the chastity bit, you know?'

Jane sighed. 'Lucky they.'

'Ah. You can see that, can you? Good. It's bred into us. Not into them. Mothers teach it, but not to boys.'

'Not fair.'

'So? When was life ever fair? What matters is to face facts, not to fight lost battles. Look, think about it in the most basic terms. We wonder, don't we, just what they've done to us, what they've left behind? Our conditioning makes us feel soiled, in a way. But they take themselves off, go for a shower, and feel clean. And clever, of course. It's part of the picture, the reason they can and do, while we can't and shouldn't. A reason why they feel they can detach themselves when it's convenient.'

'And that's all it means to them?'

'Sometimes, but not always. Julie meant more than that to David, and she knew it. You know you mean more than that too, don't you?'

'I just hope.'

'Bunkum. You *know*, Jane.'

'I do?'

'Yes. You couldn't do it otherwise. Ask yourself why he's still the only one. He's not the only wildly attractive man who's tried, is he?'

'No. It's curious. Before David they kept their distance. Now I'm pursued.'

'Of course. They knew it was useless, once. Now they smell the success, David's success. Your success too. I can see it, of course. But it never occurs to you to give, does it?'

'No. Never.'

'Why, tell me?'

'What for? It would be just a leg-over. Just sex. Just well . . .'

251

Kate smiled at her fighting shy of the word she needed. 'Ugly word, isn't it? Might be nice though?'

Jane shrugged. 'Still, just sex.'

'And with David there's something else?'

'Yes, there is.'

Kate looked at her in silence for a while. Then: 'You'll have to work the rest out for yourself, I think. That's enough of the agony aunt, except to ask whether you think *he* gives it to anyone else.'

'Or if it's just a leg-over? With the others?'

'And, if that's what it is, whether you can live with it, Jane. That's your problem.'

'Tell me . . . could *you* live with it?'

Kate waved a dismissive hand. 'Irrelevant. I'm not hooked on the man. You are. Anyway, I didn't have your upbringing. Very liberated lady, my mother. I was put into the picture very early.'

'Ah. Bike-shed?'

Kate laughed. 'No. Bedroom, parents out.'

'Convenient.'

'No. Thoughtful, rather. They liked him, thought it was time. I was seventeen. I was looked after, made safe. He was surprised, thought he'd got lucky, suddenly.' She smiled, remembering. 'Not a virgin, thankfully. But a very happy boy by the end of the evening.' Kate was silent for a moment, miles away. 'My goodness, what fun it all was. But this I can tell you: Jack was like no one else, before or since. So I know how the real thing feels, and it really is different from an ordinary lump between the legs, however effective that's been from time to time.'

'I believe you. Yes, I do.'

'Good. So you needn't prove it for yourself.'

'I nearly did, you see. I *tried* Kate.'

'Leave some poor chap without a solution, did you?'

'Not a poor chap at all, a very rich and talented one, and nice with it.'

'I'm surprised, I must say. Past a certain point it's not that easy to escape, I find.'

Jane smiled. 'Well, I didn't leave him entirely without a solution.'

'Escaped while he was recovering from his surprise, did you?'

'From his surprise among other things . . .'

They laughed, two girls together.

* * *

There'd been something left unsaid, Jane knew. Something, a puzzle unsolved, a loose end. She was sitting, thoughtful, in the first-class lounge of the ferry, its bow rising to meet the channel swell when the words came back to her. 'Such a wonderful man. Generous, *forgiving* . . .' What had Molly's husband to forgive, for heaven's sake, with a safe home, a secure future with the best possible care, a wife and kids who adored him? Would he forgive the enemy who'd crippled him? No. For him there'd be nothing to forgive. So, what, whom had he forgiven? Molly, the boys . . .

And suddenly the solution, the only possible solution. *He'd forgiven Molly for the boys.* Not adopted, as she'd assumed, not Jack's, as people must still think, but David's.

16

Her knock was tentative. The maid coming to turn down the bed, he thought. 'Come,' David said, not looking up from his book as the door opened and closed.

'Well,' said the voice 'there's enthusiasm if you like!'

He was up and hugging her. 'Kate!' How are you? How did you come? What were you doing in Salzburg . . .'

'Hey, hey, one at a time, young man. Let me find my breath!'

He put her down reluctantly. 'But why didn't they tell me you were here? The bottle's been on ice for hours.'

'Oh, an old lady like me needs time to make herself presentable, you see. Well, will I do?'

He stood back, holding her hands. 'Do? You'll do beautifully. You don't look a day older than . . .'

She laughed. 'Oh, such lovely lies! I can see why you are such a success with the ladies. Still,' she walked to the dressing mirror and surveyed the slim blonde there displayed with a certain confidence, 'I think I wear decently. It's just that it takes rather longer these days.'

He was opening champagne. 'Thirsty, Kate?'

She laughed. 'I'm not sure that fizz ever cured a thirst, but by all means let's celebrate.'

'What shall we celebrate?'

'Well, there's your *Meistersinger* triumph, your *Lohengrin* miracle, or the fact that my car survived the trip from Salzburg without getting run over by a Merc?'

He raised his glass. 'To the MG car company. I assume you still drive one?'

'What else? Newer one, though. Old faithful's getting a bit arthritic. This seemed the right time to spend on another.'

'Rich, are we? Surely you haven't parted with that lovely old thing?'

'No. It was Jack's car. But yes, I'm a little richer. My father died. There was a little money . . .'

'Oh, love, I'm so sorry.'

'Thank you. But it was expected. One gets used to the idea. It's not such a shock then.'

'I suppose not. It was a shock for me; but I was very young when Mother went, and hardly grown when Dada . . .'

'Yes, I know.'

Away with the war, then; it had left such holes in both their lives.

'So, tell me about Salzburg. Still jumping with Paris models and famous faces?'

'Yes. Isn't it terrifying? I'd no idea. I had to go out and splurge on clothes just to keep my end up. It's not easy in that company.'

'Cheaper for men, thankfully. We're allowed to wear the same suit twice, even at Salzburg. But what have you been doing there? I know, you've got a secret thing going with . . .'

'Alas. If only! You remember Joan Black?'

'Hard to forget. Wonderful voice, best thing to come out of the Valley since, well, since . . .'

'Since young Adams?'

He chuckled. 'Flattery will get you everywhere, too. Well, what about the splendid Miss Black?'

'Joan's been a friend since she was a student. I used to play for her lessons. Now I do her secretarial bits and pieces. She's Queen of the Night this year. We thought it would be fun to drive to Salzburg and motor round the Tyrol between operas.'

'Wonderful. Did you bring her with you?'

'Ah. No. She's rather occupied at the moment.'

'Not every day, surely? Only two performances each week?'

'Other preoccupations between performances. Look, you know Ardiles?'

'Oh. Jane's wonderful Argentine. It's his perform-ance of course.' Realization of what was coming dawned. His face broke into the broadest of smiles.

She sighed. 'He has this villa on top of a mountain. They never come down except for performances.'

So, the Queen of the Night, literally! 'So you've seen nothing of the Tyrol, after all? A pity. It's lovely country.'

'Oh, I've seen it. What Joan's seen one can only imagine.' She was trying to sound unconcerned, he saw that. What a good friend this was, and not only to him.

'You're not worried about her, Kate?'

'I suppose not. Not sure though. Should I be?'

'No, not at all. She's not a child. It will last as long as the opera, and then there'll be the fatherly chat about how old he is, how young she is, and how she must look after herself and he must now have a holiday with his wife who is understanding *but*. He really will not hurt her, Kate. He's a very nice man, or so Jane thinks.'

'Bright girl, Jane.'

'Yes. She'll be back for the *Meistersinger* after next. You get the next one. I'm really spoiled, this summer; beautiful ladies in all directions.'

'Careful. You'll be famous.'

'Oh please, not you too' he said ruefully. 'Jane rubs it in constantly. Her imagination runs riot.'

She sat on his dressing-stool, long legs crossed, a

pump dangling from a toe, long blonde hair tossed back with a gesture. 'Not all imagination, I think?' she held out her glass for a refill. 'No smoke, you know . . .'

'Oh, *some* fire . . .'

'Yes?'

He waved a dismissive hand. 'Not the Great Fire of London, I promise you.'

'Some ladies like to be the single spark, David. Only way to make them completely happy.'

'Who was it that said complete happiness equals complete insensitivity?'

'I don't think you've got it quite right, but the idea was Sartre's, I think. In that case Jane will never be completely happy, will she?'

'No, she won't. Nor I, nor you, I hope. Only cabbages are.'

'Well, next best thing is to be totally absorbed. Work – that's been my cure, and it's your solution and Jane's too. We'll all get by, no doubt. Now,' she became practical, 'I must eat quite soon. Do you have time for supper?'

Yes, he had, one of the nice things about a Bayreuth season being the impossibility of being professionally busy except when actually conducting. He'd show her the famous hotel. She'd be mightily amused by the whole overdone thing, and the food would be splendid.

'Kate,' he said, 'just give me fifteen minutes to put on a suit and we'll dine in style. Well Bavarian style anyway.'

'Am I dressed for it?'

'Oh, you'll do,' he said.

'Not at all what I asked. If you need a suit I need more than a twinset. I'll dig something out. A half-hour then. I told you it takes longer . . .'

It took rather less, he found, to sort out the little

black number with its single diamond pin, and to do something simple but effective with her hair. They were waiting when the limousine arrived. She was surprised and pleased. 'What fun! So this is how the great conductors live!'

'One up on sopranos?' he asked.

'Two or three, really.'

'I imagine you've had enough driving for one day?'

'Yes, rather. I'm absolutely ready to be pampered.'

'It's curious. I've never been caught up with cars. They're just a means of getting about, to me.'

'What a waste. Such lovely motor cars you could have. Joan and her friend are coming and going in the most astonishing machine.'

'I can imagine' said David. 'He's very rich, you see.'

'Despite the ladies?'

'Oh, they're nothing to do with money. They enjoy him, simply.'

'Yes, that's true of this one anyway.' The country was speeding by in effortless silence. 'He has this marvellous *energy*. Everything goes faster when he's about. Everyone on their toes, you know?'

'I know all right. It's famous. So it's the energy that gets the ladies, is it?'

'And the confidence, I think; the certainty that he's going where he wants to go, when he wants to go there.'

They drew up outside the hotel. As they alighted the ornate wooden portal opened as though by magic, the doorman bowing.

'Such a menu.' Kate sipped her champagne. 'How will I ever decide?'

He grinned. 'They intend you to take a very long time. They sell more champagne that way. Take all the time you need.'

'And all the champagne?'

'Of course. You don't have to drive.'

'I have to be able to stand up, though.'

'Hi David . . .' New York hailed from the bar, Nancy and her Dane waving gaily.

David's gesture summoned them. 'Drink?' he asked. Jonny looked carefully from David to Kate and back again, trying to decide whether or not company was wished. 'Old friend from Wales, folks,' said David. 'Mrs Jones. The wonderful lady who gave my conducting the first push. Kate, meet Nancy and Jonny, the people who really put *Meistersinger* together for me.'

Nancy shook Kate's hand enthusiastically. 'You mean you're to blame for this terrible Wagner we've been getting this year?'

'Guilty, to some extent,' said Kate, 'but I only suggested he could conduct. No one said he had to conduct *well* . . .'

'Believe me, ma'am, he's not bad,' Nancy assured her with a broad grin.

'I'm so pleased to meet you both,' said Kate, making the routine politeness sound as sincere as it really was. 'I hope he didn't give too much trouble?'

'Only problem with David was finding him,' Jonny told her. 'No sooner he puts the stick down than he's locked up in some secret *gasthaus* by himself.'

'The girls never get a look-in, that's a fact,' added Nancy, 'but I'm beginning to see why—'

Jonny's nudge was amusingly obvious. 'Mrs Jones . . .'

'Kate, please.'

'How long will you be here? Do you get to see the opera?'

'Oh, goodness yes. You didn't think I'd come just to see the boy wonder, surely? I get to *Lohengrin* tomorrow, then *Meistersinger* next day, then I have to be back in Salzburg to collect a friend and take her home.'

'Kate is travelling with Joan Black,' explained David.

Two faces lit up. 'Oh, give her my love,' said Nancy. 'She was so kind to me at the Met in the spring.'

'And we enjoyed her in Copenhagen last year,' said Jonny.

'I'll tell her,' said Kate. 'She'll be pleased.'

'I just hope she'll find time for Copenhagen again after all this excitement. We catch artists coming up and going down, you know. In between it's Covent Garden, the Met and Vienna.' He shook his head sorrowfully.

Nancy was still enthusing. 'She's been such a wow in *The Flute*. The flavour of the year, they tell me. Ardiles will be making all sorts of plans—'

Jonny jumped up, cutting her short. 'Hey, gorgeous, it's time we were gone. Frau Spiegl will be waiting.' Spiegl, in charge of the House tickets, was the lady on whom all Bayreuth hospitality depended. Jonny shook Kate's hand. 'So good to meet you. Enjoy the opera.'

'I will,' she said, and they were away.

Kate turned to David, amazed. 'How the hell does *she* know?'

'Small world,' he reminded her.

'Did you know before I told you?'

'No. I hide in my little *gasthaus* and mind my own business. But if I lived here I'd have known, yes. One of the good reasons for not living here.'

Dinner was ready. They went in. 'How lovely,' said Kate. 'A cosy corner. I was afraid we'd get one of those tables as big as a football field. We'd have had to send postcards.'

The wine waiter was offering a bottle for David's inspection. He nodded, the cork was drawn, the wine tasted, the first glasses poured. She was relaxing now, winding down after a long drive.

'Well, Kate,' he suggested 'you've escaped from the glitz. Bayreuth is different.'

She agreed readily. 'It is. Salzburg is crammed with people, all dashing about between book signings, record signings, recitals, concerts, press conferences, operas. You can't imagine.'

But he could. The ultimate expression of a music business run by record companies, where orchestras and artists lived or died at the decision of boards in New York or Tokyo. 'Bayreuth is not like any other festival, Kate. There's no point at all in coming here for anything but Wagner because there isn't anything.'

'Hmmm . . . I've never seen Wagner live.'

'Never?'

'No. I've done my homework, of course, but he's not much fun on record, is he?'

'Quite a long sort of composer. One gets tired of watching the red disc go round and round . . .'

'Indeed.'

'Your German is up to scratch, so you won't need any help with the pieces.'

'No. But tell me about them. How are they from the inside?'

They digested *Lohengrin* with the soup; *Meistersinger* with the main course.

'So,' Kate decided over the *Apfelstrudel*, 'it's awfully true, isn't it, that Wagner is all about the German people, German values, German problems and German solutions?'

'Yes,' admitted David. 'It really bothers Jane. Not a bit surprising, I suppose.'

'No, it's not. And how do you escape the problem?'

He shrugged. 'It's not my problem at all, the problem is for them.'

'Ah, but occasionally they inflict it on us, and a lot of people get hurt, don't they?'

'When they grow up they'll be all right. They're very young, only a hundred years of being Germans. They have to learn to stop shouting about it.'

'We've learned that lesson, then?'

'Yes, long ago; but we pretend we haven't. All that "Rule Britannia" at the Proms. How do you think they feel about that in Dresden?'

'Oh, David! You're not serious? If they've got any sense of humour at all—'

'Ah, but . . .' His voice dropped to a conspiratorial whisper over the table, 'they haven't. None at all.'

She was amused, not quite believing. 'Not much to be done with them, then?'

'Nothing,' he assured her confidently. 'We'll never understand each other. We are so alike in almost every way, but there's the catch.'

She looked around the room, with its plush walls and ornate limed and carved oak, its gilt mirrors and chandeliers. A set from a Strauss opera. Perhaps he was right. No one with a sense of humour could have designed it.

'Oh well, no solution?' she asked.

'No. Just enjoy the music. Nothing else to be done.'

'Well, I reckon I can do that.' The waiter was hovering with coffee. 'Yes, please,' she said.

'And cognac,' added David.

'Oh, are you sure . . .?'

'Yes. Coffee to keep you awake, cognac to make you sleep.'

'Will it? I wonder. Actually I won't need help tonight. It's been a long day.'

'You can sleep in tomorrow. Nothing to do until the opera.'

'Rubbish. I've been reading the guidebooks. There's the Hermitage, and the Margrave's opera house . . .'

'Ah. I'm to do the guided tour, I see. All right then. But there's still the cognac, and you don't have to drive.'

Just as well, Kate thought later, almost dozing off in the car. But how wonderful to live like this, in such

262

assured comfort. I wish, I wish, how I wish I'd married a conductor. This conductor, even . . .?

She climbed the stair leaning on his arm. At her door she gave him the key. He turned it, and she looked round to say good night.

'David, it's been lovely. Do I get a good-night kiss?'

He gave her his widest smile. 'If there's no more I can do . . .'

She put up her face. He took her in his arms. The kiss which began as a gesture of affection blossomed as her arms around his neck drew him close. He moved lower. Instantly she released him, smiling. Her finger tapped his nose. 'Enough, young man. I've got the message. Off you go!'

The door closed behind her. She leaned on it, breathing hard. Oh, poor Jane, she thought. What a man, what company, what fun, but what a colossal risk for a woman. Yes, poor Jane.

And, as her hands met over the dress between her thighs, poor Kate.

17

'I must say,' said Kate, relishing her mid-morning coffee, 'this is just the place, isn't it? The perfect hideaway.'

'I think so. Lovely up here, top of the house. It was meant for the family, the top floor. Now they've moved out it's kept for lucky folks like us.'

'Marvellous. Your very own ivory tower. And sun all day, with the balconies on both sides. How did you find it?'

'Lady Box told me. They came every year for a day or two. He was very fond of Germany, the old boy, ever since he was a student. After Bayreuth they used to go to the Tyrol. A village near Kitzbühel, she said.'

'*Every* year?'

'Yes.'

'Most folks like a change.'

'Most folks spend their year in one place. They have to escape on holiday. Artists usually have cottages in Wales, or Suffolk, somewhere in the UK anyway. Holidays abroad are the last thing they want.'

'The ultimate luxury, *not* to travel?'

'For me, certainly. But if one must work abroad this is a pretty good answer. It suits me, anyway.'

She looked again at the big bronzed man, reclining now, his eyes closed against the warm sunshine. David Adams, CBE, successful, assured, popular, almost indecently handsome, needing only the inevitable knighthood to complete the picture. Where had he gone, the gauche fifteen-year-old, almost too shy to lay hands on her piano?

'It's a long way from Cwmbach, all this, isn't it?' she said.

He opened one eye, looked at her, closed it again. 'Yes, it is. I've been very lucky, haven't I? And it's all down to you.'

Politeness required a disclaimer, but he wouldn't wish it, she knew. 'It was just a hunch,' she said. 'Might have come to nothing. *Would* have come to nothing but for a lot of hard work.'

He chuckled. 'Work? My old dad would laugh. He'd never have thought any of this was work. Fact is, he thought the whole point of my music was so that I wouldn't *have* to work. Anyway, to tell the truth, it's all been great fun.'

She remembered the old saying: ten per cent inspiration, ninety per cent perspiration. He'd been lucky only in that he thought the perspiration was fun. And that was in his breeding. 'Where do you go from here, do you think?' she asked.

He held up his arms in a helpless gesture. 'God only knows. Well, God and Jane, perhaps. I'd like an orchestra of my own, better still an opera house. But it's too soon, you see. Too soon for first-rate ones anyway, and we're not interested in the other sort.' She noticed the *we*. One up to Jane. He went on, 'That's the problem with early luck like mine. First-rate players are usually not spring chickens. It's not easy for them to accept direction from a youngster. Makes all sorts of trouble. And in my job we have a long way to go, ourselves . . .'

'A long way? From here? Explain please.'

'Difficult to explain. But some things do come with age. At the start everything's easy. No technical problems. Reflexes are quick, brainbox sharp as a knife, it's so easy to think there's only one answer to any musical question. In time the problems must come.'

'Why, if there are none at the beginning?'

'Because there are, you see. We're just too green to notice them. Now they're coming at me from all directions. George Box warned me.'

'He warned you about a lot of things, didn't he?'

'Yes. Not that I took him too seriously at the time, mind you. But when things happen, when things go wrong, I remember. And then I try to remember his solutions too.'

'Is there one? For lack of experience, I mean?'

'No, there isn't. But he used to say that the important thing, when there was no correct solution, was to make the honest one.'

'Isn't that true of everything?' she suggested.

'I've never thought much about it. I wouldn't be surprised. But I know it's possible to worry myself silly about a phrase or a tempo and never come to a *safe* conclusion. Then I do what comes naturally and people like it.'

'So, conducting is a matter of doing what comes naturally?' She was smiling.

'Kate, you must be joking.'

'Am I now?' she laughed.

'Oh, come on, the job's not that simple. But if the thing doesn't *sound* natural it's useless. Music should sound inevitable. As though it can't help itself.'

'Like Mozart?'

'Got it in one. All his ideas sound simple, all his solutions inevitable. Only he could provide them. But they sound, well, easy. That's why he's the universal composer, everyone's friend. Because he doesn't disturb us. He never *seems* to do the unexpected.'

She pondered this idea. 'But if he were to stop . . . leave a phrase unfinished, we'd never find the right solution?'

'No, never. None of us could have finished a tulip either. Only God.'

'So that's the secret? To do the natural thing?'

'What's natural to one of us is unnatural to another. But Mozart is natural to everyone. He's straight from God.'

God again. She was surprised. 'God? I didn't know you had the God thing.'

'I haven't. If I had, the words would mean something different.'

'So, what do you mean?'

He was silent, considering. Then: 'I mean that Mozart is nature's great achievement. A wonderful genetic accident.'

'I wonder if you're right?'

'It doesn't matter, you see. The music's enough. Ours not to reason why, nor how. Just be grateful, that's all.' He stretched luxuriously. 'Now, shall we see the Hermitage before lunch? Not much time after, if you're to see the opera today . . .'

She drove with a kind of elegance, the motor a small traditional masterpiece of the kind fast disappearing under an avalanche of modern tinplate. 'I hope you like my little car?' she asked as they turned into the gardens.

'Not just a car, is it?' he said, knowing the machine was the last tangible link with a past she'd painstakingly put behind her; a daily admission of remembrance, and perhaps her only one. She misunderstood him, carefully perhaps. 'No. More like riding, in a funny way. There's a personal connection with the machine. Very satisfying.'

'I've never done that,' he reflected.

'Oh, goodness, you must drive back, please . . .'

He laughed at her generous reaction and at her mistake. 'No, really. Not driving. Riding. I've never done it.'

'No, I suppose not.' She was brought up short, remembering again the gap between his upbringing and hers, the one he'd somehow leaped. 'It's really a sport for girls, of course,' she suggested, smiling as she swung her legs out of the tiny door.

He smiled back. 'Ah. Yes, of course. The personal connection between . . .'

She shook her head. 'Really, you have such a smutty mind.'

'Yes. Fun, isn't it?'

She giggled. 'I suppose. And it's true, of course. All that muscle between one's legs *is* pretty fascinating. Good innocent practice for young ladies.'

They walked between radiant flowerbeds, the midday sun hot on their heads. In the distance a water-sprinkler turned slowly, creating a brief recurring rain-bow as its arc reached the apogee.

'Jane thought ballet more practical,' he told her.

'Ah. Clever stuff, that. I wish I'd done it. I was more the sporting type.'

'Hockey sticks, all that?'

'Mmm, believe it or not, yes. The ugly duckling, that was me. Teeth in a brace . . .'

He laughed out loud, disbelieving.

'True, I tell you. The present state of perfection is a masterpiece of organization, and that's a fact.'

He pretended dismay, holding up his hands. 'And I thought it was all natural.'

'Like your music?'

They'd reached the great pond now. They sat on its stone edge, watching the lazy carp.

'Yes. Like Mozart. Been in love with you both, long as I can remember. You and the A major symphony. Never play it without remembering.'

'Just as well I kept my hands off you that day?'

'Just as well.'

She thought for a long moment. 'I missed out, I think?'

'So did I,' he suggested.

'Oh, I think you were doing pretty well, young man.'

'I did wish, though. But you were about as access-ible as the Queen, really.'

Yes, thought Kate. A meeting of two worlds, then. Except for the music, and that was . . . one of his wonderful genetic accidents? Was she more accessible today, she wondered?

He was ahead of her on a parallel track. 'Curious, isn't it, how the age difference shrinks?'

An alarm bell rang, soft, distant, but distinct. Care-ful, Kate. Low keys, minor themes were safest with this man. 'Yes. I reckon when you're ninety-five and I'm a hundred and ten we won't notice it at all . . .'

'Take that long, will it?' he asked.

She waved a finger. 'I'm here to keep you out of trouble, remember?'

'To stop me eating too much, I thought.'

'Ha! Believe that, you'll believe anything.' She was uncomfortably aware that in less complicated circum-stances it would take this beautiful man only an eve-ning to get her into bed. 'Speaking of food . . .'

'Lunch here, I think?'

'Oh good. I like this place.'

'It's a shame the gardens are running down,' David said over the filet, 'because there's not the money to keep them up, and very few visitors to enjoy them. A pity really.'

'So, what happens to the audiences during the day?'

'That *is* a puzzle. The town isn't overfull. Nothing to do there anyway. People all seem to come by car. Some of the towns round about are really lovely. Bam-berg, for instance . . .'

'I've seen Bamberg. On holiday, before the war, with a school trip. We had penfriends, stayed with families, you know how it was.'

He shook his head. 'Such things never happened to me.'

'No, I suppose not,' she said. 'It was the wrong

time. I was lucky. I saw how it was here. The organization, the enthusiasm, the wonderful confidence. No wonder they were taken in.'

He took her hand across the table. 'Luck comes and goes, Kate, doesn't it?' She was remembering. He could see it in her eyes, the distance and the years. He must lighten up, for them both. 'I'm the lucky one. Lovely work, lovely surroundings, lovely weather and amazing company.'

She smiled, returning to the present. 'I'm doing pretty well, myself. Two festival operas in two days.'

'Yes.' He looked at his watch. 'Come on, we have to get back to our ivory tower. The show begins in ninety minutes.'

* * *

'Such a luxury,' she said gratefully, in the limousine. 'You spoil me. I'd have driven. It's no distance.'

'Impossible,' he assured her. 'That super outfit is not for driving in. Anyway, friends of festival conductors can't walk up and down to the car park like any old tourist. It wouldn't do.'

So easy, she told herself. So easy to fall for this man. No wonder the girls tumbled. The command, the source of the talent, conditioned everything these people did. Doors opened, cars arrived, tickets materialized when theatres had been sold out for six months. Power. It was real, the aphrodisiac effect. Not that it would work if one didn't like the man.

But what wonderful fun all this was, and what fun he was, too. He was right about the years telescoping. He'd become a formidable male presence. She smiled to herself, remembering. He'd always been that, in a way, the kind of boy one would fall for if one hadn't more sense, but now? The lovable puppy had grown too strong for the leash. The leash? Was Jane hanging on for dear life? If so, how secure was her hold? The answer was all too clear. She, Jane, made all the decisions but one for this man. The big one would always be his.

'Penny for them?' he asked.

She jumped, startled out of her isolation. 'Oh . . . not worth a penny, really.'

They were slowing for the theatre approach. There were twenty minutes to the curtain. 'Time for a drink?' he suggested.

'Is there really time?'

'Yes there is. It's quite important really. Anaesthetic, I mean, before the opera. Part of the ritual.'

So they queued for the inevitable glass of hock, sitting in the sun to drink.

'Interesting people,' Kate said, looking about her. 'Well-dressed, but not dressed to kill.'

He agreed. 'When you have to sit for half a day in the theatre the choice of clothes counts, doesn't it?'

'They're here for the opera, nothing else?'

'No doubt about it. It's quite difficult, just getting here and getting in. Only people who care will make the effort. The Germans seem to have most trouble. If you want seats here it pays to have an aunt in LA or Tokyo.'

'Is it fair, do you think?' she wondered.

'It's business. But I agree, in a way it isn't fair. Wagner means more to Germans than to anyone else.' There was a stir in the crowd. 'That's the ten-minute call. Time to move. You'll find the seat, no trouble. The usherettes are wonderful. The place comes courtesy of Mr Schmidt, by the way.'

'Nice of him.'

'He begs mine on my nights, I get his. Fair's fair. You can thank him in the second interval, over a cup of tea. Now, run away. I'll be waiting here with the drinks.'

He watched her walk into the thickening crowd, a trim figure in her black trouser-suit. How old? Fifty-ish? Incredible. She'd pass for a young forty, easily. In his mind maybe she'd always be thirty, ready for a long walk on the beach with Isolde?

Now, what to do for an hour? Perhaps he ought to have begged a seat too? It was bad form, he always felt, to watch a colleague work, but the acts were long and Bayreuth short on entertainment. A telephone was the answer. He'd speak with Jane. Stage door would find him a phone.

'I rang,' she said. 'Where were you?'

'We were out to supper.'

'At Munchberg?'

'Yes. Kate loved it. All those famous faces carefully not noticing one another.'

'David, I wish I was there.'

'It won't be long.'

His voice lacked the convincing impression of loneliness for which she was listening. 'I expect Kate's keeping you entertained?'

'Kate is Kate. I've just popped her in to *Lohengrin*.'

'Schmidt back from his flu then?'

'Yes. Just as well. That's a trick one can bring off only once I think. Repetition would tempt providence.'

'David, it sounded as safe as the Bank of England. I can't think why you rehearse at all.'

He laughed. 'Any orchestra will tell you. Rehearsals are for conductors. Once the conductor knows the work the need to rehearse is gone. Now, what's happening in the real world?'

'Not a lot. I've spent most of the day looking for His Nibs.'

David's ears pricked up. 'For Ardiles?'

'Yes. He's not answering the telephone, and there

are so many things to sort out. Complications over the Israel season.'

'Jane, it's the lady. You knew there was one.' There was a long wait. 'Are you there?' he asked.

'Yes. I'm here.'

'And this is what's called a pregnant silence?'

'Something of the sort, no doubt. All right, David. Tell.'

He plunged. 'Joan Black . . .'

'My God! Is it possible?'

'Only too likely, surely? She's very beautiful and the best Queen of the Night since . . .' Her laughter stopped him. 'No joke intended. Just good information.'

'How good?'

'Faultless. The Bayreuth people know already. I'm surprised you didn't. Kate was travelling with her. She says Joan was invited for lunch and she's hardly seen her since.'

A long sigh at the other end of the line. 'I see. Oh well . . . I'll cope I suppose. How is Bayreuth?'

'Not what it was. Come back, Jane.'

'You wouldn't ask if you thought I could,' she joked. 'Kate will give you all the fun you need for a day or two. Just look after her, will you?'

'No trouble. Lovely lady, that one. Takes me back . . .'

'Not too far back, please. Your adolescence was a little *too* interesting. Give her my love, will you? And now I really must find the awful Argentine.'

'Rap over the knuckles?'

'Useless. But there's the inevitable parting present to think about. I'll just remind him that motor cars are out, grand pianos less public. One thing about pianos . . .'

'What?'

'I can get them at a discount. 'Bye now.'

The act was nearly over. He collected drinks and sandwiches. Kate was quickly out, waving to him across the courtyard.

'Well, how is it?' he asked.

'Marvellous. The whole thing is so well done on stage, and such fine playing. All one could ask really. This is so good of you, David, I can't tell you how much I'm enjoying it.' Her eyes were alight. Yes, it was an experience, all this. A musician's experience, and the better the musician the better the experience.

'Extraordinary, I agree,' he said. 'The audience makes the evening, in a way. They really know their operas, listen so well. There's nothing like it anywhere.'

'Seats are hard.'

'Famous for it. Wagner thought cushions might spoil his acoustic.'

'Some people bring their own, built in.'

'Yes. You could try putting on a little Teutonic weight before tomorrow evening. Might help.'

She was thumbing her programme. 'Second act is a bit slow, I gather . . .'

'Yes. Always a patch of heavy weather somewhere in Wagner. The two ladies have to debate for about fifteen minutes. Funny piece. It's a scrap between two women, that's all.'

'Two ideas, surely?' she argued. 'The virgin and the witch?' Material for a long and funny debate there, he told himself. Would Kate back the witch? Jane's money would be on the virgin. She'd be in there with the wooden stake, and save the prayers for later. 'So who wins?' he asked her, 'surely not the witch? Her man gets killed and she's cast into outer darkness.'

The call for the second act was sounding. She finished her wine, picked up her programme. 'Well,' she said 'she can always find another feller. Goody two-shoes should've had the man before asking her silly question. . . .' Laughing, she was lost in the crowd.

Now, how to spend an hour? What a chump he'd been, not to ask for a seat. Kate's enjoyment was infectious. These things were better shared. He'd never seen the opera – how often had he seen any opera except from the rostrum? – and to watch it with Kate would have been fun. The act under way, the restaurant around him was noisy with collected crockery. The canteen, perhaps, where the orchestra and chorus spent their breaks and ate their lunches? There would be television, perhaps.

There were curious glances as he joined the thin queue, mainly of usherettes, for coffee. Conductors were rarely seen here. He collected his cup, turned suddenly and incautiously at the till to go back for sugar.

There was a crash, a scream, and a shocked silence in which a crystal-clear Scottish voice raised to the ultimate pitch of feminine indignation asked, 'What on earth are you doing, you great lummock?' On the floor lay a tray, and around it in disarray were a broken beaker, a plate, the wreck of a salad, and a small lake of coffee. The owner of the voice was looking ruefully down at her skirt, or more properly kilt, soaked from waist to hem. Her ire showed little sign of abating, and her voice gained, if anything, in the course of protest. Verbal response being clearly useless, David reached for his handkerchief in a vain attempt to mop up the mess, belatedly realizing to his embarrassment the relatively limited area of a lady's clothing which may be mopped by a man in public.

Her voice, which had started at the level of a Sutherland in full flight, tailed off into silence. Her face showed that he'd been recognized, and that she was now as embarrassed as he. He offered the handker-chief, half smiling. She took it and mopped.

'Let me get you another salad?' he suggested.

Two brown eyes, confused beyond measure, looked up at him from beneath a dark fringe. 'Really, it's all right. Please don't concern yourself.'

'Nonsense,' he protested. 'It was very clumsy of me. Look, forget the salad. There's a much nicer one in the restaurant outside.'

'Oh, no, really . . .'

'It's the least I can do. I seem to have ruined your kilt?'

'No. It will wash.' The brogue was Edinburgh, clearly. 'Please don't concern yourself . . .'

That 'concerrrn' was very fetching. 'Look, let me replace the spoiled supper, at least? Unless you're waiting for someone?'

'Well . . .' The glimmer of a smile crept through the Scottish mists.

'That's settled, then. Come along. Let's discover how the punters eat, shall we?' He took her firmly by the arm and led her past a gaggle of her wondering colleagues to the door.

They had the choice of two hundred seats. One vigilant waiter remained to seat them. She hesitated, standing, before holding out her hand. 'Margaret Bell,' she said.

'David Adams,' he smiled back, shaking hands for-mally. 'Please call me David.'

She sat. 'In that case please call me Maggie. Every-one does. Look, I do apologize for screaming like that.'

'Not at all. I think most ladies would, don't you? Your kilt must be ruined.'

She shook her head, her hair following at the inter-val of a quarter-second. 'No, really, it's not as bad as it looks.'

'You must have it cleaned, on me,' he insisted.

'Oh no, really. Well, we'll see. But I'm sure it won't be necessary.'

'You're from Edinburgh, I think?' he asked as her meal arrived, the waiter opening its accompanying half-bottle.

She was embarrassed now. 'Really, there was no need . . .'

'Yes, there was. Modest celebration. I don't meet a fellow victim of *Saesneg* oppression every day here.'

'*Saesneg*?'

'Sassenach to you.'

Her puzzlement dissolved into a smile, occupying her whole face, wonderful to watch. 'Oh, I don't think either of us has too much to complain of the English, do you?'

'Perhaps not,' he admitted. 'Tell me, how does a Scottish lady come to be working . . .' He stopped, the question sounding too close to the traditional one.

She saw it and smiled again. 'Usherettes are students. More Germans and Austrians, but a few Brits and Americans. A Japanese even, this year. They need languages, and we have to be serious people.'

He considered. Had he been a serious student? As serious as any, he supposed, but there was something a little comic in her description of herself. His smile was nearly concealed.

She saw it and a faint defensive flush appeared in her cheeks. 'I mean they need to feel that Wagner is important to us. This place is a crash course, and very valuable.'

'So you come to rehearsals and so on?'

'Yes. Some of them. General rehearsals and the one before, anyway. We're kept away if there are . . . complications. And when it's possible to be there it's expected of us. People who do the shows and spend the rest of the time playing tennis are not popular. With the establishment, I mean.'

'Complications?'

'People fall out, don't they? Even here?' She put down her fork, the salad demolished. He waved at the waiter and the strawberries arrived. 'Oh really, you oughtn't . . .'

'There'll be straws at home now. They'll be gone before you get back. It wouldn't do to miss out,' he said. Then: 'So you know Wagner pretty well now?'

Maggie laughed. 'There's quite a lot of him, I find. But I know him better, yes.'

'But you've had enough of this opera?'

'*Lohengrin*? Yes, or nearly. There was a tremendous rush to be in at yours the other night. Great fun, to hear it done off the cuff like that. How can one?'

'Not quite off the cuff. I'd done it in America. Quite a long time ago, but it stuck, thank God. Look, the orchestra here can play all these pieces in its sleep. It makes no difference who's in there with them—'

She stopped him with a deprecating wave of her hand. 'No. It's not true. The bit about playing in their sleep is, but they're *much* better when they're awake.'

He was intrigued, but careful. This bright student was being nice to him. 'Oh, come on. I'm quite sure Mr Schmidt keeps them awake.'

'Are you now?' She was amused. 'Tell me, how often does a conductor hear a conductor work?'

'Not often,' he admitted.

'Well, in some cases you're lucky. Your *Lohengrin* was my sixth, and it wasn't easy to keep awake in the first five.'

'Well, you had the suspense factor in my case. Anything could have happened. Must have been fun.'

'The suspense factor? Oh, that vanished during the prelude. After that it was just a very good evening. By Bayreuth standards a wonderful one. A pity you were out of sight. We'd love to have seen how you did it.'

She was relaxing now, almost at ease. Would he

have been so confidently blasé at twenty, David wondered, after a month here? Perhaps, but he thought not.

'Thank you,' he said. 'It was great fun to do. I was very grateful for the opportunity. The cast is wonderful, the orchestra is great. Everything here is ideal. Anyone might fall asleep in her sixth *Lohengrin* after all.'

She smiled, eyes down, recognizing professional rectitude and his implied small reprimand. 'You'll be back, then, next year?'

'Oh yes, of course. Will you?'

'No. I'll have finished my Academy course. I need a degree. Too much to do in the summer vac. I've seen what I can of everything in the rep. Last year the *Ring*, now the rest. Except there's no *Tristan*. For that I'll have to queue up with the rest of the world.'

He was tempted, but it wouldn't do. She'd have to wait for the news and yes, she might have to queue for the opera.

'After the degree, what will you do?' he asked.

'I need a place on someone's music staff.'

'Not easy. Only two full-time opera companies at home.'

'Scottish Opera will come, I think.'

'So will Welsh, I hope; but one can't depend on it,' he said.

'There are places abroad. Even South Africa, if I'm stuck. The place where no one wants to work.'

'Will you be stuck?' he asked.

'Not if I'm good enough.' The voice was confident, the expression behind her eyes less so. A realist, this girl, with no illusions about her prospects.

'It does take luck, you know,' he said carefully, not wishing to discourage her.

'Were you lucky?' she countered.

'Indeed I was,' he assured her.

Maggie was looking at him carefully over her coffee-cup. 'Then I hope I will be. But talent is all I have to offer.'

Her meaning was clear, and charmingly conveyed. Talent and charm, he thought. And a certain openness. A rare honesty, lots of fresh highland air in it. Long might it survive in a messy business.

'So, in the end, what will you do?'

'What music staff always hopes to do. I'll conduct.'

His surprise showed. Her wry grin showed that she'd expected no less. 'I suppose you think a woman can't conduct.'

Stumped by her directness, he could only fumble. 'I suppose there's no reason.'

'Must be a reason why we don't, anyway. Women have done everything else. That's the big problem, you see. Finding out why we don't conduct, and getting over it.'

'So you think there's a reason? Apart from chauvinism, I mean?'

'Yes. There must be. Chauvinism is a fact of life. We lick it every day in most fields, if we're good enough. Still no women conductors though. It's important to find out why not.'

'I've seen women conduct,' he said. 'It looks all wrong.'

'Who cares how it looks, as long as it works?' she asked, puzzled and indignant.

'We have to care how it looks, surely?' he countered. 'How a conductor looks is how he works. If it looks wrong it just *doesn't* work.'

'Hmm. Well, if it's a problem it will have to be licked, won't it?'

The act would be over quite soon, he realized. He was reluctant to give her up. 'Look, would you like to talk about it sometime?' he offered.

Her defensive mechanism was immediate, the eyes

direct and questioning what might be a pass. That would get short shrift here. Something more formal, perhaps. 'You must let me have the cleaner's bill at least. Frau Spiegl will tell you where to find me.'

She rose. 'Thank you so much for supper. It was very good to meet you, and our talk has been most interesting. Goodbye now.' She offered her hand for shaking. Half amused, half intrigued, he watched her small shape cross the space to the theatre, purpose in every step.

* * *

Kate was surprised to find Schmidt waiting in tennis shorts and a tee shirt, the routine dress for conductors here where they were not seen by the audience. Everything else was formal enough; the tea in fine china and the very English biscuits and cake. Schmidt seemed to enjoy them too. The evening was going well, he thought. Kate was gracefully complimentary, to his pleasure, and accurately so to his evident surprise.

'One is always happy to end the second act,' he admitted. 'The third is much less trouble. Of course the trumpets before the last scene can go crazy. They have so long to wait between stage calls. And the beer is quite good. There is always a risk. We have, of course, the great sanction against mistakes, that they don't come back next year, so on the whole all is well.'

David and Kate left him with time to put on more formal clothes; he would have only two minutes to dress for his curtain call at the end of the opera, so black trousers and a shirt with a collar were always necessary for the last act. Walking in the evening sun back to the front of the House, Kate took his arm, squeezing affectionately. 'David, I'm so grateful, you know.'

He looked at her frankly. 'Not half as grateful as I've been for a very long time, Kate.'

'I was afraid I'd be some sort of lumber for you here, you see.'

He stopped walking to look at her. 'Lumber? How could you be a lumber? It's wonderful to have you to myself for a day or two. And in case you haven't noticed, I'm the envy of half the audience, having this amazingly attractive lady with me.'

She giggled. 'Flattery—'

'Will get me nowhere, I know. Never mind, I shall just keep practising.'

'To keep your hand in?'

'Yes.'

'I envy Jane, I really do.'

'Oh, she has her problems, Kate. I try to compensate, when I can.'

'The big problem is the one you never see, d'you know?'

'Tell me.'

'That she is separated so much from the most important thing in her life.'

'Hey there! The most important thing in her life is Grant and Grant. Especially since she's become both Grants.'

'Business can never be the most important thing. Even when a woman thinks it is, it can't be.'

'I think you're trying to tell me Jane's bound to get broody?'

'Don't be flip, David. It's too big a thing to joke about.' She was not pleased at his tone.

'Some things are too big to be serious about, Kate. But I know Jane wants a child.'

'Yes, of course. Your child.'

'Mine if I wish it, she says. But a child anyway.'

'Such determination. I can understand it, though. I wish I had one. Or two, or four. If we'd known . . .'

'You wouldn't have waited?'

'We didn't. It just didn't happen, that's all. Molly has the boys. Something to live for.'

'People do live for the kids, don't they? Is that always a good thing, d'you think?'

'What do you mean?'

'If we go on living for the next generation, the only generation which will enjoy life will be the last one. Seems a waste, doesn't it?'

'It's not that simple.'

'No, of course not. But it is an issue, I sometimes think. And so many of the people who've done important things did them simply for themselves, selfishly.'

'Men have a greater capacity for selfishness than women, David.'

It was time for the last act of the opera, the fanfare sounding from the portico. 'You must run along,' he said. 'The car will be waiting where we left it.' He pecked her cheek briefly, and she returned the gesture before turning away.

* * *

'A greater capacity for selfishness?' he asked her, sitting with cognac on her balcony in the near-dark.

'Yes. Surely.'

'Doesn't add up. The reverse is true, when you come down to basics. We give, you take.'

'Nonsense—'

'No. The truth, simply. Even physically. Our pleasure comes more from yours than from anything else. Your pleasure is enormous compared to ours.'

'It's not always true. Many women put up with bad sex all their lives, out of real affection. Anyway, you're just talking about sex. I'm talking about people.'

'No people without sex, Kate. But that's not all I'm talking about. Since the beginning of time we provide,

283

you take. We spend our lives providing for you and for the kids. I can't think how a woman can think men selfish.'

'But you don't provide the things we really want, David. A place in your world. Recognition that we are people, with qualities to offer. In many ways better equipped than you are.'

'You're making my case for me. We give you everything you need. Now you ask for everything we've got. Such generosity, Kate! And when it comes to skills you people do choose the ones for which you seem least fitted.'

'Tell me which,' she demanded.

'Well, this evening I met a music student from Edinburgh who is determined to conduct.'

'Well, why not?'

'Have you ever seen a woman conduct, Kate?'

'Amateurs. Choir mistresses. No, I've never seen a woman try to conduct seriously.'

'Well, I have. There are a hundred or more of them in the world now, all trying to establish themselves and failing.'

'But why should they fail?'

He took a deep breath. 'You're going to hate this, Kate. I have to tell you that the female anatomy as I know and love it is singularly unfitted for the art of conducting. All the specimens I've seen look very ungainly indeed from behind. Most of them conduct with their backsides.'

She was dismissive. 'Then they've been badly taught, that's all; most *men* conduct badly, when all's said and done. Sooner or later a woman will emerge, mark my words. Tell me about the one you met today.'

He laughed. 'Not so much a meeting, more a collision.'

Kate listened intently as he described the encounter.

'Sounds a very interesting girl,' she said at the end. 'And you do collect them with such ease, don't you?'

'Oh, Kate, not fair. Do you think I go upsetting tea-trays—'

'No, I don't. But these things happen to you. Admit it. Bayreuth is full of young men who would have loved your opportunity this evening.'

'Think so? Frankly, if she hadn't spotted who I was I think she'd have hit me with a coffee-pot.'

'Yes, perhaps. But she didn't, did she? That's what I mean. You're one of the few blokes alive who can turn any old catastrophe into—'

'Kate! I did no such thing. And that girl is about as approachable as Edinburgh Castle. One wrong word and the entire Clan Bell would arrive, complete with claymores.'

'She'll find you again, though, won't she?'

'Will she?'

'Yes. She'd be mad not to. And you'd be unkind not to show interest. In the musician, I mean, if not in the girl.'

'Show interest? What can one do? Look, Bayreuth is jam-packed with music students. Why this one?'

'Because she's from home. Because you gave her a bad evening. David, there needn't be a good professional reason. It's enough that you met, don't you see?'

'I can't think what Jane would say.'

Interesting, thought Kate. It would be so easy for him to hide this from her, and he won't. Good. *Two* up to Jane today. 'Tell her and find out,' she suggested.

'I'm not sure I can even find the girl,' he explained. 'Certainly not if she doesn't wish to be found.'

'Doesn't she?'

'I don't know. She seemed undecided.'

'Good girl, dodging a pass?'

'Yes. Yes, I think so.'

'All the more reason. In her place most music students would have moved with the speed of light.'

'She doesn't know about my attendant dragon.'

The dragon laughed. 'No, but I'm surprised she didn't try anyway.' Serious again, she asked, 'Tell me, how hard would it have been?'

He must make a serious answer. 'Hard? Well, she's pretty, she's very bright, but . . .'

'She's dangerous?'

'Yes. She is, potentially.'

'And you'd calculate the risk first. You're a hard man, David Adams.'

'You'd like me better for throwing caution to the winds? That's for a fifteen-year-old.'

'Yes, perhaps. Though I've known thirty-year-olds to do it. Incidentally, when *did* you last hear from Molly?'

'I don't hear from Molly. She's never encouraged it. I proposed myself a day trip several times when I was at college, but she never found it convenient. Christmas cards, birthdays, that's all.'

'Yes. Well, I expect she's got a lot on. The boys are grown now and at university. I wondered . . .'

'What?'

'It can't have been easy, can it?'

'No. I'm quite sure it hasn't been. Though the service has looked after them pretty well. That's as I understand, anyway.'

'Yes, it has. But this could be the time when a little positive interest might make a difference. You know, that little family is the only family you've got.'

'What can I do?'

'I don't know. You can think about it, though?'

'I will. Of course I will. Thank you for reminding me.'

She got up, stooped to where he was sitting, kissed him affectionately. 'You really are a nice man. Only a man, of course, so not entirely nice. But about as nice as they come. I envy Jane, truly.'

'Problems and all?'

'Nice problems. The sort I could do with.'

'Solve them, could you?'

'Solve one, anyway. I'd get myself pregnant, and have a lot of fun doing it.'

He stood up to hold her, kissed her.

'This is where I retreat to a safe distance and bolt the door,' she said softly. 'Good night.'

« 18 »

Jane came awake, seized the telephone. 'David, what's wrong?'

'Wrong? Why is there anything wrong? I rang, that's all.'

She breathed a sigh of relief. 'At seven? The middle of the night by your standards.'

'You're still in bed? I'm sorry . . . we're an hour later, of course.'

'And you've just woken up. Well, if you've got to be sorry, let's be sorry together, shall we?'

'I'm game,' he smiled, knowing what was coming.

'Well, I'm sorry you're not here.'

'And I'm sorry you're not here.'

'Good. Now tell me what possessed you to ring at such a time.'

'I'd like you to find my Aunt Molly, Jane.'

'Find her? We've got an address. Why? What's the problem?'

'Please find out everything you can about her, the twins, and their situation. I mean their education, how they are doing, what they will do, all that.'

'I think you mean what they can afford to do, David?'

'Yes. Just that.'

'Going to be Father Christmas, are we?'

'Jane, it's serious.'

She sobered up, audibly. 'Yes, I'm quite sure it is.'

'Can it be done quietly, tactfully? So that Moll doesn't know?'

'I expect so. With time and care and money most

things are possible. I'll talk to Isaac. He'll know how—'

'Oh, love I'd be so grateful.'

'Yes. Don't worry.'

'She's the only family I've got, Jane.'

'Yes, of course. Leave it with me. I hope to have something for you when I come.'

'In three days? Hardly.'

'Well, I'll try. What will you do today?'

'Conduct *Meistersinger*.'

'Of course. That little thing. Was Schmidt nice to Kate last evening?'

'Yes. Absolutely charming.'

'Easy to be nice to Kate, I find. I'm sorry she'll have gone before I arrive. Will she be going back to Salzburg?'

'Not a lot of point, if her friend is coming home with Ardiles. I suppose she *is* doing that?'

'I suppose, eventually. I expect he'll take her to Provence for the two weeks he's chucked. Then he's due in the States. She'll turn up in London, tired but happy.'

'In London? Why not home to Wales?'

'They always come here to me, to talk business. He's the only man I know who combined his pleasure with the lady's business.'

'Not quite, I think.'

'Oh well, present company and all that . . . yes, you give me the most amazing pleasure. Even at six hundred miles. I love you, do you know?'

'Yes. I love you too, do *you* know?'

'Yes. Yes, I do. Look, I must get up and go to work. I'll look after that problem. Leave it to me.'

'Thank you, love.'

She put down the telephone slowly, thoughtfully. Something he'd said, something . . . yes, that *Molly* was the only family he'd got? Was it really possible he didn't know about the boys? How could he not? But he'd have told her, surely? His sudden interest was Kate's doing, of course. But Kate *must* know? Well, the whole thing was in the lap of the gods. Perhaps it would be best if he never realized? Did Molly know he was in the dark? He'd been so young. No one but Molly needed to know who . . .

* * *

David was making coffee. He would need breakfast, a walk, a light lunch, his essential countdown for a performance day. Kate would be about soon. The phone rang as she knocked. He opened the door with one hand, picked up the phone with the other. It was the *Festspielhaus*. A problem. He sat down on the rumpled bed to digest it. The voice at the other end was concerned but reassuring. He made the expected response. 'Yes. Eleven o'clock. I'll be there.'

Kate saw the small worry in his face. 'Trouble?'

'A little. My second lady is down with a throat. I have to work with a change tonight.'

'Will it be all right?'

'Oh yes. Singers grow on trees here. But I have to work with her for an hour this morning. Like to come?'

'Mmm, love it.'

'Play the piano, if you like' he joked.

She returned serve. 'Oh yes. Conduct it too, if you like. I know my limitations, maestro.'

They went down for breakfast, the only English breakfasts in the house, the other residents eyeing them curiously. Kate was amused. 'Can't make us out, can they?' she suggested.

'They think you're my mother, probably?'

'You'll pay for that.'

'I know. Table's too wide for shin-kicking or I wouldn't have risked it.'

'Listen, what about your student, what's her name?'

'Bell. Maggie Bell. And she's not *my* student, thanks.'

Ah, he'd remembered her name. Significant? Perhaps. 'Why don't you ask her? Kate's eyes were carefully fixed on her plate.

'Ask her, Ask her what?'

'To play the piano, of course. This morning.'

He was surprised, dismissive. 'Out of the question. First, I can't find her. Second, she may be the worst pianist in the world, and lastly she's probably tucked up with some beefy student from the RAM and more interested in Meistersex than—'

'Don't be crude, David.'

'All true though.'

'Well, possibly. Equally possibly the Festival can find her in a brace of shakes, she may be the best pianist since Rachmaninov, and she may be eating a solo breakfast having risen—'

'From her virgin bed? All right, give in. Why you're so curious about Miss Bell I can't think.'

'If you were a woman you wouldn't have to ask. Please try.'

He gave in. 'All right; I'll see. Not to play of course. Just to listen.'

She was delighted. 'Lovely. What fun.'

'The *Festspiel* office was puzzled, but helpful and as always efficient. Yes, they would try to contact Miss Bell and invite her to attend his piano rehearsal of Magdalena's music at eleven today.

'You see!' said Kate, delighted.

'She'll be busy, or out already, or something. If I read her correctly she'll think it's a developing pass and refuse.'

Kate shook her head. 'No. That would be too silly. It's real experience for her, David.'

'We'll see,' he said.

They arrived very early. Someone was playing as they approached the studio door. 'Curious,' he said. 'They know I always play for my own music calls.'

Kate put a restraining hand on his arm. 'Listen.'

'Why?' He was puzzled.

'Just listen. Quite good, isn't it?'

Well, if Bayreuth couldn't supply a pianist to deal with this piece the world would end quite soon. Still, it was good stuff. They waited outside the door while the unknown pianist touched rapidly on Magdalena's most important passages. 'Jonny. Or Nancy,' David said.

'I suppose.'

'Someone's boobed. No need to trouble them when I can do it myself. What a pity.' He opened the door. The playing stopped abruptly as the player stood up; Miss Bell, blushing, wondering whether she was out of order and whether to apologize.

'Good morning, Maggie,' said David, hiding his surprise behind a broad smile.

'Good morning. How kind of you to invite me,' she returned, her hands folded properly and tidily before her.

'Kate, this is Maggie. Maggie, Kate. It was Kate who invited you, in a manner of speaking.'

The girl was a picture of confusion. Kate rescued her. 'Hello, Maggie. I think you've proved me right, too. So many notes! I almost thought there were two of you.'

Maggie smiled gratefully, her embarrassment subsiding as she found her feet. 'Lots of notes indeed there are.'

David sat at the piano, began to turn pages. It was an orchestra full score, not the piano reduction he'd imagined from hearing her play. So, a talent certainly.

He winked up at her as he began to play, a pianistic conspirator. 'Fun, isn't it, boiling down a score like this for two hands?'

There were voices in the corridor, Jonny with a lady in tow. The door opened and Erika entered as Erika invariably did, like the Marschallin in *Rosenkavalier*, act three.

'David, *darling*!' She advanced, beaming, arms outstretched.

He turned his smile of amusement into one of welcome, returning her hug. 'Darling! I never dreamed. How marvellous of you to help out!'

'But of course, who else, my dear? I'm covering, didn't you know? David, it's all going to be such fun! Now,' handing her coat regally to Jonny for disposal, 'where shall we begin?'

With barely concealed amusement David sat and played a few bars. 'Here?' he suggested.

Across the room Kate sat to watch an exercise in professionalism at the highest level; the conductor playing, suggesting, the artist absorbing, adjusting, her use of the voice minimal to save everything for performance later; Jonny intervening occasionally to point out movement onstage which would take time, musically. Erika had already spent time with Stolz this morning, learning the most important moves, but most would be left to her experience of the piece, fed by the rest of the cast.

Maggie turned pages for a while until on impulse David turned to her. 'Look, I've got a heavy evening ahead, why don't you play?'

She hesitated only a moment before sitting at the keyboard. He crossed the room, finding a chair where she could see him. He'd conduct now, and she'd follow, the routine for music calls when conductors were not good pianists.

Kate watched, fascinated. Jonny's interest was more

practical, critical. Where had David found this girl? he wondered. And why the interest? Was it sexual? Wasn't all male-female interest sexual? Perhaps, but there was the wonderful agent in London, and this vibrant lady too – forty-odd probably, but not one he'd kick out of bed, as Nancy would have said. But then again he'd known maestros with serious appetites: the guest conductor in Stockholm who seemed to need two women every day; the opera virtuoso who had a different friend visit him in the green room in each of the three intervals of *Traviata*. If David wanted her this would be the way to do it, no doubt. But he thought not; she was not here for her legs, remarkable though they undoubtedly were as they worked at the pedals. And she knew the piece, or she was a hell of a musician, or both. Nancy would be green with envy. All those piano calls with David and never even a pecked cheek, or so she'd assured him. An oddball, this man. Anyway, he was all professional this morning, in his amazingly relaxed way.

They'd turned most of the corners now. Some things would have to be left to chance and experience. Erika had one more worry. 'The quintet, David.'

'The quintet? What can go wrong in the quintet?'

'I can disremember, that's what.'

'You won't, of course.'

'Look, just for me, play the quintet?'

'Of course.' Maggie turned pages while Jonny and Kate wondered what use the quintet could be with four voices missing, the ones Erika would have to match, the entries she'd have to follow. The piano began the passage. A soft Scots voice began to sing, pianissimo, the soprano opening line. Nothing to do but follow suit, Jonny entering with the tenor from easy memory. Erika was smiling broadly as she made her entry, her voice so much bigger. She could find fun still, Kate saw, in working; lucky lady, after so many years of professional rough and tumble. David was singing Sachs' line. Almost a quintet, lacking only the second tenor, and that was supplied, magically, at the keyboard. The centre of attention had passed from diva and conductor to the small figure at the piano, playing, listening, responding to David's hands and singing her line in perfect tune, German words perfectly delivered, apparently unaware of the interest she was causing.

Afterwards everyone clapped, though who was being applauded no one knew nor cared. Wagner, actually, thought Kate, as they rose to go.

Jonny suggested coffee. Erika proposed something stronger then corrected herself, remembering the work ahead. David was anxious to put his performance day back into its routine.

'Off you go, all of you. I have this opera to conduct. Must get my feet up. Kate, take Maggie to lunch, if she has time? Wake me at three, will you?' and he was away, forestalling her inevitable worry about leaving him without transport. There would be a car, she realized. There always seemed to be a car or anything else the man needed. She remembered Queen Victoria, certain she could sit down anywhere, anytime, without looking round. For her there would always be a chair. The Queen and David Adams alike. Some life, his.

Conversation over coffee was the usual hilarious mixture of travel, performances, people, artists and conductor friends, often light-heartedly scandalous. Erika was already in steam for the evening, adrenalin flowing, Kate saw. Well, it would be no joke covering that role unprepared, however experienced the singer. Jonny was quieter, watching Erika with relaxed professional interest, something more personal for Maggie.

The girl was more than pretty – beautiful in a

simple, natural way. Small, straight-backed, her conversation reserved, her eyes and ears cautiously registering the world inhabited by the older woman. Erika took to her at once, wanted to know about her family, her school, where she'd learned her piano skills. Maggie's conducting ambitions produced doubting looks and pursed lips.

'Darling, it's a man's world. Something we can't get into. One of those rare situations when tits don't help.' Kate remembered David's unkind description of women who conducted with their backsides. Erika went on. 'And I'm not sure I want to be conducted by a female either. As for the men, well, tenors will expect to haul you into bed after every music call, just to show you who's really the boss.'

Maggie was determinedly unembarrassed. 'But surely it must work in reverse, sometimes? I mean, they can't *always* win?'

'Always win? Darling, they *never* win. They mustn't, don't you see? And they don't. However well they conduct or sing or whatever, we always win – at four o'clock in the morning!' Erika's simple solution to the problems of the musical sex war reduced them all to hoots of amusement. She accepted Jonny's offer of a lift, leaving Kate and Maggie together.

'Lunch?' Kate suggested.

Maggie was politely reluctant. 'Oh, you mustn't worry about me . . .'

'Nonsense. It's no trouble. Besides, I have my instructions from David. Let's find somewhere. I don't know Bayreuth. Where do you suggest?'

'There'll be somewhere in town, if you really—'

'Yes, of course. Let's look, shall we?'

They were passing the stage door. The man called to them. 'Mrs Jones? Mr Adams asked me to say that there is a table for you reserved at the Stephan. And that you are to eat,' he consulted his scribbled note, 'for the whole day.'

They thanked him, laughing. 'Well,' said Kate 'now we do have our instructions. Can you find this place?'

'Oh yes, of course. We could walk, even.'

'No, no. I'm enjoying showing these people my car. Come and see . . .'

Lunch at the Stephan, Bayreuth's best restaurant, was hardly an everyday event for this girl, thought Kate, yet she was perfectly composed. That crystalline accent, then, meant background rather than cultivation. She was accustomed to having money around her.

'David thinks you come from Edinburgh,' Kate said. 'Is he right?'

Maggie smiled, resigned. 'A curse, isn't it, the accent?'

'Try the Black Country, or Tyneside,' Kate offered. 'Much less pretty.'

'Yes. But Aedinbro always produces a smile.'

Kate nodded. Something to do with prim stone houses with small gardens, housebodies well wrapped against the wind, careful people behaving *very* properly, teacups held just so.

'Your parents must be proud of your talent,' she said.

'Not entirely. I wouldn't be here but for a Carnegie Trust grant. My folks had something different in mind.'

'Ah, I see. Doing your own thing, are you?'

'Is there any point in doing anyone else's?' asked Maggie.

Kate was thoughtful. 'One shouldn't, I suppose. But we do, don't we? Women, I mean. We usually end up doing someone else's thing. Or very much alone.'

Maggie was dismissive. 'Alone? People with minds

of their own are always alone. The other thing's for sheep.'

'Yes. But there are all kinds of alone. I'm a widow, now. Lots of friends, but alone. When you're alone on Christmas Day, that's alone.'

'Not your fault.'

'I'm not complaining. Just saying I know what alone means, and you don't. Be careful. We all need someone.'

'But not to *depend* on someone, surely?'

'Well, we all depend on everybody, I think. But your independence is wonderful. I envy it.'

Maggie was not pleased. 'You're trying to tell me I've a lot to learn.'

Kate's smile was kind. 'Maggie, you know you have. And I envy that too. Learning is fun.'

'And experience is not?'

'On the whole, no. Nor useful really, because by the time we get it there's no time left to use it. It's a short life, Maggie.'

She nodded. 'Well, that I know, at least. So I'm trying not to waste it.'

'Yes. Where will you get your degree?'

'Cambridge.'

'Wonderful.'

'Yes. perfect. But it's odd, the way academics think. Once convince the first lot and the others fall into line. Carnegie money speaks for one.'

'Not easy to get, though.'

'No. I think they liked me *because* the folks didn't want me to do it, in a way.'

Yes, thought Kate, the fact of her having got so far against the family wish would recommend her; and there would be a comforting thought at the back of everyone's mind, too, that if the going got really hard the family would come up trumps. 'What did your folks want you to do?' she asked.

'What mother did. Marry a banker, breed bankers.'
Her tone spoke volumes of contempt for the prospect.

'Are bankers so boring?' Kate laughed.

'Not to other bankers. Look, I've nothing against
bankers. I love my father dearly. But if there's something you have to do . . .'

'Yes, I know. There was something I had to do too.'

'Why didn't you?' Maggie was curious.

'I did. What I wanted to do was marry this wonderful young man and have his kids. I did it – the first
part anyway. I've never been sorry, except that I didn't
have the kids. For that blame one Adolf Hitler.'

Maggie was unconvinced. 'Kate, can one really feel
as strongly about a man—'

'As about music, conducting an orchestra? Oh yes,
yes. I know. I hope you'll know, one day.'

Maggie shrugged. 'These things get in the way.
Women get trapped.'

'Wonderful trap, at its best. I adored it.'

'Will you do it again?'

'Doubtful, at my age. One gets set, you know.'

There was curiosity behind the clear eyes, with a
well-bred reluctance to probe. 'You know David very
well, I think?' she said.

Kate smiled. 'Yes. Better than most people. Almost
as well as anyone. Maggie, he's fifteen years younger
and he's in love.'

'But he's on his own here.'

'In his job he's alone most of the time. When he
finds himself too much alone he has no trouble finding
company, believe me.'

'No. No, of course not.'

'You thought that was his game, last evening?'

'Oh no . . . oh, well, perhaps. But it wasn't, was it?'

'No. I'm sure David doesn't chase skirts, not even
kilts. They chase him. When the time is right and the
skirt sufficiently attractive he behaves as nearly any

299

man would, given his opportunity. No, he was terribly embarrassed and tried to make amends. Then he found himself interested. All things being equal, yes, you'd have no difficulty in pulling the great conductor, sometime before the end of the festival.'

Maggie was blushing furiously. 'Really, the idea hadn't crossed my mind . . .'

Kate braved the potential storm without a qualm. 'In that case you're an odd girl, Maggie. He's at the top of your tree, he's handsome, he's clever, successful, rich, and above all he's really nice. And single. What woman's mind wouldn't it have crossed?'

'Well, it hadn't.'

'But it has now, though, hasn't it?'

'You've put it there. Not fair.'

'Listen. What you do is your choice. Sleep with David if you wish, and if he wishes – not something to be taken for granted, let me tell you. But if he offers help or advice take it, Maggie. There'll be no strings attached unless you tie them on for yourself.'

'Will he? Help, I mean?'

'Perhaps. He can, easily. If he thinks you have enough talent to make it without help then he'll help.'

'But if I can make it without . . .'

'He knows talent needs luck. He was lucky, in all kinds of ways, much younger than you. If luck comes, don't stand on your dignity. Grab it with both hands.'

Maggie put down her fork. 'Look, don't think I'm not grateful. It was wonderful just to be with those two this morning. I have this horror of being patronized, that's all. It's not that I don't understand the facts of life.'

Kate smiled broadly. 'My dear, what an antique expression. Where I was brought up it meant what goes on between the sheets. The things no one ever told girls of your age, if ever.'

Her companion smiled back. 'In my family it's still

300

true. I expect I'll find out for myself, when I marry. *If* I marry.'

Kate organized her face into a semblance of discipline. 'I'm amazed. What are the young made of today that a season at Bayreuth provides no education other than the musical?'

'Oh, lots of goings-on, of course. Shared houses, flats, you know. Kids playing house. Not for serious people with work to do and somewhere to go.'

Kate wondered whether a conscienceless tenor wouldn't be good for this girl. But would one get within a mile? There must after all be honest women, and this one looked very like that nearly extinct beast. Safe to encourage David then? Probably.'

'Will you be in the theatre this evening?' she asked.

'Oh yes. Wouldn't miss it. He does it so well. Best thing this season. I suppose he knows that?'

'I wonder. He doesn't seem to have any sort of competitive instinct, so he'd never think in those terms. But he knows he's good, of course. Mad not to know.'

Maggie's eyes lit up. 'Good? Oh, he's marvellous. The whole place talks about him. Makes one proud—'

'To be Welsh?' Kate was amused again.

'Oh well, you know.'

'Yes. I know. Now, let's be practical. Has he got your telephone number?'

'No. I rather dodged that one. I'm sorry.'

'Don't be. He'll have appreciated the dodge. But do scribble it so that we can find you. I'll be away tomorrow, to Zeebrugge for the boat. But the contact may be important.'

Maggie was writing on an envelope back. 'Two numbers, one here, one at home. Kate, you're being very kind. I do appreciate it.'

'Well, let's wait and see. Now, I must do a little

shopping and get an hour's rest. These long pieces are quite sleep-inducing for us old folks, you know.'

* * *

In the second interval Maggie was waiting on the staircase, her enthusiasm bubbling. 'Isn't it the most wonderful piece? And isn't he the most wonderful—'

Superlatives, thought Kate. In a world where someone will do it better tomorrow, superlatives were for the very young. 'It *is* a wonderful piece, and I do think he's very good, yes. Do they give you time for a drink?'

'Just. If we're quick.' They walked to the buffet, queued with the bubbling audience. Maggie was surprised Kate was not upstairs with David. 'He'd rather be left alone to nap,' she explained.

'To *nap*?'

Kate laughed at her surprise. 'Of course. In a forty-five minute interval he'll sleep for thirty.'

'How can he? With the last act to think about?'

'He's done all his thinking. He'll just switch off.'

'Goodness, what a lucky man . . .'

'Yes, he is. But well organized too.'

Maggie sipped appreciatively as they talked production, singers, and the opera itself. 'Such a happy piece,' she said. 'There's a different atmosphere on *Meistersinger* nights. Wagner is so grim, isn't he? If he hadn't written this one I think I wouldn't have liked him much. As a person, I mean.'

Kate was intrigued. 'As a person? Do you think you know him?'

Maggie nodded. 'It's this place. It's sort of family. We all get to be Mr Wagner's people here.'

'Well,' said Kate, 'I'm not sure I'd want that monster for a grandfather. I know what you mean about the piece, though. It makes up for an awful lot. It's about people, for once. Perhaps after *Meistersinger* one might forgive him . . .'

The idea brought a smile to Maggie's face. 'Von Bülow said, after Wagner stole his wife—'

' "To the composer of *Tristan* one forgives everything!" ' Kate finished the famous pronouncement for her, shaking her head sadly at this ultimate example of masculine pomposity.

'Actually,' said Maggie, 'I've always thought it a bit odd that people took von Bülow seriously.'

Kate agreed. 'Yes. I think he had his tongue in his cheek. Must have been something of a handful, that woman.'

'They deserved each other, no doubt about it. Look, I must run. Thank you both for a lovely day,' and she was gone.

Settling into her seat Kate was called by the attendant. 'Mrs Jones? Something for you.' It was a manila envelope addressed to her in David's hand and labelled: 'To be opened at the arrival of the Guilds in Act Three.' It was soft to the fingers. Curious. The temptation was almost too great, but no, she'd wait. Anyway the lights were down and the great cello phrase announced the final act.

* * *

'I hope my handkerchief came in handy?' David asked, as the car pulled away from the stage door and its adoring crowd.

'Was my reaction so predictable?'

'Oh yes. Everyone weeps at the chorale, the first time. Only a heart of stone can resist it. You were bound to need a mop.'

'The chorus is unbelievable.'

'Yes. Everything else you may find somewhere else,

303

but not the chorus. Two hundred fine voices trained by the finest choral brain in Europe.'

She shook her head. 'David, that's not what does the trick. It helps, of course, but it's the music really. I was devastated.'

'Mmm. I'm quite busy just then, or it would get to me too.' He was delighted with his evening, brimming with excitement where she'd have expected physical draining. A different man from the one she'd left at 3.45.

Supper was arranged in his room, a hotplate with a goulash. He was pouring substantial whiskies before she was properly through the door, and into the second one before she'd started the first. What a problem there'd be, thought Kate, if he ever took to the bottle before the performance as had so many others.

'Whooo . . .' he sat on the bed, throwing shoes in the direction of the wardrobe. 'It's over, again. My God, Kate, it's almost more than a man can take, that piece!' He looked at the food. 'It will wait while I shower.'

He vanished into the bathroom. When he reappeared in his enveloping bathrobe she was dressed in a kaftan, her hair down, serving the steaming dish. He came behind her, leaned to kiss her cheek. 'Kate, it's so good to have you here, I can't tell you.'

She hoped he hadn't noticed her involuntary shiver at his touch. 'It's wonderful to be here. It's been a wonderful two days.' She drew up a chair. 'Now behave yourself and eat your supper.'

The food was delicious, helped down by a generous carafe. His conversation was apparently endless, about the work, the place, the people, the orchestra, the things which were wrong tonight and how to cure them next time. Hadn't Erika been wonderful? Never a slip nor a moment's forgetfulness.

'Perhaps just a little *too* knowing, for Magdalena?' she suggested.

'If you like. I think Magdalena knew her way about, though.'

'Ah. So her friend, your namesake the cobbler's apprentice, had a certain skill?'

'With more than shoes, yes. Both he and Magdalena had Walther's number from the start I think.'

'Clever girl?'

'Yes. Too clever to be innocent. I think Erika was about right, really. Experience. It shows.'

Experience indeed.

Kate wondered whether, had she not been here, Erika might have been with him instead. Or, God help the girl, Maggie. There was no way he'd have gone to bed without some sort of company for supper tonight. A woman or, heaven forbid, a bottle. He was pouring again, his steam dissipating at last. She drank again. The wine was truly marvellous. Her mind wandered to another place, another time.

'What would we have said, David, if we'd imagined all this?'

He grinned. 'But you *did* imagine all this. Isn't that how it all happened?'

'Not quite. I saw a certain talent, not to be wasted, but not quite this.'

'Well, people have been so good, you see. Nothing but help all the way. And it can be such a hard business. I've seen so many good people struggle. And it's all come to me. From you, and George Box, and Jane.'

There'd been others, thought she wryly. Jane's father, Julie, and poor Molly for whom there would be no visits to Bayreuth. Perhaps one day he'd see the whole picture?

He saw her glance at her watch. 'One last drink outside?' he suggested. 'I always do.'

So she followed him, glass in hand, to look over the

quiet dark countryside to the faint orange glow of the town. He raised his glass. 'What shall we drink to?'

'So many good things. Spoiled for choice, we are.'

'We'll drink to my fairy godmother. To you, Kate.' He drained his glass, put it down on the wooden rail. Turning, he took her in his arms, heedless of the spilt wine and her dropped glass, and they kissed. His kiss to begin, then hers as she woke to the irresistible warmth of it, then one for them both as they gave to each other. It lasted and lasted, her hands around his neck, his wandering almost unchecked until she stood back, breathing hard, afraid of the heat under the too-thin, too-loose garment, needing to think, to escape.

'David . . .' she was fighting for breath, fighting for control, 'it won't do . . .'

'Shh. Don't talk. No need.'

She stepped away, hands to her mouth, no words for him; turned and was gone.

19

Waking early, Kate had walked for a half-hour in the cool of the morning. Putting her head round his door she could hear him outside, on the balcony, telephoning.

'Where are you? Ostend? Off the early boat then? No, she'll be away long before. Meet her? How . . . oh I see. Well, I'll tell her. Where? When? Will she find it? I hope you're right. But she has a boat to catch, and dinner will be waiting here. No, of course I don't mind waiting.' A long listening pause, then: 'Jane, you're a wonder. Such a help. Please thank Isaac for me. Yes, I'll be here, of course. 'Bye now.'

He came through the door bearing the phone, dressed, shaved, the finished man. A big smile. 'Sleep well?'

'Marvellously, thank you.' The necessary polite lie tripped off her tongue. 'I hope you did?'

'Like the dead. Always do, after work. And I always wake up ravenous. Breakfast will be here in a jiffy.'

'But there's no room service.'

'There is for me. They quite like having me here.'

'Well, for the record, I've loved being here.'

'And I've loved having you.'

A knock on the door. One of the sons of the house, pushing a trolley. David gestured to the balcony and the table was quickly laid. They sat in the sun. She poured coffee. 'I'm surprised that you didn't, in fact,' she said.

He was puzzled for a moment. Then: 'Oh, I see . . . I've been wondering too – wondering why not and

307

whether or not to be sorry. And whether you're sorry.
Or not.'

'So have I.' Her smile was growing, with his. 'I'm
still wondering.'

His grin was very broad now. 'Be careful. There's
still time.'

'Yes. There's time. And there'll be more time, and
more places.'

'But not today.'

She shook her head. 'No, not today.'

It was a breakfast to remember, high in the sunshine, orange juice, muesli, croissants fresh from the
oven, cold meat, cheeses, marmalade, coffee. He
pressed more and more upon her, worried about her
starting her trip without a hot meal.

'What will you do now, for five days? With no work,
I mean?' she asked, curious. Jane would have a lot to
discuss, he told her. She'd bring the diary, all the bits
and pieces. Programmes, soloists, dates, places, ideas.

Kate was concerned about Maggie Bell. Would he
talk to Jane about her? Yes, he would. 'But is she ready
for Jane? She has a degree to get. What can Jane do?'
he asked. Jane could listen, talk to her, advise, watch
and wait, she suggested. Kate was sure the girl had
talent. Yes, obviously, he agreed, but she'd have to be
practical. Conducting? He couldn't imagine it. 'David,
I can,' she told him seriously. 'It will happen. It might
easily be this girl.'

Well, Jane would be the one to discourage her, if
anyone could. Let her try.

Kate was tuned to the same wavelength but getting
a different signal. 'Look, we know that anyone who
can be discouraged from a life in professional music
should be. The ones who can't be stopped are the ones
who will make it.'

'All right. But no one discouraged me, did they?'
he asked. 'All I got was help.'

True, she thought, and it had made him what he was. He'd worked hard as hell, but he'd cut no throats, made no enemies, spoiled chances for no one. 'David,' she said 'you are an exception to most rules.'

He knew she'd talk to Jane about Maggie, and then there'd be no stopping Jane's curiosity anyway. A man's world? Sometimes it seemed that women ran it. 'I'll arrange it,' he promised.

She was pleased. Time was getting on. 'Time to sort myself out, I think?' she said.

He got up, took her hands, pulled her to her feet. 'Oh, don't dash . . .'

'Time,' she said, releasing herself, getting up. 'The enemy, time. And I have a timetable, I gather.'

'Ah, you heard. Well, she'll have lunch late, at a place called Königswinter. Do you know it?'

'On the Rhine, the right bank autobahn.'

'There's a *Rastplatz*. How does she know these things? She thinks you can be there by three, have a meal and still catch the nine o'clock boat.'

'Quite right.'

'Sure? She may be thinking Porsche?'

'Oh no. Jane knows about cars, and about time.'

Time, yes. The unforgiving minute. He held her hands, reluctant to part with her. She pulled away.

'I mustn't keep that important lady waiting.'

He was dozing in the sun when she reappeared, ready for the road. 'Don't get up. My bag's gone down. Nothing to be done. I've made coffee.'

True realization of the distance she must drive today came to him suddenly. 'Can you really manage all this?' he asked, worried. She was confident. 'Of course. Why on earth not? Fun, David. I could drive there and back, the way I feel now.'

'Sure? Did you really sleep so well?' He stood to take her in his arms once more. 'Kate, I'm such a lucky man,' he said into her hair 'and you are the most wonderful woman . . .'

'No, David, I'm not.' She sat away from him, holding his hands, her eyes frank. 'You know where she is. Just hang on to her.' She was escaping his hands, standing up, straightening her dress. 'I'm away. 'Bye now.'

One brief kiss and she was gone. He heard the starting of the engine far below, dashed for the balcony, but the little yellow car was already turning the corner, up the hill to the autobahn.

* * *

In the tower high above the traffic Jane looked at her watch, then at her map, her face a picture of satisfaction. An average of ninety from the boat, and much of it in Belgium, where there was a limit. No policemen today. Two fifty-five. Kate ought to make it soon in that pretty roller skate of hers.

'Such punctuality,' said the voice, and there indeed she was, beaming.

They hugged, pleased with each other and with their success.

'Lunch,' said Jane, waving at the waiter. 'I mustn't keep you, but you must eat. I had a vast breakfast on the boat. You must be famished?'

'Not to worry. But yes, it's time to eat.'

The waiter advised grills for speed. 'Lots to talk about,' said Kate. 'How is our genius, well?'

'Well enough. Terribly pleased with himself and his opera.'

'So he should be. I've brought the English papers for the reviews. Wonderful. It's doing him no end of good at home, all this.'

'He had a cast change last night, the Magdalena.'

'That would be Erika,' smiled Jane.

On the ball, thought Kate, and ahead of the game.
'Yes. She did terribly well.'

'She would.'

'She seems a lot of fun.'

'Yes. But more fun for us than for the men, probably. They don't really enjoy being chased so hard, do
they? Ardiles, now, he avoids her like the plague. The
easy way for a girl to defend herself against his nibs is
to make a pass at him. That he cannot take. But he's
done it again, I gather.'

'Will he hurt her, Jane?' Kate's concern for her
friend was almost palpable.

'No, he won't,' Jane reassured her. 'At least he never
has yet.'

'But how on earth—'

'Easily. What they fall for is the energy, the
excitement, and the musicality. They *are* always singers, you know?'

'Yes.'

'And always first-rate. That's the key. It's why it
works. He couldn't pull a barmaid in a thousand
years.'

'You mean they do it for the work?'

'Oh no. Well, I suppose some do. But not usually.
He's collected some of the nicest, the least susceptible,
the happiest married, the most professionally secure
women.'

'So how?'

'Even more interestingly, how do they *stay* happily
married afterwards? I think it's because apart from the
charm and the energy he offers nothing but music and
sex. Both dynamite.'

'Well, I knew about the music.'

'Take the sex on trust. Very satisfied ladies they are.
No regrets, no . . .'

'Shame?'

'Oh no. They've always adored the whole thing.

311

The secret is in the way he allows them to think *they pulled him*. They have this wonderful sense of achievement. And then at the end he has an infallible knack of sending them away just as *they* are getting bored. Then they think that was their idea too.'

'So there really is nothing else to him?'

'Oh yes. But not for them. The real man is for his wife. But they've all been convinced that they could have kept him if they'd wished it.'

'It sounds the perfect marriage, for him at least.'

'His wife is an absolute poppet, crazy about him. "Look at him," she'll say, "he looks twenty years younger than he is. If those silly girls are what it takes, I should complain?" '

Kate sighed. 'I wonder if I could suffer a husband like that.'

Jane looked at her frankly, her smile growing slowly. 'What you're really wondering is whether *I* can suffer it, isn't it?'

Kate owned up. 'Yes. Yes, I suppose that's it. And I don't believe you can.'

'And you think that's the crunch, that I'll have to face it?'

'I hope not.'

'I told him I wouldn't, once. Now I don't know. It may be put up or give up.'

'That would be the worst solution for him, Jane. You're exactly what he needs. Anyway, I don't believe you *can* give him up.'

'No. Nor I. We'll see. Now,' she became business-like, 'Molly's twins.'

'Yes, of course. David wants to help them somehow.'

'Your idea, I think? He's been a hell of a time getting round to it.'

'Yes,' admitted Kate, 'it was my idea. And I can't think why it took him so long.'

Jane smiled her quiet smile. 'I can, I think, but

never mind. Better late than never, and I can show him how to do it, I hope.'

Kate wondered if there was anything this clever woman couldn't sort out for that lucky man. 'Good,' she said. 'It's something he must do, really.'

Time to probe, thought Jane. 'Yes, he must. Kate, that poor woman. Pregnant, with her man in hospital, and a wreck. How did she explain it? How *could* she explain it to him?'

Kate shook her head. 'I don't know. There was no one else to tell except her parents, and they may not have understood how completely Bob was crippled.'

'But what have they told the boys?' Jane wondered.

'Heaven only knows. And it really doesn't matter to anyone else. They're so close, all four. Legally they're Bob's kids, of course. Emotionally too.'

'What a man.'

'Yes. Very special.'

Now,' Jane said, brightening and waving a credit card at the waiter, 'you have a boat to catch. You'll make it?'

'Yes, of course. I get sixty into the hour. More on these roads. Sounds like a crawl to you no doubt . . .'

In the car park they sat listening to Kate's busy engine. Kate was tying her headscarf when she remembered. 'Jane, please ask him about Maggie Bell.'

'Maggie . . .?'

'Maggie Bell. No time to explain now, but please ask him.'

'Sounds a very important lady,' said Jane, puzzled.

'Could be. I'm not sure. You'll know if she is. But I was right once before. 'Bye now.'

* * *

David was asleep, the bed newly made, when Jane

arrived. She woke him, as usual, with a kiss. 'Hi. You must be getting old, all this beauty sleep.'

'Nothing else to do. All my women deserted me . . .'

'Well, if you can summon the energy, just get up and make a drink, while I shower? The bottle's on the desk. And the London reviews are with it.'

He poured two substantial measures of Glen Grant and turned to the papers.

The reviews were effusive. Any criticism was for the production. For the conducting, the playing and the singing, flowers all round. Used as he was to a good press, these crits were perhaps *too* kind. And the coverage was not limited to the critics. One of the Sundays carried a third leader comparing the success of British artists abroad – there was a brief bouquet for Joan Black's success at Salzburg – with the routine opera one so often found at home. Another gave a half-page to a discussion of the under-funding of regional opera compared with the huge sums spent in London. It was a campaign in the making.

Jane was back, towelled up and rubbing her hair dry. 'What d'you think, love?'

'Well, they seem to have been listening to something between Toscanini and Furtwängler.'

The hairdrier buzzing, she said, 'Be fair, David. Your *Meistersinger* really is very good, isn't it?'

'Yes it is. I never worked harder at anything, and I'm glad it shows. But . . .'

Praise embarrassed him; but more than that, he'd detected the smell of a small rat in the reviews. She switched off the buzzing machine and picked up her glass. 'Yes. I can smell it too. They only build up to knock down. Bitches, all of them. Bitches of all three sexes.'

'Not my business, Jane. We don't play those games.'

She stopped short in the act of snapping into her bra. 'David, you don't think *I'm* playing . . .'

'No. Of course not.'

'I never suck up to the critics, for you nor anyone. Anyway, only one in three of these chaps,' she slapped the *Observer* hard, 'has heard your performance. You're being used to hit Covent Garden, that's all.'

As ever, Covent Garden. The Royal Opera was on the anvil, and David had become a convenient hammer. 'Can't lay the Garden's problems on the Music Director, Jane. No one can produce international opera on pennies.'

She agreed. 'But do the papers care? It's all a game to them.'

'Well, it's not *my* game. Jane, we must distance ourselves from this business by any means you can find.'

'By *any* means?'

'By any fair means.'

She considered. 'Could you bear another press piece?'

'Another Sunday supplement?' He disliked the press, even when it was on his side; the *depress*, he'd called it once. 'But if the press is attacking our friends they won't stop doing it for me, will they?'

Hairbrush busy, she walked to the balcony door, pensive, stood looking out into the growing dusk for long moments. The brush slowed and stopped. She turned. 'David, the answer is television. If the game's what I think it is they *may* just fall for it. Then you could turn the piece anyway you like. An argument for British opera, for proper subsidies and for fair play for British talent, bouquets for what Covent Garden is doing on pitiful resources, an appeal to industry perhaps.'

He considered for a long time. When he turned with a decision she was dressed, putting up her hair.

'All right,' he said. 'Let's do it.'

She crossed the room to thank him with a kiss,

knowing his dislike of self-publicizing, the cultivating of the fleas that bit one. 'I'll start the ball rolling first thing,' she said. 'It must be done here, of course.'

'Here? That means in three weeks at most?'

'The Bayreuth establishment would love you for it, David. And there's nowhere better for our purpose. Anyway if I can't do it quickly the chances are I can't do it at all. Now, enough business. Am I to be taken out to supper this evening?'

'Yes, of course. I'll ring for a car. The driver will know somewhere.'

* * *

They found a small *gasthaus* five or six kilometres north. The house was modest, the menu splendid, with a cellar to match. It was still early and the room was quiet. The soup and the schnitzel dispatched, they were waiting for the strudel, enjoying the wine, when Jane remembered her promise to Kate.

'Tell me about Miss Bell,' she said.

David was pleased. 'Kate told you, did she?'

'No. You're about to tell me.'

'Yes, well . . . Margaret Bell, a student usherette here. You know students . . .'

'Yes, I know.'

'Well, the said Miss Bell met a very clumsy conductor in the coffee-shop. You know the coffee-shop?'

'Get on with it, do.'

'. . . and the said conductor made an awful mess with spilt coffee. Conversation of an apologetic nature ensued.'

'Mmm, it would. The miracle is that the said Miss Bell didn't end up in bed with the said . . . or did she?'

'You've forgotten the chaperone.'

She turned up her nose. 'Ho-ho. Very broad-minded chaperone, that one. Go on.'

316

It was time to be serious about Maggie Bell. 'She's talented, Kate. We've heard her play scores at the piano. Sings well, and good at languages. Very charming girl, completely unspoiled. Father is a banker in Edinburgh. She's studying on a Carnegie grant, against the family's wish, I think.'

'And you really think there's a special talent?'

'Yes. We all did.'

'All?'

'Kate, Jonny, Erika.'

'Such references.'

'Well yes; seriously, they are, aren't they? The downside of Maggie Bell is that she wants to conduct.'

'And of course you told her that women conductors conduct with—'

'Their backsides. Yes, I did. And they do.'

Jane snorted her disgust. '*So far* they do, yes. One day they'll learn better. But not if people like you keep putting them down.'

'Jane, come on! The whole musical world will put them down.'

'The musical world can . . . Am I to meet this extraordinary woman?'

'Girl.'

'You can tell the difference?' Her smile was growing all the time at the thought of this arch-chauvinist already half-defeated by a feminine talent.

'I *think* so, yes.'

'I wonder. Well, I gather we're to meet?'

'If you wish it.'

'How about first thing tomorrow? Do you know where she is?'

Her number's on the pad. She gave it to Kate, wouldn't give it to me.'

Jane smiled. 'A canny Scot, this one. I begin to like her.'

'Good. Now, about these two boys of Molly's. What can I do, d'you think?'

'A great deal, I imagine, with a little organization and tact.'

'Tact? Surely if Moll will accept help I can just offer . . .?'

'Well, perhaps. David, how much do you know about Moll's boys?'

'Not a great deal.'

'You've never seen them?' He was silent for a moment, looking a little sheepish, she thought. 'Some neglect there, David?' she suggested.

'I tried to find time. Honestly, Jane, it never seemed convenient.'

'To you or to Molly?'

He thought for a moment. 'Truly, Molly always had some reason—'

'And that didn't strike you as odd?'

'Jane, what are you trying to say? What's wrong with these kids?'

'Hardly kids,' she hastened to reassure him, 'and there's nothing wrong with them. They are at university, and one or other will play Rugby for Wales, they say. Both, possibly.'

'Oh, bloody marvellous!' His delight filled the room. A newly arrived family turned to examine the source of such joy and he simmered down, embarrassed. 'Tell me more,' he begged.

The ice was cold under her, and her shoes were very thin. She put one foot before the other with trepidation. 'David, let's go back, quite a long way, shall we, to that week in Southerndown?'

He was puzzled. 'If you like. Why?'

'Time matters to what I have to say. Look, how long was it, do you remember, afterwards, when the news came about Bob and his injury?'

318

'Not long. Why? Weeks, I suppose. Not long at all. Jane, how can I remember?'

'Let's not try to remember, then. I know the answers, you see.'

'Jane, what's this all about?'

'David, this isn't easy for me, and it isn't going to be easy for you. Listen to me.' She took a deep breath and jumped. 'It's quite impossible that Bob is the father of those boys.'

For some moments he seemed unable to understand her. Then he shook his head, disbelieving, dismissive. 'He must be. Of course he is. Jane, you don't know Molly. We *know* he is.'

'No, David. Everyone knows that he cannot be. *Everyone but you.*'

There was an endless silence. Then: 'No. I don't believe you. Why couldn't he? Why not?'

'He's an incapable, love. Below the waist nothing works. He simply can't . . .'

Suddenly he slumped in his chair, fighting back tears. Oh God, she must get him away, out of here. The waiter was hovering. She waved to him. '*Cognac, bitte.*'

David seemed robbed of speech, his head hanging. She wanted desperately to take his hand but he was out of reach across an ocean of white linen. She could only wait. At length his eyes met hers, his hands fumbling for a handkerchief, blowing and mopping. The words came through a fog. 'Jane, are you sure? Quite sure?'

The cognac arrived. She nodded. 'Quite sure. Drink, love.'

He took the glass and sipped, then drank deep. 'We must go,' he said, his voice hoarse.

In the car he sat apart, silent, alone with his thoughts, miles and years away, beyond her reach. There were no words until they were alone.

He was toying with his drink, his thoughts struggling for order. The big handsome boy was gone; for the first time he looked his age. Life had been kind to him, but not tonight. She waited with the few answers she had.

'But why? Why didn't I know? I thought—'

'You thought what she wished you to think. We don't know what her parents, your grandparents thought. Perhaps they tried not to think.'

'All these years. How could he bear it?'

'She's been wonderful, David. Eighteen years of nursing, and bringing up the boys too. She's a remarkable woman.'

Yes, he thought, she was all that and a lot more. 'But how is it with them? With Molly and Bob? Was it simply a bargain? That he must accept the kids if she'd accept the burden?'

'Who knows? All we really know is that she's well as can be, and the boys are big and strong and bright. But it's not surprising that you've never been encouraged to visit, is it? That might be more than Bob could take.'

Belief and acceptance were coming slowly and hard. 'He knows, then? About me, I mean?'

'David, we don't even know that. My information comes partly from Isaac's contact and partly from Kate. If Kate hadn't made her suggestion to you I'd never have asked questions. But the medical facts are so obvious that the question hardly needed asking. I've been as blind as you, David. Neither of us has given these folks a thought, have we?'

He'd thought, often. But never that he might have been responsible.

Jane went on. 'You were only fifteen, remember. Hardly more than a child. The family never imagined the kids were yours. It was literally *unthinkable*. And service wives with husbands abroad do silly things, often.'

'Not Molly.'

Arguable, but not tonight she decided. 'Bob was back quite soon. It was easier to pretend, for everyone. You accepted the pretence. You mustn't blame yourself.'

Blame? Those nights and days, long ago, were they a matter for blame? As well blame the sea for turning. In his mind there was no question of blame for the act, only of guilt for his thoughtlessness. 'Kate knows?'

'Oh yes. She must have guessed, even if Molly didn't tell her. She knew there was no one else.'

'She must think me utterly thick, or utterly selfish. Jane, something must be done, and quickly.'

'No, David. Something useful and sensible must be done, and safely rather than quickly.'

'Safely?'

'Of course. The wrong move could spoil a lifetime's work for Molly. We need to know a little more about the family, about Bob, and how it is with them. It won't be easy. You can afford a great deal, but it may be that they can't afford to accept.'

'But there must be a way. I must do what I would have done for . . .'

She smiled gently. 'For your own children? Yes, we'll find a way. But all these years of care are not to be disturbed without a lot of thought.'

He was drained, emotionally and now physically. How must it feel she wondered, after a ten-year child-less marriage, to discover that he had two strapping sons who'd never seen him, who knew nothing of him except the televised face shared with millions? Who'd lost most? Not the boys, she was sure.

'Come, love, get some rest?' she suggested. Thank God he had these days, a space in which to think this through. What he needed now was sleep. 'Come,' she said again. 'You must rest, love. Let's think in the morning. We can sort it out together, David. Trust me.'

20

David was still sleeping. Last night she'd begun to wonder if he ever would. She'd get up, have breakfast, speak to London, then with the *Festspiel*. There was so much to do. It was nearly two hours later that he woke to the smell of coffee.

'Time?' he asked.

'All the time you need. Breakfast will be here in five minutes.'

He made for the shower, shaking the sleep out of his head. When he arrived, dressed, on the sunny balcony, he seemed a little rested though worried, withdrawn. She must get him out of the way this morning. 'It's half-past ten. Miss Bell's coming at eleven fifteen.'

'Already?' His surprise was almost comic.

'You point me in the direction of the conducting talent of the century and expect me to sit here while she's snapped up by some other agent? Oy veh!' Jane gave her splendid but rare imitation of her father's hands-in-air gesture of despair.

He was buttering a croissant. 'I have this feeling that you've done a day's work already. If there are to be any more surprises for me let's get them over, shall we?'

She smiled. If his sense of humour was returning his emotional balance would follow soon. 'Surprises? From me? I'm just a hard-working girl doing her best for a slave-driving—'

'Some slave!' He gave her hand an apologetic kiss. 'Look, I'm sorry I was in such a state last night.'

'But, darling, you coped amazingly. I couldn't think how to break it to you. The shock of a lifetime, surely?'

'Yes,' he said. 'What happens now, d'you know?'

'You go for a walk. You need it, and what's more, I need you out of the way. Until twelve thirty.'

'Ah. Going to be formal, are we?'

'We are. Business.'

He laughed briefly and grimly. 'I remember the business interview. Left a scar, I can tell you.'

She grinned, remembering with him. Her father, under pressure and unwilling to accept an unformed talent, had been more aggressive than she'd ever seen him. 'Why do you think you'll make a conductor, Mr Adams?' he'd demanded.

David's reply had been rational, modest, yet confident. 'I communicate well with my hands. Orchestras understand me. I assimilate scores well. I have an instinct, I'm told. Audiences like what I do. I'm not afraid of them. I cope with occasions.'

'With amateur orchestras, students, yes . . .'

'With the Philharmonic too.'

'In an emergency. In an emergency people are kind.'

'Yes, of course. I hope they'll continue to be kind.' She remembered his smile, natural, unforced, trusting.

'GG had pressed the point. 'Have you seen my list of artists? You know it's small, that I choose very carefully?'

'Yes. I know that. I quite understand that spotting an early talent is not routine for you . . .'

A deliberate provocation, Jane wondered, or a *faux pas*? The old man had bristled, folded his arms, leaning on the big desk, the prelude to a negative, nearly always. She'd crossed her fingers under her notebook as GG asked, 'You think that I make only safe bets, Mr Adams?'

'Mr Grant, I know you are a man of experience, a

man of business and a musician too. You won't waste time on a talent unless you believe in it. I know that we wouldn't be talking but for the kind interest of your client with whom I played Bartok last week, and of Sir George. The decision is for you. It will be a businesslike one. That's as it should be.'

Partly placated, GG relaxed a little in his chair. 'Well, they were impressed. More impressed than I was, I must say this frankly. But I am one of those people who expects performance, not one who is surprised when it happens.' He glanced at his notes. 'Now, your study is not complete, I understand?'

David had smiled broadly. 'I wonder if study is ever complete? But yes, I have this opportunity in Vienna. I can't refuse it.'

'Refuse? Refuse? Of course not. Vienna is where music is made. Go, of course. Learn.'

'So,' said David, 'there is little you can do for me for some time. I'm not ready.'

Jane feared that GG would see only the confidence, where she'd recognized the tension which was producing it. He was a very young bull to be locking horns with this big one. He could not know that the reason for GG's brusque manner lay in her own insistence, her enthusiasm which had brought him here. David had hardly looked at her, unobtrusive in her corner, notepad on her knee, eyes down.

They talked of his ambition, of his engagement and his decision not to marry until his studies were over; of his fiancée's need to begin her career. Grant had warmed a little then, drawing the boy skilfully with talk of Vienna, of orchestras, of his own experience long ago. He'd make no commitment today, she knew.

'Well, Mr Adams, I will consider this carefully.' He was rising now, hand proferred. 'I will be in touch. But remember, it's a hard world for artists and especially for conductors. There are too many already, nearly all of them bad. Not a job I would recommend to anyone but the very talented. Failure makes people unhappy, sour. You have talent, of course. How much we don't know . . .'

Jane had seen David out into Wigmore Street. The old man was still sitting at his desk, doodling, when she returned.

'Pop, you were hard, do you know?'

'Hard? I'm a hard man?' His hands were expressive, wondering. 'The world, now, the world is hard. The boy has talent, this I cannot deny. But such a difficult conductor to promote. So English. He would need to be so good.'

'I know he will be, Pop.'

His smile was knowing. 'This you cannot know. Jane, you listened with your eyes. Ears are better. A conductor plays to both sexes, you know this?' She liked the boy, he could see it and it worried him. The boy was much too handsome. Liking a client made business more comfortable but it was no reason for accepting one. Women! Who could work with them? *Kinder, Kuche* . . .

'Does it hurt that half the audience likes him before he starts to play?' she asked.

'No. But it's the other half that buys the seats. And gives away the work too.'

Back in Bayreuth, several years on, David was studying her as she reflected, unusually quiet.

'Don't be too tough, Jane, will you? She's a child, really. Nice, but younger than she thinks she is.'

She's not alone there, thought Jane, starting to clear away. If GG could know how it was with David what would he have said? 'I told you so' had never been his line. 'Quite a handful for ten per cent,' more likely. She must get rid of him before this girl arrived or there'd be a very untidy discussion. 'Come along then. Time to make yourself scarce.'

'I'm not to say hello, even?'

'No you're not. Out with you.'

She watched him cross the yard. Hardly was he gone when a bus discharged a small feminine figure at the corner of the lane. She produced a note from a handbag and consulted, read the sign *Gasthaus Brauerei Blink* and made purposefully for the door.

Jane went to the staircase. There would be no one to receive a visitor at this time. 'Miss Bell? Do come up, please.'

Enter Maggie Bell, then; small, dark, nicely formed, trimly and formally dressed, bright-eyed. She looked frankly at this amazingly successful woman who'd taken over the best agency in London from her father and made it internationally influential in three years by staying up all night. A toughie; such, anyway, was the sum of the information she'd managed to gather since the phone call at 8.30 this morning.

'Tea?' Jane suggested.

'Lovely. Thank you.'

'I expect like all Scots you put in the milk last?'

'Yes.'

'And you're quite sure it makes no difference to the taste?' Jane smiled.

'Mother's quite sure. I think the argument's not quite settled.'

'It may take some time.' Jane passed a cup. 'Shall we sit outside? We always do.'

They walked out into the sunshine, settled into chairs. The *we* was not lost on Maggie, nor had Jane meant it to be. There were ground rules to be established. With David one just never knew.

The girl was admiring the view. 'What a lovely place,' she said. 'So much nicer than . . . well, you know.'

'Than the luxury hotel trade? David thinks so. I tell him it's his working-class attitude coming out. But yes, it is lovely. Tell me, did he utterly ruin your clothes the other evening?'

'Please don't worry him with that. It was an old skirt, really. He was terribly embarrassed.'

'We must buy another.'

'No. No, really. You must not. David has been so kind, and anyway, where would one buy a kilt in Bavaria?'

'Well, we'll see. Which tartan was it?'

'Macdonald. My mother was a Macdonald. It means I don't speak to Campbells. Glencoe and all that.'

Good; she was relaxing now. How uncomplicated, Jane thought, to be a Macdonald, to have an identity which made people smile. The Goldbergs had seen massacres beside which Glencoe was croquet at the vicarage. 'Tell me about your family,' she asked. 'Your father is in banking, I believe? In Edinburgh?'

'Yes. It's been in the family for ages, banking.'

'And it's not for you?'

Maggie considered. 'Well, that hadn't occurred to me, I must say, nor to my folks. Banking is for men. Women marry bankers.'

'Well, isn't conducting for men? Don't we marry conductors?'

'Yes, if that's what we wish to do. I don't. What you're saying is that if I want a fight with chauvinism I'd do better to have it on my own ground? With my family behind me'

Jane nodded. 'Yes, why not?'

'Because music is what I've got, what I've got to give, and nothing else will do. And because my family would fight harder to keep me out of banking than the entire music profession will to keep me off the box.'

'Are they so hard, really?'

'When it's a matter of conviction they are. My father

328

comes from Aberdeen. His heart's all right, but I think he has Aberdeen granite in his head.'

'Not pleased with all this, then?'

'No. I'm the lost sheep. They're waiting for me to wander home, tired and starving, so that they can sort out a comfortable future for me.'

'And it won't happen?'

'No. It won't.'

'So, three years in Cambridge for a degree. Then what?'

'I don't know. One foot before the other, that's the best I can do. So far it's been the most terrific fun, anyway.'

Guts, thought Jane. If guts could succeed she'd make it, this one. No hope without guts, anyway. But she'd have to eat. 'How about money? Do you have enough?'

The girl shrugged. 'Who has enough? That's how my family makes a living, persuading people they need more money. I'll get by. I won't get fat, and I won't run to drink, or waste expensive time, because I won't be rich enough. I'll live.'

Not an easy lady to help. There was so much pride here. 'You could earn during vacations.'

'If there's time. If the work is not so absorbing. But I hope it will be.'

'Do you have a special interest? Or are you waiting to find one? In music, a period or a composer, I mean?'

'Oh yes. I want to investigate early music. I want to know how it sounded. On those orchestras, with those players. I've done a lot of work on Handel already. You can't imagine how he has knocked about in the nineteenth century.'

Charm, intelligence, enthusiasm, scholarship, all wrapped up in one small Scots bomb. Jane was warming to Maggie Bell. 'I can, believe me. But can you get at the truth now?'

'Yes, I think so. I'll try, anyway.'

'And when, *if*, you conduct, that's what you'll conduct?'

Maggie laughed, a hearty Scottish peal. 'Goodness no. I can't imagine one would make a living in that way, can you? I'll conduct anything I can get my hands on, and grateful for it.'

'So you'll need all the music you can get in the meantime?'

'Yes. Cambridge is not so far from London. That's where it's happening. I'll listen when I can.'

Here at least was something Jane could do for her. She'd rarely have to buy a seat, and she could meet people.

'How is it with the chaps?' Jane asked lightly. 'Is there a man in the grand plan?'

The dark head shook vigorously. 'No time.'

'Most of us find the odd moment, you see.'

'It's not the odd moment, it's the total absorption. I can't spare it.'

'Hard to avoid, though? I mean, they have their attractions? Aren't you curious? Biology and all that?'

'I have four brothers. Dreadful bores, nothing but football in their heads. The curiosity factor is missing entirely.'

'They're not all like that, though I must say where David is concerned everything, absolutely everything, stops for rugby.'

Maggie nodded. 'You see? Anyway, something of my family keeps me in order where men are concerned. We're Wee Frees.'

'What's that?' The alliteration had defeated Jane.

'Wee Frees. It's a tiny, wee, Scottish free church. Very straight-laced. Men are very quickly put off by it. Easily discouraged beasties, I think. Or perhaps they find some of my friends more immediately rewarding. I had this reputation at the Academy. Maggie's wee, they used to say, but not a bit free.'

They laughed together. No wonder they'd all fallen for this very nice girl.

'Maggie, let's be practical, shall we? Do you have spare time here in Bayreuth?'

'Well, I work of course.'

'Of course. But Erika needs a pianist, and she wondered if you would like to help out.'

Maggie could hardly have been more surprised. 'Erika? Why?'

'She has a *Lieder* tour coming in the autumn. New music to learn, old music to brush up. She needs a pianist.'

Maggie's eyes showed caution. 'But doesn't she . . .'

'Yes, the place is full of pianists. But if she has to work with someone it may as well be with you. And the money will be useful.'

'You're sure?'

'She's sure, that's what matters. Do it, won't you?'

'Yes, Yes, I will of course. If you're both sure I'm up to it.'

Jane nodded reassuringly, her fingers mentally crossed over the white lie. Erika had been immediately positive this morning; it was something David wished, and that was good enough for her. If they were wrong about Maggie she could be let down gently, and two hours at the piano with a first-rate voice would prove or disprove the talent.

'We'll be away for a day or two,' she said. 'David needs a change of air, and we have five days. We'll meet again. I suppose you know he's interested in you?'

Again the guarded eyes, the careful response. 'He's very kind, isn't he?'

'Sometimes. He's a conductor, Maggie. He hardly

331

notices the world. They don't, you know. They get their own way all the time and it makes them unbelievably egocentric.'

'At first I thought, you know, that he was . . .'

'Making a pass?'

'Yes. They do, all the time.'

'But he wasn't.'

'Oh no. Not at all.'

'Sure?' Her smile was carefully organized. She hoped the fact didn't show.

'Oh yes, yes, I am. He's not a bit like that, is he?'

Jane's eyebrows rose a little. 'Oh, come on. All men are at least *a bit* like that, aren't they? And he's attractive enough.'

Maggie was confused, embarrassed. 'Yes, of course. But one can't behave like that. Especially when the man has so much . . .'

'To offer?'

'Well, yes.'

Jane got up. Maggie followed. 'Maggie, just be careful with that super conscience of yours. It can do a lot of damage.'

Maggie's eyes were frank, her gaze steady. 'I don't *think* you're suggesting that I sleep my way to where I want to be. But it does sound just a wee bit like it.'

'No, I'm not. It doesn't work, anyway. But in a world where men have most of the muscle and use it without conscience, we must use what we've got. Not without conscience. But with not too much scruple either.'

Maggie considered. 'A very difficult line to draw, isn't it?'

'Yes, it is. Not quite impossible, though. Here's Erika's number. Please ring her. She's waiting. Now, the man will be back from his walk soon. I must pack a bag for him.'

'You've been very kind, Miss Grant.'

'Jane, please. We're to be friends, I'm sure.'

They shook hands. 'I'm very grateful indeed. Thank you so much.' She watched the small figure down the stair and across the yard, down the road to the bus stop. Obligingly the bus rolled into sight. Yes, thought Jane, it would. Determination like that made its own luck.

★ ★ ★

'Packing? What goes on?' he asked.

'I thought you might like a break. Nothing to do here for a day or two. Where shall we go, d'you think?'

David grinned, knowing her too well. 'Come on. Just put me into the picture.'

'I thought perhaps the Tyrol.'

'And you've checked on the Boxes' favourite spot.'

'Predictable, am I?'

'Predictable is boring, reliable is reassuring.'

'Well, it's what I do for my reliable ten per cent,' she told him cheerfully, folding clothes into a suitcase; and more, she thought, than most wives do for the other ninety. 'We can stop in Munich for a snack. Kitzbühel for supper. Lady Box was ecstatic about the food there. And the house. Lovely, she says. Eighteenth century and nearly all original. On top of a mountain.'

'I like mountains.'

'I know.'

He was very quiet while she drove. They were beyond Nuremberg before he came out of his private world to ask about this morning's visitor. Well, he'd talk about his problem when he was ready.

'She's very sweet,' Jane told him. 'I've arranged for her to work with Erika. I'm sure she needs the pocket-money, and the experience will be valuable, won't it?

Some *Lieder*, and bits of opera, of course. Erika's learning Geschwitz.'

He was horrified. 'Jane, *Lulu* is a nightmare!'

She wondered, not for the first time, whether David's concern would have been the same had he spilt coffee over a talented boy of the same age. Just as well, perhaps, that Maggie was so sure he was *not like that*. 'Erika needs it,' she reasoned. 'She has to sing Geschwitz next spring. She's never done it before. Not too much time for it, you see. Come on, love; the girl must be stretched or we'll never know. We'll have a very thorough account of your little Scots bomb when we get back. She must sink or swim, don't you think?'

What David was thinking was that women needed men, if only to protect them from each other. If this was the sisterhood of women . . . Oh well, nothing to be done but wish Maggie luck. There was silence for a space, the autobahn traffic slipping effortlessly away behind them.

Then: 'Tell me what you know about Molly's boys,' David asked at last.

Yes, thought Jane; Molly's boys, and Molly's they must remain. That would be the hard part for David, leaving well alone, accepting that all *was* well.

'In the glove box,' she said, 'there's an envelope. Pictures.'

He opened the small package and drew out two snapshots. One of two young men in rugby kit, the other of the family; four smiling people, one in a wheelchair. She was glad to be driving, not to see his face as he studied them. He was quiet for an age. Then: 'Happy people,' he said.

She drew a small sigh of relief. 'Yes, aren't they? Hard to believe that he was expected to live such a short time? There he still is. Tender loving care is what it's called.'

'What do we know about him?'

'You know his skill is mathematics? He lectures in Higher Maths at a polytechnic. He's very, *very* good. One of the very best. Without the disability he'd have had a University chair long since.'

Yes, he remembered. Bob was the gunner, the musician, the captain. It was all so long ago, and so fresh in the memory.

'Just how bad is the disability?' He pressed on quickly, afraid she would think him about to argue again about the boys' paternity. 'I mean, how impossible is his life, really?'

She chuckled. 'Not at all impossible, I'd say, given a positive attitude and a certain sense of humour on the part of them all. Both are in evidence, clearly. Down to his hips he can move. Everything from there on down is purely decorative. Molly drives him to school, lifts him in and out of the car, would you believe, puts him to bed and so on.'

'Oh, poor Molly. She's so tiny.'

'And so strong, David, in every way. Wonderful woman. I can't wait to meet her.'

Meet Molly? Yes, he must see her soon. Perhaps they'd meet her together. 'Is she well?' he asked.

'Well and happy. She has these three chaps, all crazy about her, you see? What more would a woman want?'

A great deal more, he thought. But never mind. 'Yes, I see. Now, about the boys.'

'Tim and Chris.'

'Yes. What are they up to? Where are they going?'

'First, have you looked at them, David?'

'I've looked.'

'Unmistakable, wouldn't you say?'

'I'm not trying to avoid this issue.'

'No. But confirmation is useful, isn't it? Let's not beat about the bush; if these kids are to be part of

335

your life . . . they are quite like the young David, aren't they?'

Quite like him? They *were* the young David in duplicate. Hardly surprising when the blood-line was so precise. His smile broke through. 'Oh, they're mine all right. Can they sing?'

At last she could laugh. 'Yes. They can sing. They're Welshmen, David. It's a condition of entry at Stradey Park, I thought?'

'What else? Is there anything?'

'Music, you mean? Apparently not. Most of their leisure goes into rugby. They're very serious about that.'

'Only way to be, of course.'

'Mmm. There's a team a few miles away with an unpronounceable name . . .'

'Llanelli?'

'That's the one. They've had trials, and no trouble getting into the team. But they haven't time now.'

'Llanelli? They must be fine players, then.'

'Yes. Very big boys, very fit. One will be a mathematician. The other an economist.'

'Bright kids then?'

'Very bright.'

'I wonder what they know.'

'Yes. Perhaps even Molly wonders.'

'How would you have tackled that problem, Jane?'

For the space of a kilometre she mused in silence. She'd asked herself the question a hundred times already. Then: 'One could tell them they were adopted, when they were old enough. One could tell them nothing, except that some fool might put a foot in it later. They could have been told all sorts of lies, but the truth would emerge, wouldn't it, unless they were utterly stupid kids. And they're not, you see. Almost certainly they know, one way or another, that they are not Bob's; that Bob knows, and that Bob can live with it. I wouldn't like to be the man who cast doubts on Mother's morals with those two great lumps about, would you?'

'Wonderful. Molly, I mean. Wonderful to have made it work.'

'Yes.'

'Do they have enough money?'

'Has anyone?' She remembered Maggie's response that morning.

'Yes,' he said. 'I have and you have. Quite enough. We can either of us stop earning now and live comfortably into old age.'

'Yes. I was being flip, I'm sorry. But they are well cared for. Bob's pension is a good one. They live in a comfortable bungalow, part of the disability provision.'

'But there must be something I can do for them.'

'Yes, there must. But it's a question for Molly, David. Until we talk to her, nothing at all, I think.' It was interesting, she reflected, his lack of curiosity about her sources, his trick of assuming everything was possible to Grant's. Well, a Gray's Inn barrister could produce a speedy response from solicitors in the sticks; and having a brother close to the War Minister helped when service files were needed; but it had hardly been a routine three days' work for a concert agent.

'I feel so guilty,' he said.

'David, it was twenty years ago. You were a child, really. She ought to have had—'

He raised a protesting hand. 'Don't. You don't know how it was.'

'David, we *do* know how it was, both of us. She was starved. You were just a boy, with a boy's drive. You two had always been close. The opportunity was like a match in a barrel of gunpowder. You simply must not punish yourself now.' The edge of her patience was fraying a little, and her restraint with it.

'For God's sake, David, you didn't feel guilty about it before you knew about the boys. Why now? They make no difference to the morality of the situation.'

His fuse was short too. 'But they make a hell of a difference to the reality of it, don't they? I can provide for them. Jane, I *must*.'

'Very well. But please don't rush to conclusions about the best way to do it. It will take time. Now, here's lunch.'

Parked, they sat in silence. At length he said, 'All right. You're right, of course. It's one for Isaac, isn't it?'

Her hand on the latch, she nodded agreement, thankful that he'd begun to think rationally. 'Yes, Isaac will have the answer.'

* * *

They sat in the cool of the evening on the top of the hill, watching the tired hang-gliders circle over the little town before coming in to land on the meadow by the ski-lift. Jane was admiring. 'Terribly good at this, aren't they?' she suggested.

'Yes. Yes they are. All afternoon up there alone. Then the wife brings the Volkswagen and down they come. And all on a current of air.'

'I'd love it,' she said.

He grinned. 'Your father would have had a fit. The car was bad enough.'

She turned, surprised. 'You know about all that?'

'John told me.'

'And I thought all you talked about was rugby!'

'We talk about the most important things in our lives. Rugby, Jane Grant and motor cars.'

Jane smiled, remembering. 'He used to bring me from school, you know. We were such friends. He was a sort of favourite uncle.'

'He told me. Thought you were the most beautiful girl.'

'They had no kids, you see, John and Mary.'

'No. They wouldn't have coped with another family. Yours was enough.'

She was startled. 'Oh! Surely that wasn't the reason?'

'We'll never know, will we? But no, I shouldn't think so. Just as well though, wasn't it?'

'For us, yes. Mother was never well enough to look after us all, and GG never stopped working.' Her head on his shoulder, they were silent for a long thoughtful spell, then: 'Wonderful people. I must do something for them, mustn't I?' she said.

He smiled into her hair. 'You too?'

'Yes, me too. David, we don't stop to think, do we? What we owe people?'

He gave her shoulder a companionable squeeze. 'Oh, those two are very comfortable, surely? Do you know a happier pair? I don't.'

'I mustn't forget, though.'

'No. It's a time for remembering, for us both. Not too late. And we've been lucky, both of us. We can share our luck.'

'Work to deserve your luck, GG said.'

'Well, we have. We do, still. And we will.'

'Yes. But I'd like a little time now.'

'Yes. For a child.'

'Perhaps. David, I don't know.'

'You knew a week ago.'

'Yes. I've done a lot of thinking though. About the reason, I mean.'

He squeezed her shoulder again, reassuringly. 'You don't need a reason. It's in the genes.'

'Yes. But is it enough reason for having a child? I mean, can one say to a child in fifteen years' time, "Look, I felt broody; that's why you're here"?'

'Kids don't ask a reason for being born.'

'No. But whether it's organized or the result of whoopee over the washing-machine there's a joint responsibility.'

'Yes. Well, there's nothing irresponsible about *your* wanting a child. You can cope with one easily, in the material sense. And we love each other . . .'

'But I won't have you tied by a child, David. It would be a tie, wouldn't it? You're tied to Molly already. More tied than to me now, I think. Isn't it odd? I didn't resent Molly being so special, because the first must always be special. I could be jealous of her kids, though.'

His smile was a wry one. 'It may be a very long time before I'm allowed to enjoy them, I think.'

She shook her head. 'You're enjoying them already, love, in a way. It wasn't much fun, finding out, but the thing is growing on you. David, I thought I wanted a child for myself. Now I know that I wanted a child for us. And now it's not a special thing I can do for *you*. Only for me. And that's not a good enough reason, is it?'

'Jane,' he said. 'The thought of you with anyone else makes me throw up. If you want a child then it will be ours. Yours and mine.'

'I'm not sure, now. It needs time.'

'Darling, you're looking for that guarantee again.'

'Yes. And there isn't one, is there? I must gamble.'

'Yes. Only the small things are certainties. The big ones are always a gamble.'

'Never done it, you see. Not something GG would have liked.'

'Rubbish. He gambled. Won, too.'

'I wonder. Who knows what the next throw of the dice might have brought?'

'In that case the irresistible impulse is as good a bet as any. We're back with the kids behind the bike-shed.'

She shook her head. 'We're not kids, David.'

'No. We've learned a little caution, and a great nuisance it is, apparently. Separate rooms, then?'

'No. I came prepared.'

'Like a boy scout?' he smiled.

'Yes.' She smiled back.

'I wonder if girl guides are taught the same thing?'

'Never was a girl guide, but I imagine they're encouraged to keep their legs together, rather.'

'Like convent girls?'

'Yes.'

'Let's wish them luck, then.'

'Yes, let's.' And convent girls too, she added silently. 'Come on; it's time for dinner.'

* * *

'Lovely meal,' she said, as room-service disappeared with the remnants.

'Mmm. Lady B. was right about that,' he agreed.

'The air's so clear. And the view is a miracle.'

'Yes. You can see the Kitzbühelerhorn, three miles away.'

She chuckled. 'Bogus, did you know?'

'Looks real enough to me,' he said, puzzled.

'But bogus. Tyrolean mountains don't become *Horns* unless they reach a certain height, you see, and that one doesn't. The folks built a stone cairn on top so that their hill would qualify.'

'Well, full marks for energy anyway.'

'We'll walk up in the morning, shall we?'

'If you think my old legs can stand it, why not?'

'We'll take it easily. I know you're not as fit as . . .'

'A boy scout?'

'Or even a girl guide.'

'Prepared or unprepared.'

'So long as you have the strength tonight . . .'

341

He groaned. 'I suppose one must try. But at this rate you'll need your very own boy scout one day, darling.'

'I know. I'm collecting those knives, you know. The ones with a gadget for getting stones out of horses' hooves? They say a boy scout will do anything . . .'

'Now, *there's* an idea,' he said. 'D'you have one handy? A penknife, I mean?'

'Mm . . . in my handbag.' She rummaged and produced the small silver knife. 'Not one of the boy scout variety, I'm afraid. Will it do?' she asked, puzzled.

'Yes. Now the be-prepared gadget. May I?'

Her eyes opened wide. 'In my sponge bag. Wait a mo.' In seconds she produced the small brown object, dropped it into his palm. He opened the knife. 'Will you, or shall I?' he asked.

She smiled. 'It's your turn. I did it last time.'

He took the disc between his fingers, held it to the light and put the small blade neatly through its centre. 'These things are really not on, for a good Catholic girl,' he said with a grin.

Her face was serious. 'David, are you sure?'

'Jane,' he said, 'I've never been more sure of anything in my life.'

21

The small but entirely adequate movements slowed, stopped. She took a deep breath, relaxing, happy. 'Fun, isn't it?' she murmured in his ear.

A cricket twittered, close by. A blade of grass was tickling his other ear.

He kissed the lobe of hers softly, considered for some moments before answering. 'Fun? Well, it's caught on. I just wish you'd choose somewhere less public, that's all. Are you *quite* sure there's no one in sight?'

'No one for miles. And if there were what could they see? I'm just sitting here.'

'Hmm. I think we might give the natives credit for a little imagination, though.'

She gave a sorrowing shake of her head. 'Such ingratitude. People *pay*, I'm told . . .'

'Nothing to do with gratitude. Just trying to keep out of jail, that's all. Don't push your luck.'

She sighed. 'All right. In a mo. Can you reach my bag? Over there by your left hand.'

He reached and she delved. Triumphantly she flourished a hip flask. 'The restorative,' she said, offering. 'Drink!'

The malt went down, milk-soft. She poured another measure and sank it with the practised ease of a ghillie. Screwing the cup back into place she began to chuckle, deep reverberations causing a pleasurable disturbance. 'All right, girl guide, what's funny?' he asked.

'Just the idea of taking the two most wonderful liqueurs in the world at the same time, darling!' she

343

said, tucking away the silver bottle and producing a silk handkerchief from the depths of the bag. 'Now, love, the fun seems to be over for the moment?'

He nodded, wordless.

'Too bad that I found you in your declining years. Such fun you must have been at fifteen. The mind boggles.' She freed herself, tucking the silk carefully into place. 'There. Waste not, want not.' She smiled at his bemused face.

'You're really determined about this?' he said.

'Oh yes. Absolutely. The time's exactly right. God knows when you and I will catch the calendar again.' She bent to kiss him lightly as he fussed with buttons and belt.

He beckoned. 'Come here.' She lay down again, arms round him, clothes decorously in place now. He wrapped her tight and kissed her face, her eyes, her nose, and finally her lips. Breathless, she smiled up at him. 'Come on, own up. It really *is* the most terrific fun, isn't it?'

Such a *responsible* thing, Julie had said: but not in broad daylight, in full view of any inhabitant of St Johann who happened to be birdwatching through field-glasses. He had a sneaking suspicion that she enjoyed the act more when it was risky.

'Jane, what's this thing about the great outdoors? There's the hotel, and a comfortable bed, and here we are, struggling on the grass . . .'

'Oh, you didn't struggle *too* hard, I thought,' she grinned, her mouth an irresistible two centimetres from his. He kissed her again.

'You know what I mean,' he pressed.

'Oh, come,' she said, 'I've time to make up. Don't tell me you never did this on that mountain of yours? These are my mountains. My turn now, you see.'

Yes, he saw. The remembrance was in his face. She

laughed, taking his silence for admission. 'You see? I knew it! Come on. We've got a lot of walking to do.'

He heaved himself to his feet, offering her a hand up. The mountain suddenly seemed a long way above them, She read his thoughts. 'You'll make it,' she said.

'The mountain or the baby?' he asked her, grinning.

'You look after the mountain,' she said, 'and I'll look after the other thing.'

'Such confidence.' They began to walk, the stones of the rough mountain path rattling under their boots. 'I may not be up to it,' he suggested. 'Quality may not be what it was.'

'Just as well, perhaps,' she said over her shoulder, one foot on a stile. 'Who needs twins?' She dropped lightly to the ground, waiting for him, taking his hand as they started away again. 'Darling, I've never been so happy. I feel . . . free, complete.'

In an hour they reached the summit. She insisted on climbing the cairn too, careless of the wind in her skirt. Then down to the café for frankfurters, sauerkraut and cold beer. They sat looking at the panorama, the sun pink on the snow on top of the high alps, the river, the train, the toy cars moving through the toy town, tiny figures joining the cable car far below, growing in size as the swaying box crossed the dense firs, tumbling noisily out on arrival.

Then a voice behind them, a very English voice, faintly remembered, said, 'Miss Grant, I think? And Mr . . . Davis?' They turned, surprised. A tall stooping figure, very bald, in walking trousers and tweed hacking jacket, a hat of the same material in one hand, a stick in the other, and a small polite smile on his weathered face. David rose, his embarrassment growing with recognition as the visitor's smile developed in proportion. Jane, recovering, put him immediately at ease. 'My goodness! David, Sir Eric Keys!' She held out a hand. It was first shaken and then kissed. 'Do you know . . .?' she asked.

'Of course,' said Keys, 'He's seen my clock. You haven't, I think?'

'Your clock? No. My father used to talk about it. But how . . .?'

Keys looked at David, leaving explanation to him.

'At Cocklesea, while I was waiting for you to arrive, you remember?' he said. 'Sir Eric kindly gave me tea. And Mozart. And a lesson too.'

'A lesson?'

'A very useful one,' said David, smiling at the old man. 'Not easily forgotten.'

Her puzzlement amused the two men. 'It was all very complicated,' chuckled Keys, 'but most enjoyable. I was very glad that we met. It's rare . . . we pulled each other's legs, rather. May I sit down?'

They made room. David's offer of a beer was accepted with polite enthusiasm. 'It seems a silly question,' said Jane, 'but do you come here – '

'Often?' No. But every two or three years. Lady Keys and I used always to come on with the Boxes, after Bayreuth. People do, you know. Wagnerites are often walkers. And perhaps after all that perfumed steam one needs fresh air to clear the head. Now I go there much less frequently. It's *so* much less fun alone. But I still come on afterwards. Today's my last day. We always climbed the Horn on the last day. In fact I must fly this evening, so it's an early ride down for me. Such a waste of a splendid afternoon, but everything takes so much longer now, even packing one's bag. I expect you spring chickens will walk?'

'David hasn't quite decided,' Jane said.

'Coming up its gets one in the back,' the old man observed. 'Harder on the feet going down. Don't wear the poor chap out, will you? They'll need him for that piece again the day after tomorrow. By the way,' he turned to David with a warm smile,. 'it was splendid. Yes, no other word for it. You must be very pleased. Proud, even.'

'You were there!' exclaimed Jane.

'On the first night?' asked David.

Their surprise delighted him. 'But of course. I never miss a new *Meistersinger*. And I think this was as fine a *Meistersinger* as any I've heard. Yes, I think so.' Seeing David's rising blush he raised an admonishing finger. 'No need for embarrassment, young man. Mine is a considered opinion, not the sort of patronizing compliment of which you have no need.' The old eyes shone with genuine enthusiasm.

David was stuck for words. Jane laughed. 'One of David's problems. He's never learned to accept a compliment gracefully.'

'It's not so hard when they are just politenesses,' David offered, 'but coming from such a source, well . . .'

The old man quaffed his beer appreciatively. 'Fascinating piece, isn't it? The nearest dear old Richard ever got to ordinary humanity. If he hadn't written it we'd never have believed he had it in him. But then, there's the awful bit at the end, where he gets to his real point, you know?'

Jane nodded. '*I* know. David tries not to see it. But it's real enough.'

'Oh yes. That nice Hans Sachs offering German art, German ideas, German values as the only cure for the ills of the world. *Holy* German art! My goodness,' he shook his head sadly, 'it curls my hair every time.'

Jane's eyebrows rose, the only sign of her politely repressed amusement. 'David thinks they feel the same way about our "Rule Britannia",' she said, smiling.

'Oh no. When they hear our tune they simply build

a bigger battleship. We've no adequate reply to *Meister-singer*, I'm afraid. Too frightening.'

David was disbelieving. 'Frightening? But I love the piece!'

'Love it? Of course you do. One can hear that you love it. Anyway, how could one not? That's the problem. The old man finished his beer in a reflective silence. 'I first heard it in Munich. I was as old,' he corrected himself with a smile, 'or rather as young as you are now, David. It was the day on which that man came to power. The very day. At the end the audience sang "*Deutschland Über Alles*". Then the Horst Wessel Song twice. And every one of them with a hand in the air, giving that dreadful salute. *Every one*, including the ones who were 'never Nazis' in 1945. Awful.'

'Well,' said David, a little embarrassed at the depth of the old man's feeling, 'they've stopped doing that at least.'

The bald dome nodded slowly. 'Oh yes. It's out of fashion. But fashions are curiously cyclic, aren't they? People keep old clothes, you see. Jane knows, David. Jane will never forget. It's one of the reasons I go to hear the work when I can. So that I won't forget, either. Not the only reason, of course, but one.'

He stood, reaching for his stick. 'Oh well, I mustn't depress you two further. There'll be a car down in five minutes and there seems to be a queue already. It's been quite a climb today. Getting past it at last. Perhaps next time I'll go to Baden instead, take the waters. It's what geriatric Wagnerites do, I understand. I must run along. If you are ever in Sussex again . . .'

'One of our favourite places,' said David.

'Then come and show this young lady my clock. It plays Mozart, you know,' he added, turning to Jane before putting on his hat. He shook hands, hers first. Then he was away. They watched his walk to the cable car, and its slow descent.

'What did he mean?' asked Jane as they started back.

'About the clock? Oh, it was a rhythm that came to us both, watching the tick.'

She listened in silence to the story. Then: 'I never met his wife. She was killed in the Blitz, did you know?'

'Oh no!'

'Awful. It was the night the Queen's Hall went. There was a shelter. He went back for his cat. The bomb hit the shelter.'

'Oh, God.'

'He was months in hospital, terribly shocked. His ears were never the same again. There was no question he could ever conduct. He's "carefully balanced", as they put it.

David's memory stirred. *Not the least of the good things Hitler spoiled.* But perhaps not the greatest, either? Jane went on. 'GG knew them well. He was the second most important conductor while the foreign ones were off-limits. Really good, Father thought. For an Englishman, of course.'

David smiled at the inevitable qualification. 'He could teach,' he suggested.

'Yes he could. But he won't. His life just stopped, you see? It had been something shared. No point in it afterwards. So he went to live by the sea, and now his clock is all he cares about.'

'No,' said David.

'No?'

'No. He cares about music and he cares about people. He was amazingly kind to me when I was holding him at several arms' lengths. He knew me. He had only to say, "I'm Eric Keys . . .".'

'But he isn't, any more,' she said.

David considered. 'I wonder how that feels. To stop being someone, I mean.'

'You can imagine. If you had suddenly no talent, no work, no reputation. If you were not David Adams, CBE, famous conductor, just D. Adams, just *you*, how would it feel?'

He stopped, picked up a pebble from the path, toyed with it, tossing it from hand to hand. She waited.

'If I'd lost all those things, would I have lost you too?'

She waved a dismissive hand, walking quickly on as though to escape his train of thought. 'Darling, that is the most disturbing hypothesis. Unfair. I won't even think about it.'

He pressed on. 'It's as disturbing as yours. I'd answer yours if I could. I can't. I *cannot* imagine what it would be like to be someone else, and without my work that's what I'd be. Someone else. And to answer the question I asked *you*, of course I'd lose you, unless you can love someone else. You see?'

'You think I'm in love with the image then?' she said shortly.

It was the old question, whether he was loved for himself or for the perception of himself. Whether, without his job, he'd have a place in her life or anywhere.

He stopped walking, looking unfocused at the view below. 'No, it isn't an image, Jane. It's me. There is nothing else.' He turned to look at her, she at him, worried. 'And if there was an image, something superficial, you made it. So you have to go with it, don't you?'

She came close, put her arms around him. 'I love you, is all I can say.'

'I love you. I love being loved, too.'

'Oh, you've been loved before,' she said, happy to see his spirits rise.

He kissed her lightly. 'Yes. Not like this, though. And never loved like this, either.'

'Come on,' she said, releasing him. 'Something to show you, I think.'

Clearing the trees, the path crossed a wide meadow. A herd of cows raised incurious heads at their approach, a cowbell chiming in formal greeting. Another stile now, and on the other side a tiny wooden chapel, hardly bigger than an English potting shed.

Jane turned aside. 'Come in,' she said.

Obedient and curious he followed. There were twelve seats in pews, a small altar, a crucifix, a small statue of the Virgin and Child, some flowers.

'Extraordinary,' he said.

'No. There are lots of these hills. The cowherds live here all summer. They can't get down for Mass so they gather here, and the priest walks the hills every week, from chapel to chapel, just for the boys. Look.' She pointed to the walls, where glass frames contained small white printed cards, each with a picture, and above each picture, within each black border, a small plain cross.

'Soldiers?' he said, wondering.

She smiled a sad smile. 'Cowherds in uniforms. Not just soldiers, though. Look at the clothes.'

He shook his head. 'I don't know about uniforms.'

'No. The inscriptions will tell you. Most of these chaps were SS troops. Look, the *Liebstandarte Adolf Hitler* there, the *Grossdeutschland* division here. The élite. Members of the Party. Killed in Russia. My mother's brother was there.'

'Austrian, though?'

'Yes, Austrian. The most Nazi of all the Germans. The nice kids we passed in the street in Vienna, out shopping with their folks. Good Catholics, good Nazis.' She sat in a pew, facing the altar with its fading flowers. For a moment she seemed to be talking as much to the crucifix as to him. 'It makes for a certain confusion. To be half-Jew, half-Catholic, halfway to being one of those people except that my mother loved my father.'

'Darling, it's nonsense. You could never have been any sort of Nazi.'

'Are you sure?' She got up, turned to face him, a hand on his shoulder, looking earnestly up into his face. 'I'm not. These were just ordinary kids, like you and me. They got hold of the wrong idea, you see. Someone gave them something big to believe in, that's all. But it was something, after all, that they *wanted* to believe.'

'So, Keys is right?'

'Oh yes, absolutely.' She smiled sadly at his reluctant acceptance of the truth. 'It's hard to accept, isn't it, that music can be used, prostituted, too? But it's true all right. Art and politics are inseparable in the end, and the filthiest politics have exploited the best music sometimes. The greater the beauty the easier it spoils and the more potent the result.' Again she put enclosing arms around him, for comfort now. 'Don't be sad,' she said. 'It's not a day for being sad. It's the most important day in my life.' Her arms were round his neck now, her lips very close under his. 'Hold me, David. Kiss me?'

They kissed, long and sweet. 'Tell me you love me,' she said.

'I love you.'

'And I love you. And I want your child. Our child. More than anything. Would you marry me?'

'Yes, I would.'

'It's not possible. But it's not because we wouldn't.'

'I want no one else in the world,' he said simply.

Again the sweet kiss before her arms came away and they stood apart, looking at one another. 'Now, the visitors' book.' She fumbled in her bag for a fountain pen and wrote: 'Jane and David. Together in July 1963. With thanks to the Virgin for her many

kindnesses to us both, and for those still to come.'
Putting away the pen she asked, 'Leave me for a mo?'

He went out into the sunshine, waiting. The cows
munched on. He was alone with their small sounds
and the songs of the birds. A crocodile of schoolgirls
left the trees below, their laughter merry in the far
distance. The door opened and she emerged, smiling.

'Happy?' he asked.

Her face was serious. 'Don't ask, love. I've never
been so utterly, completely, unbelievably happy.
Thank you for understanding, for being good to
me . . .'

'Bunkum. I need you, silly. Whatever would I do
without someone to keep my diary in order? One must
make sacrifices.'

She put up her fists as though to thump his chest,
then broke into laughter. 'Impossible man. One day
we'll persuade you to show some sort of sentiment.
Oh, come on, let's get back. Time for a drink. I rather
fancy a quiet evening by the fire after all this exertion,
don't you?'

'Oh dear,' he sighed, 'I fear the worst . . .'

She grinned broadly, setting off down the path. 'Too
tired for a quiet evening, are we?'

'I thought you had it all sewn up. Firm promise
from the Lady, I mean.'

'He needs all the help she can get. It's not every
day the Holy Spirit can do that trick, you know,
especially for half-Jewish half-Catholic ladies who are
anything *but* virgins. A job for a man, I'm afraid . . .'

« 22 »

The weather had broken; it was umbrella time at the
Festspielhaus. Jane's sprint from the stage door to
the car where David waited was spectacular. 'Raining
cats and dogs and stair rods!' she said, breathlessly
handing him a pile of letters. Some from London,
some for him, some for her. All a nuisance, he
thought, sorting through them as she drove, but Jane's
curiosity was unbounded. 'Come on, open up.
London first.'

The one with the red print caught his eye. 'One
from Covent Garden, for you. Only one for me.
Rather a lot from your office, I'm afraid.'

'That's life. A girl has to live, you know. Especially
with a family to feed and a nanny to pay.'

Her confidence was complete, he realized. Well, the
event could only be delayed, and the trying was no
hardship.

She was impatient. 'Come on. Open it. The
interesting one.'

'He sends congratulations on what he calls my
double triumph. He's coming in two weeks for the last
performance . . . he'd like to talk about future plans at
Covent Garden including a *Tristan*. He hopes you'll
be there. Otherwise, perhaps you two can talk in
London.'

She let out a low whistle. 'My life! It's raining cats,
dogs, stair rods *and Tristans*!'

'Will you be here?' he asked.

'If I should be I will be, of course. I'll fly, perhaps.
We have to decide, that's all.'

More games with the master, then. There was

something about the General Administrator of the Royal Opera House which seemed to induce games. Perhaps it was because he obviously enjoyed them that people always played them? Well, she'd come out on top last time; or – David permitted himself a concealed doubt – she thought she had.

'D'you think he's heard?' he asked. 'About the Bayreuth *Tristan*, I mean?'

'Who knows? The *Meistersinger* cast knows about it. They'll have leaked to their agents. Leaking gets them brownie points. It doesn't matter, anyway. And we're not committed even to that yet.'

'I *feel* committed, though. We must arrange it, somehow.'

'Yes. All right. It'll happen, you know that. What else?'

He opened the blue envelope with the Cardiff postmark. Kate, of course; a long one to them both, with effusive thanks. She'd seen Molly and her family. All well, all thrilled with his success. Molly would come to her in early September. A pity he wouldn't be in Wales that summer, but one couldn't be in two places . . . if he could find time, though?'

Jane smiled, her gaze intent on the rainy windscreen. Time to tie loose ends then. Good. He wouldn't rest until the problem was solved. Was there a problem truly? Hadn't Molly and Bob solved it for him, long since? She must get advice from Issy very quickly.

'We must go, of course. You have the time, after all this, before Chicago.'

'Yes. Let's go,' he said. 'I'd like to walk on the beach.'

'You should be so lucky,' she said, making a face. 'If the weather's like this . . .'

He shook his head. 'No. The sun always shines at Southerndown, you'll see.'

Yes, thought Jane. It's not a real place at all, just magic sand and sun, and an enchanted boyhood remembered. None of it real, twenty years on, but it would exclude her, always. Oh well, some things one couldn't share.

'There's a note from Erika,' he said. 'And one from Maggie.'

'Well?'

'Just asking us to ring. You, rather, in Maggie's case. Erika for me.'

They drew up outside the *gasthaus*. 'Home sweet home,' said Jane. 'Now, a bag each and run like blazes.'

They ran; but the porch was small, the rain torrential, and by the time the apologetic Frau Blink was roused from her afternoon nap they were both soused. Tumbling laughing into their room they made as one for the shower. He turned on the flow. She pushed him into it in shirt and slacks, unwisely staying within grabbing distance to be hauled in in turn. Clothes were thrown out and two happy people showered in one another's arms. Kisses produced the inevitable result. Closely entwined, they tried to find a comfortable place for the obstruction between them. She stopped kissing him, looking up to ask, 'Hey, are we really going to do this here?'

'We are,' he said, 'unless one of us runs away now.'

'I'm not a runner-away.'

'I gathered. But . . .'

'Come on,' she urged, giggling. 'We managed perfectly at Rothenburg.'

'Ah. There was a wall at Rothenburg. One needs a wall really.'

He carried her with her legs around him to the bedroom. In a matter of seconds she was smiling up at him, flushed, satisfied, and still wet from the shower.

Amused too. 'Now that,' she said when her breath returned, 'was something from *Tarzan of the Apes.*'

'But not with a U certificate,' he said, rolling onto his back to relax. Smiling, she reached for a towel, began to rub her hair. He reached for his robe. 'Champagne?' he offered.

'Lovely.'

He had an effortless way with a cork, she thought, watching him from the bed. It was part of his talent; success without apparent effort. On the rostrum, with champagne corks, with women . . . was all of a piece. She raised her glass. 'To us, to the infant and to *Tristan.*' Then, her face alight with sudden inspiration, 'But of course, *Tristan.* The infant will *be* Tristan. Or Isolde, as the case may be!'

He raised his bubbles. 'To Tristan, or Isolde.' He hesitated, then with a grin, 'Or, of course, Tristan *and* Isolde.'

She shook her head, disbelieving. 'Surely lightning doesn't strike twice?'

'I don't know.'

'Is it anything to do with quantity, d'you think?'

'If it were you'd be having quads, darling. I can't think where it's coming from, and you won't be satisfied until, well . . .'

'Darling, darling, I'm utterly satisfied, over and over! You are the most satisfactory man. David Satisfactory Adams. And you do love it. Own up!'

He topped up the glasses. She looked at him over the rim of hers.

'I feel *loved*, you know,' she said, glowing.

'Loved? Of course Why not?'

'Mmm . . . sometimes loved, sometimes worshipped, sometimes simply *had*, like just now. However it happens it's all entirely lovely.'

He was not to be easily flannelled. 'Well,' he said, 'may I say, for the record, that I feel simply . . .'

'No, you may not!' she interrupted, laughing, just in time. 'I'm so glad. Now, we have calls to make. Come here.' She patted the bed, inviting, reaching for her notepad on the bedside table. 'Erika first?'

He lay, propped on an elbow while she dialled. Erika was waiting. He lay back with the phone to talk. Erika was bubbling, full of beans. 'David! You're back. How was it?'

'Wonderful.'

'I'll just bet it was.' Her chuckle was knowing. 'Fresh air, exercise, all that?'

'Fine, yes.' Jane's hand was exploring again. He seized her wrist before the goal was reached, held it firmly.

'Especially the exercise?' Erika's voice held a giggle.

He suppressed his own, trying to find a free hand with which to slap Jane's wrist. 'Yes. The exercise too. How was my Scottish friend?'

'That's what I wanted to say. She's a find, David. You have no idea what a pianist she is.'

'Well, we all thought she did very well.'

'Oh yeah, fumbling around bits of opera for us. But with real piano scores, she's something else.' She waited. He was a fighting a losing battle. Jane's head had replaced the imprisoned hand.

'Hi, you still there?'

'Yes. I'm still here. Trying to think. She's good, eh?'

'Good? You'd better believe it. Look, that's what I wanted to ask you. I have this tour in the winter, you know? In South America? A month. Eight concerts. Begins Mexico City, ends at the Colon in Buenos Aires. Can I ask her to come?'

David thought quickly. 'To play, you mean?'

'Yes, what else?'

'You don't have an accompanist yet?'

'Not really. I asked Jonny. He was interested, then suddenly he wasn't . . .'

One up to Nancy, thought David.

Erika was still talking. 'It would be a help, David. We're so good together, and we have another three weeks here to work out. Unless you have other plans?'

'Other plans?'

'For Maggie, I mean.'

Jane was winning now. He must get off the line before his condition became audible. 'Erika, I have no plans at all for the lady. She's her own person. Not even an agent. Have you asked her?'

'Nope. But I have to make a decision soon, before going home. Plenty of pianists in N'York, of course.'

'Let me talk to her. Or better still, Jane. Give us twenty-four hours?'

'See ya tomorrow, David.' She was gone, just in time. He gave himself up to Jane. When he opened his eyes, on the blissful other side of ecstasy, she was still in possession, looking up with the smile of a satisfied cat.

'Come here, idiot,' he said.

She crawled up his body to kiss him.

'Now you have to ring Maggie,' he reminded her knowingly.

'Oh dear . . .'

'Fair's fair,' he said.

'David, she'll know.'

'Erika knew. She must have known.'

'I do hope so. But Erika's Erika.'

'Yes. Too nice, our Maggie, you think?'

'Yes, of course. Much too nice.'

'Then she's going to have an interesting time, travelling with Erika, isn't she?'

'Travelling . . .?'

'Just ring and ask her to come for a chat, darling. All will be revealed.'

'All is already revealed. And accessible. That's what's worrying me,' she said.

'Shouldn't have started this, then.'

The slow smile at the corners of her mouth grew in confidence. 'All right, damn you. Do your worst. Or your best. Or whatever. Give me the phone.' She lay back on the pillows. 'Well, call the lady,' she commanded.

He dialled, handing her the phone. He could hear the faint ringing and Maggie's Scots 'Hello'. A long time, he reflected, since sex had been such wonderful simple *fun*.

★ ★ ★

'Is David out?' asked Maggie, sitting demure and precise in a new kilt and sipping her orange juice, all she could be persuaded to accept at one in the afternoon.

'Asleep,' Jane told her. 'On performance days he walks for one hour, has a very light lunch and sleeps for two.'

'Goodness. He's very organized, isn't he?'

'Yes. They are, you know. Singers too.'

'They sleep, you mean?'

'Some of them. At least one lady on my list won't *speak* on her concert days until she begins her warm-up. She sends notes to people.' Not the time to tell her, Jane thought, about the one who always spent the last fifteen minutes before her call to the stage closeted with her husband, the door fast locked.

'Goodness,' said Maggie again. What a lot of goodness about this lady, Jane thought. Some of it would have to go, so much first-rate art being of quite different origin. 'Does that really help?' asked Maggie.

'What?'

'Not speaking, I mean?'

'Physically, about as much help as a rabbit's foot in her handbag I expect. But if she thinks it helps then it helps.'

'Yes, I see. Does David have one of those? A rabbit's foot?'

Quite a bright girl, this one, thought Jane for the tenth time. 'No,' she replied, 'but he takes a lot of care. He'll wake up thinking Wagner and he'll go on thinking Wagner until the last note tonight. There'll be no significant conversation between waking and the overture. It'll take him a half-hour to shower and dress because he won't be thinking of what he's doing. He won't drive himself to the theatre and whoever drives will drive very quietly.'

Maggie was wide-eyed. Jane waited for another dose of goodness, but no. 'It must make him quite difficult,' said her friend.

'Difficult? All men are difficult, Maggie, aren't they? Quite odd people. And extraordinary men are usually extraordinarily difficult. We have to find the one with the attractive difficulties I suppose.'

'Well, he's certainly attractive.' The girl's eyes were alight. 'And a wonderful conductor,' she added, as a precautionary afterthought.

Jane considered. 'Wonderful? He's not Karajan, nor Klemperer, nor Bernstein. Now they *are* wonderful. But David's very very good. At thirty-five, he's that at least. One day he'll be wonderful, I expect.'

'The cast loves him, Erika especially.' That was all one needed, Jane thought. 'And the orchestra too,' Maggie went on. 'We can tell.'

'Yes. I rather care for him myself,' said Jane, staking her claim while there was still some David left.

'You must know him awfully well.'

Jane smiled. Nice, this girl, simply nice. 'As well as anyone. I think. Maggie, how are you getting on with Erika?'

'Well, she's interesting to work with. Not just the voice, but she's musical. She's clever too. She listens. Yesterday I showed her something in *Lulu* and she got the point at once, although it made the thing much harder to sing.' Jane's eyes widened at the thought of this child changing the artist's mind in a passage of Berg, but Maggie enthused on as though it were the most natural thing in the world. 'So much better,' she said, 'and it would have been nearly impossible the other way. For the clarinet, I mean.'

'For the *clarinet*?' Jane was lost.

'Yes. He'd never have made it fit, you see . . .'

Time to re-establish some sort of businesslike contact, Jane thought. The available bomb would do that effortlessly. 'Would you like to work with Erika after Bayreuth, Maggie?' she asked.

'Afterwards?' The girl's surprise was complete.

'Yes. In New York and on tour in South America. She needs an accompanist and she likes your work.'

The girl put down her glass, her eyes wide, holding her breath for an age before letting it out with a rush.

Jane laughed. 'Is it such a bad idea, Maggie?'

'Bad? It's wonderful. Oh, how kind of her! My goodness, how good everyone is!' There were tears in her eyes and she was groping for a handkerchief in her sensible handbag. 'Oh dear, but my degree . . .'

'Look at the dates,' suggested Jane. 'You'll find most of them fall in the vac. And we can ask your Prof for a day or two if we must. University's not a grammar school, you know.'

'But the work . . .'

'You'll have endless time, hanging about on tour, and in the air. Erika will sing only every three days at most.'

'Oh,' said Maggie, 'what a lovely idea. Lovely.'

'Good. Then that's settled. You'll have to talk business, of course.'

Maggie was suddenly silent, her eyes doubting. 'Oh dear. Can't I leave that to Erika?'

'Yes, you can if you like. Erika won't let you down. But let me make a suggestion?'

'Oh, please.'

'It's what I do, you know?'

'Yes, I know.'

'Let me talk to Universal Consolidated.' Seeing her baffled look Jane explained. 'Erika's agent in New York. Then she won't even have to think about it. Much nicer for her, you see?'

'Oh yes. Much.'

'You'll need perhaps two thousand pounds a week on tour, with your travelling and hotels found, I think. And because you'll have to get yourself to New York you'll need the first week in advance, won't you. And the rest at the end?'

Maggie's eyes widened with every word. What was that expression Jane had heard from a North Country artist? Eyes sticking out like chapel hat pegs? 'Believe me,' she said, 'you'll need money, Maggie. It's an expensive life, this one.'

Maggie took a deep breath. 'Oh Jane, how can I thank you?'

'Ah,' said Jane. 'Now here's the sting in the tail. I'd like you to become a Grant artist. And until you graduate we won't put time into you except in a quiet way, to build a picture for you. A background, you see? Because there's not much you can do in the next four years.'

Maggie nodded wordlessly.

'And until then we won't take a percentage, either.' She held up a hand to still the remonstrance rising to the girl's lips, 'because you can't afford it, and we don't need it. Don't worry, my dear; when the time comes we'll be quite expensive, so don't have a conscience about it.'

'I don't know what to say,' said Maggie, her eyes shining.

'Just say thank you to David. That's all. It was all his idea. Now, there's something else.' Poor girl, she thought, it must feel like Christmas already, and there was still a present at the bottom of the stocking. 'I'm going home tomorrow. Next week a television crew will arrive to make a film about David. You'll be needed for that, if you can find time. Can you?'

'Oh yes. Of course. All the time in the world.'

'Well then, you and I have a lot to talk about before our talented man wakes up.'

* * *

'How was it with our Scots protégé?' David called, from the distant shower. The performance over, the last autograph signed and the congratulations of the Bayreuth establishment fading into the past, he could think about the future for the first time today.

Jane sipped her champagne. 'It went very well,' she said, as the flow stopped, providing the silence she needed.

'Good. She seemed pleased this evening. For a moment I thought she was about to kiss me.'

Jane handed him his glass. 'Yes. I thought she might. You'd have hated that, I imagine?'

'I'd have suffered in silence. You know me. She's not given to kissing other ladies' men, though, I would think.'

No, thought Jane, and just as well. 'We have it all arranged. She'll be here for the TV people, and she'll go to America with Erika.' He arrived in his robe, towelling his hair, kissed her cheek en route to the opposite chair, and sat with his glass balanced on its arm. 'She was surprised, then?'

'Oh come *on*, David, she was simply stunned.'

'Yes. She would be. Who wouldn't? At eighteen, my goodness.'

Jane laughed. 'Don't you start, for heaven's sake!'

'Start what?'

'My goodnessing. She does it all the time.'

'Ah. Couldn't find anything else to say, I suppose.'

'No not a lot except thank you. And that's what she'll say to you when you meet tomorrow.'

'Tomorrow?'

'Yes. You have work to do before the fun starts. She'll be at the theatre at eleven. I'll drop you before I go.'

He groaned. 'It's all *go*, isn't it?'

'Yes it is. But she'll give you a lot of fun besides making her face famous. The lucky lady studying Wagner at Bayreuth with Britain's brightest. Lots of pics for the papers, with her at the piano and you looking helpful.'

'Sage.'

'What?'

'Sage is what I must look. I'll need to talk a great deal to her before those people come, I think.'

'Yes. Meanwhile there are things I can tell you. First, she's not a Bell.'

'Not . . .'

'No. Nearer a glock than a bell. She's only been a Bell for thirty years.'

'Darling, what on earth are you talking about? The girl is eighteen, no more.'

'Her grandfather was a violinist in the Berlin Philharmonic. He saw the trouble very early and arrived in Edinburgh in '29 with his considerable family. Name of Steinberg. Jacob Steinberg. Changed it to Ian McCaulay Bell. Played in the old Scottish Orchestra, under Barbirolli. His sons went into finance.'

'So! That's where the music comes from!'

'Yes, that's where.'

'Funny choice, Bell.'

'He liked it.'

'Obviously.'

'David, you're very slow tonight. He liked Bell's whisky. Hence the name.'

He laughed so heartily that she feared for the safety of his glass, precariously perched. He rescued it just in time, taking a mouthful as his hilarity subsided and choking on a treacherously recurring giggle. She slapped his back enthusiastically until both choking and laughing stopped. 'Oh dear,' he said, with what diction he could muster, 'it's so funny, Jane.'

She was by no means so amused. 'Funny, yes. Not *that* funny, though, surely?'

'But for *two* people to do it, don't you see?'

'Two . . .'

'Steinberg and Goldberg.

Stunned, she sat silent, agape. Then: 'I don't believe it. It can't be true. It can't!'

'Darling, your wonderful father liked Scotch. All the world knows he chose Grant because of Grant's Standfast.'

She was indignant. 'Standfast! He wouldn't have drunk Standfast if he'd been marooned on a desert island with a crate of the stuff. *Glen* Grant, David.'

His laughter showing signs of bubbling forth again, she made for the shower in high dudgeon, leaving him chuckling. Returning ten minutes later, slippered and house-coated, she stopped in the doorway, smiling quietly. He waited.

'David, I cannot believe this. Do people really think – '

'Darling, they know.'

The smile broadened, became a grin, and she broke into laughter with him. 'Do'you know, none of us ever asked?'

'Isaac knew.'

Her laughter ceased. 'He knew?'

'He told me.'

She made a face. 'Some family, I must say, to hide important secrets like that from one another.'

'Yes, awful thing. Now, what else about Maggie . . .'

'Bell?'

'Yes. Mind you, Steinberg would probably advertise better.'

'It might,' she agreed. 'Well, she was worried about you. Thought you were making a pass, you know. I told her you wouldn't.'

'And she believed you?'

'Yes. I gave it to her in the only way she could understand. We've been secretly married for two years, I'm pregnant. You're utterly faithful, always have been, and all rumours to the contrary are purely propaganda.'

'And she liked that?'

'Not altogether. Wee Frees, or whatever they are, don't care for the divorce and remarriage thing. Interesting people. I must find out – '

He held up protesting hands. 'Love, please don't bother. Aren't two sorts of religion trouble enough?'

'Anyway, she won't worry about it now. And she won't try her luck either.'

'Sure?'

'One can't be sure. But she has a good idea of what I'll do to her if she does. What's more, her hard Scots head will tell her that it would be the worst possible business.'

'Ah. Another genius added to your list?'

'GG would have hated it, wouldn't he?' she smiled. 'Actually, she asked me why we were being so kind to her.'

'And you told her it was just business?' Grinning, he held up his hands in the GG gesture.

'She's not that stupid, love. No; I told her that she had a real talent, that we liked her a lot, that everyone needed luck, that life was all chance, and that you'd had yours. Lots of luck and many chances, in fact. And that what one had to do was spot them, grab then, exploit them, and work like mad to deserve them. All of which we're sure she'll do.'

'Wish her luck, then?'

'Yes. The sort you had.'

'We're nice people, it would seem,' he said.

'Yes. I think so.'

'Mustn't let on, must we?'

'No. Not the sort of reputation one needs, in our business.' She ruffled his hair.

'Look, must you really go?' he asked.

'Must. His nibs is to talk with the BBC in two days, before he goes to the States. He'll collar that job now, I think.'

'I'll be back in two weeks.'

'I suppose I can wait that long . . .'

'I can't,' he said.

She sat up, shocked. He began to laugh again. 'Jane, you don't have to go for twelve hours more.'

'I give up,' she said. 'Don't you know pregnant ladies are not to be upset?'

'Sure, are you? That we rang the bell, I mean?'

'As sure as a girl can be. Done my homework, you see. Dates are my thing.' She was silent, thinking, then: 'Yes, I'm sure. There are times and times. Times when one feels . . . d'you think it happens to lots of people?'

'Yes. I think it does. But not on our scale, love. We are, well . . .'

'Erika would say *something else*.'

'Yes,' he agreed. 'That's what she'd say.'

'She's a danger, isn't she?'

He shook his head, surprised. 'Erika? No, of course not. Not at all my sort of lady.'

'But she's clever and beautiful, and she makes the running. Those are the ones who score with you.

That's why Maggie's safe. She's too nice to try and if she doesn't try you won't.'

'Nice to know I've been thoroughly sorted out,' he said with a wry sort of smile. 'Erika will broaden that lady's outlook, I think.'

'She's begun already. Poor girl arrived early for a call yesterday and caught Jonny hauling on his zip, looking very embarrassed, and our friend very flushed and breathing hard.'

'Poor Jonny.'

'Poor Nancy, surely?'

'No. Nancy's a winner. Jonny may be randy but he's not stupid. How did she react? Maggie, I mean?'

'Went away, came back in ten minutes. Erika was not a bit embarrassed, Maggie said. And she thought Erika sang really especially well.'

'Our girl's learning fast.'

'Yes. I hope it goes well for her.'

'How can she fail, with all that talent and the best agent in the world looking after her?'

'I mean the other thing. More than any girl I've ever met, she needs the right man, David.'

'Made a study of these things, have you?'

'Maggie's like me, and she'll have to be lucky, like me. I hope she will be.'

'I'm not allowed to volunteer, I gather.'

'No, you're not. I have this feeling that if you did there'd be two of us. We're so damnably alike, Maggie and me.'

His head shook, side to side, very slowly. 'Jane, there are none like you. And if there were it wouldn't matter a damn. You're enough. No one could ask more than I've got. I'm lucky. I know I am. A man would have to be very stupid, you know, to throw this away. Marry me, Jane.'

Her eyes were wide and suddenly moist. 'David . . .'

'Don't talk about it, Jane, just do it.'

'Oh, David, I can't. You know I can't.'

'Darling, I'm offering the commitment. Don't you want it?'

'More than anything.' Her voice was very low.

'Well, the commitment will always be there. There will never be anyone else.'

'Always? David, I can't tie you. It wouldn't be fair . . .'

'You're right. You can't. I can tie myself. We can tie each other. Not with promises, not with the form, but with love.'

Her head fell slowly to his shoulder, the tears coming freely now. He held her tightly in one arm, the other searching for a handkerchief. Between the sobs came the words, 'Kiss me, David.'

'Not while we're sitting in this chair,' he said. 'About to do myself an injury, I am.' She got up, giggling and crying at once, trying vainly to shake away the happy tears. He followed, pulling her belted robe undone before putting his arms around her. 'Bed?' he suggested.

'Oh yes please,' she said. And then, 'What's the time?'

He glanced at the clock. 'Twelve fifteen,' he said, puzzled.

'Oh, goody! Come on.' She was leading him, opening the balcony door. 'The street light on the corner goes out at twelve.'

'What it is,' he said, 'to be well-managed.'

The afternoon sun was losing its battle with the September breeze. David turned up his collar as he walked. She was waiting where the cobbles met the sand, a small, oddly familiar figure. Sensing his approach she turned, smiling.

'Hello, David. Coming for a walk, are you?' She held out tiny hands for his big ones to hold, and he kissed them both. Her face had gained a few lines, and the hairs which strayed below the cap had their share of grey among the black, but her eyes were bright and her smile held the remembered promise of ready amusement.

'Lovely day for it,' he said, catching her mood. 'Getting cooler, mind you. Back to school soon.'

She took his arm as they began to walk. 'School, yes. Big schools now. I've been packing clothes for days.'

'You'll miss them,' he suggested.

'It'll be very quiet, yes. But I'll get used to it.'

'It must have been a shock when two turned up?'

She laughed. 'It was a shock when I knew *one* was coming, I can tell you.'

'I was the only one who didn't understand. Slow, I was.'

'Get on with you. Only a boy. How were you to know?'

'Well, I didn't.'

'No. Well, never mind. You had a lot to think about, didn't you? Working so hard. You've been busy, David. We listen on the wireless. Lovely to see you on the telly. The boys love it.'

'I should have come to see them.'

She shook her head. 'No. Our fault that is, not yours. But too much for Bob, you see. He didn't say, mind you, but I thought it was best. There'll be time, David.'

'I hope so. Big boys, are they?'

'Big as you, David, big as you. And still growing they are.'

'Good for the game then?'

'Great. Very useful they'll be at University. Bob is a bit worried in case it's all rugby with them and no work.'

'One to Oxford then?'

She laughed. 'And one to Cambridge. We'll have to wear one colour each.'

'I must come to the varsity match.'

'Oh, you'll be in Japan, or America, or somewhere, as usual.'

'Perhaps not. I must find time for Jane. I don't have to work so hard, really.'

'Sure, are you?'

'About Jane? Well, I can't imagine anyone else.'

'Oh, she's the one all right. But about finding time, I mean. Being busy suits you both.'

He smiled. Wisdom here. Wisdom which argued with Julie's warning that he should take time to live. 'You think she'll get fed up with me if I hang about?'

'Possible. No, that's not what I mean. I mean she's got a lot to do and so have you. It's important to both of you.'

'I see.'

'If you were not so clever, had lots of time, I mean, would she be interested in you?'

'I hope she would, Moll. But who knows?'

'Well, would you have taken notice of her if she'd been a typist, not this business marvel?'

'I might.'

'Yes, you might. You might have taken her to the pictures and home to bed, if she'd tried hard enough. But there'd have been the end of it. No, you are two for a pair, no doubt about it. Get on with it and don't waste time. I told you before, time is what we haven't got, none of us. 'Specially her.'

'She wants a family.'

'Don't you?'

'I've got one, haven't I?'

She stopped short, turned to face him, looking up into his smile with an expression of firm determination. 'No. No, David, you haven't. The boys are Bob's. Always were, always will be. You can't have them.'

'But I must do something . . .'

'No, you mustn't. Not for a long time anyway, and not while their father is alive.' His face showed his hurt and hers melted a little. 'David, they don't *know*. Or anyway, they've never been told. They're happy. They worship him. They know he won't make old bones. It's a miracle he's done so well. There'll be a time for explanations. But not yet.'

'Are you sure? That they don't know, I mean?'

'They are not daft, boy. They must *think*. But no one told them and no one will, now, until I do. What they've had from him is far more than kids ever got from a father. He had time, see. Men never have time with kids. He'd die for those two.'

'And you'd die for them all.'

She laughed again. 'It won't come to that, I hope. Things are always easier when they're away. He keeps reminding me what fun we have.'

Fun, thought David. What a life.

'Molly, surely there's something I can do? For you all?'

'No. Not now. Not without spoiling it all. Time will come, perhaps. Stop worrying, there's a good boy.'

'Are you sure they have enough money? It makes a difference, you know, having a bob or two in your pocket, even at university.'

'David, stop worrying yourself. The grants are very good. The education people have made them an extra one each, because they are pleased with them. It was quite a surprise. We heard only last week. Anyway, they will have enough. Too much, Bob thinks.'

Well done, Isaac, thought David. But they mustn't know. 'I can't stop worrying,' he said. 'I feel . . .'

'Guilty? Don't be daft. It was all my doing. A bit of madness. And something else too.'

'Something else?'

They'd reached the breakwater, the turning-point in their walk. Molly dusted away the sand in that tidy way she had before sitting down. He sat beside her. 'It was different for Kate,' she said.

'For Kate?' She'd lost him.

'Yes. For Kate and Jack. Jack knew he wouldn't come back. He knew. He never said, of course, to Kate. But she knew it was in his mind. But Bob knew *he'd* come, thank God. Never had a moment's doubt about it. That's why we didn't try, you see.'

'Try?'

'For a family, boy, before he went. He knew there'd be time after, and he didn't want me having a baby when he was away. No sense in a child without a father, he used to say. Wanted to be there when it happened he did.'

'But Kate and Jack . . .'

'Yes. Kate wanted a child. She didn't believe Jack wouldn't come back, but she wanted a child anyway. They tried very hard before he went. It was a joke between the four of us that they never got out of bed. Jack used to say he wasn't safe out shopping even. She'd try in the car park.'

'And no luck.'

'No. Bob and I had the luck, see.'

He was beginning to see. 'But you didn't *know*?'

'Of course not. But we hadn't heard from them, and they always wrote. We were worrying when you were here, both of us.'

'I didn't know.'

'Well, why should you? David, you were only a boy, I keep telling you. How could you know *anything*? I didn't *know*, myself. But I think that had a lot to do with . . . well, you know. You and me.'

Yes, he knew now.

'So Bob and I were lucky. Kate was the unlucky girl. She knows that.'

'And I was the lucky boy?'

'More lucky than you know. It could easily have been Kate, not me, you see. And she'd never have let you go, you know. She had nobody. As it was . . .' She stopped, confused.

He pressed her. 'What? Come on, tell me.'

'Well, I suppose . . . you didn't know about the money, at college?'

'What money?'

'Oh dear, I shouldn't be telling you.'

'Well, you'll have to, now.'

'You mustn't let her know I told you. She'd never forgive me, David love.'

'Molly, just tell me.'

'Well, when you won the scholarship, to Vienna . . .'

'Yes, what then?'

'The extra money.'

There was a glimmer at the end of the tunnel. 'The grant from college funds?'

'Not really, you see. But we knew you wouldn't have enough. To live properly, and travel about, and go to concerts . . .'

'So, it was Kate's?'

'Yes.'

He was stunned. 'But it was two thousand a year, for three years, Molly.'

'Was it? I knew it was a lot. She didn't want to tell me about it at all, but there were formalities. I was the only family, David.'

'But she must have it back. Now, I mean, today.'

She sighed. 'David, stop for a minute and think. She didn't want you to know then, and she doesn't want you to know now or she'd have told you herself. It was something she wanted to do. She felt responsible, you see.'

No, he didn't see. 'How was she responsible?'

'She started it all, boy, didn't she? She did what a mother would do if she had a clever son, to give him a start. All that teaching in Cardiff, the help from the BBC, everything.'

He had no words. Molly pressed on. 'She had to see it through, David. She was so excited.' She smiled, remembering. 'Used to ring up once a week and talk about nothing else. David this, David that. Just like you were her own. She said it was like seeing a ha'penny on the beach, picking it up and finding it was a gold sovereign. She knew you had talent, she said, but not like that.'

'I don't know what to say, Molly. I owe you both so much.'

'No. No, you don't. Look, where would I have been without the kids? What would Bob have done with his life? Dead in a year, he'd have been, like they expected. And Kate had nothing, nothing at all, only money. Not a fortune, but quite enough. Her family were not short, nor Jack's neither. She has a nice pension and she can play and teach. Mind, I'm not saying it was easy to give. Far too much for that. But it was money she had. It was the best thing to do, you see. Something to live for.'

He shook his head, only half believing. 'You're telling me that you're both happy with it all?'

She laughed. 'Well, it's not quite perfect. I would like a pair of legs for Bob, if you happen to know where we can pick them up cheap! And Kate would like Jack back, I expect.'

'I'm sorry. I didn't mean, you know . . .'

'I know what you mean, and you are right in a way. But it was all our doing, love, not yours. Even if you'd been of an age to be responsible you did no harm. Nothing but good to me, David. And you've given Kate someone to be proud of. That's what she wanted, what Jack couldn't give her.'

'But not her own. Yours are your own, Molly.'

'And yours, David, one day. But not yet.' Her voice took on the old light tone. 'And of course I had you, didn't I? Wasn't it fun?'

'Molly, it was the most wonderful thing that ever happened to me. Can you believe that?'

She chuckled. 'It wasn't bad, young David. God knows I needed it. Clever boy you were.'

'You were the clever one. Every boy should have an auntie like that.'

'With twins after? No thank you. But it was something I had that Kate didn't. You know she had trouble keeping her hands off you?' He made a noncommittal noise and she went on: 'She told me. Shocked I was, I told her. But she knew about us, of course, when I fell for a baby. No one else, you see. And no one since, of course. A bit easier for her than me, in that way.'

'Yes. There must have been . . .'

'Yes, of course there were, with Kate. But it's a bit of David I had and she didn't.' She got up and dusted herself down. 'Time to be getting back. Otherwise they'll think we've been at it again, won't they? And you've got a plane to catch.'

He stood, taking her hands. 'Give me a kiss, David?' she asked.

He took her in his arms. They kissed for an age. The kiss of the fifteen-year-old, the kiss of the man, the kiss of a lover and of a friend.

'Mmm . . .' she said at length, nodding, 'I remember now. Very easy it was. Very easy it would be again, too. But it will have to wait . . .'

They began to walk. 'Will you marry Jane?'

'She won't marry me.'

'Won't she? All right in the head, is she?'

'She has her reasons. I understand her point of view. It's all very complicated.'

Molly waved a dismissive hand. 'Not my business, so I won't stick my long nose in. I suppose you'd marry her if she would, though?'

'Yes.'

'David, tell me something?'

'Yes, of course.'

'Do you ever make a decision? Outside music, I mean?'

'What? I'm not quite with you, Molly.'

'Well, let's start at the beginning. Who made a man of you, David?'

He was silent, considering. 'I thought . . .'

'Yes, it took two. But I did it, didn't I? Think, now. If I hadn't, would you have made that one move?'

'Molly, how could I?'

'Easily. Many boys of that age would have had me hours earlier, with half the encouragement.'

'Rape, you mean?'

'Oho! A woman puts herself in a boy's bed, goes to sleep, what can she expect? To wake up full of a man, David, that's what.'

'You'd have stopped me.'

She chuckled. 'Would I? Well, I might have struggled for two ticks, just until I started to enjoy it.

But you didn't try, did you? Now tell me, with Julie, who decided?'

That was easily remembered. 'I'd promised you, not until it was safe. And I wasn't old enough.'

'So, Julie decided?'

'Yes. Yes, she did.'

'Then Kate decided what you were to do.'

'It's true. I've been very lucky. Look, I'm grateful to you both.'

'I know.' She was impatient. 'But that's not the point. Come on, boy. Was it Julie who decided the wedding must wait? And that there would be no family for a long time?'

'Well, it was for the best.'

'And Julie decided that the marriage was over. Did you fight?'

'Oh, Molly, it was best for her. How could I fight it?'

'Lots would fight. Most men would feel injured, insulted, that she wanted another man.'

'But there'd been – '

'Other women? Of course. But she knew that. Not many women chuck their husbands because of a bit on the side, you know. By the way, how often did you do the chasing?'

'That's a theory of Jane's.'

'Clever girl, that Jane. What's the answer?'

'There isn't an answer, Molly, you know that.'

'There's an answer all right, if you face it. The answer is, not very often. The answer is that everything in your life, music apart, has been decided for you, by me, Kate, Julie, and now Jane. Funny, that you haven't realized it yet. Or is it that you don't care?'

He sighed. 'All right. Where does that get me? Have you worked it out?'

'It's for you to work it out, David, not me. But if you let Jane go you'll have to find another one like her. And she'll always be in the way of that.'

'Let her go? There's no question of it. There are no more like Jane, Molly.'

'So. There's a decision to be made. Make it. Whatever she thinks about it, make it. She can't have her own way all the time, David.'

'Molly,' he protested, 'she's not like that, really. And she's had a hell of a life.'

'We've all had our share of hell, David; Kate and Jane and me. And Julie too, in her way. Yours has been nearly all sunshine, hasn't it?'

'Well, yes, nearly.'

'Don't worry, rain will come if you wait long enough. Then you'll understand us all a lot better. In the meantime, decide. After all, whether it's heaven or hell, there's some consolation in knowing you made it yourself.' They stopped at the end of the sand. She took his hands again. 'That's what I did, you see.'

Jane was waiting in the car, talking with Kate. The motor started as they approached. 'We've been for a ride in Kate's car,' said Jane. 'Marvellous.'

'Like one, would you?' he asked.

'Too late, darling,' she grinned. 'Give me three months and there won't be room for this lump behind the wheel.'

He kissed Kate and Molly, climbed in, and they were away. In her mirror Jane saw them waving frantically. She stopped and they ran the short distance to the car. Two faces appeared at the windows.

'We nearly forgot,' said Kate. 'Many happy returns, David.'